A WORD ABOUT
WHITE PALACE

continued. . . .

MORE WORDS ABOUT
WHITE PALACE

"BRISK."
—*The New York Times*

"ACCOMPLISHED."
—*The Washington Post Book World*

"EXTRAORDINARY."
—*San Francisco Chronicle*

"MARVELOUS."
—*Los Angeles Daily News*

"GREAT."
—*Rave Reviews*

"ENDEARING."
—*Impact, Albuquerque Journal Magazine*

"SPARKLING."
—*Newsday*

"SATISFYING."
—*Publishers Weekly*

See the Next Page
for a Scene from WHITE PALACE. . .

ON THE COUCH

"Nora, you're being irrational."

"And you're being a regular tight-ass."

"Look, I don't want to argue about this. Just leave me to my root beers and I'll leave you to your vodka tonics. How's that?"

"Fine with me."

"Good."

"Just don't go trying to tell me what to do."

Max sighed. "I'd have to be more of an idiot than I already am to try to tell you what to do," he said.

She crossed her arms. "What does that mean? Does that mean you think you're an idiot for seeing me?"

"Come on, Nora. Don't do this."

"Because if that's what you think, we can just break this thing off right here and now. I got me enough problems in my life without having to put up with a man who thinks he's too good for me."

"What am I doing here on your couch if I think I'm too good for you?"

"That's a good question, isn't it?"

What Max said next he must have said under his breath, for Nora's expression softened, and her hand went to her earring, and she said, "I don't think I heard you right."

"I said I'm the one who's not good enough for you."

"You'd better go easier on those root beers," Nora told him. "I think you're getting carbonation on the brain."

Max took her into his arms. He almost wished she would have fought him off, for the sake of her own dignity. But she relented. . . .

BANTAM NEW FICTION

WHITE PALACE

GLENN SAVAN

BANTAM BOOKS

NEW YORK · TORONTO · LONDON · SYDNEY · AUCKLAND

WHITE PALACE

A Bantam Book
Bantam New Fiction trade edition / July 1987
Bantam paperback edition / October 1988

Grateful acknowledgment is made for permission to reprint excerpt from "Lullaby" by W. H. Auden: Copyright 1940 and renewed 1968 by W. H. Auden. Reprinted from W. H. AUDEN: COLLECTED POEMS, edited by Edward Mendelson, by permission of Random House, Inc.

Library of Congress Cataloging-in-Publication Data

Savan, Glenn, 1953–
  White palace.

  (Bantam new fiction)
  I. Title.
PS3569.A837W4   1987   813'.54   86-47902
ISBN 0-553-27659-X

Published simultaneously in the United States and Canada

Bantam Books are published by Bantam Books, a division of Bantam Doubleday Dell Publishing Group, Inc. Its trademark, consisting of the words "Bantam Books" and the portrayal of a rooster, is registered in U.S. Patent and Trademark Office and in other countries. Marca Registrada. Bantam Books, 666 Fifth Avenue, New York, New York 10103.

PRINTED IN THE UNITED STATES OF AMERICA

RAD   11   10   9   8   7   6   5

But in my arms till break of day,
Let the living creature lie:
Mortal, guilty, but to me
The entirely beautiful.

—W. H. Auden
"Lullaby"

PART ONE

CHAPTER ONE

Janey had never seen his high-priced apartment in west St. Louis County, much less lived in it, yet each evening when Max Baron arrived home from work, her absence still hit him like a piece of unexpected sad news. As usual, things had altered slightly while he was away. The evening sun threw a honey-colored rectangle across his glass-topped coffee table, lighting up a new film of dust, though he had dusted only two days ago. His philodendron plant which, according to his watering schedule should have been doing just fine, had lost a certain waxiness and sheen, and drooped a little. He checked to see that his black and gold Oriental rug was still perfectly flush with the cracks in the hardwood floor; it was not. Something, maybe the rotation of the earth, maybe the hand of a subtle poltergeist, had shifted it slightly out of whack. Max nudged it back into alignment with the heel of his shoe.

It gave him a kind of nervous satisfaction to see his basic grievance against reality confirmed once again by reality itself; nothing held still. Every time you turned around, something else had gone rotten, or fallen into disrepair, or disappeared entirely. In a universe that couldn't be trusted, that could at any moment just as likely as not blow up in your face like a bomb, you had to carve out your own island of order and control, however arbitrary, however illusory, just to keep going. The fatalistic Japanese, with their absurd and deadly serious tea ceremony, understood this. Max understood it as well, and although he had to begin getting ready for the bachelor party of his closest friend, Neil Horowitz, which would be starting in less than an hour, he took the time out to water his

3

philodendron, dust his coffee table, and by way of these ritual chores, pretend to keep chaos at bay.

Then he sat on the edge of his brass bed and undressed. He set his shoes side by side on the floor with their polished toes pointed in the same direction; he dropped his dirty things into the hamper; he hung up his slacks where they belonged—in among the other brown clothes. From left to right, the wardrobe in his closet formed a carefully graduated rainbow. This passion for organization could be seen all over his apartment. His bookshelves were arranged alphabetically, by author, and within each author's territory the books were lined up chronologically, like the children in a family portrait. His record albums were arranged the same way, with those eighteenth-century masters of sweetness and light, Bach, Haydn, Vivaldi, and Mozart, taking up most of the space. In his kitchen the copper-bottomed cookware hung separately from the aluminum pots and pans, and in his file cabinet the canceled checks and bank notes, the recipes cut from newspapers, the letters from friends on general topics and the letters of condolence, and the bundle of snapshots of Janey—which he did his best not to look at—were all relegated to their proper manilla folder. Since his childhood, when his room had been the only clean one in his mother's maniacally disordered house, Max had trained himself in neatness. But following the death of his wife, this tendency had deepened to obsession, and now if his living space wasn't as logically laid out as a library, as immaculate as an operating room, he found that he couldn't sit still.

His days were as strictly arranged as his apartment. His work as an advertising writer took care of the first ten hours. It was the remainder of the day that he'd had to worry about, especially since the flood of dinner invitations that started after Janey's funeral had slowed to a trickle and finally dried up sometime last year, when the novelty of his widowerhood had worn off on everyone he knew except himself. There were basically six hours to get rid of before sleep. After straightening up his apartment and taking his second shower of the day, he would listen for a half an hour—flat on his back on the sofa with a black sock over his eyes—to Bach or Mozart or Vivaldi, until the flotsam and jetsam of his day at the office had been pretty well cleared from his head. After that it was time to watch the news, and after that, time to make dinner. Max refused to eat like a bachelor, and the care that he gave to his cooking usually insured that it was eight or eight-thirty before he sat down at the table. To carry him through until bedtime (eleven o'clock) he had devised a reading program. The idea was to choose a major author—Tolstoy, Dickens, Twain—and read everything by that writer he could get his hands on, however marginal, however dull. This established a small goal for him each evening, and moreover, relieved him of having to wonder what to do, whom to read, where to start, in those long silent hours before sleep finally took him from himself. Three weeks ago he had begun on the collected works of Shakespeare. He had thus far put behind him the sonnets, *Venus and Adonis, Troilus and Cressida*, and *Two Gentlemen of Verona*, and was now into the third act of *Romeo and Juliet*. In another life, prior to Janey's death and his career switch to advertising, Max had been a high school English teacher, and he hadn't looked at *Romeo and Juliet* since teaching it. He found that his allegiances had changed. He used to identify most strongly with Romeo, and so, too, naturally, did his adolescent and hormone-crazed students, who viewed Romeo's morbid lovesickness and impetuous disregard for consequences as perfectly normal. But now Romeo made Max uncomfortable, and it was circumspect Juliet, instead, who came away with most of his sympathy. Her common-sense reply to Romeo's complaint on the balcony, *"O, wilt thou leave me so unsatisfied?"* had become, over the past two evenings, the mantra which had finally dipped him into sleep: *What satisfaction canst thou have tonight?*

Of course he wasn't happy. But he had given up on happiness since the rainy October night almost two years before when Janey had rolled her Datsun into a ditch off the side of Mason Road, and had never shown up again, not even as a corpse—for the coffin, in accordance with Jewish law, had been closed. He was, at least, surviving with dignity, and while he never kidded himself into

thinking this was enough, it was certainly better than
some of the alternatives. He had not lost his mind, or his
will, or his decency, or, he hoped, his sense of humor.
He had simply lost his taste for life, and that, he'd discovered, was not a prerequisite for living.

Max showered. Then he got out the rented tuxedo—
mandatory dress for Horowitz's bachelor party—and put it
on in front of his full-length mirror. As short as he was,
with broad shoulders, short arms, and no ass at all, nothing ever fit Max before it was extensively altered. He
hadn't given nearly enough lead time to the tuxedo shop
to get the job done right, but it still irritated him that he
was going to have to show up at a party—never mind that
it was only a party of drunken young men he had known
since childhood—in something that didn't fit. The seat of
the pants was baggy, and the bottoms sagged over the
tops of his shoes. The shirt-sleeves were so long he had to
roll back the cuffs before he put in the studs. Still, there
was nothing to be done about it. Max affixed the white
carnation to his lapel.

He had to admit that he was fond of his own good
looks, and that he was probably far more vain than men
less handsome than himself. One of Janey's favorite teases
had been to call him her little Ken doll—although tonight
he looked more like something that had jumped off the
top of a wedding cake. His hair was a dense carpet of tiny
black curls, and his face was baby-smooth, with large
black long-lashed eyes and a petulant, feminine mouth.
The trauma of his grief had failed to show up in his face.
At the age of twenty-seven, many people still took him for
twenty-two or twenty-three, and back in his days as a
teacher he'd worn a full beard in order to bolster his
credibility with his students. Now he was clean-shaven,
and just as fresh-looking as ever. Max sometimes wished,
when he was wallowing at the bottom of his grief, that his
looks were more emblematic of his fate, that he bore
some kind of facial badge that was adequate to his loss—
maybe a jagged scar, or a missing eye, from having sur-
vived the accident. But he had been nowhere near the site
of the accident when it happened. He was at home,
cleaning up after dinner, when Janey, on her way to her

aerobics class, had made whatever fatal mistake she had made. Neither Max nor anybody else would ever know exactly what had happened—whether she had sneezed, or braked for a dog, or fiddled with her radio too long, or simply let her attention drift away at a critical moment— for Janey had died alone. And now his handsome, un-lined, unscarred face should have belonged to someone else: someone, perhaps, who was still involved in the pursuit of women, and could have at least put it to some good use.

Max left his apartment, stopping outside the door to make sure it was securely locked. Then he got into his Volvo, reputed to be the safest car on the road, and drove east toward the city of St. Louis with his speedometer at fifty-five, both hands on the wheel, and his shoulders hunched with apprehension—so that anyone driving be-hind him could have easily mistaken him for a little old man.

———————

Horowitz, who had taken it upon himself to plan his own bachelor party, had booked a room at the Cheshire Inn—which was where, some fifteen years before, in a much larger room, his bar mitzvah party had been held. He did this, he told Max, partly for the sake of poetic symmetry, but also to prove to the frightened and un-happy thirteen-year-old boy inside himself that even fat ugly men could wind up getting what they wanted. Horo-witz had remained a virgin until the scandalous age of twenty-four, and in marrying Rachel Fine, he was finally saying I-told-you-so to all the kids on the old block, starting with himself, who had doubted his manhood.

Max had grown up on that block—three doors down from Horowitz on seedy Raymond Street in University City—and he had been at that bar mitzvah party. As he crossed through the lobby of the Cheshire Inn, with its suit of armor and its tapestry of a unicorn hunt, Max remem-bered certain things so vividly, they might have happened

an hour ago: how the feast had consisted of the unkosher
combination of hamburgers and milk shakes; how he had
found Horowitz cowering in the men's room and feigning
diarrhea because he did not want to be forced to dance
with anyone; and how he had stolen away at one point
with Janey Roth, who wore a yellow ribbon in her hair,
and coaxed her into a janitor's closet somewhere in this
hotel, and how, when she finally consented to kiss him,
her breath had been redolent of potato chips. That had
been an important moment. He had never fully realized
before that girls were just as human as boys—that if they
put something into their mouths, and you kissed them
soon afterward, they would taste of it. Now, riding up the
elevator, Max felt the thirteen-year-old boy awaken inside
of him; the boy was staring with incredulity through all
the intervening years at his rigid, mournful, twenty-seven-
year-old self, who was no longer the sort of guy to exuberantly cajole a girl into a closet, and it didn't like what it
saw. He was not supposed to have ended up like this.

Max walked down the hallway, watching for Horowitz's room number, and tried to shake his gloom. He
was happy for Horowitz—never mind that he himself
didn't feel happy—and did not want to do anything to
sour the party. He experimented with putting a jaunty
bounce into his step, but the pathetic insufficiency of this
only depressed him further. He found the room and
knocked. Horowitz yelled out to come in.

Max stepped into a bad smell. It was a stale, meaty
stink, as if several couples had spent several days in this
room engaged in a strenuous orgy without ever opening a
window or breaking to bathe. The source of it stood in the
middle of the room, in the middle of a card table: three fat
white sacks surrounded by a litter of the small white
cardboard boxes in which White Palace hamburgers were
served.

The three tuxedoed young men avidly feeding there—
Larry Klugman, Marv Miller and Horowitz—comprised,
along with Max, the old first string of the high school
debate team which had made it to the Missouri State
Semi-Finals on the strength of their handling of the topic
Resolved: That the Federal Government Should Continue

to Provide Tax Incentives to Corporations. They were the best team University City High had seen in years, and it was generally agreed that they would have gone all the way had Larry Klugman not lost his mind at a critical moment. Max had witnessed few things as painful to watch as Klugman simply standing there with his hands in the pockets of his checked sport jacket, his eyes glazed over and his mouth hanging open as if he were in silent communion with his ancestors, for the entire minute and a half of his final rebuttal. It was still, after all these years, the one thing you did not kid Klugman about. While Max had gone on to become first an English teacher and then an advertising man, and Horowitz had turned his hobby of photography into a lucrative profession (his specialty was gorgeous commercial photographs of food), Klugman and Miller had remained true to their original vision, fulfilled their early promise, and both became tax attorneys. For four men as young as they were, there was plenty of money in this room.

Horowitz wiped his mouth, rose from his chair, and came over to Max, his enormous landslide of a body straining at the confines of his tuxedo. The two of them embraced, and Max was lost in a wall of fat. Since Horowitz's engagement to Rachel and the dinners at her apartment every evening, he had grown more obese than ever. Max, on the other hand, had been slowly and steadily losing weight. It had been their odd sizes—Horowitz a hulking grizzly bear, Max a tiny doll—which had first drawn them together as children. Nobody ever wanted them on their teams.

Max told Horowitz how happy he was for him. Horowitz grinned and shrugged.

"Are you nervous at all?" Max asked him.

"I'm kind of sad, if you want to know the truth. I'm not sure I want to say good-bye to the rest of my life leading up to this—as rotten as it was. I'm having a heavy attack of nostalgia. Are you hungry?"

Max glanced at the carnage on the card table.

"I don't think so," he said, and went over to greet Klugman and Miller. He shook their hands, asked how they were doing, and then asked after their families. Miller—

the brilliant captain of their debate team, who had studied law at Stanford—already had two small boys and a prematurely middle-aged wife. He nodded his head emphatically in response to Max's questions; his mouth was too full for talking. Klugman showed Max a slow-spreading smirk, which was his favorite facial expression, and said, "Sherri's on a sexual strike again."

"How come?"

"Probably because she's figured out how much I like it."

There could have been more than a grain of truth in this. How Klugman had ended up with Sherri, who was not educated, not pretty, and not in any way likable, was one of the great mysteries. She was a tall, morose, evasive woman with liver-colored scoops under her eyes. Talking to her was like yanking teeth, and when she did come out with something, it was almost always negative. Max felt badly for Klugman, not simply because he was married to Sherri, but because he was so obviously and painfully in love with her. When they were out together, Klugman treated her with such anxious attention, you would have thought they were on their first date.

"That's a nicely understated tuxedo you've got on," Max told him.

"Why, thank you," Klugman said, and took a drink of what looked like scotch and water from a plastic tumbler. His tuxedo was shocking pink, with glittery silver lapels. "I thought I'd go for something muted."

Horowitz was back at the table, stuffing a White Palace into his mouth. "Sit down," he said to Max. "Eat."

Max took the chair between Klugman and Miller, tugged straight the creases in his loose pant-legs, then removed a White Palace hamburger from its box and inspected it. The bun was very soft, and when he pulled it away, bits of bread stuck to the meat, which was a flat dead-looking gray, scored with holes and sprinkled with translucent onions. The stale sex-smell was too much for him, and he held it away at arm's length. "Anybody want this?"

Miller snatched it away from him. Miller was an owlish, bony, largely humorless young man whose air of constant aggravation Max attributed to the fact that Miller already had everything that he could possibly want for the rest of his life except for more money which would come along anyway if he simply sat still. He had two supernaturally well-behaved boys, aged two and three, a wife who was as dependable as Gibraltar, a house in Creve Coeur, a restored Bentley in his garage, and a junior partnership in one of St. Louis's most prestigious law firms. Yet Miller walked, and even sat, with a pronounced stoop, as if all of this early good fortune were nothing but an unfair burden, and the Rolex around his wrist merely an upscale manacle. He blinked at Max through his thick horn-rimmed glasses. "You don't want any?" he asked.

"No."

"Now, wait a minute," Horowitz said. "I paid twenty-four cents apiece for these things. It'd be a sin to let them go to waste. You should think about all the children in Ethiopia going to bed tonight without their White Palaces."

Max laughed. "Horowitz, I'm sorry—but I just don't have the digestion of a twelve-year-old anymore. How can you guys consciously put those things into your mouths?"

"It's interesting," Klugman said, staring at his half-eaten White Palace. "Why do we eat these things? You know they're garbage, you know they're going to end up giving you the shits—and then they do give you the shits, and then the next thing you know, you've got a bag full of belly-bombers on the seat of your car, and you're stuffing your face with them again. Why? Could it be their very awfulness that makes them so attractive? They taste like sin would taste, if you could eat it—don't you think?"

"It sounds like you're talking about a certain kind of woman," Max said.

Klugman thought about this. "I'm probably talking about Sherri," he said, and finished off the rest of his hamburger.

"Well, anyway," Horowitz said. "Rachel hates these things. If I come home smelling like White Palaces after we're married, she'll probably file for divorce. So this could very well be my last hurrah." He took two White Palace boxes from a sack and lobbed one in front of Max.

"Come on, Max—don't you remember going to White Palaces at three in the morning back in the good old days? Just eat one for the sake of nostalgia."

"If I do, I'll be feeling nostalgic about it for the next two days."

"Then have some cheese fries."

"No thanks."

"I hate to say this, Max—but you're really turning into a prig."

This cut. It was the truth.

"Will you at least have a drink with me?" Horowitz said.

"Sure," Max told him.

He followed Horowitz's lumbering body over to the wet bar. Here stood a half-gallon of Chivas Regal, a water pitcher, an ice bucket, two stacks of plastic tumblers, and nothing else. Max asked him if he had any club soda.

"You mean to mix with your scotch?"

"I mean to drink by itself."

"Oh no you don't," Horowitz said, and picked up the bottle. "This is my bachelor party and you're drinking with me tonight—and I don't want to hear any crap about the evils of alcohol or the dangers of drunk driving."

The problem was, Max was wary of what alcohol did to him. He had not gotten completely drunk since the night of Janey's accident. Horowitz had been the first person he had called after the police had called him—he couldn't have dealt with his mother at that point—and once his ordeal with the police, with Horowitz there the whole time at his side, was over, Horowitz had run out for a bottle of Wild Turkey, plucked the phone from its plug, and forced Max to drink until he passed out. Since then, after more than two drinks, panic had set in. But it had been months since Max had taken more than two drinks, and it was entirely possible that he'd gotten over that period of his mourning. Besides, he owed it to Horowitz to give himself over tonight, as far as he could, to celebration.

"All right," Max said, putting his hand on Horowitz's shoulder. "Pour me a drink."

"Now you're talking."

"But make it light."

"Fuck you," Horowitz told him, and poured out two or three fingers worth into a tumbler. He added water and handed it to Max. It was the color of honey.

"I'm making a toast," Max announced.

Klugman and Miller picked up their drinks.

Horowitz ducked his head slightly and plucked at his drooping cossack moustache.

Max had no idea what he meant to say. But having been a teacher for three years, he knew that the only way to start was by opening his mouth.

"To Horowitz," he said, "who I love—well, who I love better than any person I know." Love did not enter into his feelings for his mother. That was purely a matter of duty, pity, and guilt. Now he drew a blank. Beside him, Horowitz rearranged something in the pit of his throat, and Max simply started all over again. "To Horowitz," he said, "the world's slowest bloomer. It took him twenty-four years to get laid, and twenty-eight years to get married, and now I'll just bet that his happiness lasts for the rest of the years of his life. He certainly has it coming to him. *L'chayam*."

Miller applauded, Klugman whistled, and everyone drank. The whiskey jolted Max.

Horowitz guided him back to the table with his big arm draped around his shoulders, then took a seat, reached into a sack, withdrew a box, and stared into it. "Well, how do you like this," he said. "It's empty."

"How could it be empty?" Miller asked him.

"Take a look for yourself," Horowitz said, and tossed the box over to him.

Miller handled it as if it were a piece of state's evidence. "You'd better look at the rest of them," he advised Horowitz.

Horowitz shook out the sack and five empty boxes dropped soundlessly onto the table. "What the hell," he said. "I'm still hungry."

The sight of those empty boxes touched a sore spot inside of Max. He hated to see mistakes made, things overlooked. It was carelessness, after all, that had killed Janey, and it was going to be a moment of pure dumb, unthinking carelessness, he was sure, that would finally trip the switch on Armageddon and blow down the whole house of cards. He took another taste of his scotch. "You've been cheated," he told Horowitz.

"I know," Horowitz said sadly, and went on staring at the boxes.

"Well, what are you going to do about it?"

"What do you mean?"

"Aren't you going to go back there and get it straightened out?"

"Max, I'm having a party for chrissakes. I'm not going to suddenly get into my car and—"

"But you've been cheated, Horowitz."

"It's six lousy White Palaces. Cool down."

But Max was hot. "Do you know what this is? It's the typical passive St. Louis attitude. Why do you think nobody in this town uses their horns?"

"What?"

"You've driven in other cities. People use their goddamned horns in other cities. But not in St. Louis. You could run a red light and mow down an old lady and I guarantee you wouldn't hear a single horn. It's the same damned thing in movie theaters—nobody ever turns around to tell loudmouths to shut up. They just sit there and suffer through it like it's their civic duty to be timid. And how about when that thirteen-year-old girl was raped in the fountain at Forest Park with a whole crowd of rubbernecks just standing there gawking?"

"Max, what the hell are you talking about?"

"I'm talking about how nobody in this city has the imagination to even know when they're getting crapped on."

"Look—I just got crapped on to the tune of a dollar and a half, and I don't care. All right? And if that's a typical St. Louis attitude, then I'm a typical St. Louisan. Now, will you please just drop the whole thing? We're trying to have a party here."

Maybe he was overreacting. But maybe he wasn't. Big things were built out of small things; and it was always in the small things first that principles were compromised away until they were compromised away entirely.

"Doesn't anybody here give a damn about principle?"

"Are you kidding?" Klugman said. "I'm a lawyer."

Miller, who did not laugh easily, hooted at this.

"Which White Palace was this?" Max asked Horowitz.

"I'm not telling you."

"Fine."

Max searched the three sacks until he came up with the receipt. It was the White Palace at Grand and Gravois—right in the heart of redneck South St. Louis. He put the six empty boxes along with the receipt into one of the sacks and stood up.

"I'll be back as soon as I can," Max told Horowitz.

"Max, what the hell do you think you're doing?"

"What the rest of you are obviously too complacent to do," he said, and walked out of the hotel room.

Max punched his tape deck and Bach came on—the fourth Brandenburg Concerto. The serene interplay of the notes was as rational and soothing as the conversation of angels, and Max wondered why they didn't play such music, to the exclusion of everything else, in shopping malls, supermarkets, dentists' offices, elevators. It might have tamed the world.

Or maybe not. He was headed, after all, into the heart of darkness (it didn't matter that this South St. Louis neighborhood was mostly white), where the young men looked like roadies for heavy-metal bands, and the young women, already dragging one or two dirty toddlers behind them, were pregnant again, and where the drivers along Grand Avenue were even more savagely ignorant than usual. They waited to make their turns by jutting out halfway into intersections; when they weren't double-parking they were lurching out of spaces along the congested street; they wove over the lines as if they were drunk, which they most likely were. Why couldn't people understand that they were sitting inside of deadly weapons? Max's own profession, advertising, was partly at fault; cars were fun, cars were excitement, cars were penises, cars were expressions of your life-style and weltanshauung, cars were everything, in fact, except what they were: huge hunks of metal hurtling through space with no regard for human life, usually commandeered by mental deficients.

Max crept along. He wondered why South St. Louisans were so much uglier than people, say, in Clayton or Ladue. It wasn't simply a matter of bad childhood nutrition; there were the barbaric beards and shaggy hair, the Budweiser T-shirts, the cheap rubber sandals from Woolworth's, the tattoos, the glum faces, the general uncleanliness to account for. Max, too, had grown up poor, if poor meant simply not having enough money. His father, a faceless peddler of women's clothing (his mother kept no pictures of him), had deserted them when Max was an infant, never to be heard from again, and his mother made so little at her cashier's job at Rexall that there was seldom a period in Max's childhood when he wasn't delivering newspapers, collecting bottles and cans, mowing lawns, shoveling snow, or selling subscriptions to *Grit* to help out. But that had been one kind of poor, and down here, south of Highway 44, was another—Max had never been deprived of the benefits of civilization. His gut reaction to what St. Louisans (not to be confused with people from Indiana) labeled as "hoosiers," poor white trash, made him wonder what caliber of mind he really had. He didn't like these surly downtrodden sons and daughters of laid-off brewery workers and transplanted farmers from the Ozarks; they made him uncomfortable; he had a hard time thinking of them as full-fledged human beings. Part of this was due to his Jewish upbringing—Jews were generally democratic only at a distance. But such a prejudice, he knew, wasn't worthy of a tolerant and compassionate soul, not to mention someone of Max's leftist political sympathies. In conversation he was always ready to champion the wretched of the earth, but in reality he did not like to be in their vicinity—especially on a September evening as hot as this one. Heat, for some reason, seemed to be the natural element of hoosiers. It brought them out of doors, sat them down on stoops, increased their intake of Busch beer, melted what was left of their mentalities, and made them still more dangerous behind the wheels of their jacked-up, rusted-out Oldsmobiles and Impalas.

Max suddenly braked for a long-haired young man who was crossing the street without looking at the traffic—as if this stupidity were some kind of proof of his manhood—and honked his horn at him. Then he nosed forward again with his jaws clenched.

The White Palace came into view. It was indeed a small white palace, replete with battlements and turrets, which looked to have been built of enormous bathroom tiles. The parking lot was sprawling and chaotic. Max pulled in and remembered, with a pang, the last time he had been here.

It was another night of celebration. Janey, after six restless years, had finally graduated from the University of Missouri at St. Louis with a degree in general studies, and they had gone to have dinner at Tony's, St. Louis's only five-star restaurant. It was a Saturday night, and the wait for a table was long. Janey, who wore a navy blue dress and the string of real pearls that her parents had given her (along with a brand-new Datsun) as a graduation present, was in an expansive mood, and each time the bartender checked in on them, she ordered another whiskey sour. Max remembered basking in the radiance of her smile and drunken eyes, and feeding on a happiness stirred up by thoughts of yet more happiness to come. They had been married for almost two years, and this was the first time, now that Janey's education was behind her, that they had talked seriously about having children. An hour and a half went by, and still the maître d' hadn't summoned them to a table. Janey leaned against him. "I'm smashed," she said. "If we don't get something to eat pretty soon, I think I'm going to pass out in front of all these beautiful people." Then she sat up, taking her pearls between her fingers, and laughed. "Hey—I've got a great idea. Screw all this high-rolling bullshit. Why don't we go to a White Palace?" And so, dressed to the nines, they had waited for the parking lot attendant to pull their car around, then drove into South St. Louis and gorged themselves at this very same White Palace restaurant, perched here on the corner of Grand and Gravois. Of course they were as sick the next morning as a pair of debauched sailors. But it made a good story, this cheerful descent from top to bottom, from glitter to gutter, and it showed Janey off in her best light: funny, unaffected, surprising. For the four remaining months in which she had left to live, Max told it often.

Now he turned off his tape deck, undid his seat belt, and got out of his Volvo. The heavy damp blanket of heat, after the air-conditioning, nearly knocked him over. He straightened the carnation in his lapel and went into the White Palace, carrying his sack full of evidence.

The smell was fierce. Except for that, and except for the crowd of unhealthy, badly dressed, poorly washed hoosiers all around him, this place could have been a morgue: the walls were of white linoleum tiles, there were gleaming aluminum railings and counters everywhere, and the bitter antiseptic light that was pouring down from the ceiling would go on pouring all night long. These places, like morgues, never closed. Max got into line. In front of him was a stooped old woman with a goiter on her neck the size of a tangerine and he lifted his gaze, instead, to the menu above his head. You could eat here for less than a dollar—how many indigent people on the verge of starvation had White Palaces kept alive over the years? Max, who paid attention to slogans, noticed that the one under the White Palace logo was new, and he had to admit that it was a pretty good one: *White Palace—One Taste and You're Hooked*. He wondered who did their advertising.

"Take your order?"

The woman was not young, and she wore a peaked blue cap; beneath it the bun of her black hair had come partly undone, and two strands of it licked at her neck like tendrils. She looked tired and impatient. Max remembered that he was wearing a tuxedo and saw himself through her exhausted dark blue eyes—another smirky West County slicko down in these parts on a slumming expedition. He sat the sack on the gleaming metal counter between them, which was probably intended to come up to most people's chests, but reached only the middle of Max's neck.

"Hello," Max said. "I have a complaint."

The woman waited.

"Would you please take a look inside this sack?"

The woman's blue-painted eyelids came down a notch; she wasn't in the mood for this. She took a grudging look inside the sack. "Well, Katy-bar-the-door," she said without the slightest intonation of surprise. "Six empty boxes."

Max showed her the receipt. "I paid for thirty White Palaces," he said. "And you gave me only twenty-four."

"Is that right?"

"Yes. And I'd like my money back."

Now the woman showed him a crooked half-smile. "Honey, how do I know you didn't just go and eat those six White Palaces you say we didn't give you?"

Max did not like to have his honesty doubted, even by people who didn't know him. "You're just going to have to take my word for it," he said.

"Now, why should I do that?"

"Because I'm telling you the truth."

"And what if *I* told *you* I was Marilyn Monroe?"

"If I worked in this restaurant and you were one of my customers," Max said through his teeth, "I'd ask you to give my regards to Joe DiMaggio. Now, I'd like my money back, if you don't mind."

The woman looked at him with what seemed to Max an inappropriate curiosity. One of her hands had gone to her ear to toy with the tiny earring there.

"Look," Max said. "If you won't take my word for it, why don't you just smell one of these boxes? If there was ever a White Palace inside of them, they'd stink of it, wouldn't they?"

"Honey, my nose is so full of White Palaces, I couldn't smell one if you pushed one in my face."

Max's patience had run out.

"I'd like to see your manager," he said. "What's your name, by the way?" He'd noticed that this woman, unlike the other women engaged in their furious dance behind the counter, wasn't wearing a name tag.

"Why would you want to know?"

"Because once I get my money back, I'm going to complain to your manager. You've been extremely rude to me."

The woman's wide mouth settled into a straight line.

Then she punched the register, a bell rang, and she handed him the money. "Here's your refund, sir," she said with a heavy emphasis on the sir. "I'm sorry if we caused you any inconvenience."

"How much were the six White Palaces?"

"A dollar forty-four, plus tax."

"You gave me a dollar seventy-five."

"Go buy some lifts for your shoes with it," she told him, then turned to the restless crowd behind him. "Next!" she called out.

———————

"And there," said Horowitz, "is the bar mitzvah boy."

The projector was set up on an end table which Horowitz had moved to one side of the room; the screen was planted in front of the canopied bed. There stood a plump thirteen-year-old Horowitz with a yarmulke on his head, a tallith around his shoulders, an enormous Torah cradled in his arms, and his pink tongue pointed at the camera.

"This is the one my parents never hung in the hallway," Horowitz said.

"Next slide!" yelled Klugman, who was by far the drunkest of the four of them.

Max was into his second drink and already feeling light-headed. The dollar seventy-five which the woman at the White Palace had handed him was still in his pocket; Horowitz, infuriated with what he called Max's "Abraham Lincoln complex," had refused to take the money. So his descent into South St. Louis had in one respect been for nothing, but in another respect had not: justice, at least, had been served—not that anyone cared except Max.

The projector whirred and clacked.

"My bar mitzvah party," Horowitz said. "At the Henry

the Eighth Room right here at the Cheshire Inn. There's Max, dancing with Mindy Ladinsky, and there's me, standing in the middle of it all and wishing I was invisible. It was the first party I'd ever been to with girls, and I was scared shitless. As I recall, I didn't score that night—notwithstanding the fact that I'd just become a man."

"You didn't score for the next ten years," Max reminded him.

"Next slide!" Klugman shouted.

Here was a picture of Max dancing with a very thin, very pretty girl with straight blond hair and a yellow bow in it, making the V sign behind Max's head and laughing at the camera.

"Is that Janey?" Miller asked.

"That's Janey," Max said.

"Look at how skinny she is."

"When the hell did you start going with her?" Klugman asked. "In kindergarten?"

"Just about."

"I remember you two being such a hot item in high school, but I had no idea you were childhood sweethearts. It's so wholesome, it makes you want to puke. Didn't you ever go out with anybody else?"

"Sure," Max said. "But I always wound up going back to Janey." He took a sip of his drink; his heart was beating strangely. The slide was still up on the screen. "All right already," Max said to Horowitz. "Can't we look at something else?"

"The projector's jammed."

"Well, what's wrong with it?"

"That's what I'm trying to find out."

Max had to go on looking at Janey—her hand, as he danced with her, was sassily planted on her own narrow hip—and he felt a peculiar sort of jealousy. It was himself, in another life, that he was jealous of.

"Is the projector broken or what?" he said.

"Just hold your goddamned horses." Horowitz gave the projector a couple of knocks, and the next slide came on. This one—of Rachel Fine standing in a very lush garden, maybe the Climatron—was from a much later period in Horowitz's life. There seemed to be no particular order to the slides in this presentation, which Max found vaguely unsettling. Rachel was wearing a pair of sunglasses and a flowered tentlike dress.

"Jesus, she's fat," Horowitz said.

"She's nowhere near as fat as you," Klugman told him.

"We're both fat, and so we make a perfect couple. It bums me out sometimes when I think about it."

"I don't see what you've got to complain about," Miller said.

"I'm fat, she's fat, we're going to have a big fat wedding and slap a big fat down payment on a house and raise a bunch of fat kids, and for the rest of our lives, we'll be in fat city. It's too damned *pat*. Everybody on both sides of the family is fat, except for my father. You should see us when we all get together and eat—we look like a bunch of happy peasants from a Brueghel painting. And wait'll you see the wedding. All of Rachel's *bridesmaids* are fat. I wouldn't be surprised if the whole goddamned synagogue sinks into the core of the earth next Sunday."

"You shouldn't be talking like this," Miller admonished him. "Rachel's a very sweet woman."

"Miller, how the hell did you ever get into Stanford? I'm not saying that Rachel isn't sweet. I'm simply complaining about all the genetic engineering that goes on in this culture. Fat people marry fat people, ugly people marry ugly people, and beautiful people marry beautiful people. Look at our Laughing Adonis over here. You think he'd ever hook up with a woman who wasn't gorgeous? Why *should* he? Even when she was thirteen, Janey looked like a Jewish Grace Kelly. And look at Max—he's a mannequin out of *Gentlemen's Quarterly*. Why do you think Janey married him anyway? Her daddy's one of the richest Jewish robber barons in town and Max was just a midget pauper from Raymond Street. She married him because he was the only other person at U. City High who was as beautiful as she was."

Horowitz wasn't very far off the mark. Bill Roth owned the largest chain of movie theaters in the St. Louis area, among other things, and at least as far as the subtle stratifications of local Jewish society went, Max had married above his station.

"Do we have to keep harping on this?" Max asked.

"Sorry," Horowitz said, and put up the next slide.

Bad luck: here was another shot of Janey. Max remembered the event. It had been a horse show out at Queeny Park, and Janey had taken home two blue ribbons. He sipped his scotch and filled his lungs with air. Horowitz's camera had caught her at the apex of a leap over a white fence, on the back of a long-legged elegant black horse. Her riding crop pointed away from her armpit. Her face was a blur. He remembered the horse's name: Nightmare.

The projector whirred and clacked.

Here was Janey grinning as she whisked off her riding cap, and her hair, with the sun behind it, was a flurry of spun platinum.

Clack.

Here was Janey seated in the wooden stands, her chin cupped in her hand, looking worried about something.

Clack.

Max's tolerance for alcohol was low, his glass was empty, and this was probably what started him crying. It was not one of those wrenching, lung-heaving episodes, but a quiet, almost a contemplative cry, and Max probably would have gotten away with it—sitting in the dark with his face in his hands—if Klugman had not staggered up from his chair and switched on the light on his way to the bathroom.

Horowitz had one hand on top of the projector and was staring at Max. "Miller," he said, "would you mind turning off the light?"

———————

Klugman spent a good part of the next hour hugging the toilet bowl, and Miller finally drove him home. Now it was just Max and Horowitz at the card table, the bottle of Chivas Regal between them. Since the slide presentation,

Max had been carefully regulating his intake of liquor. Horowitz had not. His tuxedo jacket, cummerbund, bow tie, and wilted carnation were strewn across the canopied bed, and his big red face seemed to sag with the weight of the booze in his blood. "Do you know who you're turning into?" he said. "You're turning into that crazy old woman in Dickens. The one who just sits there in her rotten wedding dress staring at her rotten wedding cake— Miss Hammershlammer, or whatever the hell her name was."

"Miss Havisham," Max said.

"Well, that's who you're turning into."

"Let me ask you this, Horowitz. Just when is the recommended deadline for men to stop mourning their wives?"

"Whatever it is, you've passed it." Horowitz picked up the bottle and tipped it into his tumbler. "Max, I can understand you cracking up at a picture of Janey six months, maybe even a year after she died, but not two years, for godsakes. It's becoming pathological. I'm sorry to tell you this, Max—but I'm getting sick and tired of watching you lick your wounds."

"What do you suggest I do?"

"Start living again."

"I'm alive."

"You know what I mean. When was the last time you even had a date?"

Max sighed and leaned forward onto his crossed arms. "I gave it a shot for a while, Horowitz. But it just wasn't any good. I wasn't ready."

"You didn't answer my question. When was the last time you actually had a date?"

"Around Christmas."

"Who with?"

"One of the women at the office set me up with her cousin."

"And?"

"She was very pretty, which was a surprise, and we had a nice dinner at Spiro's, and then she invited me back to her apartment."

"Did you fuck her?"

"No."

"Why the hell not?"

"Because I picked up this collection can she had sitting on her coffee table—you know, with a slot in the top for coins. It had a photograph of a sunrise on it and a headline that read something like HELP SPREAD THE SUNSHINE. And then I noticed at the bottom, in very small print, that you were supposed to send your contributions to a Christian foundation in Lynchburg, Virginia."

"So fucking what?"

"So Lynchburg, Virginia, in case you didn't know, is where Jerry Falwell has his headquarters. The woman was a Fascist, and I guess I must have told her as much, because she ended up asking me to leave."

"You blew a chance to get laid because of *politics*?"

"You're damned right I did, Horowitz. Come on—would you go to bed with a neo-Nazi?"

"I'd go to bed with *Eva Braun* if I were in your shoes, Max! Don't you realize that I'm the world's foremost leading expert on the ravages of prolonged horniness? I know what it can do to a person." Horowitz took a swallow from his tumbler and wiped his mouth with his sleeve. "Why don't you just stop this marathon mourning session of yours and go out and get laid? It'd be the easiest thing in the world for you. All you have to do is go stand in a bar and take numbers."

"What if I told you I wasn't interested in getting laid?"

"Interest in getting laid is the human condition, for chrissakes."

Max made a steeple of his hands; it was the gesture he used to fall back on when explaining a particularly thorny concept to his students. "This is going to shock you, Horowitz. But here it is: I've made a conscious decision to be celibate for a while."

Horowitz frowned at him and tugged on his moustache. Then he finished off what was left in his tumbler. "What?" he said.

"I've thought it over, and it's just the best thing for me right now. I'm still scared, Horowitz. I'm scared of complications and messiness and things getting out of control—and that tells me I'm not ready for a relationship. And if I'm not ready for a relationship, then I'm not interested in going through the whole dishonest routine of dating women who I have no intention of taking seriously. All right? There's your explanation."

Max watched Horowitz slop more scotch into his tumbler.

"Why don't you just go out and find some woman who has no intention of taking *you* seriously?" Horowitz said.

"Why would I want to go out with a woman who doesn't take me seriously?"

"For the simple brute pleasure of fucking, goddammit!"

"Horowitz, you just said it. It's a simple brute pleasure. I can live without it right now."

Horowitz knocked back his whiskey, blinked at Max, and belched.

"You're going to kill yourself, drinking like that," Max told him.

"Are you Max Baron?" Horowitz said. "Have we met?"

"Come on, Horowitz."

Horowitz slumped forward on his elbows. His eyes had puffed into slits. "Do you want to know what this thing really is? This isn't celibacy we're talking about. This is necrophilia. As long as you're not making love to anyone else, you're still being faithful to Janey. That's the whole thing, right there in a fucking nutshell."

Max turned away to absorb the blow. He stared into a darkened corner of the hotel room. He had to tell himself that Horowitz's words had been spoken in love, and that, moreover, they were probably true. But how true? It was important not to mistake a part of the truth for the whole. Yet Max couldn't find any argument against it. For all intents and purposes, he was still the faithful husband.

When he turned back to the table, Horowitz was asleep on his big crossed arms. His mouth was open, and spittle had already begun to collect on the sleeve of his frilled white shirt. Max roused him to the point where he could dance him to the bed—the incompetent trainer with his drugged bear—and managed to dump him across the mattress. He undid the studs from his shirt, yanked his belt away, and took off his shoes. He set the shoes side by side on the floor with their toes pointed in the same direction, and then, as if this had flipped a switch inside of him, he went on to clean the rest of the hotel room. By the time he was hanging Horowitz's tuxedo jacket in the closet, the room was in near-perfect order. Except for one small thing: there was a White Palace box on the floor beneath the card table, which he had somehow over-looked. Max started for it, then stopped himself. What did he think he was doing? There could be no sane explana-tion for cleaning a hotel room when a maid would be coming around in the morning. But on the other hand, it was absurd to leave the White Palace box lying where it was, as if this proved some kind of principle. Max went over to it, bent down, and his heart seemed to crack with weariness. Enough of this.

He sat down at the card table, picked up his tumbler, and drank. The second drink had made him slightly drunk. The third had landed him in a kind of intensified sobriety.

Horowitz had been right about everything. Max was in love with his own misery; Max was a secret necrophiliac; Max was a prematurely aged little old man. He was sick of this half-dead life he was living, sick of his half-dead self. Now another, nearly blasphemous thought came to him. What he was really sick of was Janey. It was true. He was hugely sick of her—sick of her death, sick of her absence, sick of all the endlessly picked-over images in the junk shop of his heart. The dead clung closer than the living. The dead were insufferably demanding. Nobody nagged like the dead. At least when Janey was alive, he'd been able to get away from her on occasion.

The thing to do—but what was there to do?

The thing to do was to get drunk. Never mind why.

There were two bars right here at the Cheshire Inn, but Max wasn't interested in drinking at any decent estab-lishment. He wanted a lowdown dirty drunk in a low-down dirty dive—someplace where Janey, had she been alive, would not have been caught dead at.

CHAPTER TWO

Cousin Hugo's, which squatted across the street from a Venture discount store in Maplewood, was a sad green clapboard building with a floodlit parking lot as bright as a prison yard. Some years ago it had been the scene of some kind of appalling murder (Max wasn't clear on the details), and the air of old tragedy he imagined to be hanging over the place, along with the fact that it was the sleaziest bar he could think of within a short drive from the hotel, drew him there. He pulled into the parking lot full of Jeeps, pickups, Trans-Ams, and what looked to be the very same jacked-up, rusted-out Oldsmobiles and Impalas that had been going for his throat in South St. Louis. But this was not South St. Louis, with its century-old redbrick houses crumbling in the shadow of the Anheuser-Busch brewery—this was Maplewood, near Dogtown, with the defunct Scullin Steel Mill as its centerpiece, a downtown shopping strip that had last been fashionable before World War II broke out, and its own peculiar atmosphere of seediness.

Max sat in his Volvo and contemplated a few more bars of "Eine Kleine Nacht musik." Then he left his car and looked for the entrance to Cousin Hugo's, and as he stepped beyond the reach of the floodlights, the starlit sky opened out above his head like a fan. The constellations were as clear as he had ever seen them in the city. There, hanging low in the sky, with his unmistakable belt of three stars, was Orion the Hunter—another accident victim. His lover, the moon goddess Artemis, and quite a hunter herself, had carelessly shot him through the heart as they

were stalking a lion together (she had somehow managed
to mistake him for that lion) and in apology she had
installed him in the heavens among the other immortals. It
must have been a whole lot easier, Max thought, to account for senseless fatal accidents back in the Classical
Age, when the gods themselves were known to be klutzes.
Most likely they still were. Max had no patience with the
Judeo-Christian concept of a consistent, judicious, grand-
fatherly deity. Give him a wild and fickle universe rampant
with mischievous demons and self-indulgent demigods—
all the good evidence pointed to such a model.

He went into the bar. It seemed that he was going
from one foul-smelling room to another tonight; here was
a heady concoction of stale beer, cheap perfume, frying
hamburgers, and sweat. The bar was full of young salt-of-
the-earth blue-collar types—the sort who had voted twice
for Reagan, if they voted at all, because he fit their image
of a cowboy—and amid these cowboy hats, seed-corn
caps, halter tops, and blue jeans, Max's tuxedo must have
been so anomalous as to render him invisible, for nobody
so much as gave him a glance as he made his way to the
bar and took a stool. Behind the bar was a hand-lettered
banner that read CONGRATULATIONS CHUCK AND JOAN—IT'S A
BOY! and in a corner was a small grill upon which a few
hamburgers were sputtering. If this evening were a fugue,
hamburgers, smelly rooms, and hoosiers would have been
the central themes to which the music kept returning.

An angry-looking bartender with a beard and a Grateful Dead T-shirt took his order: Chivas and water in a tall
glass.

He sipped his scotch—which tasted sweet, as scotch
tasted only when you had drunk too much of it—and
noticed that a woman, sitting at the far corner of the bar,
was staring at him. She wore a slinky maroon dress that
exposed her bony shoulders, and held a streaming cigarette in her uplifted hand; behind the rising arabesques of
smoke her stare was as bold as a child's.

Max, not knowing what else to do—except ignore
her—raised his glass in a friendly salute.

Abruptly the woman's hand went to the black bun of
her hair and patted the place where a wild strand was

poking out; then she ground out her cigarette, picked up her purse, and left her stool. She walked past Max without glancing at him, and he turned to watch her weave her way through the thicket of tables in the adjoining room, the small of her back indented with what he took to be offended dignity. She was strangely built. Her shoulders and waist were very narrow, and yet below that waist, suspended like a ripe pear, or maybe a fat inverted valentine, was a rump all out of proportion to the rest of her. It bounced against itself within the clinging membrane of her dress, passed beneath the blue neon rest-room sign, and jolted out of sight.

Callipygian, Max thought, turning back to his drink. It was one of those arcane and basically useless words dear to the hearts of English teachers and ex-English teachers everywhere. What it meant was big-assed. Max found such outsized asses vaguely repulsive—Janey's boyish, athletic buttocks had always been his ideal. Still, there was something sordidly fascinating about such a monumental rear end on such an otherwise waifishly built woman, and Max wouldn't have minded getting another look at it. Not that he had any designs tonight on this woman, or any other woman. He told himself that his interest was purely, if perversely, esthetic. Then he wondered what there could have been in that innocent gesture of raising his glass which had so offended that Callipygian woman. Had she taken it as a sexual come-on? Or had she been hoping for a sexual come-on and felt rebuked by the simple friendliness of the gesture? He had lost touch with women to the extent that he couldn't tell. The language of sexual signals was like any other language: let it fall into disuse and it deserted you. Of course, he had no more need of that language these days than Chinese. Nevertheless, it bothered him that that woman had so completely misread him. Or maybe he was off the mark entirely. Maybe she had simply been seized by an urgent need to visit the john.

Max dropped the whole matter and picked up his drink.

Somebody tapped him on the shoulder.

Max swiveled on his stool and faced the Callipygian

woman in the cheap maroon dress. She was grinning at him wetly, her eyes shone, her purse was pressed to her chest beneath her crossed arms, and she was swinging from side to side on the broad fulcrum of her hips like a little girl coyly applying for a favor. She wore too much makeup, too much perfume. He noticed that the wayward strand of hair had been tucked back into her bun. Whoever she was, she was vaguely, disturbingly, familiar.

"Hello," Max said, and gave her a polite smile.

"Well, hello to you. My Lord—what a tiny little world."

"Is it?" Max asked, maintaining his smile.

"Honey, don't you know who I am?"

"You're going to have to refresh my memory."

"All right," she said, and laughed. "Have you got a dollar seventy-five to buy a lady a drink?"

Max felt his smile evaporate. He had probably failed to recognize her because she was out of uniform. On the other hand, he hadn't really been paying close attention to her face back at the White Palace. It was a hard face, almost masculine, with severe features: strong nose, high cheekbones, firm jaw, wide mouth. Her skin was deeply tanned, and her almond-shaped eyes were a disconcerting shade of dark blue—disconcerting because they didn't seem to belong in that face. She might have been the improbable offspring of an Apache and a Swede. He guessed she was somewhere in her late thirties, although it was entirely possible that he was off by five years in either direction. He couldn't say if he found her attractive or unattractive; she certainly wasn't pretty, at least not by any conventional standard.

"Are you going to invite me to sit down?" the woman asked him. "Or are you still mad at me?"

To tell the truth, he *was* still mad at her—as much for that cheap crack about his height as for her assumption that he had been lying—but he did not want to think of himself, or appear to anyone else, including this strange woman, as a man who held petty grudges. Max asked her to have a seat.

"Why, thank you," she said. "I don't mind if I do."

She set her purse on the bar and settled down on the

stool beside him, her big butt mushrooming. She patted
her hair, opened her purse, took out a pack of Winstons,
and went on smiling at him. "Well now," she said, lighting her own cigarette—Max never carried a lighter—"isn't
this just the strangest thing, running into you again like
this?"

"It's strange, all right," Max said with a smile, although for some reason it didn't feel that strange at all.
There was some kind of justice in it.

"I guess I owe you an apology," she said. "I mean
for what I said about you getting lifts for your shoes. That
wasn't very nice of me, was it? But you see, I had me one
hell of a rotten day, and I was just dog tired, and you just
came in at the wrong moment, I guess. I'm what you'd
call short-tempered." She laughed—it was actually more
of a hoot—and covered her mouth. "There I go, talking
about short again. Are you very sensitive about that?"

"I've always had more important things to worry
about," Max said.

"Well, good. Because I'll tell you—if there's one
thing I can't stand, it's a short man with a short man's
complex. I think the meanest bastards I've ever met have
been short men with chips on their shoulders about it. But
you don't strike me that way."

"Keep harping on it, and you'll probably *give* me a
short man's complex," he said.

The woman laughed. "Lord, I do go on, don't I? You
see, the truth is, I've already had me a drink or two."

"So what are you drinking?"

"A vodka tonic, if you don't mind."

Max hailed the dyspeptic-looking bartender and ordered their drinks.

The woman put her elbow on the bar, her chin in her
hand, and leaned toward Max. He picked up, through the
haze of her perfume, another, more fundamental smell,
grittily female, as though she had made love within the
last hour and neglected afterward to bathe. It might have
been the residual atmosphere of White Palaces still clinging to her. Whatever it was, Max didn't find it, in spite of
his usual fastidiousness, all that unpleasant, and he had to
wonder why.

Their drinks arrived. The vodka tonic came to a dollar seventy-five. There was nothing unusual in this. There must have been dozens of cheap bars in this area where mixed drinks sold for a dollar seventy-five. But the coincidence gave Max the feeling of being the butt of some kind of practical joke.

"So how'd you end up in Cousin Hugo's anyway?" the woman asked him. "This doesn't seem like exactly your kind of place. You look to me like one of those West County types."

"Now, is that nice?" Max asked her. "What if I told you that you looked to me like one of those South City types?"

"You wouldn't be far wrong." She went on smiling at him and he went on inhaling—almost tasting—her gritty scent. Max had always been afflicted by an overly judgmental nose, but this was one smell that he couldn't seem to come to a decision about; was it repulsive or attractive? And which category, for that matter, did this woman fall into? He couldn't even figure out if he really wanted to have a conversation with her, or would have preferred sitting alone. It was unusual for Max to be talking with someone of a completely different social background (St. Louis, unlike, say, Chicago or New York, contained worlds that seldom overlapped) and perhaps the novelty alone was enough to keep him feeding drinks to this drunken, rather slatternly woman—all right then, to this hoosier— whether he actually enjoyed her company or not.

"So come on," the woman said. "How'd you end up in this dump?"

"Pure serendipity," Max said.

"You'd better say that in English."

"It means a lucky accident."

"Oh? Why lucky?"

She had him there.

"It sounds to me like you've been to college," the woman said.

"Have you?" Max asked her. Stupid, clumsy question. But something about this woman was putting him off balance.

"Sure, honey," the woman told him, picking up her drink. "I just graduated from Harvard last week."

She indented the small of her back again as she polished off her drink and Max noticed—why hadn't he noticed it before?—that beneath her tight-fitting dress her breasts were practically nonexistent. The woman caught him looking and gave him a questioning smile. Blood came to his face.

"I could use another drink," she said. "That is, if you don't mind."

Max signaled the bartender.

Max watched her as she watched the bartender and he thought, for just an instant, that she was not bad-looking at all. Then she gave a different angle to her hard profile and he had to revise that judgment. Instant by instant he vacillated between thinking that she was coarse, common, and slightly repellent, and that, in some peculiar, mercurial way, she was actually lovely. Her face kept changing like a face in a dream.

He asked her what her name was.

"Why would you want to know?"

"So I don't have to call you Mildred," he said.

"How do you know my name isn't Mildred?"

"Is it?"

"No."

"Then what is it?"

She took a deep pull on her cigarette and let the smoke roll out of her mouth.

"Nora," she said.

"Nora what?"

"Just Nora."

"Don't you have a last name?"

"Well, of course."

"But that's classified information."

"That's right. You catch on fast." A new vodka tonic appeared in front of her. "And what's your name?" she asked him.

"Mildred," he said.

"Come on," she said, and lightly slapped his arm.

"It's Max."

"Max what?"

"Max Baron."

"I like that."

"Why?"

"Oh, I don't know. It's kind of short and cute—and so are you."

Max decided to let this pass.

"So how come you're wearing that monkey suit?"

"I was at a bachelor party."

"Who's getting married?"

"A friend of mine."

She watched him over the edge of her tilted glass. "Are you married?"

"Uh—no."

She noticed his hesitation. "*Were* you married?"

"Yes."

"Divorced?"

"No."

Nora's eyes appeared to grow rounder.

Max leaned forward onto the bar and put his palms together, forming the old pedagogical steeple. "My wife died a couple of years ago," he said.

Nora was frowning at him. "But you're so young," she said. "What did she die of, if you don't mind my asking?"

"It was a car accident."

"Honey, that's just—well, I'm sorry. How old are you, anyway?"

"Twenty-seven."

"So you were twenty-five when she died."

Max nodded.

"And how old was she?"

"The same age."

"Well, shit."

Max picked up his drink again; all the ice had melted. Even when he set out to get drunk, he couldn't seem to bring any genuine recklessness to it.

"Maybe you'd like to change the subject," Nora said.

"Please."

"It looks to me like you're still hurting."

"I thought we were going to change the subject."

"Sorry," Nora said, and got out another cigarette. "How about I buy the next round?"

"It's my treat tonight."

"So what do you do?" Nora asked him. "No. Wait. Don't tell me—you're an actor."

"Nope."

"Well, you oughtta be. You look something like Tony Curtis. Anybody ever tell you that? When he was younger, I mean. You ever seen him in *Some Like It Hot* with Marilyn Monroe? Well, that's who you look like—when he wasn't wearing a dress in that picture, I mean."

Max laughed. "I've been told I look like a Ken doll," he said, and felt, superstitiously, that he had somehow betrayed a confidence between himself and Janey. He tried to joke himself out of this. "Except, of course, that I happen to have a navel."

"I'll bet you've got the rest of it, too," Nora said, and laughed her hooty laugh. "So if you're not an actor, what are you?"

"I'm an adman. I work for Spindler Advertising, if you've ever heard of it."

"What all do you do there?"

"I'm a writer."

"You mean like for commericals on TV?"

"Radio, TV, newspapers, the works."

Her mouth came open. This was glamour.

"Well, how do you like that? You ever wrote any commericals I might have seen?"

"I haven't really done a lot of TV work yet," Max said. "This is just my second year in the business, and television is usually reserved for more senior writers."

"Well, how about that?"

"Have you ever heard any radio spots for Baumann's Hams?"

"Sure. You mean like the one with all those kids in that orphanage?"

"Right. That one's mine."

"That's a pretty strange commercial."

"You don't think it's funny?"

"No. Just strange."

"Well, it was supposed to be funny," Max said peevishly. He prided himself on his ability to write humorous advertising. Of course, he had to remember where the criticism was coming from. He felt, nevertheless, deflated. He picked up his watery Chivas.

"Do you know you're the first advertising person I've ever met? Hell, it's almost like talking to somebody famous."

"I wouldn't say that," Max told her, still wondering why she hadn't found his spot funny. He began to go over some of the dialogue in his mind.

"Lord, just wait'll I tell the girls at work that I was having me a drink with a real advertising man. They'll probably think I'm some kind of pathological liar."

Max looked at her. He was surprised by her use of the word *pathological*. Just how intelligent was this woman, anyway? His curiosity awakened on a number of fronts. "So tell me something about you," Max said. "Are you married?"

"Do you think I'd be sitting here with you if I was married?"

"I have no idea."

"That shows you don't know me very well."

"I don't know you at all," Max said. "So you're not married."

"I'm not saying."

"I thought you just *told* me you weren't married."

"You shouldn't go jumping to conclusions," she said, and held up the back of her left hand to show him the ring on her finger.

"Now, let me see if I've got this straight," Max said, annoyed at this childish game. "You're married and you're not married, and you have a last name but you won't tell me what it is. Do you have any children? Or do you have them and not have them at the same time?"

"How come you're asking me all these questions?"

"How come you're not answering any of them?"

"It's a free country, isn't it?"

"Would you like another drink?"

"Yes."

"You answered that one fast enough."

Nora raised her chin. "If you're going to take that

tone of voice with me," she said, "I can always just go sit someplace else."

But he didn't want her to go sit someplace else, and he couldn't say why not. Why was he being so belligerent with her? It could have been leftover anger from their encounter at the White Palace, but that wasn't all of it: this woman got under his skin in some way. "I'm sorry," Max said. "I didn't mean to be rude."

"Well," Nora said, "I'll accept your apology. And who knows? Maybe after this next one I'll open right up and tell you all about my miserable life. It's a humdinger, let me tell you. One of these days I'm going to write it all down in a book, and I wouldn't be surprised if it turns out to be a bestseller."

"So tell me," Max said.

"Maybe I will."

But Nora kept to her evasions. She told him that she lived in St. Louis, but would not disclose which area; Max guessed it was around here, or farther south—she was not, after all, one of those West County types. Had she always lived in St. Louis? No, her family had moved up here from a small Missouri town when she was a child. Which Missouri town? She wouldn't say. How long had she been working at the White Palace? Too long, she told him. What did she think of working there? She answered this with a derisive snort. Well, did she have any other ambitions? She sure as hell wasn't planning on working at Shit City for the rest of her life, she said. Then what was she planning on doing? This turned out to be none of his beeswax.

Max had lost patience. "Do you know that it's very difficult carrying on an intelligent conversation with you?" he said. "I feel like a dentist yanking teeth." He thought of Klugman's wife, and for some reason his heart gave a flutter. "Is there some reason why you're being so mysterious?"

Nora's wide mouth was set in a straight line and her dark blue eyes looked as flat as poker chips. "What kind of soap did your wife like to use?" she asked him.

"I'm sorry?"

Nora lit a new cigarette. The lighter clacked beneath

her palm against the bar. "That's not such a hard question, is it? Every woman has a particular kind of soap she likes to use. What did your wife like? Ivory? Camay? Something fancier?"

It was called Pure Castile soap. Janey bought it at health food stores, where she bought so much of the high-priced merchandise that filled their refrigerator and medicine cabinet. It came in a blue plastic bottle, and it contained peppermint oil. That was how she smelled when she came to him at night—her mouth all peppermint from natural peppermint toothpaste—her sweet weight rocking the bed. The recollection sent a cascade of shivers down his back.

"Cat got your tongue?" Nora said. She picked up her drink. "I guess there's just no telling what some people consider too private to talk about, is there?"

This drunken and most likely uneducated woman had just cannily scored a point against him via the Socratic method, and Max lost all sense of whom he was supposed to be talking to.

Nora listed toward him. She was smiling again. "You know, I'm glad I ran into you here tonight. I'll be damned if I know why, but I like you for some reason—even if you are hard to get along with." She put her hand on his thigh. "Ooh. Just feel you. You're as tense as a little boy who's about to get a shot."

"I wish you'd take your hand off my thigh."

She raised her eyebrows.

"Don't you like being touched?"

"I'd just prefer to keep this friendly."

"Honey, that's all I'm being is friendly."

"Then why don't you take your hand off my thigh?"

She complied and shrugged and readjusted her big rump on the stool. "So where's your girlfriend tonight?" she asked without looking at him.

"I don't have a girlfriend."

"Oh, come on—a guy as handsome as you? You don't expect me to believe that, do you?"

"Yes I *do* expect you to believe that. I expect you to believe everything I tell you, as a matter of fact. I'm kind of strange that way."

"No reason to get all riled up," Nora told him. "It just seems to me that a man as good-looking as you would have women just falling all over him all the time." Now she laughed and bumped shoulders with him. "Hell, I get any more drunk and I just might fall all over you myself. How would you like that, Max Baron? How would you like it if I fell all over you tonight?"

The thing to do was to set the record straight as quickly as possible, and in no uncertain terms. "Nora, it's got nothing to do with you. I'm simply not interested in going to bed with anyone tonight."

She raised her eyebrows. "Well, that's telling it like it is, isn't it? You haven't gone queer, have you?"

"I've just—lost interest in women since my wife died."

"I think you mean to say you're not interested in me." She turned away and watched the hamburgers sputtering on the grill. Her hand went up to her right ear, and she began twisting the tiny earring there, around and around, as if she were trying to screw down a loose thought in her brain. "What's wrong with me?" she asked him. "Am I too old? Too ugly? Too drunk, or what?"

"Why don't you believe anything I tell you? It's not you, Nora. It's me."

"Uh-huh. Well, I guess I was just out of line, thinking I could interest a slick young West County type like you—an *advertising man* and all. I guess I was just way out of line."

The conversation had nowhere to go now. He certainly hadn't set out to hurt this woman's feelings, but what was he supposed to do? Go to bed with her for altruistic reasons?

"Nora," Max said, "it was nice running into you again like this, nice talking to you—but I've got to go now."

"Oh, stay and have one more drink."

"I think I've passed my limit."

"You don't seem drunk to me. Come on, Max—just one more drink? I'll even pay for this one, how's that? I just—well, I'm not ready to go home just yet, and there's nobody else in this dump I feel like talking to."

He was surprised by the surge of compassion he felt

for this woman, whom he didn't even particularly like. Look at her: drunk, middle-aged, desperate, hitting on a man maybe ten years her junior in a sleazy bar on a Saturday night, and failing in that, begging for ten minutes more of conversation. It wasn't going to kill him to stay for one more drink.

But it was not one more drink, at least not on Nora's part. Max had switched to water, but Nora kept putting away the vodka tonics, and as she grew drunker she grew more candid—although only to a point. She had chosen to tell him about what had to have been the absolute low point of her life: the death of her thirteen-year-old son of leukemia, and her husband's subsequent desertion of her. It had happened, he gathered, about five years before— but that was just about the only detail he was able to extract from her. She spoke only in the most broad and hackneyed ways about the events—so that her angelic son and her no-account son of a bitch of a husband might as well have come straight from central casting. She wouldn't tell him what kind of student her son had been, or what her husband looked like, or what kind of relationships had been going on between the three of them, or what the course of her son's disease had been like. Max had sympathy enough to give her, but it was hard to sympathize with a family of ciphers. He went on probing, unsuccessfully, until the lights came on and the bartender began barking at everyone to leave.

Now, in the unforgiving light, her makeup looked clownish, and she appeared older, drier, more desolate. "You know," Nora said, "I only told you about all that so you'd realize I got some understanding of what-all you've been through. I know what that kind of hell is like. Believe me, I do."

Max didn't bother contradicting her, but he was very tired of hearing that particular sentiment. Nobody knew what he was going through because nobody else had been Janey's husband. People liked to believe that tragedies were interchangeable, that they bought you entrance into some kind of brotherhood of grief, where empathy among the members was exalted, telepathic, but this was probably only because they needed to believe that tragedy taught you something, that it wasn't a total waste, that the prize you received in lieu of your loss was a new level of understanding. Max didn't view his bereavement as particularly educational, however. All he knew now that he hadn't known before was what he should have known in the first place: no one was safe.

Her fierce odor came into his nostrils again; Nora was leaning against him.

"Hey," she said. "Gotta ask you a question. You think I'm too drunk to drive?"

"You're probably too drunk to stand up," Max told her.

"Well, do you think you could maybe give me a lift home? Or is that asking too much? I don't live far from here, you know. Just a few blocks. Could you do that for me, Max? Could you be a real gentleman and take me home?"

Again he sensed that some elaborate practical joke was being worked on him. Nora's head was lolling like an underwater flower.

"You wouldn't want me to go and have an accident, would you?"

She smiled. She had him. She knew it.

"Where do you live?" Max asked her.

CHAPTER THREE

Nora, as it turned out, could walk just fine. She pointed out her car as they passed it in the glaring light of the parking lot—an ancient, lavishly dented Impala mottled with islands of missing paint—and Max hoped he never had the bad luck of meeting up with her at a four-way stop. She didn't seem nearly as drunk as she had in Cousin Hugo's. It was possible that she was simply finessing this ride home in order to afford herself another opportunity to try to seduce him, but that didn't matter at this point. Max had promised to drive her home, and so drive her home he would. Besides, what was she going to do—attack and overpower him?

Nora proved to be anything but a gracious passenger. First she put up an infantile fight when he insisted that she buckle herself in. Seat belts, she complained, made her claustrophobic. Max calmly explained to her that she had her choice: she could either put on her seat belt, or sit there in his car until she was sober enough to drive, whichever came first. Then, once they were on the road, Nora asked him if he couldn't find something else to play on his tape deck.

"This is Mozart," he said.

"Well, it's giving me a headache."

"It's not Mozart that's giving you a headache. It's all those vodka tonics that are giving you a headache. Why don't you just relax and listen to it for a few minutes? This is called 'Eine Kleine Nacht musik'—a little night music—and it's some of the best music ever composed."

"Well, maybe so. But it doesn't appeal to me."

"What would you rather listen to? What kind of music do you like?"

43

Nora shrugged and fussed with her shoulder strap.

"You got any Oak Ridge Boys?" she asked him.

They compromised and listened to nothing.

It turned out, of course, that she lived much farther away than just a few blocks. Nora lived in Dogtown, the rundown little area south of Forest Park which, according to St. Louis legend, had been the campground for the workers who had built the 1904 World's Fair. There were as many explanations for the origin of the name as there were tellers: Dogtown was called Dogtown because the immigrant laborers had been Lithuanians who ate dogs; they had been Chinamen who ate dogs; they had been Blackfoot Indians who ate dogs. Others maintained that this had been the site of the city's original dog pound. Still others insisted that the neighborhood had simply always had a lot of dogs in it. Nora failed to enlighten Max on this score. "It's probably called Dogtown," she said, "because nobody lives there unless they're in the doghouse."

Then, giving off her complex atmosphere of ciga-rettes, cheap perfume, and loamy womanhood, Nora launched into an unexpected subject: Marilyn Monroe and the mysterious circumstances surrounding her death. She brought a real passion to the topic and had evidently done her homework. She knew, for instance, that Mari-lyn, who had been obsessed with the upkeep of her breasts and so had made a lifelong habit of sleeping in her bra, had been discovered nude on the morning of her supposed suicide. Why, she wanted to know? Max sug-gested that maybe Marilyn hadn't cared what her breasts were going to look like after she was dead. Nora snorted at this and went on: Did Max think that Jack Kennedy, in an attempt to protect the reputation of his younger brother (for it was well known that she and Bobby had been carrying on an affair), had enlisted the aid of the CIA to have her discreetly bumped off? And what about her famous diary, which so mysteriously disappeared? And why would Marilyn have killed herself at that point any-way, just as things were starting to turn around for her? On and on Nora speculated, in a devout torrent of minu-tiae, pausing only to take a drag on her cigarette or to guide him through the narrow, rather spooky streets of

Dogtown, past the tiny bungalow houses and the darkened confectioneries and the dilapidated corner bars, until Max, who had been driving with the exaggerated caution
of a guilty drunk, allowed himself the brief luxury of
rolling his eyes heavenward as he started the turn into her
driveway and plowed straight into her mailbox.

His Volvo seemed hardly to be moving at the moment of impact, yet he and Nora flew forward and back
like dummies in a crash test, and the sound of the collision was like a gunshot in his ears.

He had had an accident.

Max looked at the scene from some vantage point
outside of his body. This was one accident, evidently, that
was not going to turn out tragically. Both of them were
still upright in their harnesses; the windshield was intact;
he felt no pain; Nora had her hand over her mouth and
was laughing.

"Bingo," she said. "How do you like this? It's the
drunk driving the drunk."

"Are you all right?" Max asked her. His voice sounded
extraordinarily low.

"Hell, I'm all right. I think it's your car you got to
worry about."

"You're lucky I made you put on your seat belt," he
told her.

"My hero," Nora said, in falsetto.

Max opened the door and got out on wobbly legs to
inspect the damage. The mailbox itself had flown away,
and the iron stem was bent down, as if it were stooping
to have a look, toward the jagged black socket where
his headlight used to be. Speckles of shattered glass fan-
ned out at the mouth of Nora's driveway like a fallen
constellation.

Her house was on a cul-de-sac of identical small
boringly rectangular houses that looked like the houses on
a Monopoly board. Behind Nora's house rose the haggard
outline of the abandoned Scullin Steel mill. Max sat down
on the lawn with a groan and lowered himself onto his
back. The neighborhood was certainly noisy; there was a
thick chiming of crickets and, like an angry canine mob,

the yapping and barking of all the dogs of this Dogtown neighborhood, aroused by the sound of his collision.

He heard the door to his Volvo slam shut, and soon Nora was sitting beside him on the grass.

"I hope you got insurance," she said.

She pronounced insurance with the stress on the first syllable.

"It's illegal to drive without insurance," Max said.

"Honey, it's illegal to drive when you're drunk."

He went on listening to all the dogs of Dogtown.

"I got an idea," Nora said. "Why don't you come inside and I'll fix you some coffee? You don't want to go driving home in this condition, do you?"

Max turned his head to look at her, silhouetted against the starry sky. Somehow she knew instinctively which arguments would best work on him; and somehow she was getting him where she'd wanted him all along—in her lair. He tilted his head in the other direction and looked at his wounded car. She was right; he wasn't going anywhere without three or four cups of coffee in him. "That's a fine idea," he told her, and sat up.

"Well, come on then."

He followed her heavily switching buttocks across the lawn, up the small stoop, and into the house. She didn't bother with any keys; she had simply left the door unlocked.

Nora flicked on the hallway light and Max stopped in his tracks. While this wasn't quite his mother's house—his mother was a pack rat, a lifelong accumulator of junk, with a house so high piled with useless booty that some rooms were simply impassable—in the chaos that prevailed, this wasn't far from it. The place might have been trashed by a goon squad. Strewn along the floor of the front hallway and spilling over into the living room, like the debris of some indecent parade, was a fallen wardrobe of nylons, pastel panties, blue jeans, tennis shoes, and skimpy bras of black and white and tan. The living room was a disaster. On her coffee table stood dirty plates and glasses, ashtrays peaking with butts, and crumpled cellophane junk food wrapped. There were twisted-up sheets on the sofa, magazines flung everywhere, and the carpet had received a steady rain of ashes, glints of plastic, bits of paper, yet more nylons, and balled-up Kleenex. The scene unnerved him; he felt like a fireman gazing at a blaze that he wasn't licensed to put out.

The woman's taste in art was wondrously appalling. At the back of the living room hung an enormous painting of a livid maritime sunset. There were three velveteen nudes of exotic women with gigantic gravity-defying breasts, each with a different-colored flower in her hair. These must have belonged to her husband—it was impossible that she had chosen them herself—but if so, what were they still doing on the walls? Opposite the sofa, near the picture window, was a black and white poster of Marilyn Monroe in a matador's hat. And here, where he stood in the hallway, was nothing less than a photographic shrine devoted to her. There must have been three dozen small photos, all framed, of Marilyn making love to the camera in various outfits, various moods, various stages of her career: Marilyn skipping on the beach, sipping champagne in a bathtub, nuzzling Joe DiMaggio's ear, dancing with Carl Sandburg, listening pensively to a pipe-smoking Arthur Miller.

"Just what exactly is there between you and Marilyn Monroe?" he asked her.

Nora shrugged. "I guess she's just my favorite person."

"How come?"

"Hell, I don't know—I guess because she was so beautiful, and so screwed-up, and her life was so tragic. I've seen every single one of her movies at least twice."

Max cautioned himself against making any wisecracks; he was, after all, an unbeliever loitering in the Holy of Holies.

"How about that coffee?" he asked her.

Nora led the way into the kitchen, all apologies for the condition of her house—she'd hardly had time to think this week, much less attend to her housework—and started clearing off the small square formica table that bore the half-petrified remains of a meal: a dish with a dried orange dollop of what looked like canned spaghetti, a partially eaten sandwich made with white bread, a glass coated with milk, a jar of mayonnaise. There was a moldering hill of dishes in the sink.

He asked Nora the way to the bathroom.

Here was a surprise. The bathroom was scrupulously clean. There was a plastic dish filled with never-before-used eggs of colored soap; the towels were neatly folded, and looked fresh; her shelves of cosmetics were tidy; the sink gleamed. The top of the toilet was covered with blue fur, as was the oval toilet seat. Max lifted it, took a long vigorous piss, and remembering that he was in a woman's house, dutifully closed it again. What could possibly explain such an oasis of cleanliness and order in such an otherwise filthy house? Houses, he supposed, like human personalities, contained anomalous corners that refused to fit in with the rest of the general pattern. In her house-keeping habits Nora was like a brutal serial murderer who nevertheless went to Mass every morning and never forgot her mother's birthday.

Coming back into the kitchen, he found Nora seated at the table before a bottle of Smirnoff Silver, a bottle of Schweppes tonic water, and a pink ceramic swan-shaped ashtray—the bowl between the lifted wings—in which yet another Winston sat burning. She had let down her hair in his absence, and its beauty shocked him. It fell, gorgeous and thick, to the small of her back, so lustrously black that as she shifted in her chair to pick up her drink, it gave off winking highlights of blue.

He looked at her and felt a queer pressure in his chest.

"I'm afraid I got you in here under false pretenses," she told him. "I could've sworn I had me a whole new can of Folger's coffee in the cabinet, but it looks like I was mistaken."

"You don't have any coffee at all?" he asked her.

Nora shrugged. "Sorry." Now she smiled for him. "How about if I fix you a drink instead?"

"For crying out loud, Nora—I'm trying to get my ass home in one piece."

"So you don't care for another drink?"

"No thank you," Max said, and took off his tuxedo jacket; the house was hot, and his own body temperature

had just gone up several degrees in the past few seconds.
He sat down across from her and sighed.

"Can't you make it home without your coffee?"

"I'm afraid of tempting fate twice," he said.

"Well, why don't you call a cab?"

Max checked his wallet. Three dollars—nowhere near
enough to get him all the way out to Kirkwood. How
much money had he spent on this woman's vodka tonics,
anyway? Then he remembered that he had been drinking
Chivas Regal.

"Let me check in my purse and see what I've got,"
Nora said.

"No," Max told her. "I don't want to take your
money."

"It'd be a loan, honey."

This woman was obviously too poor to lend him the
twenty dollars—or whatever it would take—to get him
back to his apartment; and besides, taking her money
would involve another visit back here, or at least an
exchange of phone numbers, and Max did not want to
open that door. "Just keep your money," Max told her.

"Well, what-all do you want to do?"

He saw that he had little choice but to spend the
night (the invitation was imminent) in this dirty house,
under the same roof with this partly repulsive, partly attractive, inexplicable woman who was probably going to
do her damnedest to seduce him. He looked down at his
carnation, which had finally wilted. He lobbed it toward
the overflowing trash can, where it landed on a box of
Hostess Ding-Dongs and slid into the mouth of a blue egg
carton. Throwing in the towel, he thought.

"I tell you what," Nora said, pulling on her cigarette.
"Why don't you just spend the night here? I got me a sofa
in the living room that folds into a bed, and we can put
you up there. How's that?"

"Well, I appreciate the offer," Max said.

"What else are you going to do, honey—walk home?"

"I'll accept on one condition."

"What's that?"

"You have to promise to be nice."

"You mean no hanky-panky?"

"That's right."

"All right," Nora said, grinning at him. "I promise to be nice." Her dark blue eyes moved over him in a bemused, proprietary way, as if he were a puppy in a pet store window which she had just decided, on impulse, to buy and take home with her. "Well," she said, "seeing as how you're not going anywhere, how's about sharing a little nightcap with me?"

Max asked her if she had any scotch in the house.

———————————

The dream he had was this:

The Spindler office Christmas party was being held, for some reason, between the gargantuan gleaming legs of the St. Louis Arch. The heaven-high swooping structure was festooned with green and red crepe paper, a gigantic wreath was fastened at the apex of the legs, and at the very top sat a waving Santa Claus. The crowd was vast and rowdy, and for a while Max wandered through it, feeling slightly panicked because he didn't recognize anyone. These were not the sort of people you'd expect to see at an advertising function. They were unwashed, sick-drunk hoosiers stumbling around with pails full of Busch beer. Party crashers, Max thought, and then his boss, Rosemary Powers, took him by the arm.

"How do you like it so far?" she asked him.

"I don't know," he said. "And I can't understand why we're having this down by the Arch."

"It's the Gateway to the South," Rosemary told him.

Rosemary had this wrong. The Arch was known as the Gateway to the West. But even so—how did this explain anything?

"You're late," Rosemary told him.

"I was finishing up some work in my office."

"You know what they say," Rosemary said, wagging a cautionary finger at him. "All work and no play makes Max a dead boy."

Max laughed at this, idiotically, for he had no idea what she meant.

"There's someone here to see you," Rosemary said. "Someone very, very special."

And now they were in what looked like the waiting room of a doctor's office. There were vague figures slumped in chairs around the perimeter of the room, which contained potted ferns, magazine racks, and an antiseptic odor.

"Here comes the bride," Rosemary sang.

Here came his mother, as alarmed and frantic-looking as always, leading by the hand a pale woman in a blue hospital gown.

"Look!" his mother bellowed. "Look, Max! Look who I brought!"

His heart contracted. It was Janey. But it wasn't the Janey he remembered. She was as thin as a specter and her hair was hay-colored, and stood around her head in a wild halo, like that of a crazy woman.

"She was sick before," his mother said. "But now she's as good as new."

But she was not as good as new. Her head was bowed and her shoulders were hunched; she was ashamed to be seen by him in this condition.

He felt nothing but pity and horror, but still, she was his wife, and he had to act like her husband. He took her hand in his; it was tiny and cold as the charm off a bracelet. "Janey?" he said.

Now she lifted her face to him and he saw from her eyes that she was dead. Some kind of terrible mistake had been made.

She opened her mouth and a hoarse, animal groan came out.

"Janey—what do you want?"

"Satisfaction."

"What satisfaction canst thou have tonight?"

She tore away, with one movement, all of his clothes, and slammed against him, their breastbones clacking, until he was on his back on the floor and she was sliding her face down his chest, down his belly. Go back, Max thought. You have to go back. You're dead.

Janey gave out another deep-throated growl, took hold of him, and buried him in the heat of her mouth.

Go back.

He opened his eyes and there was Marilyn Monroe.

No—it was only a poster of Marilyn Monroe, lasciviously smirking in a matador's hat. The sensations of his dream raged on; he was being swallowed, sucked, milked, and then he raised his head and saw the iridescent black hair fanning across his belly and the upraised fleshy, coppery ass rising and ducking behind it, and he understood, without knowing if he were grateful or outraged or what, that Nora was in the process of raping him.

CHAPTER FOUR

He watched her in amazement, as if he were grappling with an angel. His nostrils were full of her: blood, earth, tobacco, cheap perfume. A hot patch of sunlight, boiling with dust, fell over them where they lay upon the sofa-bed, and gave to Nora's skin an unreal, honeyed glow. Her broad haunches were raised high; her freckled shoulders wedged his thighs apart; her right hand gripped the root of his yearning hard-on while her left hand clasped her blue-black hair in a ponytail behind her neck; her head nodded slowly and deeply above his belly, as if in emphatic agreement with some undeniable truth coming clear at the back of her brain.

Had Nora been any less forceful or unhesitating in her assault, Max might have recovered the presence of mind to defend himself. But by the time he struggled out of his dream and saw clearly what was happening, Nora was already so far along in her work, and he himself was already so aroused, that the call to resist sounded as far-off, tinny, and ridiculous as the voice of a soapbox madman on a street corner three blocks away. Resist on what principle? For what purpose? To whose benefit? Yet somewhere he had a grievance. Then he remembered that this was an attack, a violation of his person and a breach of promise, not to mention a display of extraordinary chutzpah—and then Nora, as if to counter these objections, bore in on him still further, pushing, pushing, pushing, until something came unlocked at the back of her throat with a definite tactile click, and she swallowed, along with the whole length of his prick, the last of his defenses.

Max's head hit the pillow. Oh, whatever else this

woman was, she had a talent when it came to this. Max's sexual experience, in spite of all the opportunities his good looks afforded him, was not wide; he had spent most of his adult life being faithful, on the whole, to Janey. His only genuine period of promiscuity had been during his two years at Tulane—which he cut short in order to finish his education at Washington University in St. Louis—largely because the long separations from Janey had become too hard to take. He supposed, although he never actually stopped to take count, that he had been to bed with a dozen or so women, but never had he been in the hands, or the mouth, of such a matter-of-fact master as Nora. Janey had brought to this act an air of sweet, hesitant, hopeful performance, rather like a little girl induced to do a tap-dance before a crowd of half-drunken adults. But there was nothing apologetic in Nora's approach. She wasn't doing him any favors. She was doing this because she liked it. He even sensed that she didn't particularly care whose cock this happened to be, nor would have much cared if he simply ignored her, went back to sleep, and let her go on with her business. This notion excited him still further, sent still more blood sluicing down to his groin, and he sat partway up, gripping her hot, freckled shoulders, and spoke her name.

She looked up. Her eyes were dramatically bloodshot. She let him slip away with excruciating slowness, millimeter by aching millimeter, from the grip of her throat, the caress of her mouth, the lingering light pinch of her teeth, until he flopped free, and showed him a crooked grin. "I sure do like having breakfast in bed," she told him.

"Good morning," Max croaked.

"You're not mad at me, are you?"

"I really don't know."

"You want me to go on?"

"Yes."

"Say please."

"Please."

"Now say pretty please."

He knew what she was up to. She wanted evidence of his complicity that would stand up in court. But that didn't matter; what mattered now was that he was stranded in the unembracing air, and it was torture. He swallowed—his mouth was dry as paper—and said, "Please."

Nora flicked her tongue around his straining, purplish crown, and plunged down on him again.

Max's head hit the pillow once more—the same cheap spongy pillow she had issued to him the night before, most likely knowing full well what she intended to do with him in the morning—as she drew from the depths of his guts a resonant groan. He gave his pelvis a twist and dug his hand down between the cushion and the back of the sofa, seizing hold of what felt like a small cellophane bag. He withdrew it and held it above his face. It was a half-eaten package of barbecued pork rinds. The brand name was Ozark's Best, and the logo featured a cartoon hillbilly snoozing under a tree. So he was being sucked off by a woman who not only ate such a thing as barbecued pork rinds, but lost packages of them behind the cushions of her sofa. And yet in spite of this, or maybe, perversely, because of it, he was about to explode in her mouth like a fireworks stand.

Max chucked the pork rinds over the side of the sofa-bed and sat up, taking Nora's fiercely indented cheeks between his hands. "Nora—"

Nora lifted her face and released him. "No," she said. "Don't say nothing and don't do nothing. I just want you to lie back and enjoy this. Well, go on—do like I say."

He tried to comply, but soon he couldn't stand it anymore. He had to be inside of her, joined at the juncture of those monumental thighs. He drew her up by the armpits and she wriggled forward until her mouth was over his. Her breath was stale and brassy, and he did not want to kiss her. But he did, and oddly, she tasted sweet.

With their tongues softly wrestling, they massaged each other's loins, and it seemed to Max that Nora's hot wet ferny opening breathed out a small breath into his hands like another mouth. She took hold of him and guided him in. Then she sat back on her heels, arching her back, and gave her coal-black hair a prideful toss. In the slanted square of sunlight she shone like burnished bronze. Her thighs were solid, her thin arms rounded, but in her slightly wrinkled neck, her loose belly, and the fatty corrugations at her waist, her age—whatever it was—was apparent. She was pleasingly pear-shaped, like one of Botticelli's Graces, although even Botticelli would have endowed her with larger breasts; her coffee-colored nipples stood out on rises of flesh no deeper than the sections of a quilt. Her pubic patch was dense and luxuriant, as blue-black as the hair on her head. Max pressed his palms into it, hooking his thumbs beneath her pelvic bone, and upon this fulcrum Nora rocked herself.

She picked up speed and intensity like a locomotive, let out a little cry, and fell over him, her breath pumping hard at his ear. And then, as she fought toward her climax, she began to speak.

No—she wasn't speaking at all, at least not in any language that Max had ever heard. She was letting loose a stream of fervent syllables that had all the cadence and inflection of speech, but no more meaning than the babbling of an infant or the entranced gibberish of a Pentecostal speaking in tongues. It was guttural as German, fluid as Italian, odd as Swahili, singsongy as Chinese. She pleaded, she questioned, she chided, she praised—and all in the medium of these wild prelingual noises, as if she were in rapt conversation with some older, lower part of herself, the reptile or the bird. Max listened, fascinated, astonished, impressed, until it seemed that he was no longer feeling the interlocked struggle of their lovemaking so much as hearing it, and then Nora took him with her, seized him, as it were, by the ears, and flung him into the still center of a hurricane.

Sometime later her odor, powerfully enriched by sex, snapped him back to consciousness like a whiff of smelling salts. She was a vast moist weight on top of him, and he was unable to expand his rib cage all the way. Outside the window, maybe in the next yard, a radio was going, tuned to the Cardinals baseball game; so it was already afternoon. On the ceiling above him was a water stain in the approximate shape of the continent of Africa, and down to the right was another smaller stain, which might have stood for Madagascar. A dog barked, and then a whole platoon of dogs, like an answering chorus, took up with it.

So here, after two years of self-imposed celibacy, on a sofa-bed in a filthy house in Dogtown, he had finally been fucked, and what was amazing was that he was so flatly unamazed. He had forgotten the old discovery you made each time you entered the body of a woman; this was the most profoundly ordinary of all human acts.

Nora stirred and gave a reluctant little moan—like a child awakened against its will—and then pushed away from him. Their bodies came unstuck with a gluey smack. She smiled down at him, holding her hair away from her face.

"You're so beautiful," she said, "it almost hurts to look at you."

Max wished he could return the compliment. Her imperfections—her bottom-heaviness, her flabby waist, the startling flatness of her chest, the strange pairing of her hard brown Navajo face and those intensely blue, albeit bloodshot, Scandinavian eyes—intrigued and aroused him, but there was no complimentary way of telling her this.

"You're just a regular firecracker, do you know that? I swear you blew the top of my head clean off."

Max grunted and smiled at her; he didn't feel capable of talking.

"I guess you must think I've got my nerve."

"Uh-huh."

"But there wasn't no way I was going to talk you into bed, was there?"

"No."

"Are you sure you're not mad at me?"

"You did break your promise, you know."

"What promise?"

"You promised last night you were going to be nice."

Nora grinned at him. "Wasn't I nice?"

So he was dealing with the devious, hair-splitting mind of a natural lawyer.

"Yes," he said. "You were very, very nice."

"Well, then."

Nora found a place for her bottom on the sofa and began fishing through the clutter on her coffee table until she came up with her pack of Winstons and a lighter. He watched her suck on her cigarette as she lit it, and the sight of her indrawn cheeks made his groin stir again.

"Do you always talk that way during sex?" he asked her.

"Talk like what?"

"Don't you remember? You were talking a blue streak."

"What was I saying?"

"Nothing. At least, nothing intelligible."

Nora frowned at him. "I don't remember saying nothing," she told him.

He believed her. She had no more recollection of her rapture—and rapture seemed a pretty good word for it—than someone coming out of deep hypnosis. Was this the first time she had fallen into such a trance while making love? Or was he simply the first man straightforward enough to mention it to her? Nora scratched her ribs. The curves and angles of her body, eclipsing the sun that was pouring through the window, were outlined in gold. She appeared to be a living riddle, a sphinx, so honeycombed with secret passageways and hidden chambers that she was a mystery even to herself. Nora reached down to scratch her ankle, her spinal column bumpling beneath the thin translucent skin, and her mythical luster disappeared. She was suddenly something bitterly prosaic: a middle-aged, unbeautiful, hung-over woman in critical need of a bath, rousing herself from yet another one-night stand in the trash dump of her living room. Just the thought of trying to synthesize those two visions exhausted Max, and he lay back and blinked at the map of Africa floating in the cracked sea of her ceiling.

Nora's cool long-fingered hand closed lightly over his testicles.

"I think I'm ready to get the top of my head blown off again," she said.

The rust-colored square of sunlight had moved away from the sofa-bed and up along one wall to imperfectly frame the poster of Marilyn Monroe in her matador's hat. After such olympic exertions, Max should have been as dead to the world as Nora—who lay snoring with her majestic rump aimed in his direction—but instead he stood naked amid the wreckage of her living room, feeling rubbery, purged, and supercharged with curiosity. He took another look at Nora to make sure she was sleeping soundly, then took up his tuxedo pants, which he had carefully folded over the back of an overstuffed armchair before going to sleep, and drew them on. He intended to take inventory of her house.

If Max had to write out a list of his faults, snoopiness would come in somewhere near the top. Both his mother and Janey had lit into him routinely for reading their mail, inspecting their purses, rummaging through their drawers, invading their glove compartments. If nosiness were a sin, it was a minor one, although Max preferred to think of it as the exaggeration of the virtue of intellectual curiosity; what was science, after all, if not applied nosiness? Certainly he was about to violate Nora's privacy. But it wasn't as if she'd shown any respect for *his* privacy. Having just been ravished, he felt he had the right to know something about his ravisher. Besides, had Nora been any more forthcoming about herself, he wouldn't now have to stoop to this espionage. Armed with these rationalizations, he went directly to her refrigerator.

He did this first because he was ravenous—he hadn't had anything to eat since before Horowitz's party—but second because it seemed to Max that what people kept in their refrigerators was every bit as indicative of their personalities as what they kept on their bookshelves. He doubted this woman even had any bookshelves, and in lieu of that, this seemed a fruitful place to start. It was an old General Electric, as outmoded and bulky as an upright sarcophagus. What he could see in the freezer—which hadn't been defrosted since the Ice Age—was a bag of Ore-Ida french fries, several Swanson pot pies, a Tombstone pizza, and a can of Minute Maid orange juice. All brand names, which came as no surprise. He had learned from advertising that poor people were fiercely brand conscious. They wasted their money on advertised products because they were deathly afraid of wasting their money. It was only in the affluent suburbs that generic labels moved well; Max's apartment was full of items that had no names. So. The main chamber of the refrigerator was a depressing revelation. Aside from a stick of butter, a carton of eggs, a bottle of Schweppes tonic water and a jar of Kraft mayonnaise, there was nothing to be seen but products from Oscar Mayer: Oscar Mayer bacon, Oscar Mayer bologna, Oscar Mayer chopped ham, Oscar Mayer hot dogs. That was it—no pickles, no cheese, no vegetables, no fruit. What a desolate, unimaginative, passionless mind such a diet would have to feed—yet Nora's sexual nature was nothing like this. In bed she was a regular Julia Child.

Max made a thick sandwich of Oscar Mayer coldcuts and Wonder bread. It was so bland it was almost good. He continued his investigation, grimly chewing. Stored within her cabinets were cheap sky-blue plastic dishes, plastic cups and saucers, and an array of promotional glasses she had picked up at places like Wendy's and Burger King featuring such characters as E.T., Luke Skywalker and Darth Vader, the Flintstones and the Smurfs. He hadn't thought of it before, but such marketing tie-ins were a boon to the poor. Evidently Nora was one of those women who lined up at the grand openings of supermarkets, banks, and car dealerships to raid them for whatever goodies she could carry away: complimentary ashtrays, calendars, umbrellas, candy dishes, balloons—it hardly mattered what, so long as it was free. His creative director, Rosemary Powers, had told him of that certain sector of the market who could always be depended upon to move their measly accounts from financial institution to financial institution simply to cash in whatever giveaway was being advertised that month—and Max had had a hard time envisioning what sort of people would actually apply themselves to such low-grade piracy. Now, three times in succession, he had just made love to one of them. His sandwich was going dry in his mouth. He got himself a glass of water and went on inspecting the contents of her cabinets. There was a good stock of sugared breakfast cereals, horrible canned pablum like Franco-

American spaghetti and Hy-Power tamales, and box upon box of Hostess cupcakes, Twinkies, Ding Dongs and Ho Hos. You'd think the woman was ten years old. With a diet like this, how in the world did she ever get the energy to fuck like she did? It was a miracle that she was even still breathing.

Max started down the hall, which was where the family gallery of portraits should have been hung. But aside from Marilyn Monroe and the three velveteen nudes, he had seen no pictures of anyone in the house. He could understand there being no photographs of her ex-husband. His mother kept no pictures of his absent father, and Max—as a means of protecting himself—kept all of Janey's pictures in the bottom drawer of his filing cabinet. But what of Nora's beloved dead son? You'd think that a mother's nurturing instinct would seek to keep his presence alive—that shrine to Marilyn in the front hallway should have been a shrine to her brave dead angel. Maybe she kept the photos in her bedroom. He tried the last door on the left, beyond the bathroom, and came into a room as exuberantly trashed as the rest of her house.

Clothes were heaped around the floor. The bed wasn't made. A clattering fan turned in the open window, which looked out onto a backyard that needed mowing, and beyond that, to the Scullin Steel mill. Her nighttable bore two dirty Flintstones glasses, half-opened flowers of used pink Kleenex, and an ashtray so high-piled with butts that Max couldn't resist emptying it into the wastebasket standing below it, which also wanted emptying. He tested absentmindedly the surface of her mattress and nearly fell over as it sloshed away and rolled back at him. A water bed. What was this woman doing with a water bed? Absolutely nothing else about her smacked of hipness. Then he wondered what it would be like to fuck her on this loose, rollicking, thigh-slapping surface, and the base of his throat went tight with renewed lust. It was impossible that he could want her again so soon; no pair of testicles in the world could refuel themselves so fast, after having been so ruthlessly emptied. This was the excrescence of a brain that had gone too long without sex. He was merely readjusting to the habit of desire. And yet—

Max opened the single drawer in her nighttable. Oh boy. Here was a big plastic bottle of massage oil, and next to it, three dildos. His heart thumped. One of them was about his size—he'd been told that he was pretty hefty for being such an otherwise tiny man. Another was as big and curved as a banana, with three sets of rubbery fringes down the shaft, like fern fronds. He flexed it a few times—it did not have much give. The last was shaped like a snub-nosed missile, and was surprisingly heavy. There was a switch at the bottom. Max flicked it. The missile buzzed. There were three speeds and he tried them all.

He tried to imagine Janey keeping such toys for her own private pleasure, and could not. She had not been a prude, but neither had she been what you could easily call a sexpot—nor, for that matter, had he. Their lovemaking, like so much of their marriage, was governed by a certain ceremoniousness. They were both neat, careful people, and perhaps because their marriage had been so young, they treated it as something breakable. Just as he knew that when he returned from the high school each afternoon Janey, like the prototypical American housewife, would be there to greet him with a kiss, or just as he knew that they would spend each Sunday morning on the sofa with The New York Times he had picked up in Clayton, reading in silence and nibbling on lox and bagels, he knew that when it came time for sex (always at night, never in the morning) Janey would light a candle by their bedside and retire to the bathroom, Max would put on a piece of music like Wagner's Tristan and Isolde, or Rimsky-Korsakov's Scheherezade, undress, and wait under the sheet, and then Janey would come to him in her nightgown, having just brushed her teeth and sweetened her crotch with feminine hygiene spray, and in a slow, stately swoon of peppermint, clean sheets and bodies, fine music, candlelight, and mutual protestations of love, possess each other like newlyweds. He had never (my God, did he have to think about this now?) fucked her in the ass, or ripped away her clothes, or even climbed into the bathtub with her. They had never made love in any particularly dangerous locations. The one time they had watched a porno movie together, on the VCR at Klugman's house, Janey had risen from her chair in disgust and joined Sherri in the kitchen, leaving Max and Klugman to their dry throats and wisecracks. Janey had even told him—and he believed her—that she had masturbated only a few times, and had not found it particularly satisfying. Their sexual life had kept within its bounds. There was decent, appropriate sex and there was lewdness and nastiness, and they had both encouraged each other's natural inclinations to stay on one side of the line.

Here, however, was a woman who didn't know the meaning of the word *lewd*—no more than did a goat or a monkey in heat—whose sexual nature pervaded her from the dirty bottoms of her feet to the ends of her lustrous blue-black hair, who took to copulation as avidly and guiltlessly as an animal took to its food, and there was nothing, he suspected, that she wouldn't do for him or for herself; he could tie her up, piss in her face, have her ream his asshole—not that any of those notions necessarily appealed to him. Yet his heart was pounding. He wanted her again.

Max switched off the vibrator—the palm of his hand still tingling—and set it back in the drawer, which he closed as quietly as he could. He tried to relocate his attention. Across from her water bed, on a rickety-looking stand, was a small old-fashioned plastic record player, much like the one he had bought as a child with the money he'd made one winter shoveling snow. He knelt and flipped through the record collection below it: Tammy Wynette, The Oak Ridge Boys, Loretta Lynn, Hank Williams Junior and Senior, Willie Nelson, Charley Pride: this was an auditory slum. On one corner of her bureau sat a small stack of books. None of the titles surprised him: Norman Mailer's *Marilyn,* Fred Guiles's *Norma Jean,* something called *When Bad Things Happen to Good People,* a romance novel entitled *This Shining Promise,* and what was probably Nora's equivalent of a well-thumbed family bible, *The Joy of Sex.* On the floor beside the bureau stood a knee-high stack of women's magazines, a *Cosmopolitan* on top, and next to that, with its mouth sagging partway open, sat her purse.

Max crossed his arms as he stared at it. Inside would

be her billfold, her driver's license, her full name, her age. Yet to root through this woman's purse went beyond simple snooping; it bordered on thievery. But how else was he going to find out what he wanted to know? And moreover, why did he want to know it? Was he actually thinking of seeing her again?

Down the hall the toilet flushed.

Max fled the bedroom, slinked past the bathroom, and without thinking why, made straight for Nora's front door and stepped out into the blinding sunlight. There was a cacaphonous blast of heavy-metal rock and roll from somewhere, a lawn mower grumbling, the yapping of dogs. He realized then that he was standing out here in his bare feet and bare chest. He withdrew again into the front hallway. Nora was waiting for him with crossed arms.

She wore a frayed crimson bathrobe. Her hair was fastened back in a ponytail and her face had been scrubbed free of makeup. She was even older than he had suspected. She had hardly any eyebrows at all—plucked down to arched hints of hair—and the skin of her cheeks was as rough as a plaster wall. She wasn't smiling.

"Looks like you're in such a hurry to leave," she said, "that you just plumb forgot your clothes."

Max decided to make a joke out of this, if he could.

"Well," he said, "it's a hot day."

Nora didn't grace this insipidity with a response. He felt, with the groundless certainty of a paranoid, that she knew all about his surreptitious exploration of her house, that she had been lying awake with cocked ears, listening to every move he made, to each opening and closing of every drawer and cabinet.

"Am I ever going to see you again?" she asked him.

He dropped his eyes and watched her veiny hands pumping the muscles of her forearms through the red material of her robe, the knuckles going from yellow to pink to yellow again. She had, of course, every right to ask this question, but the bluntness of it, and the bitter tone in which she asked it, unstrung him.

"It's a simple enough question," Nora said. "Am I ever going to see you again?"

He waffled. "Why does this have to be all my decision?" he asked her.

"Because I'm the one doing the asking. And that gives you all the power. Or didn't you know that?"

He put his back to the wall and his hands into the pockets of his tuxedo pants. Around his feet lay curved, like a sleeping snake, a pair of her fallen panty hose. He felt unfairly cornered. The only thing he could possibly do was to thank her for a memorable afternoon, kiss her good-bye, and get the hell out. What else could he do? Ask her for a date? But he raised his eyes again to that unpretty, destroyable face and lost his courage.

"How old are you?" he asked her.

Nora lifted her chin. "Take a guess."

"Please, Nora—no guessing games. Just tell me."

"I'm older than I look—or so I've been told."

"And how old is that?"

"I'm forty-one," she said. "I'll be forty-two come this December. And you're how old? Twenty-seven? Lord, there's one hell of a spread there, isn't there? I'll bet you've never been with anyone near as old as me, have you?"

"No," he said. "I haven't."

"So what-all else would you like to know about me? Hell, you've just taken me for a test drive—now it's only natural you'd want a look under the hood. So just ask away."

She waited.

"Why don't you just interview me like you did last night? You already know what I'm like in the sack—or is that all you're interested in knowing?"

"Now, wait a minute, Nora. Let's not forget that you were the one who seduced me. I didn't ask for this."

"You didn't put up much of a fight, either."

"I was outmatched."

She leaned against the wall beside her shrine to Marilyn Monroe and let her arms hang down at her sides, as if she were daring him, through this defenseless stance, to do his best to hurt her. "You think I'm just a dumb ignorant hoosier, don't you?"

"Nora—"

"Don't bullshit me. That's what you think, and that's what I am. I never got past the ninth grade, and I've been working at that White Palace for going on six years now because I'm not qualified for any other kind of work. And I'll tell you something else about me. I'm not in the habit of picking up men in bars. Oh, I used to be. I used to be in the habit of doing a lot of things, which I'm sure you'd rather not hear about. But I just got so sick and tired of all the fucked-up rednecked bastards I kept falling in with that I just gave up on men entirely. Do you know you're the first man I've been with in over a year? Not that I haven't had my share of offers—I've had plenty, let me tell you. But lately I've just gotten this funny idea about myself. I've started thinking that maybe I deserve better than the only kind of man who's likely to be interested in me—which is a laugh, I guess. And then I met you." She crossed her arms again now and kicked away a lone red shoe that was lying at her feet. "I'm sure I'd have to be an even bigger fool than I already am to think you'd want to have anything to do with me. After all, I'm not exactly your type, am I? But there's just something about you. I'll be damned if I know what it is—but there's just something about you." She stared at Max, blinked at him once, and sighed roughly through her nostrils. "So when you kept on sitting there and drinking with me last night at Cousin Hugo's, I thought to myself, well hell, Nora, stranger things have happened. That's what I thought. Stranger things have happened." She shrugged. "So there you are. I'm too goddamned old for you, I'm poor, I'm ignorant, I'm not pretty, and I'm sure you'd be ashamed to introduce me to any of your friends. So what are you going to do, Max?"

The impossible, diabolical thing was, he wanted her. He wanted her right now, just as she was, with her exposed face and her plucked eyebrows and her lingering stale smell of sex; he wanted to take her right here on this floor, down among the litter of shoes, panties, crumpled Kleenex, fluffballs of dust—he wanted to damn all common sense and circumspection and descend once again into that oblivion.

But he also knew what he had to tell her.

"Nora—I'm sorry."

She showed him a half-smile of contempt.

"Do you know," she said, "for a minute there I really did think you were going to up and surprise me?"

PART TWO

CHAPTER FIVE

"Can I offer you something, Max? A Snickers? A Kit-Kat? How about one of these amaretto macaroons? They're from the Missouri Bakery down on the Hill, and they're positively orgasmic."

"No thanks, Rosemary," Max said, taking one of the overstuffed chairs in front of her desk. "I just had lunch."

Rosemary smiled at him. "*Did* you?"

She plucked a macaroon from the big walnut bowl on her desk which she always kept brimming with assorted sweets, popped it whole into her mouth, and settled back in her deep leather-covered swivel chair with a heartfelt little moan of pleasure. Rosemary was a dedicated sensualist. She nibbled ceaselessly throughout the mornings, and yet always managed to bring a healthy appetite to lunch. She smoked strong, aromatic imported cigarettes, English Ovals or Balkan Sobranes, and she had the capacity for booze of a hard-bitten Irish wardhealer. For several years she had been living openly with a woman much younger than herself who also happened to be (Max found this perfect) a professional masseuse; and yet, for all of this habitual overindulgence, she looked quite good for a woman of forty-four. She had round gray attentive eyes, a canny and rather boyish freckled face, and close-cropped hair the color of baby carrots. She could not have weighed much more than a hundred pounds. Her office was designed to accomodate her hedonism. Her chair, deliciously comfortable—Max had sat in it on occasion— cranked all the way down to a flat horizontal. Her mahogany desk was curved like a boomerang so that everything could be easily reached from where she sat. Her couch, wide and plush, was made for a living room and not an office, the chairs in front of her desk were the sort you could take a nap in, and instead of shingling her walls in typical advertising fashion, with awards and plaques and framed ads and *New Yorker* cartoons satirizing the business, Rosemary had hung on opposite sides of the room two enormous, intensely relaxing reproductions of Monet's water lilies. This was the room where, like a warm kitchen, people naturally tended to congregate at the tail end of Spindler office parties. And to make it still more inviting, there was a small bar and a stereo system behind Rosemary's swooping desk.

In a business where people tended to slam phones, charge down hallways, and pace the floors of their offices like inspired lunatics, Rosemary simply glided along with the languor of a well-fed lioness. Max wasn't sure how she managed it. It wasn't that she ignored the pace and the pressures. She seemed, instead, to ride them like a snarling wave, with a surfer's curious repose. It might have been her detachment that carried her through, for Max had learned that despite Rosemary's high standing in the St. Louis advertising community, her heap of local and national awards, and the seminal and unorthodox campaigns she had done in the sixties and early seventies, for which she was still remembered, Rosemary fundamentally despised advertising. She claimed that she never watched television, and seldom listened to commercial radio—the ads drove her crazy. But plumbers, she liked to tell him, did not have to be especially fond of pipes and toilets in order to ply their trade. Like a good plumber, she knew her business, enjoyed her own proficiency, and did her best not to think about the purpose of it all—which was, like plumbing, to move a lot of shit from one place to another. Max only half-believed Rosemary's explanation. But then again, he sometimes couldn't understand what he himself was doing in the business, for on the whole, he didn't like advertisements any better than Rosemary did.

He knew well enough what had driven him away from teaching; he had been working far too hard for the money, and the money wasn't nearly enough. Had Bill and Sara Roth not been funneling funds to them throughout the years of their marriage, things would have been a lot rougher, and Janey, God forbid, would have had to finish up college in four years instead of six and put herself, like a commoner, into the job market. Yet Max himself, for all of the ten- and eleven-hour days he had put in as a teacher, was guilty of a certain indolence, for it was not until Janey's death that he finally built a fire under himself and sought other work. His life now lay in pieces, and the only good effect of this was the liberty it gave him to put those pieces back in any arrangement he desired. Max thought of advertising because he knew it was lucrative, because he trusted his ability to write, and because most of the local ads he heard were so utterly moronic that he figured he would have to be a moron in order not to top them.

Sara Roth had put him in touch with a friend of the family's, Bernard Wine, a retired art director, who agreed to help Max get together a portfolio of speculative ads. Kindly, asthmatic Mr. Wine claimed to be impressed with Max's native talent, gave him every encouragement, and graced his clumsy headlines and florid copy with layouts and illustrations that might have come straight from a 1957 edition of the *Ladies Home Journal*. Thus armed with his dubious portfolio, his complete ignorance of the business, and a few names supplied to him by Mr. Wine, Max began to get politely turned down by every agency he visited. Once he'd used up Mr. Wine's contacts—two of whom turned out to be dead—Max simply went to the Yellow Pages and started dialing, starting with the A's. By the time he got to the S's—and Spindler—he was merely going through the motions, spurred on by a certain angry obstinacy, but was already becoming resigned to a lifetime as a teacher. He suspected that he was only using the job search as a way of deflecting attention from his own mourning. But his interview with Rosemary Powers surprised him. He was in luck first of all because a writer there had just given notice a few days before, and on the morning he called, Rosemary hadn't gotten around to putting an ad in the paper. And luck was also with him because he walked into her office so wearied by rejection that he answered her questions with the complete candor of a person who had nothing to lose.

Rosemary leafed through his portfolio without a word, smoking her cigarette down to the butt and lighting another, then closed it, pushed it aside, and asked him what he thought of his own work.

"I think it's lousy," he said.

"So do I."

"But at least I can write a decent sentence."

"Yes, you can."

"And I know how to follow out an argument logically."

"I agree."

"But I don't know the first thing about advertising."

"No, you don't."

"So I suppose you're going to tell me to stick with teaching, right?"

Rosemary shrugged. "I don't know."

"Well, what else could you possibly say? It's obvious. I'm not qualified."

She narrowed her eyes at him and smiled. "Is that why you asked for this appointment with me? So you could come in here and tell me why I shouldn't hire you?"

Max laughed. "All right," he said. "I think you should hire me purely on the basis of my potential, because that's all I've got. Are you convinced?"

"Tell me why you want to stop being a teacher."

"Money."

"Understandable. Do you like teaching at all?"

"I love being in the classroom, I love the material, I like most of my students—and I've run out of patience with everything else."

"What makes you think you'd have any patience for advertising?"

Max sat forward in his chair. "Look, Miss Powers—"

"Call me Rosemary."

"All right, Rosemary—I'm burned out as a teacher. I can't promise you I'd be good at this, but I can promise you that I'd bring all of my energy and enthusiasm and concentration to it. I need—well, I need something new in my life."

"Why?"

Without intending to, he found himself telling this woman about Janey.

Rosemary fell silent for a few moments, taking this in. Then she offered him a cookie. He declined. She cranked herself back a few notches, chewed on her cookie, and addressed the ceiling. "You don't know the first thing about advertising," she said. "That's in the minus column. But advertising's no great mystery—it can be learned. What's in the plus column is your obvious intelligence, the fact that you can write, and the fact, too, that you're a teacher. Teachers make the best students, don't they? And the other thing is that I like you. But let me ask you this. You seem hungry, and that's good—but are you hungry enough to starve for a while? If I were to hire you—and that's a big if—you'd have to work at a coolie's wage for as long as it took until you proved yourself. Could you do it?"

"Yes."

"You can't run a business on intuition," Rosemary said. "But on the other hand, you can't run a good one without it." She tilted her face and looked closely at him with her clear gray eyes. "Of course, if I were to hire you, and you turned out to be good, you wouldn't be working at a coolie's wage for long. A young writer can make a shitload of money in this business." She laughed. "In fact, that's why I do what I do. I have extremely expensive tastes. But do you know what my real ambition was when I was a few years younger than you?"

"What was that?"

"I wanted to be an English teacher."

She had hired him the following week—at seven thousand dollars a year. Under Rosemary's tutelage Max had flourished beyond his own expectations. He discovered that all advertising writing really required was common sense and a certain facile cleverness, and that both of those qualities, even among seasoned writers, were rare. Max began to shine early, and in less than two years at Spindler, he had already gotten four raises and his own account, Baumann's Hams. It didn't matter that, like Rosemary, he had no sense of mission when it came to bringing his clients' messages to the masses; the challenge of learning a new discipline eclipsed every other consideration.

Rosemary was his champion at Spindler, and he, in

turn, was her prize pupil. While she often confounded
him, Max's admiration for her was complete, and he
sometimes thought that had things been different—had
Janey never existed, had Rosemary been twenty years
younger and not so dead-set in her ways as a lesbian—he
might have easily fallen in love with her. Or maybe, in a
way, he already was.

This afternoon Rosemary had called him into her
office and asked him to shut the door behind him. Closed
doors around Spindler usually signified trouble: a firing, a
salary dispute, a severe dressing down. Now, as usual,
Rosemary was taking her own sweet time in getting around
to the point.

"Where'd you have lunch?" she asked him.

"At home," he said.

"I went to O'Connell's and had one of their big
bloody roast beef sandwiches. I think I could live at
O'Connell's, if they had someplace where you could sleep."

"Rosemary, why is the door shut?"

She gave an ambivalent shrug. "We have some things
to discuss in private. Some good, some bad. Bad things
first. Why don't you have a look inside that manilla folder
on the corner of my desk?"

Max opened it onto his lap.

"As you can see, it's addressed to Lou Baumann. He
passed it on to me, and he's very seriously upset about it.
Now, read it, and please—no wisecracks."

The letter was typed on stationery bearing the Missouri State Seal.

> Sir:
>   This is in reference to the supposedly "humor-
> ous" radio commercial you now have running on
> KMOX—the one that takes place inside an "orphanage"
> and and operates from the absurd and insulting
> premise that chilren in the care of a state insti-
> tution would actually refuse to eat ham (they are
> lucky to get ham at all) because it is not a Baumann's
> ham.
>   I have been a social worker for the past twelve
> years and have dedicated myself to the problems of

the disenfranchised children of this city. While I believe that I have a healthy "funny bone" like anyone else, I find nothing to laugh at in this commercial. On the contrary, I find it appallingly tasteless and insensitive. Those of us in the social services have enough trouble doing our jobs without commercials that propogate the idea—unfortunately, quite widespread in this conservative decade—that so-called "orphans" dependent on state funds are somehow undeserving of our attention and care.

I cannot imagine how such a cruel and potentially very destructive advertisement ever found its way onto the airwaves and I assure you that I will do everything in my power to see that my family, my friends, and my professional associates follow my lead in refusing to purchase your product.

> Sincerely,
> Dr. Robert Hamilton,
> Assistant Director, Missouri State
> Foster Care Programs

P.S.: I am forwarding a copy of this letter to Mr. Robert Hyland of KMOX radio.

"I'll bet he didn't like *Oliver Twist* either," Max said.

"I told you—no wisecracks. Now, here's what's happening. Mr. Baumann has decided to pull the spot."

"What?"

"You heard me."

Max found himself emptying Rosemary's pewter ashtray into the wastebasket beside her desk.

"Would you care to vacuum the rug while you're at it?"

Max shrugged and stuck his hands into his pockets and began to pace her office. "Rosemary, how many people heard that spot? Two hundred thousand? And one solitary crackpot complains, and so they yank the commercial? What the hell kind of reasoning is that?"

"What counts is the solitary crackpot."

"Why?"

"I wish you'd sit down. You're only making both of us more agitated."

He sat and crossed his legs.

Rosemary had cranked her swivel chair all the way down. This was the position, with her sharp Irish nose aimed at the ceiling, from which she preferred to deliver her talks on the nature and theory of advertising. "It was a good spot, Max."

"You're damned right it was a good spot."

"But it was bad advertising. I'm afraid Dr. Hamilton is right. I never should have let that spot go through. Advertising should never admit to any kind of controversy. It needs to be as deodorized and idealized and devoid of reality as, say, some sort of Nazi vision of the millenuium with a bunch of blond-haired blue-eyed demigods frolicking on an Alpine mountainside in lederhosen."

Max laughed.

"People *want* to believe in a world like that, Max. How do you think Reagan got reelected by such a landslide? He didn't run a campaign. He ran a commercial. And that commercial, like all good commercials, assured us that all was right with the world." Rosemary lit a new Balkan Sobrane and shot a column of smoke toward the ceiling. "The only kind of suffering we admit to in advertising is the kind brought on by dandruff, or not getting your Express Mail on time. There is no insanity, no divorce, no murder, no war, no rape, no anything that would interfere with the idea that all of our problems can be solved by one simple trip to the supermarket. Because if consumers don't believe—at least for the sixty seconds when we have their attention—that happiness is easily *achievable,* then how are we going to convince them that brighter teeth are going to fix up forever their history of failure with the opposite sex? If we don't sell achievable happiness, we don't sell toothpaste. It's as simple as that. And so we present as the background to our sell a lovely, unreal, impossible vision of lobotomized American bliss, and that vision doesn't allow for things like orphanages. In a perfect world, every little boy and girl has a mommy and a daddy. That's why I never should have let that spot go through."

Rosemary blew a perfect, hovering smoke ring.

"What do you think?" she asked him.

"I'm thinking it through," Max told her. Rosemary had a tendency to exaggerate—as people in advertising, he supposed, should. But you had to be careful with her. There were always enough handholds of truth in what she said to make her arguments appear rock-solid, until you thought about them for a while. But Rosemary had been thinking about this for twenty years, and for the moment, Max could see no gaps in her logic.

"Now, here's the upshot," Rosemary said, and cranked herself back into a sitting position. She looked at him with a kind of apology in her eyes. "Mr. Baumann wants you off the account."

He was facing an expanse of Monet's water lilies, whose depthless mixed ovals of orange and green and violet suddenly took on depth, and he felt himself sinking. He twisted back in his chair to face Rosemary, heated with the injustice of it: in the year he'd been handling Baumann's hams, they'd gone from fourteenth to seventh place in the St. Louis market. But Rosemary was well aware of that. She was sitting forward now, with her hands clasped on top of her desk pad.

"Please try not to take this too much to heart, Max. Like I told you, there's good news for you, too. And anyway, this has nothing to do with your performance. Your performance on this account was top-notch, and don't let anyone around here tell you otherwise. It's just that someone's been working on Mr. Baumann, and I have the feeling it's his son, who's a prize horse's ass—and he's come to the conclusion that humorous advertising doesn't work for his product. Never mind the sales figures, of course. He refuses to be confused by the facts. So humorous advertising is out, and you're out along with it, because all he knows about you is that you write humorous spots."

"I can write any kind of spot, Rosemary—it's only the funny ones that take something extra."

"I told him that, Max. I spent all morning pleading with him. But he couldn't be moved. He wants new blood on the account. And so I've decided to give him some old blood instead—I'm giving Baumann's hams to Eddie Labodiak. Eddie couldn't write a really funny spot if you put a gun to his head, and so I figure we're safe there. And meanwhile . . ." Rosemary ground out her cigarette, sat back in her chair with crossed arms, and narrowed her eyes at Max. "Meanwhile, I've decided to give you Fidelity Federal. Now, I know that you're just a junior copywriter. But frankly, I think you're well on your way to being better than Eddie ever was, and I'm willing, as usual, to take a chance with you. Of course, I'll remain the senior writer on the account, but you'll be doing most of the work. We might have some trouble with Marv Keller over at Fidelity Federal—he's used to Eddie and Eddie's style. But I'll stand behind you." Now she offered him one of her rare, open smiles; Rosemary's teeth were her worst feature, crooked and yellow. "So how's that, Max? Does that make it up to you?"

For the past five years Fidelity Federal had belonged to Eddie Labodiak, an aging, rumpled, pretty well burntout case, with whom Max had never gotten along. Fidelity Federal was far and away Spindler's largest account, billing over half a million dollars a year. Max's back crept. He was going where he wanted to go. It was odd, but the sensation of realized ambition was not unlike the sensation of fear; he felt the floor flowing under him like water.

"Well?" Rosemary said.

"Well, I'm flattered."

"I'm not doing this to flatter you. Do you think you can handle the account?"

"I don't know," Max said. "For one thing, I don't know the first thing about financial advertising."

"I'll teach you," Rosemary said. "Do you want the account or don't you?"

"Of course I want it."

"Then you've got it."

"What about Eddie?"

"Oh, he'll threaten to quit. Or maybe he *will* quit, and then show up the next morning as usual. You know Eddie."

As little as he liked Eddie Labodiak, Max didn't like the idea of using Eddie's failure as a stepping-stone to his own success. But that, of course, was how business worked, and he, of course, was now a businessman. Still, he didn't savor the inevitable confrontation with that round-should-ered, musty-smelling, wild-haired old incompetent in the hallway tomorrow; he would have to think of something conciliatory to say to him.

"You look disturbed," Rosemary said.

"I'm just sorry about Eddie," he said.

"You'll get over it. Meanwhile, we'll start with Fidel-ity Federal this week, and then in a couple of months, once we see how you do, we'll talk about a raise."

Max thanked her effusively.

"That's enough," Rosemary told him, and he thought, in his excitement, that she was dismissing him from her office.

He rose to go.

"Just one minute, hotshot. We've got one more little item of business."

Max sat back down. Rosemary inspected him for a moment, then got up from her chair, clasped her hands behind her back, and stood in front of her big picture window, looking out onto Clayton Road. "I know you're going to think this is terribly petty—especially having just shown my trust in you by giving you Fidelity Federal. But it's bothering me, and I feel I have to bring it up." Her hands worked behind her back. "You were late coming back from lunch by an hour today, and yesterday you didn't drag yourself back to the office until well after two. I'd like an explanation."

"Rosemary, don't you think this is kind of unfair?"

"How am I being unfair?"

"Well hell, Rosemary—you know what goes on in this office. Everybody else around here habitually takes at least—"

"I'm not talking about everyone else around here. I'm talking about you." She continued to look out the win-dow; in her dark green suit, with her close-cropped hair, squared shoulders, and hands knit behind her back, she reminded him of a drill sergeant. "You've been the abso-lute model of virtue ever since you started working here, Max. You don't take two-hour lunches—or at least, you haven't up till now. You never bitch about staying late when I ask you, you never crab about your workload, you've never missed a deadline—I don't think you've ever even *flirted* with a deadline. I've got three other writers back there studying their navels or gossiping like old ladies, and you're in this office every five minutes with another piece of copy or another idea. It's not *like* you to take liberties, Max. And when a saint gets a parking ticket, it's front-page news. So I'd like an explanation for your late lunches these past two days." She turned and faced him now; she looked a little sheepish for some reason. "You're wearing a tie today," she said.

"Rosemary, I always wear a tie."

"That's right. So much for my writerly powers of observation. All right then, I'll just ask it—are you looking for another job?"

"What makes you think that?"

"What am I supposed to think? You're obviously not drinking your lunches."

"Rosemary, I'm happy here. I'd have to be out of my mind to be looking at other agencies." Then he wondered if Rosemary had given him the Fidelity Federal account as bait to stay on with Spindler; possible, but unlikely. She wouldn't have given him the account if she didn't think he could handle it. Besides, it wasn't worth worrying about: Fidelity Federal was his.

Rosemary resumed her place in her leather-covered chair, picked up a pencil, and began twirling it between her hands. "Well, if you're not out job-hunting and you're not out getting smashed, just what in the world *are* you doing for two hours at lunch?"

Max felt himself coloring.

Rosemary flipped her pencil over her shoulder and burst out laughing. "Whoops," she said, "I must be getting stupid in my old age." She was having some trouble getting the smile off her face. "Anyway, no more matinees, all right? Just do your screwing after work hours, like the rest of us."

Max nodded.

"Max? Can I ask you a question which is absolutely none of my business?"

"Go ahead."

"Is this serious?"

"I think I'm in the process of finding out."

"Ah."

He heard Rosemary take a deep breath through her nostrils.

"One more inadmissible question and then I'll drop the whole thing," she said. "Is this the first woman you've been serious about since Janey?"

"I don't know if I'm serious about her," he said again. "But yes. It's the first woman I've been involved with since Janey died."

"Thought so. I don't know what made me think so, but I thought so." Rosemary was looking at him with undisguised maternal concern. "Will you do me a favor?" she said. "Will you try and be careful? After all you've been through, I imagine it would be very, very easy to go overboard."

"Why shouldn't I go overboard?"

"Purely selfish reasons. I need your brain. And I know what happens to my brain when I'm in love."

"Please, Rosemary—don't go jumping to the conclusion that I'm in love."

She raised her eyebrows. "All right."

Max stood now. "Is it all right if I go?"

"Of course. And congratulations."

He wasn't sure if she were congratulating him on Fidelity Federal, or his new love affair. Rosemary's instincts were right: his mind was probably going. He opened the door.

"Max?"

"Yes?"

"Just be careful," she told him.

CHAPTER SIX

Max had tried to be careful. But you couldn't duck what you couldn't see coming, and there was no way he could have predicted that this inexplicable obsession for Nora would invade his system like a virus, or that the only relief from the fever, however temporary, would lay in another massive dose of the infection.

Max had left her house that Sunday afternoon—left her standing in the doorway, wrapped in her crimson bathrobe and blazing like a fiery pillar of accusation—and felt in his pocket for the folded slip of paper that bore her phone number. "You still owe me a brand-new mailbox," she told him. "I know I sure as hell can't afford to buy me one." He had every intention of making good on his debt to her—never mind that it was only at Nora's insistence that he had driven her home from Cousin Hugo's. She was poor; he was not. And so he would deliver the mailbox, and be constrained to see her one more time.

Knowing this was what probably left a door in his mind ajar, through which Nora, like a persistent and unwelcome caller, kept intruding. He had gone to make his obligatory Sunday visit to his mother's house that evening, and even she had noticed his abstraction; she kept asking him every few minutes if he was feeling all right, if he wanted a cup of tea, if he wanted to lie down. Finally, pleading illness, he cut short the visit and went home. Once in his apartment, he put on the most soothing music he could think of—the Goldberg Variations—and yet the thought of Nora, like a ghost demanding to be recognized, followed him as he paced from room to room, breathing down his neck, rattling her chains, drowning out the sweet, measured, rational strains of Bach. In bed, struggling unsuccessfuly for sleep, he thought of Janey only to marvel at the fact that he hadn't been thinking about her. For once he was free of her. But he wasn't free. He had been transferred, like a prisoner in shackles, from one cage to another, and his grief had been supplanted by this gnawing hunger for that middle-aged woman who worked at a White Palace and lived in a house as filthy as his mother's, who pronounced insurance with the accent on the first syllable, who harbored lost bags of pork rinds under the cushions of her sofa, and who, as far as he could tell, he didn't even like. He tossed in his bed and tried to reason with himself. Surely it was only the sex. What else could it be? The woman's grace, intelligence, and charm? He had to remember that he'd been without a woman for nearly two years; it was only natural that he would become irrationally attached, like a newborn chick, to the first biologically suitable individual who happened along. Any woman would have served as well as Nora. But if that were the case, if sex were the only thing, why wasn't he—now that his flesh had come to know itself again—engaged in a wide-ranging erotic reverie involving all kinds of women? He was once again a sexual animal. Why wasn't he thinking about the despoliation of the entire zoo? Horowitz was right—all Max had to do was to stand in a bar and collect numbers. Or easier still, he could simply get back in touch with all the women who had tried to hit on him since Janey's death: there was Janey's best friend, Judy Solomon, who had given him a call not one month after the funeral; there was Linda in the media department, Sheila at the receptionist's desk— Spindler offered him a virtual harem to pick from. There was also that actress he'd used for a Baumann's ham spot, Katherine or Kathleen, he couldn't remember which, who had given him her card at the end of the recording session and suggested they get together some evening and share a bottle of wine. But Max didn't want any of these women. He wanted Nora. He wanted her coffee-colored nipples, her veiny hands, her Callipygian ass, her maddening, swampy smell.

Max threw his sweaty pillow at the wall, got out of bed, considered picking up the pillow and putting it back where it belonged, decided to leave it there, and went downstairs to fix himself a cup of cocoa. He carried it into the living room, set it on a coaster on the coffee table, sat down on the sofa, picked up his volume of Shakespeare, and opened it to the last act of *Romeo and Juliet*. This was a lousy choice—never mind that it was what he should have been reading according to the program. To hell with the program. The last thing he needed was to read about a pair of star-crossed lovers. He tried *Twelfth Night*. *If music be the food of love, play on*. No good. None of the comedies would be any good— they all had romantic themes. He turned to *Lear*. But it was useless. Nora kept slithering like a serpent between the lines.

Max put the book down. His regimented system had abruptly broken down, and he didn't know what to do with himself. He thought about cleaning his apartment, but it was already immaculate, and moreover, he didn't feel like putting anything in order; what he felt like doing was tearing down his bookshelves, emptying his wastepaper basket onto the floor, dumping his file cabinet over, smashing his dishes against the wall. The clock read eleven. Most likely she was still awake; few adults he knew went to sleep as early as he did, and Nora, furthermore, had not even woken up until sometime this afternoon. The thing to do, he thought, was to call her, make arrangements to bring the new mailbox by, and get this thing over with just as swiftly as possible. And who knew? Maybe he would luck out. Maybe when he saw her again in the flesh whatever delirium was possessing him would have vanished, and he would see her for what she was, and feel nothing. The sooner he put himself to the test, the better. He'd see about coming over tomorrow night, after work. And what if his madness were still there? He put the thought out of his mind. He took the slip of paper with her phone number on it from his wallet, and dialed. The phone rang for an eternity.

He tried her again from the office on Monday morning. This time, after the tenth ring, she answered.

"Yeah?" Her voice was thick.

"Nora, this is Max."

"Who?"

"Max. You know—the guy you slept with yesterday."

Nora laughed. "I don't remember doing no sleeping."

He swallowed. "Did I wake you up?"

"Uh-huh. I had a shift at Shit City last night, and I
didn't get home till this morning. Max. What a nice surprise. I didn't expect to ever hear from you again."

"I told you I'd bring you a new mailbox," he said.

"Honey, men have told me a lot of things."

"That shows you don't know me very well," he said,
and realized he'd borrowed one of her lines from Saturday
night.

She returned the favor by borrowing one of his lines.
"That's true," she said. "I don't know you very well."

He was becoming increasingly nervous. He looked
down at his desk pad and saw what he'd unconsciously
been doodling: boxes within boxes within boxes. He
dropped his pen. "I, uh, was thinking of maybe coming
over this evening with the mailbox," he said.

"Well, how sweet."

"Except that I've got to buy it, you know, and I don't
even know what your last name is."

"Why don't you just bring me a whole batch of
letters, and I'll stick 'em on myself?"

"Why don't you just tell me what your last name is?"

"All right. It's Cromwell."

He decided, in his nervousness, to be funny. "How's
Oliver doing these days?"

"Who?"

"Oliver Cromwell."

"I don't believe he's related to me. Does he live here
in St. Louis?"

"No," Max said.

"Well, where-all do you know him from?"

"Oliver Cromwell is dead," Max said.

"I'm sorry to hear that. Was he a friend of yours?"

"Not really," Max said, and was overcome with a

flood of depressed shivers. Did it matter if this woman knew who Oliver Cromwell was? Not if he meant only to deliver a mailbox. But what did he actually mean to do? And if what he meant to do was to plunge into bed with her again—*then* did it matter if she knew who Oliver Cromwell was? But who gave a shit if she knew who Oliver Cromwell was?

"So you'd like to bring me that mailbox tonight?"

"Yes," Max heard himself say.

"Well, what time do you get off work?"

"Five."

"I'll be here all evening."

"Then I'll be there around six."

"Well, good. You remember when I told you yesterday that I had a feeling you were going to up and surprise me? Well, you did. It just came a day late, is all."

"Nora," he said. "All I'm doing is bringing over a mailbox."

"Uh-huh," she told him, and hung up.

On Thursday evening, four days into their affair—or whatever it deserved to be called—Max showed up at Nora's house bearing a bag of groceries, two bottles of champagne, and the good news about his acquisition of the Fidelity Federal account. As he came through the front door, which she habitually left unlocked, he noted once again that the pole, the pail, the mailbox, and the small bag of concrete he had dutifully purchased at Central Hardware and brought over on Monday night were still sitting untouched in a corner of her front hallway: a monument to the impatience of their lust. They had not been able to keep their hands off each other for long enough to grab a sandwich from the kitchen, much less to go out and install a new mailbox on her lawn. *As prime as goats, as hot as monkeys* was the line from *Othello* that kept occurring to him. For the first time since the first weeks of his marriage, Max's penis stung when he handled it while he was pissing, and his entire pelvic area felt bruised; it was all he could do to keep from walking bowlegged at the office. Even Nora, who Max had begun to think was an indestructible sexual workhorse, had finally shown signs that she was mortal; this afternoon during their hurried lunchtime assignation, she had complained of pain and asked him to withdraw. It was then that she had revealed to him her collection of sexual trifles and showed him how to apply the buzzing missile, set at the third speed, just to the front of her, and had him bring her off in that way as she reclined on a jumble of pillows like a sleazy odalisque, with her rough gray armpits exposed, and wildly encouraged him in her private nonsensical language of ecstasy. The two of them, he thought, had been fucking as people aboard the sinking *Titanic* must have fucked as the band on the slanting deck played "Nearer My God, to Thee," or as the citizens of Moscow must have fucked upon hearing that Napoleon had reached the suburbs—fucking each other past all awareness of some relentlessly approaching disaster. And the disaster they were both trying to put out of their minds, Max thought as he picked his way through the fallen wardrobe on the floor of her front hallway, was that of getting to know each other better and realizing, as they had to, that this liaison of theirs was congenitally doomed. They had barely managed to sustain a five-minute conversation since Sunday.

Tonight was going to be different. He had brought an assortment of props to keep his hands innocently occupied; he was going to clean her kitchen, light candles, break open the champagne, serve her something decent to eat, and insist that the two of them talk. He really felt too sore for anything more strenuous than that. He called out for Nora.

"Max? I'm back here in the kitchen. I got my hands full, so just come on back."

As he approached the kitchen he picked up—could it be?—the scent of ammonia. And here was Nora, kneeling in jeans, a Charlie Daniels T-shirt, and a red-checked headscarf, cheerfully scrubbing the floor like an energetic, efficient housewife in a Johnson's Wax commercial. Achievable happiness.

She sat back with a grin and pressed the palms of her hands into the small of her back. "Surprise," she said.

The kitchen was clean.

"Here's to your new promotion."

"Well, it's not exactly a promotion."

"Then here's to whatever the hell it is. Good luck, Max. Get rich."

They clinked Star Wars glasses emblazoned with the Burger King logo.

"You know," Nora said, "I got me some nice china coffee cups over there in the—"

"Nora, stop it. I like drinking champagne out of my Darth Vader glass. Besides, it's no good if you can't see the bubbles. How does it taste?"

"Almost as good as you."

He could see she wasn't going to give him any help tonight. Nora's hair was up, and for that he was grateful; had it been down, the lush iridescent cascade of it might have incited him directly to her water bed. As it was, she wore a skimpy sleeveless rose-colored blouse, and the utter vacancy beneath it where her breasts should have been was already undermining his resolution. He kept his eyes on her face.

"So," Nora said, "now whenever I see a Fidelity Federal commercial on TV, that'll be something you wrote all by yourself?"

"Well, not all by myself."

She shook her head at him. "I didn't have me no idea I was screwing such an important man."

Max smiled at this, but the effect of it was to make his elation over his new account seem ludicrously inflated. He didn't think there had been any irony intended there, but he wasn't entirely sure. He was having a hard time determining just how intelligent Nora really was.

"Do you know if I told the girls at the White Palace

that my new boyfriend was a bigshot advertising man, why, I'd bet they'd just laugh in my face.''

"It's really not that big of a deal," Max said, disturbed by her use of the word *boyfriend*. But what else was she supposed to call him? Something bluesy and mildly pornographic would have described him better: *my sweet jelly roll, my kitchen man, my deep-sea diver*. No man answering to such a description would have to bother about carrying on a relationship beyond the confines of the bed.

"Honey, if it's not that big of a deal, why the champagne and all?"

This drew a sheepish shrug and smile from him. "All right. It is a big deal. But part of what all of this is about is, I want to talk to you."

Nora's eyes went flat. "Talk to me about what?" she said carefully.

"Hell, I don't know—anything. The point is, we've hardly said a hundred words to each other since Sunday."

Nora sat back and exhaled. "I thought you were going to tell me you didn't want to see me again," she said.

He had to think about this. Here, of course, was an opening. But he did want to see her again. He wanted to be with her now; he wanted to stay with her tonight, never mind that one day, and one day soon, he would certainly have to tell her good-bye. "Talk to me," he said.

"All right."

They stared at each other.

Nora began tracing small circles on the table with her fingertip. "Why don't we talk about what went on today?"

"All right. What went on today?"

Nora raised her eyes to him. "I thought about you," she said. "That's what went on today."

"I thought about you, too," Max said.

"And what were you thinking about in particular?"

"About how we needed to talk."

Nora laughed and slapped the table. "I just don't know about you," she said.

I just don't know about you, Max thought.

She picked up her Luke Skywalker glass and drank up

the champagne. Max picked up the bottle and refilled it for her.

"Say, I've got me an idea. Why don't we gossip?"

"About whom?"

"Hell, anybody. I don't know—how about that Oliver Cromwell friend of yours who died? You know any good dirt about him?"

As he got dinner ready, Max obliged her with some seventeenth-century English history, but Nora quickly grew restless. He knew from teaching the sense of having lost his audience, but something obstinate inside of him insisted that he go on. She watched him for a spell as if he were a television show she wasn't particularly interested in, then got up to empty the pink swan-shaped ashtray—was she already picking up nervous tics from him?—resumed her seat, finished off what was in her glass, and poured out the last of the champagne. Max rattled on as he minced the garlic, irritated with Nora for being bored, with himself for being boring, and with the two of them for failing in the commonplace endeavor of carrying on a normal conversation. Was there simply too much sublimated sexual energy squirming around the room? Should they have fucked first and talked later? Max went on with his lecture.

"Honey," Nora said. "Where'd you put that other bottle of champagne?"

"In the refrigerator," he said, and scraped the garlic into the sputtering olive oil. "By this time," he went on, "it looked like Cromwell's luck had pretty well run out. . . ."

Nora came over to him with the champagne bottle. "Could you open this?" she said. "I'm afraid I'm all thumbs."

"You don't seem terribly interested in what I'm talking about."

"I guess I'm not."

"Aren't you even curious to know if Cromwell gets beheaded?"

"Well, I imagine he does, doesn't he? Max, I *am* sorry, but all this talk about England and Puritans and the rest of it is just giving me a headache."

Everything he cared about seemed to give this woman

a headache. Mozart had given her a headache. "So you don't care about history," he said.

"I guess not."

"What are all those books you read on Marilyn Monroe about? Isn't that a certain kind of history?"

"Well, I suppose so, but it's different."

"How?"

"I care about Marilyn Monroe." She handed the champagne bottle to him. "Would you open this, Max? I think we could both use some."

"I tell you what," Max said, sitting down with the bottle between his knees. "When people don't have a sense of history, they're bound to screw things up in the present. Look at Ronald Reagan." He worked the bottle open, and the launching of the cork and its frothy aftermath gave vent to a certain portion of his frustration. He filled the two Star Wars glasses, and brought them over to where Nora was standing. "What was I talking about?" he asked her.

"Ronald Reagan."

"Well, if that man has ever cracked a history book in his life, I'll eat this glass."

"I like President Reagan," Nora said.

Max caught his breath. "You what?"

She shrugged and sipped her champagne. "He seems like an awfully nice old man."

"What the hell kind of difference does it make if he's an awfully nice old man?"

She looked at him. "Why are you yelling at me?"

Why was he yelling at her?

"I'm sorry," he said. "I just get very worked up when I talk about Reagan."

"I think you get very worked up when you talk about a lot of things."

"I suppose I do," he said.

"Well, what's wrong with Reagan?"

"Maybe the fact that he is such a sweet old man, and that his policies are so misguided and vicious."

"I guess you voted for Mondale or something."

"Yes, I did, as a matter of fact."

"Well, there was a real winner for you."

"Nora—" Max lowered his voice. He intended to be soft-spoken and reasonable. "You're poor—you barely make over the minimum wage. And if Reagan had his way, there wouldn't even *be* a minimum wage. Not only that, but you're a woman. Don't you understand that that man is your natural enemy?"

"Honey," Nora said, fitting herself beside him against the counter. "Ronald Reagan didn't make poor people and he's not going to unmake them, and neither is anybody else. Do you really think I'd be any better off if someone else was president? Hell, no—it's all nothing but a big fat joke. Everybody's always ranting and raving about what goes on in the White House or over there in Israel or what-have-you, and none of it really makes any kind of difference. It's like the World Series. You remember how steamed up this city got about the Cardinals? Lord, the way people carried on, you would have thought the world was coming to an end. And then the next morning we all woke up and everything was just exactly where we'd left it. It's the same damned thing with politics, if you ask me. Much ado about nothing."

He didn't know what bothered him most, her glib know-nothingism or her unconscious use of Shakespeare. He knew that her argument was fatuous, and yet, from where she stood, she was right; no president of the United States was going to make her life any easier. Nora bumped shoulders with him.

"So what're you making for supper tonight?"

"It's called spaghetti carbonara."

"Never heard of it."

"It's from Italy—a Roman dish."

"Well, I figured it was Italian from the spaghetti part."

She pronounced it eye-talian, like some South St. Louis waitress—which, of course, was what she was.

She asked him what was in it.

"It's basically pasta with bacon and eggs."

She made a face of disgust like a little girl.

"You'll love it," he told her.

But she did not love it. She poked at it and rearranged it on her plate and took a few experimental bites—protesting all the while about how very good it was—and then let most of it grow cold. Maybe he would have had more luck if he'd told her it was Spaghetti à la Oscar Meyer. In compensation she consumed several bowls of salad, nearly all the garlic bread, and once the champagne was gone, washed down her food with a vodka tonic. The main topic of conversation (now that they had finally gotten the ball rolling, Max almost regretted it) was Nora's grievances at work. The abuses committed against her were manifold and petty: scheduling problems, sexual come-ons from her manager, real or imagined, her failure after six years in the organization to become a manager herself, and in every instance Nora came out looking well-intentioned, cruelly misunderstood, and gloriously in the right. He noticed that she had the self-centered habit of dragging people into her narrative by their first names without having first established who they were, as if all the trivial details of her life were supposed to be common knowledge. His mother, to his constant exasperation, did the very same thing when she talked. Max kept having to interrupt Nora for clarification. "So then I say to Sheila—" "Wait a minute. Who's Sheila?" "She's the woman I work with who's carrying on with Marvin." "Who's Marvin?" "I told you—Marvin's the night manager who I'm going to haul off and slug one of these days if he doesn't learn to keep his cotton-picking hands to himself." And on it went. Max soon grew as weary of Nora's epic catalogue of complaints as she had been of his history of Cromwell. Unlike Nora, however, he did his level best to appear interested, and that, he thought, was a matter of breeding. He felt a hot flush of dislike for himself. Who the hell was he to talk about breeding? He had never even met his own father. And this was a class act indeed, pretending interest in this woman's bitchy monologue so that later, as sore as he felt, she would admit him to her bed, and all the while secretly despising her. Just what was he doing at this woman's table if that was how he felt? But he wasn't at all sure that this was how he felt. He wasn't sure of anything at all, except that even the depressing experience of his first real meal with this woman was doing nothing to tame his monstrous desire. He wanted to pass his hands lightly up behind that rose-colored blouse, bend back that middle-aged and finely wrinkled throat, and bury his guilt and bewilderment in the tobacco-tasting depths of Nora's kiss.

Nora's face was softened, sweetened, by the amber glow of the candle on the table; her eyes shone. She looked happy.

"You know," she said, "this was really awful sweet of you." She reached across the table and took his hand; her hand was much larger than his. "Thanks for making dinner, Max. It was wonderful."

He snuck a look at the spaghetti carbonara which had congealed on her plate. He had been wrong to force this dish on her; he should have brought over some prime steaks instead. The point, after all, should have been to please her—not to educate her palate.

"I want to tell you something, Max. This may sound corny, but I just don't care. You're just about the nicest man—you probably *are* the nicest man I've ever been with. I mean that. Oh, I know we've only known each other a real short while, but all the same, I just want to tell you that you're kind and you're sweet and you're thoughtful. You're—well, a gentleman. Except when you shouldn't be, that is." She squeezed his hand and laughed. "Of course, you just might turn out to be a rotten son of a bitch like the rest of them. But for right now, I'm just real glad I met you." Now she released his hand and got out a Winston and lit it in the candle flame. "Do you know this is the first time a man's ever cooked dinner for me?"

This touched him. "You're kidding."

"Scout's honor."

"Didn't your husband ever cook for you?"

She snorted. "That'd be the day. Oh, he barbecued for me and the like, but this is the first time a man's ever whipped up a whole nice meal like this, just for me. It was nice, Max. It made me feel . . ." She carefully set her Winston between the wings of her swan-shaped ashtray. "It made me feel pretty."

"Let's make love," Max said to her thickly.

They were both still bruised and scraped, and in their care not to hurt each other, their lovemaking took on a new tenderness. It seemed like hours before either one of them came. Afterward Nora went into the kitchen to rustle up a cigarette, and she looked contemplative as she came back into the bedroom, naked and pear-shaped, her Winston hanging from her mouth, and the question she asked him when she sat down on the edge of the bed made him bark with startled laughter.

"Are you Italian?" she wanted to know.

———————

On Friday his work finally suffered. He'd been given his first assignment for Fidelity Federal, and it wasn't a very interesting one. It was a newspaper ad for a "line of credit" loan, which allowed savers to borrow money up to a certain limit simply by writing a check. Rattled by sleeplessness, bleary-eyed, and still drenched in the residual presence of Nora, Max engaged all morning in maddening word-play until he finally came up with a headline which, if it wasn't anywhere near brilliant, was at least serviceable: *The Pen Is Mightier Than the Loan Officer.* He borrowed a felt-tipped pen and a pad of layout paper from the art department, wrote out the headline, added a childish cartoon of an anthropomorphized fountain pen, and brought it in to Rosemary.

"I'm not sure Marv Keller is interested in pornographic headlines," she told him.

"What are you talking about?"

"The penis—mightier than the loan officer."

"It's supposed to read 'the pen is.' "

"Not the way you've got it here, sweetheart." Rosemary smirked at him. "And look at this. You've even added a nice little drawing of an erection."

"That's supposed to be a fountain pen," Max said.

"Oh? Silly me. Well, anyway, I don't think this is quite the approach we're looking for." She handed back the pad to him. "Something on your mind today?" she asked him.

Rosemary had been right; he'd somehow gotten the spacing wrong between the letters. He sat down on her wide sofa and blinked at his crude attempt at an ad. "I'm stuck, Rosemary."

"This happens every so often to every writer."

"It hasn't happened to me before."

"There—you see? You're human after all. Have a chocolate." She proffered her box of Godiva chocolates. Max shook his head. Rosemary selected one for herself and poked a hole in the bottom with her fingernail. "Oh, good," she said. "Coconut cream. My favorite. Isn't it awful, sneaking peeks inside chocolates as expensive as these? Bad habit." She watched Max fidget on the sofa. "I have an idea," she said. "Why don't you just take the rest of the afternoon off?"

Max's right knee stopped jiggling. "You're kidding."

"Not at all. Go to the zoo. Go to the art museum. Go pretend you're unemployed. It looks like a lovely day outside."

"I can't just leave my work like that."

"Why not?"

"Well, it seems unprofessional—sloppy."

"Max, I wouldn't be suggesting this if I couldn't spare you this afternoon. It's one of the few slow days we get around here, and you'd be smart to take advantage of it."

Max stood. "Thanks, Rosemary. But I'm feeling defeated right now, and I don't want to walk out of here feeling defeated."

"I wish you'd sit down," Rosemary said, and there was command in her voice. She waited until he got settled again and said, "I don't suppose I have to tell you that you're a perfectionist."

"Is there anything wrong with that?"

"Only if you take it too far. Max, I want you to pursue excellence, of course. But I want to warn you against taking it to the fanatical extreme where you begin to unconsciously reward yourself with occasional little doses of failure. Lighten up on yourself for once. Do you know what's going to happen if you go back to your office and tackle that ad again? You'll fail. I know how it works. Your mind isn't clicking, and the harder you push it, the less it'll click. Why fail today when you can take the afternoon off and enjoy a walk in the park instead? Go easy on yourself, Max. Go to the zoo."

Max stood up again. "Is that an order?"

Rosemary sighed. "It's a request."

Max went back to his office and fought with the ad until closing time.

———————————

"Lord, you're a bitch tonight. I'm afraid to open up my mouth around you."

"I don't like that word, Nora. And I'd prefer if you didn't use it around me."

"It's just a *word*."

"What do you think words are? Soap bubbles? Words happen to *mean* things. People kill each other over words."

"Look, I already told you—I don't got nothing against nobody because their skin is black. But there's black people and there's niggers, and if you grew up in the city like I did, you'd know the difference. Hell, any black person will tell you the same. That son of a bitch who came into the White Palace today and started slapping that poor girl around—right there in plain view of everyone—what the hell else do you call that except a nigger?"

He was standing at the open kitchen door, glaring out into the hard-driving rain. The silhouette of the steel plant seemed to flutter like a ragged black flag. He turned back to Nora. In the flat light of the kitchen her makeup looked absurd, whorish. He wanted to take her by those frail shoulders and shake the stubborn ignorance out of her. "If he's a son of a bitch, then fine—he's a son of a bitch. What the hell does that have to do with him being black?"

Nora rolled her eyes to the ceiling and strode back to the counter to get her drink. "Well, I am sorry—but his skin *was* black, and he *was* a son of a bitch, and in my book, that makes him a nigger. You didn't see the way he was laying into that poor child. It was enough to make you sick."

"That's not the point, goddammit!"

"Well, what is the point?"

"How it makes you sound when you come out with a word like that."

"All right, then." Nora crossed her arms and fit her back against the counter. "How does it make me sound?"

Max sucked in his cheeks as he looked at her.

"Well? How does it make me sound? You were going to say ignorant, weren't you? Isn't that what you were going to say?"

"Yes."

"Then why the hell don't you just come out and *say* it?"

Max could no longer be in the same room with her. He picked up his scotch and water (his drinking habits, thanks to Nora, had changed radically in the past week) and retreated to the chaos of her living room. He cleared away from one of her dusty armchairs a copy of *Cosmopolitan,* an empty Doritos bag, brushed some fallen cigarette ash from the seat, and slumped down in it. He took a deep swallow of his drink. This was as far as it went. They had run up against the thick brick wall separating their worlds, and from this point on the relationship—the whatever it was—could only deteriorate. He had been way out of line to let it start up in the first place, and if he had any sense, or any courage at all, he would tell her good-bye tonight.

Nora entered the room silently and sat across from him on the sofa. Her hand went to her ear and she began to twist her earring. Of all the particulars about her which would come to pierce him when he was away from her— her swaggering, bottom-heavy walk, her infuriating odor, her singsongy Missouri twang—this singular mannerism was perhaps the most potent. With each tiny twist that she gave to her earring, she further unscrewed his resolve.

"I don't want to fight with you," she said.

"I don't want to fight with you, either."

"No?"

"No."

"Then let's make love?"

"Don't you think we ought to have some dinner first?"

"I don't think dinner is going to make us feel any better," she said.

———————

She woke up screaming.

The rain muttered steadily and there was no light in the room. Max crawled on top of her and tried to restrain her against the rocking surface of the water bed, whispering, "It's all right, it's all right." Finally she quieted and sank back onto her pillows. Her breath was still panicked and her mouth was making dry clicks. Max groped along the floor until he found the Flintstones glass she always kept by the side of the bed when they made love, and lifted her head to help her drink the stale water. She nodded, as if to let him know that she was cognizant again, and finished the water on her own. He put his hands on her belly and felt her rib cage shuddering. Then he lay beside her.

"Nora? What was it? What were you dreaming about?"

She only shook her head.

"Do you remember?"

"Yes."

"But you don't want to tell me."

"No."

"I'll get you another glass of water," he said.

She seized hold of him. "Max—?"

"I'm here."

She relaxed a little. "You know what I want?"

"What?"

"A bath."

He drew it for her. He watched on his knees as the water hit the tub and began to swirl and eddy, and as the heat pushed into his face, he thought that for the first time since this started, his heart was empty of misgiving.

Nora came into the bathroom wearing her crimson bathrobe. She looked as pale and weak as a sick child.

"How come you're so good to me?" she asked.

CHAPTER SEVEN

On Saturday morning he awoke alone in the water bed (Nora was pulling a double shift at the White Palace and would not be back until late) and remembered, as he stared at the forlorn cracks in her ceiling, what day this was: it was the second anniversary, on the Jewish calendar, of Janey's death. It wasn't Max who kept track of such things, but his mother. For all of her apparent addleheadedness, she had a memory like a tribal historian, and there was not a family birthday, death date, wedding anniversary, or even phone number or address, current or obsolete, that she did not keep stored in her vast mental file. No cousin was too distant, no brother or sister so estranged, that they could not count on getting a card from her on their birthday, Hannukah or Rosh Hashanah—never mind that in return they generally ignored her. That his mother might let Janey's yahrzeit slip by without notice was unthinkable. Janey had been one of the few people in her life—perhaps the only person—who had shown his mother any genuine affection (Max's displays of affection were merely productions of filial duty), and so his mother had loved her, and still loved her, like a favorite child. During last Sunday's obligatory visit to her house, his mother must have reminded Max a dozen times of his promise to take her out to the cemetery this afternoon, and had pressed upon him, just as he was leaving, the fat fleshy-pale yahrzeit candle which he was supposed to have lit last evening at sundown. While Max had no use for religion, he had plenty of use for ritual, and he certainly would have lit the candle, just as he did the year before, had Nora not intervened.

Max hadn't been back to his apartment since Thursday, when he stopped by after work to pick up some toiletry items and a few changes of clothes. In fact, he had completely forgotten about this day until now. A week in Nora's arms had befuddled his memory like a week of shock treatments; he could barely even remember what his life had been like, just seven days ago, before he met this woman.

Max sat up amid her twisted sheets, sporting a full-blown morning erection, and found his wristwatch curled behind the stinking ashtray on her nighttable. It was already eleven. He had promised to pick his mother up at noon; he would have to get moving. Instead, he continued to sit cross-legged in the bed, staring through a heap of dirty clothing on the floor.

Two years dead. It was like a birthday wrenched wickedly inside out. Each time it came around, Max would be one year older, while Janey, stopped by death like a butterfly sealed in amber, would never be any older than twenty-five; instead of celebration, there would be grief; instead of Janey blowing out her candles, candles would be lit in her memory; the party, such as it was, with just Max and his mother in attendance, would take place in that crowded corner of that overpopulated Jewish grave-yard in University City, in this first week of October, just as the sweet smell of the season's decay was beginning to bite through the air. Janey had died in the fall, and would always die in the fall, like Persephone. But would Max always mourn her?

Time would have to answer that; he knew only that right now, sitting naked and tumescent in this water bed with Nora's odor, as persistent as garlic, still clinging to his skin, he wanted no part of any graveside visit. He saw something monstrously deceptive in going to pay his respects to his dead wife's bones after this week of avidly knocking bones with Nora; it was nearly as cold-blooded as a Mafia boss bearing a wreath to the funeral of the rival he himself had ordered murdered. Besides, hadn't this volcanic reawakening of passion finally overwhelmed his stubborn grief and acted, in a sense, as Janey's second burial? Let her stay buried, he thought. He could always call his mother and plead illness.

But of course, he couldn't do that. He had given her his promise. And furthermore, she had no other way out to the graveyard, thanks to Max. A few months after Janey's death he had convinced his mother that she was too nervous to drive, and had confiscated her license. As a result, Max often had to act as her chauffeur, to the supermarket, to her bingo games, to her meetings at the Jewish War Veterans building, to the graveyard, and while this was certainly an inconvenience for him, at least there was one less crazy woman out on the road.

He got out of bed, picked his way through the flotsam and jetsam on Nora's bedroom floor, went into her bracingly clean bathroom, and showered with the care of a man who had spent the day at a toxic waste site: he did not want to pick up any hint of Nora's scent as he stood before Janey's grave.

Both he and Janey, Max thought as he drove down to University City, would have been far better off had they somehow been able to switch childhoods. They were both only children, and so the trade would have had a certain neatness about it. Max could have taken Janey's enormous room on the second floor of the ugly Tudor-style mansion in Ladue, with its fairy-tale-princess canopied bed and its blue and gold trimmed French Provincial furniture; Janey could have settled into the sunroom at the back of his mother's tiny shotgun house, which Max had made into a sanctuary of cleanliness and order during the years of his growing up—and the cramped austerity probably would have been good for her. They both possessed missing places in their characters, Janey a certain toughness and realism, Max an ability to let go and relax, which such an exchange, as in the story of the prince and the pauper, might have gone a long way to correct. Max could have given up his constant scratching for extra money, his rabbinical study habits, his ceaseless surveillance of his mother, and taken time out for tennis, a coming-out party now and then, or a riding lesson or two. It was doubtful, too, that he would have abused, had he been given them, the charge cards for Saks and Neiman-Marcus that Janey had so irresponsibly wielded since her sixteenth birthday. Janey, on the other hand, could have taken up his paper routes and his lawn-mowing clients; instead of having a maid, she would have known what it was like to play maid to his mother; after living for long enough on his mother's awful food—canned tomato soup, overly mayonnaised tuna salad, blackened grilled cheese sandwiches—she might even have learned how to cook.

Both mothers, too, would have been happier had they made the swap. Janey was just the sort of daughter his mother's explosive temperament required: patient, cheerful, undemanding, easy in her affections. Max was the intellectual companion Sara Roth had been unable to discover either in her husband—genial Bill Roth, as indisposed to introspection as a friendly cartoon bear—or in Janey, whom she habitually condemned for her materialism, her vanity, and her lack, as far as Sara could see, of mental discipline. "She has the mind of a debutante," Sara once told him. "Frankly, I don't understand why she doesn't seem to bore you." Sara had been too hard on Janey, who was considerably more intelligent than she gave her credit for, but by the same token, Max was probably far too hard on his mother, or so Janey used to tell him. Janey's ability to hear out his mother's endless complaints with that bright look of interest her face was so good at maintaining, to quietly and lovingly douse the flames of his mother's incipient hysteria, or even to willingly spend as much time with her as she did, having lunch, playing cards, or acting, every Tuesday night, as her bingo partner, was something Max found as incomprehensible as magic.

And as long as these roles were being shuffled around, wouldn't Max and his mother have been much better off if he had been the natural parent, she the child? The transference of authority had started when he was very small. He could remember at five or six screaming at his mother to wash the dirty dishes that had been languishing for days in the sink, and when she refused, standing on a chair and

learning to wash them himself. It had been Max who ran
the vacuum cleaner, Max who scrubbed the floors.

When he was in grade school he would periodically
come home at lunch and surreptitiously clean the house.
His mother was an inveterate hoarder, incapable of throwing away anything, and the house was usually so crammed
with useless trash—shopping bags stuffed with enough
toilet paper, aluminum foil, Q-tips, and cotton balls to
outlast a siege, countless yellowing stacks of old newspapers, piles of salvaged gift wrap, obsolete mail-order
catalogues, broken appliances—that Max was too embarrassed by the mess to even have Horowitz over. Each time
his mother came home from work at the Rexall store to
find that he had cleaned out the house in her absence, she
would fly into a rage, call him a sneak, a thief, a dirty
little back-stabber, and then as often as not storm into the
backyard, where her hoard of treasure lay piled in and
around the garbage cans, and truck it all doggedly back
into the house. It was Max, as a teenager, who made sure
that she got her car inspected on time, who canceled the
subscriptions to magazines she couldn't possibly be interested in which some door-to-door salesman had suckered
her into buying (like *Trout and Stream* or *Hot Rod*) and
Max, who figured out, when he was fourteen, what all the
dunning phone calls and letters were about, and began
his lifelong campaign of haranguing his mother about her
finances; from then on it was Max who saw to it that she
paid her bills each month, Max who balanced her
checkbook.

As often as he made the trip to his old neighborhood
north of Heman Park, the discrepancy between its present
reality and his childhood memories still surprised and
saddened him. Everything had shrunk from the epic proportions of his childhood, and looked shabbier, more
embarrassed for itself: the dumpy little houses, most of
them no bigger than Nora's, the unkempt lawns the size
of swimming pools, the cracked sidewalks, the weary-
looking trees. His old grammar school, University Forest,
now rudely boarded up, looked too absurdly small, too
ruined, to have contained all those years of his life, all
that early flowering of his mind. Max had been one of

those peculiar children who had actually loved going to
school, and to see the old building shuttered up, of no
interest or use to anyone but vandals, gave a twist to his
heart each time he drove past it. The neighborhood, too,
had changed hands. Once fairly divided between Jews
and German Catholics, it had been annexed in the middle
seventies by blacks from the near North Side. Most of the
Jews living here, eager, perhaps, to preserve their liberal
ideals, had joined in a latter-day exodus to Creve Coeur
and Olivette in West County; the only whites still remaining were those, like his mother, who were too poor to go
anywhere else. Driving down Partridge Street, he passed a
wiry, slate-colored old man in a straw hat, laboring in his
tangled little garden; he passed a knot of black kids playing
corkball in the middle of Plymouth Street; he drew up
behind a tall young woman in a turban pushing a baby
stroller down the sidewalk, and slowed his Volvo for a
better look at her ass. It was impressive, all right, like two
bowling balls trapped in the seat of her jeans, and it put
him in mind of Nora. What would she do if he told her
she didn't have a white woman's ass? Probably break his
nose, Max thought, and made the turn into Raymond
Street.

His mother's tiny house looked from the front like the
archetypal house children drew in kindergarten: a square
frame, a peaked roof, a door in the middle, and two
windows flanking the door. All that was missing was a
chimney with a crayon squiggle of smoke rising out of it
and a dog perched in front, wearing a human smile. Max
parked on the street, as the driveway was too spotted with
chuckholes to be negotiable. He would have to get that
taken care of, when he had the extra money—probably
not until the spring, when the problem would be twice as
bad. His mother still worked, after twelve years, at the
Rexall store in Olivette (how they had managed to put up
with her for all that time was past his comprehension) and
she took home only a hundred dollars a week. Max made
up the rest. He did this despite the fact that his mother
squandered a good portion of it on the Missouri State
Lottery, her bingo games, and her occasional senseless
purchases—like the sewing machine gathering dust in the

dining room (his mother didn't sew) or her memberships in various book clubs (she didn't have the patience to sit through a book). Their arguments had been going on for years, and more than once Max had threatened to teach her a lesson in thrift by cutting her off. But he had never made good on his threat. His mother was incapable of learning a lesson; and Max, in turn, was incapable of defying his own guilty sense of duty. She could be flushing her money down the toilet, and he would go on sending her more.

He knocked on the door and waited as his mother unlatched, unlocked, and unbolted the baroque system of barricades she lived behind in abject terror of the *shvartzes*. He wasn't sure how safe or unsafe this neighborhood actually was, but his mother was probably better off with her exaggerated fears than with a glib carelessness. What neighborhood, after all, was safe? Max made a mental note to start giving Nora more trouble about leaving her front door unlocked, and then his mother's door came open.

Her rosy moon face appeared, her eyes rounded, as usual, with anxiety. The girlish sausage curls quivering at her neck looked a deeper shade of brown than they had last Sunday; maybe she'd gone to the beauty parlor again. His mother's hair had begun to go gray in her thirties, and now, at the age of fifty-six, there couldn't have been anything left but gray beneath all those applications of dye. She looked younger than she was, with very few wrinkles, and the blurred, unfinished features of a woman who had grown old without having ever grown up.

"You're early!" she said. "You tell me twelve-thirty and here it's only twenty after twelve and I'm not ready yet! Why are you always rushing me like this?"

His mother shouted this. Shouting was her normal tone of voice. Whether she did this because she feared that no one ever listened to her, or because no one ever *did* listen to her because she shouted all the time, was a classic chicken-or-egg question that Max had long ago despaired of puzzling out. He ignored her yelling, stepped into the house—which smelled sharply of his childhood— and gave his mother a hug. She clung to him.

"How have you been?" he asked her, knowing what sort of response was coming.

"Well, I shouldn't complain—" his mother started out.

"Then don't," Max told her, and sat down in the old armchair that was the color of a golden retriever.

His mother recited her litany of ailments as she ponderously relatched and rebolted her door: aching feet, sinus trouble, constipation, dizziness. "So I go to Dr. Dorfman and what does he tell me? He says it's all in my imagination—I'm healthy as a horse, he says."

"You *are* as healthy as a horse," Max told her. His mother had never been hospitalized for anything, and even Janey's death, while it sent her spinning into a depression as long as Max's, had never actually affected her physically. She was wearing a baggy black dress, and an old woman's black tie-up shoes, and the energy emanating from her round, solid body—as misdirected as it always was—was nonetheless considerable.

"Don't talk to me about Dorfman—that goniff! I pay him my money and what does he give me? Nothing! He tells me to take aspirin and to stop worrying so much."

"That's good advice," Max said.

His mother turned around from the door with a look of surprise on her face. "I have to go to the bathroom," she told him, and hurried out of the living room.

Max took a look around. While the accumulation of junk in the living room was nowhere near some of the levels he had seen it reach, the place was still being used as a dumpsite. There were perhaps a half a dozen shopping bags standing like drunken sentinels in various spots around the floor, and copies of the *Post-Dispatch* were building up by the side of the sofa. The dining room table supported a mountain of cardboard boxes. And then he noticed something else: her pictures had been brought upstairs again, and were standing, as usual, on the coffee table, the mantel, the TV set, and every inch of shelf space that wasn't already taken up by an arrangement of plastic flowers, a cheap plaster figurine, or a souvenir ashtray from someplace where his mother had never been.

Soon after Janey's death his mother had removed her

photographs, along with the photographs of the rest of the
family, and stored them away in the basement. Max hadn't
seen them again until now. He arose from his chair and
went over to inspect them: here were her beloved dead
parents, whom Max had never known, posed formally
side by side in their medieval Jewish garb (the photograph
had been taken in Russia); his grandfather in his black hat
and dirty-looking patriarchal beard, his grandmother looking grim and Asiatic in her peasant dress and babushka.
There were no pictures of his father, although his mother
had told him (he wasn't sure if he believed this) that he'd
been a dead ringer for Errol Flynn, which was the only
reason she'd gone ahead and married him. There were
some smaller photographs of his aunts and uncles and
cousins in Chicago, who may as well have been living in
Siberia for as often as his mother saw them. The lion's
share of the pictures were of Max and Janey; Janey, in
fact, might have had the numerical edge. It was easy
enough to understand why his mother had put Janey's
pictures away; they pained her too much. But why the
rest of the family would have had to follow her into
seclusion was another question, and one for which his
mother had no better answer than "It didn't look right,
everyone there except Janey." But Max thought he knew
why. His mother hadn't been able to bear the thought of
Janey sitting it out all alone in that dark, cheerless basement, and so had sent the rest of the relatives down to
keep her company. His mother's Jewishness was simply a
matter of habit and form; at heart she was a primitive, an
animist, and these family photographs were her living
household gods.

   Yelling, pulling at her girdle, the toilet roaring behind
her, his mother came back into the living room. "That
Dorfman! I tell him how I have to make water all the time
and does he give me anything for it? No, he—"

   "Mom—"

   "—tells me take aspirin and calm down. How is that
supposed to—"

   "Mom!" Max shouted.

   She stopped where she was and stared at him.

   "How come the pictures are back?" he asked her.

"Is it too soon?"

"Of course not. It's been two years since you've—"

"It's too soon! I knew it was too soon! I never should have brought them up before—"

"Goddammit, Mom—will you please lower your voice and listen to me?"

Her mouth crumpled and she blinked at him.

"Why did you decide to bring these up now?"

She shrugged. "I had a dream."

"What was the dream?"

His mother came up beside him and took down from one of the shelves a slick professional photo of Janey in her riding outfit. He could hear the breath whistling in her nostrils as she stared at it. "I had it Wednesday night," she said. "I dreamed I came home and there was Janey sitting right there on the sofa—just as alive as anybody. You should have seen her, Max. She looked—just beautiful. So beautiful. And so we talked a little and played some gin rummy, you know, just like in the old days, and then she looked up and she said to me, 'Mom—where are my pictures?' And so I told her how I'd taken them down to the basement, because, you know, she'd died, and Janey just laughed and laughed. 'What makes you think I'm dead?' she told me. And you know what, Max? I woke up right then and I felt so full of joy—I really did think for a few minutes that I'd gotten it all wrong and she was still alive. And—I don't know. That day I just brought the pictures up, that's all. I missed them."

"I missed them, too," Max told her.

"So it's not too soon?" she asked him.

"No," Max said. "It's not too soon."

The roll call of the headstones was as rich and piquant as borscht: Pinkus, Mandlebaum, Fish, Ladinsky, Protzel, Adelman, Zucherman, Blitz . . . no mildly recumbent, blissfully snoozing Smiths or Joneses here. As Max kept pace beside his mother through the thicket of monuments in the Chesid Shel Emeth cemetery, he imagined these comical, undignified Goldfarbs, Nachmanns, Shlotzkys, and Mermelsteins still reeking of onions, chomping cigars, talking profit and loss, complaining of back pain and dealing out the pinochle hands beneath their six feet each of packed earth. Even the look of the graveyard was Jewish—eccentric, anarchic, with the headstones as closely packed as teeth, sprouting up wherever space would allow. If gentile graveyards, as serene and open as golf courses, were the suburban country clubs of the dead, then this place was surely the Lower East Side at the turn of the century, just barely able to sustain the influx of immigrants from the other world. His mother, on familiar ground, led them through the mazy pathways without a moment's hesitation to Janey's grave.

"Oy, God," she said. "Look what they've done to her!"

The grave was indeed in sorry shape. Knee-high weeds burst from the mound, one corner of which had been mashed flat by some kind of vehicle with treads.

"Those people should be shot," his mother said. "It was just like this when I came out here last week with my girlfriend Delores—"

"You come out here with your girlfriends?" Max said.

"Of course. Why not? And it was just like this! And so I called those goniffs and they promised they'd fix it up—and now look! And those people call themselves Jews!"

"I'll have the Roths take care of it."

"The Roths!" his mother said derisively. "They're too busy counting their money to bother with a thing like this."

"For God sakes, Mom—it's their daughter's grave."

"A lot they care—those bigshots."

His mother stooped and began to fiercely uproot the weeds that were sprouting from the grave. When the mound was mostly cleared, she tore up two fistfuls of grass and stood, red-faced and panting, offering Max his portion of grass. He took it carefully into his hand. A strong wind was blowing at their backs, fluttering the square of black lace pinned to his mother's hat. She tossed her grass toward the grave; the wind dispersed it. Grunting, she knelt, ripped up another fistful of grass, and this time patted it onto the grave.

"Now you throw yours," his mother told him.

"Do you have any idea what this is supposed to mean?" Max asked her.

"It's to show your respect for the dead."

He had seen her do this every time they came out to the graveyard, and had never been able to get any kind of sensible explanation for this ritual. Nevertheless, he stooped, like his mother, toward the grave, and let the wind filter the grass toward the mound. They stood in silence for a spell. Aside from the unacceptable perversity of the birth and death dates—much too recent to have been carved into granite—Janey's grave left him unmoved. This boringly official monument had nothing to do with her; they should have commemorated this day by visiting the apartment on Wydown where Max and Janey had spent the years of their marriage, or U. City High, or the riding stables out in Fenton, or the women's department at Saks. This grave was as bland and impersonal as a statistic. Yet today, with his desire for Nora coloring the whole of his consciousness, it was easy to imagine Janey beneath this bed-shaped bump in the earth, sitting upright among the worms with a quizzical look on her face. *Why her of all women, Max? I'm surprised at you. I always liked to think you had good taste.*

His mother rooted through her purse until she came up with the tiny pamphlet that bore the mourner's prayer, Kaddish, in Hebrew and in Hebrew transliterated into English. Max knew the gist of it. There was no mention of death anywhere in the poem. It was instead a jubilant paean to the creation and to the Creator—a Creator Max would have refused to praise even if he'd believed in His existence—and so when his mother took the yarmulke from her purse and tried to press it upon him along with the pamphlet, Max kept his hands in his jacket pockets.

"I'm not going to say Kaddish, Mom."

"You're the husband. Who else is going to say it?"

"Mom, we go through this every time we come out

here. I don't believe in God, and I'm not going to pray to a God I don't believe in."

His mother glared at him. For some reason Max's apostasy, despite the fact that he'd been openly maintaining it since his early adolescence (he'd refused, resolutely, to go to Hebrew school and be bar mitzvahed) always came to his mother as a complete surprise.

"What are you—a goy?"

"Goys believe in God."

"Don't say that out here!" his mother hissed, and then, over her shoulder, another woman appeared, coming down the narrow path with precise, urgent steps, her head down. It was Sara Roth. She wore a small boat-shaped black hat in her salt-and-pepper hair, with a veil that reached to the tip of her nose, and carried a bouquet of daisies, Janey's favorite flowers. When she spotted Max and his mother, the smile she produced looked forced; she had not expected to have her privacy impinged on here.

Partly to act as a buffer between the two women, who loathed each other, and partly because he was so moved to see Sara, Max left his mother's side and met her on the path.

He had not seen Sara since late July, after she confessed to him one evening following a heavy dinner and several glasses of brandy that their weekly meetings had become too painful for her to bear. "You make her too real for me," she said. "The rest of the time she's some angel or ghost, or just a memory, and I think that's the only way I can take it, Max. Maybe that's what we have to do with our dead in order to go on living—make them unreal. But when I'm with you, she's my flesh-and-blood daughter all over again, and it just tears the wound wide open. Please, don't hate me, Max. I'm just feeling weak these days and I think I need to retreat for a while." Max had kept his distance after that. And while he often felt an acute yearning for Sara's company, he couldn't really blame her for his banishment. It wasn't for him to say how much or what kind of pain she should have been able to take; in losing Janey, he had not lost a daughter, and furthermore, had not lost a daughter with whom he had never gotten along, and to whom he hadn't had the chance to become reconciled before it was too late. There was unfinished business between Sara and Janey that would always remain unfinished.

He embraced Sara—crushing the daisies between them—and her thin back was tense beneath her dark cloth coat.

"I'm sorry I've been such a stranger, Max."

"How have you been, Sara? You look—"

"No. Don't tell me how I look. I know how I look."

She had aged in the past two months. Her face looked more closely drawn to the bone, and the sickle-shaped smudges of sleeplessness under her eyes were dark enough to be seen behind her veil. She had always had trouble sleeping, but in the past two years her insomnia had grown worse. She was still a handsome woman, however, and her face still echoed Janey's: the same high patrician molding of the cheeks and brow, the same nose, a lovely touch too wide at the bottom, the same powder-blue eyes, with their characteristic look of astonishment.

"I've missed you," Max told her.

"It hasn't been healthy, our not talking, has it?"

"Not for me, anyway," Max said.

Sara glanced at his mother, who was standing a few yards away and watching them indignantly. "I'd better go say hello to your mother before all hell breaks loose," she said, and went over and took his mother's hand.

"Edith, it's good to see you. How's your health?"

For once his mother failed to recite her epic catalogue of miseries. She shrugged. "I can't complain, I guess."

"Good. I'm glad to hear it. Could you excuse me for a moment while I have a word with your son?"

Sara's formality intimidated her. His mother made a vague, uncertain gesture, and Sara returned to him on the path. "I want to have lunch with you," she said. "Do you want to have lunch with me?"

"You know I do."

"No. I *don't* know you do. I don't forgive as easily as you do, Max, and I think I've hurt you."

"Forget it," Max said. "Let's have lunch. I need to talk to you."

"What about?"

Suddenly he knew what about. He had a ferocious need to talk to her, to talk volumes, and what he wanted to talk about was not Janey—that had been talked into the ground often enough—but Nora. He didn't know why he was about to choose Sara as his confessor. But she was the one he wanted to reveal himself to—not to Horowitz, not to Rosemary, but to his ex–mother-in-law, who was probably in a position to understand him the least.

"Why don't you meet me this Saturday at Chez Louis? Can you make it?"

"Sure."

"Do you know where it is?"

"Don't you remember? You took Janey and me there right after we announced our engagement."

"That's right. She infuriated me, I remember. She wouldn't eat."

"She was nervous."

"Janey didn't have any nerves."

His mother, angry at having been ignored for so long, hustled over to Sara and tugged on the sleeve of her coat. "Do you know that today is Janey's yahrzeit?" she shouted.

Sara took a step back from her. "Of course I know, Edith. That's why I'm out here today."

"Well, did you know that you have to light the candle twenty-four hours before—"

"I lit it last night."

"Do you need any more candles? Because I picked up some extra at the Schnuck's store because I thought that maybe—"

"Thanks, Edith. I've got all the candles I need."

"You got all you need?"

"Yes."

His mother fell silent and plucked at the girdle beneath her black dress; this was all the advice she had to give, and none of it had been needed.

Sara brushed past her and laid the daisies on the grave. She considered the arrangement briefly, with crossed arms, and Max joined her. "I don't know why I bother

coming out here," she said. "It never does me any good."
Now she noticed the flattened corner of the mound. "What
the hell happened here?" she said.

His mother, hearing her cue, rushed over and let rip
her jeremiad against the cemetery owners, bellowing to
be heard over the wind. Sara endured it for a while, the
wind pressing her veil to her face, and finally raised her
hand for silence. "I'll get it taken care of," she said.

"But you don't know these *schmendricks* like I do!
You call and you call and you—"

"I *said* I'd get it taken care of," Sara said too sharply,
and Max saw it coming.

"Don't you shout that way at me!" his mother said,
puffing out her chest. "How dare you shout that way
at me!"

"You're the one who's shouting, Edith."

"Shut up, Mom," Max told her.

She jabbed a finger at him. "You keep your nose out
of this!"

He took his mother by the shoulders. "I don't want to
hear another word of this."

His mother ignored him. She shook a finger at Sara's
impassive face. "Now, you just listen to me, Mrs. Roth!
Maybe I'm not rich and classy like you and maybe I don't
live in Ladue and belong to Temple Israel and go around
with my nose stuck up in the air—but I'm a human being,
too, and I deserve a little respect! Because when all is said
and done, Mrs. Bigshot Roth, your shit smells just as bad
as mine!"

Sara stared at her through her fluttering veil. When
she spoke, it was from depths of weariness more than of
anger. "Edith, I really don't care how you speak to me,
because frankly, you're not all that important to me. But
my daughter's memory is important to me, and I promise
you that if you ever, ever create another scene like this
before my daughter's grave, I'll see to it that you're never
allowed on these grounds again. And don't think I can't
make that stick. Do you understand?"

His mother understood; she was staring at the ground.

"And one more thing you should know, Edith. When
you're as rich as I am, your shit doesn't smell at all."

Sara gave Max's elbow a squeeze. "I'll see you Saturday at noon," she said, and made her escape from the graveyard.

He didn't know what made him start to do it. Maybe it was all the conflicting tensions from his afternoon visit to the graveyard; maybe it was simply the acid of his passion eating away at the last supports of his self-control; but on Saturday night, as he was fucking Nora from behind and listening to her entranced, ecstatic babble, he opened his mouth, stepped off the edge of himself, and started to babble right along with her. It was as easy as falling. The syllables flooded out—electric, staccato, senseless, unstoppable once they started. He listened with disbelief from some far corner of himself to the two of them going at it. They were jabbering and chattering like a pair of monkeys in a burning cage. And then he lost all sense of himself, all sense of what was happening, and he didn't even seem to be present when his orgasm finally shuddered him inside out.

Horowitz was married on Sunday, in a ceremony that started twenty minutes late, with Max as his best man and all of Rachel's plump, flushed, teary-eyed bridesmaids in their peach-colored dresses, like a gathering of overgrown cherubim, in attendance. The altar area failed to collapse, although Horowitz gave it one hell of a shake when he stomped the wineglass to powder beneath the heel of his shoe. The reception at Le Chateau was chaotic, exuberant, and giddy, and the theme of love ruled the atmosphere. Everyone seemed to assume that Max's period of mourning was long past, and everyone wanted to know, especially Judy Solomon, Brenda Ladinsky, and Teri Fox—

all women he had known since high school—what his dating habits were these days. Max tried his best to be vague in no uncertain terms: he wasn't really back to dating yet, whatever "really" meant, and at certain points during these friendly interrogations, he almost wished he had Nora at his side to put a halt to the inquiries.

But he had not invited Nora to the wedding. He had told her, instead—his first lie, a milestone—that he would be spending the evening at his mother's house. It was not until he was driving home from the reception, slightly drunk, that he faced up squarely to the reason for his lie. He had not invited Nora to the wedding because he did not want to be seen with her. Nora had been right: he was indeed ashamed to introduce her to any of his friends. He cared what people thought.

Now he had to think about Janey. If he was so fearful for his reputation as to keep Nora hidden away from public view, like some two-headed monstrosity shut up in an attic, then hadn't his reputation been one of the secret considerations when he'd decided to marry Janey? Certainly in winning her, he had won the loudest applause of his life. Men wanted her, women envied her, parents approved of her, and when he presented her at a party, he may as well have been showing off a five-foot golden trophy. And of course Janey had not only been beautiful; there was nothing about her he'd had to apologize for. Viewed against Nora's towering imperfections, Janey appeared almost saintly, and like a saint, Max thought, turning off his tape deck so he could better hear his reverie, there had been something fundamentally uninteresting about her. Lovely Janey, sweet Janey, cheerful Janey, simple Janey. Maybe Sara Roth had been right about her. How long, really, could he have lived with a woman like that?

Their marriage, too, now looked suspiciously problem-free to him, suspiciously placid, like the surface of a lake where nothing stirs. What had they argued over? Money— Janey's favorite hobby, outside of riding horses, was shopping for things she didn't need—but they had never argued about it with any genuine vituperation, for thanks to Janey's parents, there had always been plenty of money close at

hand. Had there been other bones of contention? Max
searched for old grievances between them, and could
come up with nothing of any substance. There was something peculiar, and again, suspicious in that, as though
they had not been fully conscious during the years of their
marriage. And yet, having known Nora just over a week,
he already had enough grievances against her to fill a file
cabinet, and grievances, furthermore, that only seemed to
stoke his passion. And here was the other thing, perhaps
the salient thing: while he had no doubt that he had loved
Janey, and could not conceive of actually loving Nora, he
had never felt this kind of gnawing desire for his wife, had
never been so utterly brain-sick with the thought of her.
And why not? Max could reason it out only in this way:
Janey had been patently lovable, Nora was patently the
opposite, and maybe a love for a woman so deserving of
love was bound to prove unexceptional. In his feelings for
Janey there had been no ambivalence, no misgiving, no
conflict, no friction, and so, perhaps, no fire.

This argument hounded him all the way back to his
apartment. Max had made up his mind to sleep alone
tonight, just to prove to himself that he could get through
a twenty-four-hour period without the problematical comfort of Nora's company. But once he'd hung up his tuxedo
and stood before his brass bed, contemplating the cool
inhuman expanse of space that awaited him there, his
determination dissolved. He pulled on a pair of jeans and
an alligator shirt and left his apartment, slamming the
door.

CHAPTER EIGHT

Nora's Monopoly-board house was lightless, a dim rectangle set against a darker sky. But there was her rusty Impala parked in the driveway; she must have been asleep. Max went in through her unlocked front door. It was as black in here as a carnival funhouse. He minced his way—almost slipping once on what felt like a nylon—to the wall where her Marilyn Monroe shrine was hung, passed his fingers lightly over the pictures, and then found the light switch and flicked it. He remained in darkness. Was the light bulb spent? He called out for her; there was no reply. He groped along the turn in the wall, continued down the hallway and stepped into her bedroom. Here was enough light coming in through the window to see; her bed was empty; the fan in the window was stopped. Max retraced his steps, testing the velvety darkness before him like a blind man approaching the edge of a sudden precipice, and was suddenly struck by a powerful presentiment of her loss. He was going to lose her—if not now, if not soon, then certainly someday, and this abandoned, panicked groping in the dark was his rehearsal. He kept calling out her name.

"Out here," Nora finally said.

Max was in the kitchen; the voice had come from the other side of the screen door, out on the patio. It was a moonless night, and her backyard was nearly as dark as the house. The neighborhood dogs were carrying on their nightly argument. The black hulking mass of the Scullin Steel mill seemed to rear up right at the edge of her property. She was lying in her lawn chair; the orange tip of her cigarette floated somewhere above her body. He couldn't tell if she turned her head to look at him.

"I sure as hell didn't expect you to show up here tonight," she said.

"What kind of greeting is that?"

All he heard in response was the sound of ice cubes rearranging themselves in her glass.

"Dark enough for you in there?" she asked.

"I almost broke my neck. What happened?"

"Electricity's out."

"How come?"

"Because I didn't pay the bill, that's how come."

"How long was it overdue, Nora?"

"Long enough, I suppose."

"Come on—how long?"

"Three months."

"Oh, Jesus, Nora."

"Poor people certainly are disgusting, aren't they?"

He had not heard this low, grinding edge to her voice before. Here was another Nora, one she'd been carefully hiding from him: bitchy, self-pitying, mean. He thought he could feel actual physical waves of hostility rolling out from her body and lapping at his shirt—but then he realized it was only the wind. The tip of her cigarette made a slow arc through the gloom and burned brighter as she drew on it. "I guess they must have shut it off while I was off at Shit City," she said.

"Nora, why didn't you say something to me about it?"

"You mean beg you for a handout?"

"I would have given you a loan."

"Thanks, but no thanks."

"Why not?"

"I don't want to have to be beholden to you," she said.

"I would have *given* you the money."

"I don't need your charity, or anybody else's. I'm doing just fine on my own, thank you."

"This is what you call doing fine? What's doing great? When they repossess your car?"

Her cigarette shot out into the dark.

"You know," Nora said, "these ice cubes in my glass are just about melted. Why don't you go on inside and fetch me a new glass of ice? I've noticed you don't mind fetching things. Will you do that for me? There's a bag of it in the sink."

He wanted to challenge her, ask her why she was being so hostile, but he was afraid of any answer she might give.

"I really do wish you'd fetch me that ice," she said. "And while you're at it, you can bring out that bottle of vodka."

Max went back into the kitchen, wondering why he was acting so contrite. Of course he knew that he was guilty, but what could Nora know? Could she smell it on him as animals were supposed to be able to smell fear? He filled two glasses full of ice—he wanted a drink himself—and brought the vodka bottle out with him. Nora neither looked at him nor thanked him when he handed her the glass. He took a lawn chair that stood folded against the house, opened it out, and sat beside her, picking up the vodka bottle and pouring a small shot into his glass.

"Did you have a nice time at the wedding?" she asked him.

Max carefully set the bottle onto the concrete patio. He sat back in his chair and closed his eyes; it was almost a relief to be so justly nailed. It gave the illusion that the world was a well-ordered place.

"How did you find out?" he asked her.

"I called your mother. No—I wasn't checking up on you, if that's what you're thinking. I mean, I didn't have any reason to think you were lying to me, did I? It's just that when I got home and saw I didn't have no electricity, well, I got upset and I wanted to talk to you. So I called up information and got hold of your mother, and surprise."

Max's eyes had adjusted well enough to the light so he could make out her profile. Her strong Indian face looked closed and unappeasable.

"Why did you lie to me?"

Nora picked up the bottle and tilted it into her glass; two glugs. She set it down and waited. "Cat got your tongue?" she asked. "Well, then, maybe you can answer me this: Is this someone you just met or have you known her for a while?"

It took Max a moment to figure out what she was driving at; then he almost laughed from pure surprise.

"Lord, you're quiet tonight," Nora said. She took a swallow of her drink. "Tell me all about her, Max. What's she like?"

"Nora, you're—"

"No. Don't tell me. Let me guess. I like guessing games, in case you haven't noticed. Let's see . . . first of all, she's young, of course. Probably just a baby like you. And she's pretty, too—she'd have to be pretty, wouldn't she? Nice and young and fresh and pretty, with big boobs and a nice tight little ass—am I getting close? And I'll just bet she's a college girl, too, someone you can talk to about books and history—"

"Listen to me, Nora. You're wrong."

"Oh? She's not a college girl? You mean to tell me you go slumming all the time?"

Max absorbed this blow in silence.

"But I'll bet I got one thing up on her," Nora said. "I'll bet she can't hold a candle to me in the fucking department, can she? I may be a dumb hoosier, but that's one thing I know how to do, isn't it? And you like that, don't you, Max? You like that plenty. Hell, there's not much else to like, is there?"

"Nora, goddammit—that's enough!" He was on his feet and facing the Scullin Steel mill with his drink in his hand. He turned to look at Nora. Her big knees were raised in front of her where she lay on her lawn chair and he could see the whites of her eyes through the murk. "There's no other woman. Do you understand that? I almost wish there were another woman—but there isn't. My God, I can't even look at another woman without thinking how much I want you instead."

"You're going to have to do better than that."

Max chucked his drink, glass and all, into the backyard behind him, and found himself kneeling by the side of her lawn chair. "Nora, I don't know what's happening to me, or why it's happening—half the time I don't even *believe* it's happening—but this is the truth, and you'd better believe me. I've never wanted any woman as much as I want you. Never. Not even my wife."

Nora drew her knees up still higher and stared at him.

"Don't say that. How can you say that?"

"It's true."

"Are you drunk? Is that it? Did you get drunk at that wedding?"

"Do I seem drunk to you?"

"You seem crazy. Your eyes look funny."

"You're *making* me crazy, Nora."

She shifted uneasily in her chair and gave her hair a guarded toss. She looked over her shoulder at him. And then she suddenly came around and bent forward, clasping her hand behind his neck and drawing his face close to hers. She smelled of booze, cigarettes, herself, and—naturally she hadn't bathed after work, in the dark—the meat and onion stink of White Palaces. It was perversely intoxicating. "Max, don't say something like that if you don't mean it. I mean what you said about your wife. That could just tear a person apart . . . if you don't mean it."

"You know I mean it."

"Honey, how can you say you love me more than your wife?"

Max sat back on his heels. "That's not what I said."

"Well, what *did* you say?"

"I said I wanted you more than my wife."

"Well, just what the hell is the difference?"

"I don't know what the difference is."

"Then how do you know it isn't love?"

"Nora, I *don't* know. I know only that when I'm away from you, I'm a total wreck. . . ."

"And when you're with me?"

"Then I'm a different kind of total wreck."

"And how about when I wreck you in bed?" She asked this without a touch of humor in her voice. "Does that put you all back together again?"

"For a while."

She gave a shiver and lit a new Winston and stared off in the direction of the steel mill. Her upraised knees began to wag. She appeared to Max both slovenly and regal, with her big thighs emerging from a pair of ugly checked polyester shorts she might have bought at K-mart, and her unbrushed hair hanging in tangles all down her back, like a mane of seaweed, or of vines. She was part slattern, part Olympian, and he wanted to take her in his arms and crush away the contradiction.

He asked her in a thick, grainy voice if she loved him.

She blew a plume of smoke from her mouth. "Lord, I just don't know. I wish to hell I did know. But I'll tell you this, Max. Every time we make a date and you show up here like you said you would, right on time like you always do, why, I'm just so grateful, it's downright sickening. Because I don't expect you to show up at all, you know. I keep thinking—well, Nora, tonight's the night he's going to come to his senses, and that's the last you're going to see of him, and you may as well be happy that it lasted as long as it did. Just a nice little break in the middle of your rotten life. And then when you *do* show up, the feeling I get—well . . ." She sighed. "That's when I think I just might love you. But then I remember that I met you only last Saturday night, and then I just don't know all over again." She shrugged and smiled at him. "How's that for an answer?"

"What does it matter how long we've known each other?"

"Nobody falls in love in one week's time, honey."

"Sure they do. Do you know how long the action of *Romeo and Juliet* takes? Three days. That's it. Just three days."

"Max, that's just a play."

"It's not just a play—it's Shakespeare."

"Well, be that as it may, I don't believe in love at first sight and all that romantic hogwash. It doesn't happen, Max—at least not to grown-ups."

"Are you sure?"

Nora finished off her drink. "No," she said. She set her empty glass onto the patio. "You still haven't told me why you lied to me."

Max was an unpracticed liar, and here was the problem with lies: one led inexorably into another. He could hardly tell her the truth, not if he ever wanted to see her again—or to come totally clean, not if he meant to go to bed with her tonight.

He asked her if she'd ever been to a Jewish wedding. She snorted. "Not recently," she said.

He went on to explain how the two of them would have been relentlessly cross-examined from every side about their relationship, and how he hadn't wanted to put her through such a trial so early on in their affair. It frightened and amazed him how smooth and plausible it sounded. Rather than bring up the subject of the wedding, he went on, only to tell her that he wasn't inviting her, he figured—and now he knew he was mistaken in this—that he simply wouldn't bring it up at all. He admitted that he'd taken the easy way out, that he'd been absolutely wrong, and he asked her forgiveness.

Nora looked at him warily. Then she shrugged.

"Well hell," she said. "Every wedding's like that— Jewish or not."

Max was ashamed of his easy victory. Maybe he was born to be a professional warper of the truth; he probably should have started in the ad business directly out of college.

"I just want you to know," Nora said very quietly, her eyes directed again to the steel mill, "that there's nothing I hate like having somebody lie to me. I think I'd rather have a man beat me up than lie to me—at least there you have a chance of defending yourself. You know, Max, I really did think you were honest. But I guess I was mistaken, wasn't I?"

She knew just where to slip in the knife. He had found a teacher in Nora worthy of teaching a teacher. First she had destroyed his illusion of self-control, and now she was going after the illusion of his self-image. It was no longer safe to presume anything at all about himself.

"I wish you'd say that you forgive me," he said.

She left him dangling for a spell on the hook of her silence.

"I'll forgive you once," she told him. "But I'll be damned if I'll forgive you twice."

CHAPTER NINE

"I wonder sometimes about my intelligence," Rosemary said. "I always seem to be the last person to find out what's going on around me. You remember when Bill Sampson in the art department married what's-her-name? That anemic little media buyer?"

"Denise," Max said.

"Right. You know when I found out about them? When I got the wedding invitation. Here they'd been carrying on a torrid affair for months practically right outside my door, and I didn't have the vaguest clue. Not that I'm terribly interested in that sort of thing, but still you'd think . . . well, anyway." Rosemary opened the bottle of Jameson's Irish she'd taken from the liquor cabinet behind her desk and poured hefty shots into both of their glasses. "So naturally when Marv Keller announced his retirement, I was the only person in either organization who hadn't been expecting it. Of course I knew he was diabetic, Max, but I had no idea how bad it was getting. It was hard to tell with Marv. He was always so quiet, so unopinionated and pliable, I just didn't take any notice when he sat there like a fading ghost during our meetings. I thought it was his *style*." She sighed and picked up her drink. "So after eight years at Fidelity Federal, Marv Keller's gone, and they expect to choose a new marketing director within a few weeks. Let's hope it takes a lot longer than that."

"Why?"

"Drink your drink."

"Rosemary, I just don't understand your gloom. All right—so Marv Keller retires and they hire a new marketing director. So what?"

Rosemary showed him one of her controlled smiles, masking her bad teeth. "You know, I tend to forget that you're still just a novice in this business—until you come out with something like that."

"What did I get wrong?"

"This is the classic textbook way that agencies lose accounts, Max. Whoever this new marketing director turns out to be, he or she is going to have to quickly flex their muscles by making certain dramatic changes. It's a matter of establishing your turf. And the easiest, swiftest, and least painful way of doing that is to dump the old agency and bring on a new one bearing your personal stamp of approval. I can't tell you how many times I've seen it happen. How do you think we get half the accounts we do? We hear about a shake-up in management somewhere and we dive in like vultures." Rosemary knocked back her whiskey with an abrupt, mannish toss of the head, then set her glass onto her desk pad and slumped forward on her crossed arms. "I'm worried," she said. "I haven't been this worried in a very long time."

Max refused to be infected by her moroseness. "Rosemary, we've had the account for over ten years. Doesn't that count for anything?"

"Not in this business."

"What about the job we've done for them?"

"All a client wants to know is, what did you do for me this morning?"

"We're still dealing with human beings, aren't we? There's got to be such a thing as loyalty."

His drink was still standing on her desk. Rosemary pushed it closer to him. "Have some whiskey," she said.

Max took it and tasted it. "So you think we might lose the account?"

"Fifty-fifty."

"But you don't even know who this marketing director might be."

"That's why I'm being optimistic and calling it fifty-fifty."

"What if he turns out to be a reasonable human being with a reasonable-sized ego?"

"Then I'll dedicate the rest of my life to the service of

the Holy Mother and make a pilgrimage to Lourdes."
Rosemary laughed. "People with reasonable-sized egos
don't become MBAs, Max. They sell beer at the ball-
park—or something."

Max shivered. So his sudden rise at Spindler—through
no fault of his own—was now in danger of taking just as
steep a dive. He took another swallow of his whiskey and
asked the question he was afraid of having answered.
"What happens if we lose Fidelity Federal?"

"We lose one-third of our billing."

"And then?"

"We lose one-third of our people."

"Me?"

"Probably. You are the new kid on the block, you
know."

"You?"

"It's possible."

"Well, what can we do?"

"Nothing, except to wait and see." She summoned
up another smile for him and poured more whiskey into
their glasses. "We can also stop scaring ourselves silly,"
she said, "and have another drink."

He did not leave Rosemary's office until after seven,
and was drunk when he came through Nora's door. She
was sitting on the sofa in her frayed scarlet bathrobe,
vodka tonic in hand, the television not three feet away
from her. The show was *Hee Haw*, and when she laughed—
never mind that Max didn't catch the joke (Buck Owens
cracked it)—it was at something he was certain he would
not have found funny. He kissed her, his Daisy Mae, his
Minnie Pearl, and judging by the slackness of her jaws
and the wild animation of her tongue, she was just as
bombed as he was. This wasn't unusual, for the two of
them to be drunk so early in the evening. They had
entered into what Max would later cordon off in his
memory as their alcoholic phase—or more rightly, *his*

alcoholic phase; you could hardly call Nora's hard drinking a phase. He had not been anywhere near this dissipated since his debauched sophomore year at Tulane, when his long separation from Janey had torn him loose from his moorings. Now it was another woman who had set him adrift on a sea of booze. From that first night at Cousin Hugo's, liquor had figured heavily into their relationship, but only now was Max starting to match Nora almost drink for drink. And Nora, perhaps encouraged by this new recklessness on his part, had upped the ante, and was drinking all the harder. On a typical evening (Max clocked this period by the length of the Horowitzes' honeymoon to Mexico, with which it coincided almost perfectly) Nora would hand him his scotch and water—he now kept his own bottle of J&B in her kitchen cabinet, nestled in among the Ding Dongs and Froot Loops—and they would go on drinking, sometimes with a break for dinner, sometimes with an excursion to one of the neighborhood Dogtown bars, until the two of them fell heavily into her water bed, where, as often as not, they would forgo lovemaking until the morning, leaving their lust to simmer all night, and awaken and fuck with the blunt impatience of animals. Much of it, Max had to admit, had been fun—the kind of impulsive, dangerous fun which his life until now had been plentifully lacking. He was suddenly more of a teenager than he had ever allowed himself to be in his teens. One warm October night they had taken Nora's battered Impala, with the hole in the floorboard and the defective muffler, and ridden it out to the Holiday Drive-In, where they intermittently drank vodka from the bottle, ate corn dogs, caught snatches of something called *Truck Stop Call Girls,* and made awkward, squealing love in the filthy backseat—the first time Max had ever completed the act in a car. On another night they took go-cups from the McCausland Tap, along with a sleeping bag, to the serene, unpatrolled grounds of Concordia Seminary and screwed behind the towering back of a statue of Martin Luther; they went out to the great wrought iron egg-shaped birdcage on the outskirts of the zoo, a relic of the 1904 World's Fair, and toasted the posturing flamingos by the light of a fat yellow moon; they had pork brains and scrambled eggs early one morning at Irv's Good Food, and watched the walls of the diner turn roseate as the dawn reared up behind them; more than once, drunkenly and perhaps foolishly, they had declared their love for each other.

On a Friday night midway through their marathon bacchanal, Nora announced that she wanted to go dancing. She made Max wait in the living room as she changed, and emerged, strutting and laughing, in jeans, an embroidered western shirt, a yellow scarf tied at the neck, and a pair of high-heeled pointy-toed cowgirl boots, and then took Max down to the South Fork Saloon on Grand Avenue, just a few blocks away from the White Palace where she worked. The place was barnlike, dark, and dirty, and after a few minutes of taking it in through his tolerant, inebriated senses, Max decided that it was the genuine article. Nobody here was pretending to be a redneck; he was the tourist from another culture in his Brooks Brothers woolen jacket, his tie folded up in his pocket, surrounded by real McCoys. The band, notwithstanding the tripe they were playing, was surprisingly good; the licks were clean, the voices bracingly masculine, the harmonies sweet. There were as many old people as young people on the dance floor, and the Texas two-step that prevailed allowed for a kind of democracy that didn't exist in discos or ballrooms. Here, for once, the beautiful did not attend strictly to the beautiful, the ugly were not stuck with the ugly; old leering men with their shirts coming out of their pants danced with lithe young butt-twitching girls; fat middle-aged women in ten-gallon hats clasped the narrow waists of high-stepping cowboys; twosomes became threesomes, threesomes became foursomes, and rows of dancers with their arms at one another's shoulders hopped and kicked as they turned like slow-swinging gates. Here, Max thought, as he sipped his Chivas Regal, was the egalitarian frontier vision of America in living action—never mind that there wasn't a single black face in the crowd. Even Utopia had its limits. Nora was in her element. Her eyes glittered, her lips, wet with vodka tonic, mouthed the lyrics to the songs, and her left hand, in none-too-discreet a way, massaged his crotch beneath their rickety wooden square of a table. She leaned into his ear and shouted, "Let's dance." "I can't dance like that," he shouted back. "I'll teach you." "Next song." "Why?" "Because of this," he yelled, and pressed her hand against the stiff curve of his hard-on.

Nora laughed and dragged him by the wrist onto the densely populated dance floor. Max wasn't any kind of dancer, but Nora's firm guidance, and his own loose booziness, allowed him to manage a certain hopping, scuffling motion which he didn't think was too far off the mark. Nora kept throwing her head back with laughter—whether in ridicule or appreciation of his clumsy attempts to follow her movements, he didn't care. She was display-ing a grace and a skill that he didn't possess, and the sight of it warmed him. His aging cowgirl, his hoosier queen. The yellow kerchief at her throat was particularly lovely, a fragile, momentary banner of brightness around that vul-nerable neck, and he watched her with an aching wonder that he could interpret only as love.

A fat bald man with a belly like a twenty-gallon drum cut in on him, and Max happily stepped back to watch the two of them dance until he realized that his hard-on had failed to subside. He went back to their table and lost sight of Nora in the crowd.

When the music stopped, Nora plopped herself down beside him and loosened the scarf at her neck. "Why didn't you save me from that creep?"

"Which creep?"

"The fat one. You know what that son of a bitch did? He started playing grab-ass with me out there. I tried to knee him in the balls, but his goddamned belly got in the way." Nora picked up her drink and glanced over her shoulder. "Lord, I can't stand it when some pig starts to paw me like that."

"I think you can take care of yourself," Max said.

Nora shrugged and downed her drink.

The fat man, tolling heavily from side to side like a bloated bell, approached their table. He wore a red-checked shirt on the verge of bursting its buttons, and his face was like a Tartar's: slit eyes, bulbous cheeks. He nodded meaningfully at Nora, then bent down, placing the flats of his palms on the table, and looked at Max.

"I wanna talk to your girlfriend," he said.

"I got nothing to say to you," Nora told him.

The man went on peering at Max. His face was no longer human. It was as broad, blank, stupid, and implacable as a concrete embankment. "Go get me a beer," he said.

Max's heart was hurling itself against his rib cage. "I'm sorry?"

"You're sorry? What the *hell* are you sorry about?"

Nora put her hand on the back of Max's neck.

"I didn't—I'm not sure I understood what you said."

"I *said,* go get me a beer."

Max dislocated from himself. He seemed to be hovering a foot or so away behind his own shoulder. "Why don't you go get it yourself?" he heard himself say.

"Because I asked you to get it."

"I'm not a waiter. You see that woman over there in the cowboy hat? With the tray? She's a waitress. Why don't you ask *her* to get you a beer if you're too fucking lazy to get it yourself?"

He expected the blow, for some reason, to land on one of his eyes. He willed himself not to blink.

The man lifted his palms from the table and frowned at him. Then he gave a heavy roll to his shoulders and extended his hand. "Name's Clark," he said.

Max shook. The fingers were as fat as a baby's. "Max," he said.

"I'm drunk."

"I can see that, Clark."

He shifted his weight to another foot. "Buy you a beer?"

"No thanks."

"Why don't you just go off someplace and fuck yourself?" Nora said.

The man actually looked wounded. "I didn't mean no harm," he said. And then he lumbered, heavily rocking from hip to hip, back into the crowd.

"Let's get out of here," Nora said.

It didn't hit Max until they were out on the street, and

it manifested in a strange sort of giddiness. Along Grand Avenue the streetlights drooped like low-hanging moons; Max's head was in the stratosphere. "Hooo-weee!" he said as they moved down the sidewalk, Nora gripping his elbow, the heels of her boots rat-tatting on the pavement. "Hot damn!" he said. "I do declare!"

"I thought for sure that son of a bitch was just going to tear your head right off," Nora said. "Don't you realize how big you are?"

"Honeylamb," Max said. "I'm just as big as all Texas!"

Nora laughed. "I swear to God, you're crazy."

"Yes, ma'am, but I shore don't mean no harm. What I am is an ignorant unwashed hoosier from South St. Louis way, and I'm mighty awful proud to make your acquaintance. Name's Clark—yessiree bob, goddamn and you bet!"

Nora tugged on his elbow. "Come on," she said. "Stop it now."

But Max couldn't stop. "Now, lookee here: I cain't help it if I'm an australopithecene evolutionary throwback with a brain the size of a pea. The good Lord in his wisdom just made me that way. My mammy and pappy were brother and sister, and we all growed up on a diet of cornbread and dirt—"

"Stop it," Nora said. "I mean it."

"—and I spent my whole childhood shucking groats and wishing I could shimmy like my sister, Kate—who I'm going to marry one of these fine days if she'll have me— and setting cats afire with gasoline. I didn't get me no education because I was too busy humping old Bessie the cow, who's the best goddamned woman this side of the Mississippi and a damned sight smarter than the rest of the clan—"

Nora stopped walking. "Shut up," she said.

"Hell, back where I come from we used books for toilet paper and we'd lynch anybody who had a vocabulary of more than—"

Nora slapped him. It was hard and stinging and caught a piece of his nose. The streetlights exploded into supernovas; he nearly lost his legs. Then Nora's arms were around him. "Just shut up," she said.

"Nora—"
"Just shut up."

———————————

They went on drinking. By the middle of the second week of this routine, Max was in a state of constant mottled fatigue and his kidneys felt like they were bruised. Yet his work at Spindler continued, diabolically, to shine, and this egged him on. It was clear in certain ways why they were soaking their love affair in liquor. It eased the spots where their personalities scraped and softened their visions of each other, blurring their fundamental incompatability. It added a new conspiratorial dimension to their relationship; they were now drinking buddies as well as lovers, collaborators in dissipation, the strangely matched pair getting sloppy in the back booth at the McCausland Tap, or simply two sick bodies coming to consciousness in the stale arena of her water bed, their heads clanging in sympathetic unison.

But Max had another reason for keeping this bender on a roll. Booze made Nora talk. She had let go in the first week with certain dribs and drabbles; by the second week she was confiding in him. He found out, for starters, that her ancestry was pure Irish, aside from one great-grandfather who had married a full-blooded Osage Indian.

"It's one hell of a combination, let me tell you, Irish and Indian, especially for a family that liked to drink like mine did. One part can't stop drinking, and the other part can't handle the liquor." They were at their favorite booth at the McCausland Tap, with their empty glasses lined up in front of them like a dazed regiment of soldiers awaiting orders. Nora's almond eyes were shining. "Lord, you never saw such a pack of drunks. My daddy drank, all right, but my mother had him topped by a long shot. She was a lush from the word go. But hell—look at me, talking about drinking. But I'm not a drunk, you know."

"You're doing a pretty good imitation," he said.

"Look who's talking. Anyway, you should have seen me when I was a little girl. All the Indian blood in the family just went straight to me. I had this perfectly straight black hair that my mother used to put up in two braids— that is, when she was sober enough to give a shit how I looked—and it used to just drive my daddy straight up a wall. He hated the fact that we had nigger blood in our family. He figured anyone who wasn't white was a nigger— that's how dirt-ignorant he was. He used to call me Pocahontas when he got drunk, and take it out on me with this special kind of meanness. He used to thrash my brothers and my one sister, but when it came to me, it was like he sat up all night thinking of inventive things to do."

"Like what?"

"Like this," Nora said, and took both of Max's hands and pressed them around his glass. "He'd make me hold my hands like this, and then he'd fill up the glass with boiling water and make me hold it till the tears were popping out of my eyes."

"For what?"

She shrugged and picked up her drink. "Who the hell remembers?" she said. "Oh, I was a wildcat, don't let me tell you any different. I probably deserved half the things that bastard did to me."

"Is he still alive?"

"He died when I was eleven."

She told him how he had cut his hand on a piece of machinery at Scullin Steel, and refused medical attention for so long that by the time he got to the hospital, the blood poisoning killed him. "So if you're ever wondering where I get my stubbornness from, it's my daddy. I'm just as headstrong as that son of a bitch ever was."

Her mother, he found out on another night, died of cirrhosis of the liver a few years later, and Nora spent her adolescence bouncing from one foster home to another until she met and married Jack Cromwell at the age of seventeen.

"What about Jack Cromwell?" he asked.

"What about him?"

"What kind of guy was he?"

She snorted. "Do you really want to hear about all this?"

The man she described could hardly have been more villainous: drunk, violent, ignorant, and surly. He worked at the brewery, lived at the bars, and only came home, it seemed, to use her as a punching bag. "And what a lover he was," Nora said, laying back on her water bed against a hill of pillows, a fresh vodka tonic on her chest. "He had the knack of making you feel like a fence post with a knothole in it. And the son of a bitch was so potent that I seemed to get pregnant every time we screwed. That's how we ended up getting married, in fact. The first time we did it was in the back of his car in the back of the VFW Hall in Maplewood, and bingo, I was knocked up."

"So you were never happy with him?"

"Hell, no."

"Not even in the first few months?"

"I think it all turned to shit the day we got married. For one thing, I lost the baby. I think that's when he first started getting really violent with me—like he waited until I was in good enough shape to give him a decent fight. And then in no time flat I was pregnant again, and for a while there he kept his hands off me. But it was always like that. He'd lay into me when I wasn't pregnant, get me pregnant again, and lay off for a few months. It got so I went to bed with him again only so I could get myself pregnant and have me some peace." Nora took a swallow of her drink and looked at Max. "It turned out I had a weak uterus," she said. "But of course that was too damned technical for Jack to understand. All he knew was, he wanted a son, and I wasn't giving him one. When he got oiled up real good he'd accuse me of losing the babies just to spite him, and I'll be damned if I *wouldn't* have, if I could've arranged it. That's how much I hated him by then. I even gave him to understand that there was something sickly about his own manhood that was causing me to keep miscarrying. And the son of a bitch was so dumb, I think he believed me."

"When did you finally have Charley?"

"I got to tell you about this one thing he did first."

"All right."

She took a long contemplative swallow of her drink and worked her shoulders around against her pillows.

"What he used to do was, he'd go off on these long benders with some of his horseshit buddies from the brewery, and sometimes he'd be gone for days. No phone calls, no nothing. The first few times it happened, I was scared out of my wits, let me tell you. I mean, there I was—maybe seventeen or eighteen, and most likely pregnant, with no family and no real friends to call, just wandering around the house and picturing my husband lying dead in a ditch somewhere. But it went on like that for years, and finally I got to the point where I was hoping he *was* lying dead someplace. And then one time when he was off galavanting around, I had another miscarriage. This time I was almost six months along and my body was just a wreck, and I started hemorrhaging like a regular son of a bitch. I was all alone with no money for cab fare and nobody to call—and for some reason it never occurred to me to call an ambulance. So what I did was, I prepared myself to die. I remember getting into the bathtub because I didn't want to ruin the bed—can you imagine? And I must have passed out, because when I opened my eyes, there was Jack, drunk as a lord and blubbering like a baby, and by the time he got me to the hospital I'd lost so much blood that it was nip and tuck there for a while. The doctor said if he'd gotten to me an hour later, I would've been dead. Well, after that I decided it was Jack who was dead. Nothing he could do could ever hurt me again, because he didn't exist, you see. He was just a dead man I happened to be living with. And then Charley was born."

And here was where Max finally ran aground against her silence. No matter how much vodka he plied her with, he could not get Nora to talk about her son in any but the most vague and idealized terms. He had been as good and sweet and loving as Little Eva in *Uncle Tom's Cabin,* and like Little Eva, had died a saintly and uncomplaining death, and had ascended, Max supposed, directly to heaven, escorted by a throng of jubilant angels. He began to entertain doubts that Charley had ever existed at all. Where, in fact, was the concrete evidence? There were no pictures of him anywhere in the house, no schoolboy mementos on the walls, no yellowing comic

books stuck between her stacked *Cosmopolitan*s, no baseball gloves collecting dust in the closet. It made no sense,
unless Nora was hiding something, and whatever she was
hiding—having already delivered up to him so many sordid secrets—it probably surpassed all the rest in ugliness.

So after all these carefully orchestrated, booze-sodden
hours of gentle interrogation, he had yet to crack the
internal code of this woman with whom (he no longer
bothered trying to talk himself out of it) he was falling ever
more helplessly in love.

CHAPTER TEN

"So," Sara Roth said, fishing the cherry from her manhattan, "tell me all about her."

Max had intended to do just that. For the past two weeks (Sara had canceled their meeting last Saturday on the grounds that she was feeling "too morbid" to face anyone), Max had been mentally rehearsing this interview. But now, sitting here in this hushed, creamily lit restaurant, he realized that he had miscalculated, either in the timing of his confession or his choice of a confessor. Nora did not want to be dragged into the light. And Sara, moreover, did not look ready to receive any jarring news. Almost as soon as she joined him at the table, she told him that she hadn't been able to get any real sleep all week, and apologized ahead of time for anything "unhinged" that she might say. She wore a simple lemon-colored blouse, no jewelry outside of her wedding ring, and very little makeup, as if she'd made the decision to present to him unadorned the evidence of her losing fight for sleep. Her eyes were puffed, her mouth drawn. Max took a sip of his vodka and grapefruit. He was still feeling rocky from last night's saturnalia with Nora, and the small infusion of alcohol failed to steady him.

"Am I going to have to pull teeth?" Sara was smiling at him now. She had read into his reluctance to talk something cute: the tongue-tied young man in love.

"It's not going to be easy to talk about her."

"Is that because I'm your former mother-in-law?"

"It's because I'm a coward," Max said.

Sara raised her eyebrows. The waiter appeared soundlessly at their table—a tall, straight-backed young man whose lank blond hair, Max noticed, needed trimming at

141

the back. "We're not ready to order yet, Julian," Sara told him. "But you can bring another round in a few minutes." The waiter slipped away. Sara returned her attention to Max. "Come on," she said. "Just start talking. What's she like?"

Max made a careful steeple of his hands. "Well," he said, "she's different."

"Different than what?"

"Than Janey, for instance."

"Did you think that I expected you to find another Janey?"

"There are no other Janeys."

"Oh, don't be so pious. There are scads of other Janeys."

"What the hell is that supposed to mean?"

Sara shrugged. "I've just grown awfully sick and tired of hearing her eulogized, idealized all the time. She wasn't what you could honestly call an exceptional young woman. She was a fairly conventional Jewish American Princess who was in love with horses and tennis and her own reflection in the mirror and everything money could buy. I loved her, of course. But I refuse to make her over into something that she wasn't. And it's been very hard to hold the line against that type of delusion these past two years, Max. It's very hard to keep your memory in place when everyone around you is constantly rewriting history. My God, you should hear poor Bill talk about her; you'd think she'd been a combination of Mother Teresa and Albert Einstein."

"That's funny," Max said.

"What?"

"Janey told me once that she'd have to win the Nobel Prize in order to get your approval."

"She wasn't in much danger of winning that."

"Your approval or the Nobel Prize?"

Sara blinked slowly at him with her blue, fatigued eyes, then took a sip of her manhattan. "I'm sorry," she said. "I didn't mean to get us talking about this. I warned you I might fly off the handle, didn't I? We weren't talking about Janey. We were talking about this new friend of yours."

"I'm sorry I'm so edgy today," Max said.

"You're no edgier than I am. Come on. Tell me about her. Is she Jewish?"

Max smiled. "No," he said.

"She's pretty, of course?"

"Not really—actually, I don't know. That's something I can't seem to make up my mind about."

"That's more than a little bit interesting. How intelligent is she?"

"I can't seem to make up my mind about that, either."

Max, aware that Sara was watching him, obsessively knotted and unknotted his limp plastic swizzle stick. He had opened the door on Nora a crack, and he knew that if he didn't completely clam up right now, he wouldn't be able to get it shut again; one more admission and everything would come tumbling out, slapstick-style, like the contents of an overstuffed closet.

"How old is she?" Sara asked him.

Max tossed his swizzle stick onto the immaculate beige tablecloth. "She's forty-one," he said.

"What?"

"You're not supposed to betray your shock."

"Well, I'm sorry—but my God, Max, that's practically my generation. Where on earth did you find her?"

"I was trolling for a date at the old folks home."

"All right. I suppose I should be cooler about this. But Max, with all the fresh young things around, what would you want with an old broad like that? I'm sorry. I really am putting my foot in my mouth, aren't I?"

"No," Max said. "It's a perfectly legitimate question. What do I want with an old broad like that?"

A busboy came by and picked up his swizzle stick.

"Maybe it makes a certain kind of sense," Sara said, "your taking up with an older woman right now."

"Does it?" This was just the sort of feedback Max had been hoping for. "How does it make sense?"

"Don't jump down my throat when I tell you this."

"All right."

"After all you've been through, you just might be in the market for a mother." Sara waited. "What do you think about that?"

"I already have a mother."

"No you don't, honey. And you never did."

Max finished off his vodka and grapefruit. It was true that he'd had a lifelong habit of attaching himself to older women. There was hardly a female grade school or high school English teacher who hadn't adopted him as her pet. And here he sat with his ex–mother-in-law. Even when Janey had been alive, his closeness to Sara had been odd, singular. Then, of course, there was Rosemary Powers to think about; once again he'd been made a protégé of a teacher/mother/protector figure. So far, so pat. But what about Nora? Max abruptly laughed.

"Sara, you couldn't be more wrong. If anybody's the mother in this relationship, it's me. I can't imagine her nurturing anybody."

"That's an odd thing to say."

It was indeed, Max thought.

"Let me try this on you," Sara said. "Young women can be a hell of a lot of trouble. But an older woman who's been around the block a few times—well, maybe she can make things very cozy for you. Is that it, Max? Is it comfortable?"

"It's about as comfortable as a roller-coaster."

"Oh? Do you fight?"

"We fight, all right."

"Who usually starts it?"

"Me."

"You? I find that hard to believe. What do you fight about?"

Max sighed. "I can't seem to accept her for what she is."

"And what is she?"

Had he stopped to consider Sara's likely reactions—amazement, horror, disgust—he might well have dried up. Instead, he flattened her into a distant, unknown listener, a pair of exhausted blue eyes across a table in a restaurant with no more power to judge him than a painting—and simply opened his mouth and started talking. The more he disclosed, the more daring he became with his disclosures, and he left out nothing, as far as he could tell, of importance; he told Sara about everything

from their first meeting at Cousin Hugo's to their recent
drinking spree, from Nora's worship of Marilyn Monroe
to the rapturous babbling of her sexual transports. He
ate his food—a square of fish pâté followed by as-
paragus—without tasting it, and drank his vodka and
grapefruit without restraint. Sara listened wordlessly to
his fevered monologue until the busboy had cleared away
the dishes and Max was winding down his story, then
reached across the table and squeezed his hand.

"We need some fresh air," she said. "What do you
say we go for a walk?"

Drunk once again, drained, strangely exhilarated, Max
allowed Sara to lead him by the arm out of Chez Louis
into the dazzling sunlight. It was a Saturday, and the
streets of the Clayton business district were largely deserted. In the precise silvery light of the high November
sun, the office buildings glittered like sugar cubes. Sara
led him across Forsythe Boulevard and over to a bench in
a shaded parklike area down from the library. They sat
there for a spell, observing the sparse traffic through a
frame of rattling bronze leaves, absorbed in their own
separate silences.

Finally Sara spoke. "Would you like to hear what I
think?"

The unexpected thing was, having finally purged himself of his secret, the burden, for the moment, had been
lifted, was no longer a problem, and he found that he
wasn't particularly interested in what Sara had to say. But
of course he was obligated to listen. He sat up straighter
against the cool back of the bench, worked his fists around
in his jacket pockets, and tried to corral his attention.

"I'm going to be harsh," Sara said.

"All right."

"I'm also a little bit tight right now."

"No apologies."

"All right, no apologies." She took in a breath. "Get
out of it," she said. "Get out of it today if you can. For
godsakes, Max—the last thing you need is another catas-
trophe in your life. And from the sound of everything
you've told me, you're just begging for it."

Already he was hardening himself against her.

"You make it sound like I'm doing this on purpose."

"You are. Unconsciously, you are."

"How is it that you've got a handle on my unconscious mind?"

"Please, Max. You told me about this woman because you wanted my opinion. Please don't block me out before you've even given me a hearing."

"I'm sorry," he said. "I'm just—a little frightened."

"You should be."

The wind was picking apart the frame of dead bronze leaves even as he stared through it; the ceaseless dry rattle was like the sound of distant applause.

"What kind of woman is this, Max? From everything you've told me she's nothing but poor white trash. I'm sorry—I told you I was going to be harsh."

"Go on."

"You can't be friends with her. You don't even seem to *like* her. You come from two entirely incompatible backgrounds and live two entirely incompatible lives. The relationship's got absolutely nowhere to go but downhill. And I'm not telling you anything new. You *know* all this, Max. So why do you persist in keeping it going?"

"Tell me."

"You're scared to death and you're trying to protect yourself."

He laughed. "This is one hell of a way to protect myself."

"It *is* one hell of a way to protect yourself, Max. Just listen to me. There must be thousands of suitable young women in this city just dying for the chance to go out with a young man as attractive and intelligent and *decent* as you. So why aren't you dating any of them? I think it's because you're frightened. I think you're terrified of getting close to any woman who might be right for you, with whom you might have the chance for a real future—and then have that woman turn around and abandon you just like Janey did. Your system couldn't take another loss like that, or doesn't think it can. So what do you do? You latch onto a woman who's impossibly wrong for you—a woman you can't help but secretly despise. You commit yourself to a relationship that's doomed to fail from the moment it starts, and so you really haven't committed yourself to anything at all. What do you lose if you lose this Nora? Nothing but a bad problem, a mistake. You actually come out ahead—or at least, that's the neurotic logic of it. But the reality is very different. The reality is purely destructive. You're playing with this poor woman's feelings, Max, and you're playing very, very dangerously with your own. It's all a terrible, contorted, dishonest way of pretending to be in love when it's really love that you're afraid of—and I say get out of it just as quickly as you can, cut your losses, and find yourself a healthy relationship with a woman who can really *nourish* you. Just how much punishment do you think you're built to take?"

"I guess I'm going to find out," he said.

Sara touched his arm. "Please don't shut me out, Max. I'm not saying this to hurt you." She turned to better face him on the bench, looking stricken and a little fearful. "Was I too harsh?"

"No. In fact, everything you said made perfect sense."

"Did it?"

"It made perfect sense. The only problem with it is, it's all shit." Max stood and faced Sara, charged with a wild, pulsing certainty. "It's all Psychology 101, Sara— nothing but a lot of fine-sounding psychoanalytical bullshit. Do you think if you were anywhere close to the truth you'd be coming up with such elegant, airtight arguments? We're all messes inside. There aren't any straight lines. You can't read a human personality like it's a fucking blueprint."

"Please don't rave," Sara said.

"I'm not raving. And so what if I *am* raving? It's about time I raved a little." He was pacing in front of the bench with his fists jammed into his pockets; Sara looked frail and doll-like bundled up in her fur-lined jacket. He wanted to pick her up and fling her into the center of what he knew to be true. "Let me tell you what Nora isn't," he said. "She's not my mother, she's not Janey turned inside out, and she's not some kind of receptacle for my neurosis. You make it sound like she's some kind of *category* of woman, something entirely interchangeable. I can go down to any sleazy bar in South St. Louis and pick myself up another low-class middle-aged woman, and it wouldn't make any kind of difference just so long as she satisfied this sicko need inside of me to be with a woman I fundamentally despise—isn't that what you're really saying, Sara?"

Sara only stared at him.

"Well, it's Nora who I want. I want that particular woman who works at that particular White Palace at Grand and Gravois and lives in that particular filthy little house in Dogtown. That's who I want. Don't give me any reasons for it. Why does there have to be a reason? Janey died. I fell in love with Nora. There are your two events. All right? There are your two events. Now you give me a good, elegant, airtight argument as to why they happened!"

"Max—"

"Tell me why they happened."

"They're not related."

"Oh, yes they are."

"How?"

"They both happened without any reason for happening and I can't do a goddamned thing about either one of them and both of them are fucking up my life—"

Max meant to go on, but he was suddenly crying. There had been no transition. One moment he had been strutting and bellowing at Sara, and the next moment he was on his knees with his face pressed to the cool, rough, perfumed material of her skirt, trying to find his breath between his sobs.

Sara neither touched him, nor spoke to him, nor pushed him away, nor drew him any closer. She simply sat there, and the strongest sense he received from her was that of a detached and pointed curiosity.

Max did what he could to regroup and regain some sense of control. For the first time in weeks he thoroughly dusted and straightened his neglected apartment; he had his Oriental carpet cleaned; he finally took his Volvo into the shop to have the headlight replaced and the front fender repaired; he reestablished contact with the Horowitzes, and made a date for later that week to see the slides of their honeymoon in Mexico; he stopped drinking altogether, and replaced the J&B in Nora's kitchen with two six-packs of A&W root beer. The first night he declined to drink along with her, she accepted without a quarrel his explanation that his liver and kidneys were overdue for a rest. But on the second evening of his abstinence, as she sat with her drink watching *Dallas*, and Max sat beside her, leafing through one of her women's magazines, she abruptly shot a fierce sigh through her nostrils, flopped her weight against the back of the sofa, and said, "I'm bored."

"Why don't you turn the channel?" Max said. "Or better yet, why don't you just turn it off for once?"

"And then what?"

"I'll read to you." Max leaned over, switched off the TV, and opened the magazine to the first article he found. "Ah," he said. "Here's the article we've been waiting for. 'The First Time He Comes Over—What To Do with Your Place to Win a Place in His Heart.' I hope you're paying strict attention, Nora."

She grunted and took a swallow of her vodka tonic.

" 'Make sure your house or apartment is absolutely immaculate. And that means everything—no cheating! —floors, walls, windows, and even the top of that refrigerator that you haven't dusted since Carter was president.' This is good advice, Nora. I think there's real wisdom here. 'Don't don't don't leave any of your personal items where he can see them! Put away the Tampax you left on top of the toilet and the spermicidal jelly laying out on your nighttable. And for goodness' sakes, get those depilatories out of sight! This is a night for romance, illusion, fantasy. The pedestrian reality—if all goes well this evening—will set in soon enough. Arrange fresh flowers—' "

Nora stood up. "Why don't you put down that goddamned magazine, get rid of that goddamned root beer, and have a real drink with me?"

"I don't want a real drink," he told her.

"Well, it's no fun drinking alone like this."

"Then why don't you have a root beer with me?"

She touched her earring. "You think I'm an alcoholic, don't you?"

Max set the magazine aside. "I think you drink too much."

"Lord, look at the pot call the kettle black! Just who *was* that getting smashed with me every night for the past two weeks if it wasn't you?"

"I'm stopping," Max said.

"I'm not a drunk. Nobody knows better than me what a drunk is. I just happen to like it. I have myself a drink and I feel better—what's wrong with that?"

"I didn't say there was anything wrong with that," Max said carefully.

"You don't have to say it. All you have to do is sit there with that goddamned root beer looking all holier-than-thou."

"Nora, you're being irrational."

"And you're being a regular tight-ass."

"Look, I don't want to argue about this. Just leave me to my root beers and I'll leave you to your vodka tonics. How's that?"

"Fine with me."

"Good."

"Just don't go trying to tell me what to do."

Max sighed, and it was just the sort of defeated sigh that he gave out when he was arguing with his mother. "I'd have to be more of an idiot than I already am to try to tell you what to do," he said.

She crossed her arms. "What does that mean? Does that mean you think you're an idiot for seeing me?"

"Come on, Nora. Don't do this."

"Because if that's what you think, we can just break this thing off right here and now. I got me enough problems in my life without having to put up with a man who thinks he's too good for me."

"What am I doing here on your couch if I think I'm too good for you?"

"That's a good question, isn't it?"

What Max said next he must have said under his

breath, for Nora's expression softened, and her hand went to her earring, and she said, "I don't think I heard you right."

"I said I'm the one who's not good enough for you."

"You'd better go easier on those root beers," Nora told him. "I think you're getting carbonation on the brain."

But Max knew that what he'd said was true. If he were really good enough for her, he would not be ashamed of her; he would have invited her, for instance, to the slide presentation at the Horowitzes' tomorrow evening; he would not have been carefully, secretly, avoiding any spot during their two weeks of drunken meandering where they might have been seen by someone he knew; he would have been strong enough to admit freely to his love, and to admit Nora—whatever the cost to his reputation, that prissy monster—into his world. Moved by a surge of desire and remorse, Max left the couch and took her into his arms. He almost wished she would have fought him off, for the sake of her own dignity. But she relented.

They were looking at the tenth or eleventh slide of the ruins at Chichén Itzá. Bright-eyed, bubble-cheeked Rachel Horowitz, wearing a sombrero and a loose dress splashed with tropical flowers, stood in the foreground, as she had stood in the foreground of more than half the slides so far. Her placement at center stage, eclipsing these melancholy ruins rising behind her, carried the suggestion—as such *tourista* slides, Max supposed, always carried—of gentle imperialism, implied ownership. Look what we discovered! She was the contemporary Jewish-American version of the conquistador, and the booty that traveled home with her was this photographic record of her triumphant presence there. That Horowitz, a professional photographer after all, would stoop to such vulgar and self-congratulatory compositions was something that Max was pleased to see; Horowitz, evidently, had allowed his artistic integrity to be swamped by his ardor as a new husband. So Max was not the only one here who had lost track of himself in the blizzard of his passion.

"Next slide!" Klugman called out.

Over on the shadowy sofa, beneath Klugman's outstretched arm, Sherri stirred and lit a cigarette. In the momentary light Max saw that she was frowning. "I wish you'd stop that," she said in a voice that had almost no breath behind it.

"Stop what?"

"Yelling 'next slide' between every slide. It's childish and it's annoying."

"Well, shit—I'm just trying to keep Horowitz awake over there."

"I think he's awake. Are you awake, Neil?"

"Sure," Horowitz said carefully.

There was a brief silence.

The projector whirred and clacked.

Here was a shot of a window, framed by a dull white stucco wall, which looked out onto a featureless stacked arrangement of sea, horizon, sky.

"What the hell is that?" Klugman asked.

"That," Horowitz said, "is the view from our bathroom window. As you can see, our hotel was right on the beach."

Sherri pulled on her cigarette in the gloom; the swift downward arc it traced was like an orange shooting star. "I don't—why would you take a picture out of your bathroom window? I don't get it."

"And let's hope you never do," Horowitz said. "This was basically the only sight we took in during the last three days of the trip."

"You drank the water?" Max asked.

"No," Rachel said. "We were very careful about that. And I wouldn't let Neil eat at any of those filthy taco stands, either. I think we just got it from breathing the *air,* or maybe touching the *doorknobs*—I don't know. You just couldn't believe how dirty everything was down there— even in Acapulco. The whole country smelled like a backed-up sewer. Of course, I wasn't expecting it to be *clean,* but still, it was a shock to see how those people actually lived."

"I thought it was very romantic," Horowitz said.

"After all," Max added, "what's true romance without a little squalor thrown in?"

For a senseless instant he thought he had given himself away. But of course nobody here could have the slightest inkling of how that last statement resonated in his obsessive, secretive brain. He had not made any mention of Nora, or even hinted that he was involved with a woman—much less that the woman he was involved with was, in her own way, just as alien, impoverished, uncivilized, and lacking in decent hygiene as the most backwater village in Mexico. Nora was pulling a shift this evening at the White Palace, which made things neatly convenient; Max would not have to account for his whereabouts during her work hours when he saw her later on tonight, nor would he have to invent an explanation for failing to invite her to this gathering. They were all at the Klugmans' house in Olivette because Rachel—who was still in the process of furnishing and decorating the new apartment—had insisted that their place wasn't ready yet for public viewing. So in a way this party had been foisted upon Sherri, who, unlike Rachel, was not a natural hostess. All evening long the Klugmans had been bickering, and the volleys of veiled jabs that had passed across the dinner table had grown as heated as a championship tennis match. Horowitz and Rachel had been merely made uncomfortable; Max, on the other hand, had been watching the Klugmans go at it with the uneasy intensity of a man studying his own face in the mirror.

"Well, anyway," Rachel said. "Believe me—there's nothing romantic about spending your honeymoon on the toilet."

"Think of it," Klugman said to Sherri. "Someone actually had a honeymoon that was shittier than ours."

No one laughed.

The projector advanced the slide.

"Now, here's what we did to cheer ourselves up when we got back to St. Louis—after taking a day out to recuperate, that is. You might call this our second honeymoon."

The shot was of a billboard, backed by a dusky sky,

which read: CINDY'S MOTEL—WATER BEDS, MOVIES, HOT TUBS, FAMILY RATES.

"You actually went there?" Klugman asked.

Rachel giggled. "I don't know where Neil comes up with these ideas."

Horowitz advanced the projector. "Here, as you can see, were our lovely accommodations. Water bed, replete with black satin sheets, black-light posters, and an array of strategically placed mirrors. I've come to see mirrors in a whole new light. They're not just for shaving anymore."

"And you should have *seen* what they had showing on television," Rachel said. "I mean, we thought it would just be something R-rated, you know? But when I turned on the TV, I almost fell over. There it was—the whole *schmeer*."

"What did they charge you for the room?" Klugman asked.

"You saw the sign," Horowitz told him. "Family rates."

"What do you say, Sherri? It's probably cheaper than a sex therapist."

Sherri did not respond to this.

Nora, Max was thinking, would go absolutely hog-wild in a room like this—and so, for that matter, would he. Just a month ago such a notion would have been as unthinkable as a trip to Jupiter. But now he was making a mental note to bring the idea up with Nora. She could even bring along her collection of dildos, and they could make a real picnic of it. He shifted his weight in the armchair and picked up his glass of wine.

"I just—you didn't really do that, did you?" Sherri said. "I mean, on your honeymoon?"

"It was *fun*, Sherri," Rachel said. "In a nasty kind of way, it was some of the most fun we've ever had."

"It just doesn't seem right. Not on your honeymoon, anyway. It seems like you were—I don't know. Making fun of your marriage or something."

"Oh, really, Sherri. Neil and I have been going together for almost two years. It's not as if—"

"Well, maybe you all think I'm a prude, but it just seems to me that you'd want to take your honeymoon more seriously."

"Sherri's got a point," Klugman said, and took a swallow of his scotch. "Honeymoons are not a laughing matter. Ours certainly wasn't—unless you happened to be watching. And neither, for that matter, is marriage a laughing matter. Tragic, maybe, or maybe tragicomic, but certainly not—"

"Can we see the next slide?" Sherri asked.

"There you go again," Klugman told her. "Always yelling for the next slide between slides. Don't you realize how annoying that is?"

"You've had too much to drink and you're making a fool of yourself."

"*Au contraire*. Does anyone else here think I'm making a fool of myself? Let's see a show of hands."

"Please stop it."

"Stop what?"

"Talking."

"Well, I can't very well do that, can I? We're hosting a party here, and it's customary at parties for people to do a lot of talking. It's part of—"

Sherri abruptly arose from the couch; she was a tall, hollow-eyed shadow in the gloom. "I'm sorry," she said. "You'll all have to excuse me."

And then she moved soundlessly out of the room.

Rachel and Sherri were commiserating upstairs in the kitchen; Klugman, Horowitz, and Max, who had retired to the paneled den ostensibly to play a game of pool, were instead, at Klugman's rather shrill insistence, hunkered down around the glass-topped coffee table, snorting up lines of cocaine. This wasn't the first time Max had tried coke, but it was the first time he had acquiesced to doing it without a lot of prodding from those present. One act of recklessness, he supposed, primed you for another—and what was a noseful of cocaine compared with a willing noseful of Nora? Not much on the recklessness scale. During the first round of toots, Klugman had delivered a boring panegyric on the purity of the stuff in his black plastic film canister—he had scored it from one of his clients, a neurologist, who could not be bothered with anything less than a clinical quality blow. He was now laying out more lines as thick as baby worms directly onto the glass surface of the table. He handed Max the rolled-up dollar bill and said, "See you in Bolivia."

"Thanks, Klugman. I think I've had enough."

"Mr. Moderation-in-Everything, right?"

For some reason Max rose to this bait. He accepted the makeshift tube, gave a shrug, and bent down and vacuumed up two more lines.

Horowitz loudly began to pluck at his thick walrus moustache. "Klugman," he said, glancing at the door to the game room which Klugman had insisted on locking, "how can you possibly keep a thing like this a secret from Sherri? How much of this stuff do you normally do, anyway?"

"The answer to the first question," Klugman said as he took the dollar bill from Max, "is that I *don't* know that she doesn't know—let's hope to God she doesn't know. And the answer to the second question is, probably too much." He leaned down and snorted deeply.

Max was on his feet with his hands in his pockets, his backbone glowing like a neon tube. He hoisted himself onto the edge of the pool table. The gaily-colored travel posters that ringed the paneled room amounted to a visual shout. "Doesn't this seem to you awfully adolescent," Max said to Klugman. "Hiding your furtive little habits from your wife?"

"*Au contraire,*" Klugman said. This seemed to be his pet phrase for the evening. "Deceiving the marriage partner is a time-honored tradition among adults." He glanced up suddenly, blinking his red-rimmed beagle's eyes, and raised a hand for silence. "Did you hear somebody come downstairs?" he asked.

"It's the storm troopers," Horowitz said. "Anne Frank, the jig is up."

"Okay, laugh—Sherri would have my balls in a fucking jar if she knew about this."

Max swallowed an acrid residue of cocaine, taking a

close look at Klugman. He was used to thinking of Klugman as an eternal seventeen-year-old, hardly changed from the agitated wise guy he had been back in high school; but now he appeared—hunched over his precious hoard of cocaine, his colorless bald spot showing—as he was: a disappointed man approaching thirty whose emotional reserves were already dangerously depleted. Could Sherri be blamed for this? Or had Klugman done it to himself, merely utilizing Sherri as the whip for his self-flagellations? Or would he have arrived anyway at this itchy, unhappy state regardless of whom he happened to fall in love with? Max pushed a billiard ball across the table and gave Klugman another look.

"Why do you stay with her?" he asked him.

Klugman sniffed and wrinkled his nose. "Come again?"

"Why do you stay with Sherri? You two obviously don't like each other."

"Can't we find something else to talk about?" Horowitz asked.

"No, it's a good question." Klugman was nodding. "That's one hell of a good question, Max. Why do we stay together? Just what sort of witch's spell is this that keeps me so enthralled?" Klugman bent over, pressed a nostril shut, and snorted. He flopped upright against the couch beside Horowitz—who looked grouchy and restless—and raised his eyebrows. "It can't be her cooking—she doesn't cook. It can't be her sense of humor—she doesn't have one. And it can't be her beauty—let's face it, guys, my wife looks like a depressed Jewish goose. Then is it the sex?" Klugman sniffed and swallowed. "Yes—that has to be it. The sex. I must be staying with her on the off chance that one of these days she might fuck me again."

"Do you love her, Klugman?"

Klugman raked his fingers through his lank hair. "Give me a second to think about that," he said.

"Why don't we get off this subject?" Horowitz said.

"What's wrong with this subject?" Max asked him.

"Come on, Max. This is none of our goddamned business."

Horowitz, too, sat before Max in an altered light; the old angst, the old role of the fat, cerebral outcast with the self-deprecating sense of humor, which had always played such a nice, corrective counterpoint to his own role as the luckier, better-adjusted of the two, had been shuffled off like an old skin. Here was Horowitz now, unworried and unhaunted, and content to sink down into a thoughtless middle age, snugly surrounded by his possessions, his respectability, and the love of his perfectly suitable wife. Max felt a sudden, biting dislike for his friend. "What would you rather talk about, Horowitz? We've already covered your new apartment, your new furniture, your new camper-van, and your trip to Mexico—what's left along those lines? The pattern on your new china?"

Horowitz sat forward. "What the hell is wrong with you, Max?"

Max shrugged. "It's the cocaine."

"No, it's *not* the cocaine. Something's going on with you. What is it?"

He felt Horowitz's scrutiny blow through him like a cold wind. He was about to get caught. You don't hide things from someone who's known you for twenty years. Max took in a breath and decided to beat Horowitz to the draw. "I'm . . . seeing somebody," he said.

Horowitz's eyes grew round. "You mean a woman?"

The cocaine was skittering up and down his spine. "No, I mean a sailor. His name is Olaf, and he's this big, strapping Norwegian fellow—"

"Max, how long has this been going on?"

"A while."

"How long is a while?"

"I met her the night of your bachelor party."

"Where?"

"At a bar."

"What bar?"

"What does it matter, what bar?"

"Max, I can't believe this. You've been going with a woman for over a month and you haven't even mentioned her to me? Why the hell not?"

"Because," Max said, and let out a breath that seemed to have no bottom to it, "you're not going to like her."

CHAPTER ELEVEN

Max took to his work as a penitent monk takes to his cell. In the outer world, where Nora held sway, all was madness, chaos, and unshackled instinct—a regular thirteenth-century plague-ridden Europe, steeped in darkness and coming apart at the seams, where gangs of flagellants whipped themselves into pieces, rabid dogs roamed the streets in packs, heretics burned at the stake, lunatics wore the crown, and the unwashed drunken populace conducted its orgies on the palace stairs, in the public fountains, and on the altars of the great cathedrals. But here in the quiet solitude of his office, or in the hushed intensity of the recording studio, were refuge, contemplation, devotion, and sweet discipline. Beyond work his life was all genital impulsiveness, but within his work—in the invention of a headline, the consultation with the layout artist, the creation of a marketing concept, or the cutting of a radio spot to the precise length of fifty-nine and a half seconds—were the comforting anal pleasures of measure and control. Never mind that the commercials he created were for the most part insipid and insulting—the meaning was in the doing, and in the doing, momentarily at least, Max found himself again.

The period during which Fidelity Federal conducted its search for a new marketing director turned out to be, just as Rosemary had predicted, a kind of creative honeymoon. Soon to retire, Marv Keller basically released the controls to Rosemary, and for once Max was able to work with her without the niggling interference of a client. For the first time Rosemary allowed him to produce a television commercial entirely on his own. It was a premium offer for Oneida silver, involving a dinner party shot wholly in tight close-ups, and cut to thirty seconds worth of Vivaldi. Max applied himself to the project with such single-mindedness that he stayed home alone in his apartment for two nights running—standing fast against Nora's bitching—to insure that he was fresh and rested for each morning's shoot. The final product turned out to be just as slick, sparkling, and fluidly rhythmic as Max had envisioned it, and Rosemary was so pleased that she negotiated for him another two-thousand-dollar raise. Professionally, at least, he felt that he was at the top of his form and the top of his luck. But the honeymoon ended two weeks before Thanksgiving, when Rosemary appeared in his office wearing her leather jacket with the mink collar, her cheeks slapped pink by the cold, and informed him that she had just had her first meeting with the new marketing director, a woman in her middle thirties named Stephanie Deluc.

"I just wish she weren't a woman," Rosemary said.

"That sounds like a sexist remark."

Rosemary shrugged and took a seat, sinking down into her fur collar. "It's just that women who rise to positions of authority in this business so often turn out to be ballbreakers. I suppose in a male-dominated field, it's hard *not* to become a Lady Macbeth once you arrive—"

"What about Rosemary Powers?"

She smiled. "I'm probably much too full of the milk of human kindness," she said, and drew out her box of Balkan Sobranes. "Do you mind if I smoke?"

Max pushed the clean glass ashtray on his desk closer to her.

"So who is this woman?"

"She was a product manager over at Ralston Purina. I don't know if it was dog food or pig food or what she was handling—but I do know she's accustomed to dealing with D'Arcy, which, as you know, is fifty times the size of Spindler." Rosemary blew a column of smoke out of the side of her mouth. "So, right from the start she thinks she's dealing with a bunch of small-time amateurs."

"Did she indicate that?"

"No. Of course not."

"Then what makes you assume it?"

"I'd be stupid to assume anything else."

"Well, how does she strike you personally?"

"She's very brisk, very cool, very no-nonsense. She has an MBA from Tulane—"

"Tulane? That's my old alma mater."

"It is? Good. Remember to mention that. Or *I'll* mention it. Although evidently you didn't have the same professors. You should hear this woman talk, Max. She's a walking marketing textbook. Things come out of her mouth like 'interface' and 'impact' used as a verb—it's almost frightening. We're having a meeting on Monday morning, by the way, which according to her lingo isn't a meeting at all, but an 'orientational conference.' "

"Am I invited to come and interface at this orientational conference?"

"Yes. I praised you up and down, Max—so please, just sit there and look like a wunderkind and keep your mouth shut. Not that I expect you to say anything asinine. It's just that we're going to be on unknown ground, and I'd prefer it if you left the talking to Mr. Spindler and me." Rosemary ground out her cigarette and sank still lower in her chair; with her hands shoved deep into her jacket pockets, her close-cropped red hair, and her knees set apart, she looked at that moment like an overgrown, sulking tomboy. "I'm worried," she said. "I'm afraid that we already dislike each other. You should have seen us circling around each other at that meeting, Max. The two of us kept grinning like a couple of Cheshire cats. My jaws are still aching from it. And the damnedest thing—" Rosemary laughed and shook her head.

"What?"

"The woman has B.O."

Max laughed. "Come on."

"I know," Rosemary said. "I know it sounds impossible. But I walked into that meeting and here she is, surrounded by Marv Keller and Mr. O'Brien and half the board of directors, the toast of the town and the belle of the ball—she's a very attractive woman, by the way—and I'm *smelling* something. Well, I'm thinking, it's one of the men, or there's a gas leak somewhere, or God forbid it's *me*, and then Ms. Deluc comes over in her perfectly tailored skirt and jacket and takes my hand and there's no doubt about it—the woman *smells bad*. I couldn't believe it, Max. I still can't believe it. Who knows? Maybe she just slipped up this morning and forgot her deodorant, or maybe she's got some kind of glandular problem. All I know is, it struck me as awfully, awfully strange."

Max was thinking of Nora's own fierce odor. Was it possible that this Stephanie Deluc had simply come from lunch at a White Palace?

"I can hardly wait to meet her," Max said.

"You'll get your first whiff of her on Monday," Rosemary told him.

He began to buy her gifts, but Nora turned out to be a tough woman to shop for. Flowers left her curiously unmoved. He tried geraniums, then, in defiance of Janey's memory, daisies, and finally a dozen roses. She received them all with a polite reserve. He later learned that one of Jack Cromwell's favorite ploys to win back her favor after a period of treating her like dirt was to bring her flowers; the association lingered. Candy, however, was a sure-fire thing. Nora was mad about peanut brittle, white chocolate, heavenly hash, and chocolate-covered cherries most of all, and went at them not with the guilty furtiveness of a grown woman, but with the straightforward greed of a child. It seemed to both thrill and sadden her when he gave her a silky cream-colored blouse with a Halston label which he had found on sale at Saks—even marked down it had cost him sixty dollars. She complained that she didn't have anything nice enough to wear with it. "So don't wear anything at all," he told her, and they were soon making love on the littered floor of the living room, Max naked, Nora in her Halston blouse. On the day he received his raise he went to Wehmueller Jewelers and purchased a pair of tiny beehive-shaped black coral earrings, testing the grip to make sure she could twist them with no trouble during her absentminded reveries. Nora was touched. She wore them, along with her Halston blouse, out to his apartment, where he had two bottles of champagne and a pair of lobsters in a bucket waiting for them.

This was her first time out to his place. He had been forestalling the inevitable invitation on symbolic grounds; once she had taken one step into his world, there would be no more keeping her out. Now that he had revealed her existence to Horowitz—although he'd left most of the salient details to Horowitz's imagination—there was no reason not to lift the quarantine completely. The burden of concealment, and of his own guilt for concealing her, had grown too heavy; he was ready to shrug it off and let things take their course. It was Nora that he was worried about now. Once the affair was in the open, she would become an object of wonder, speculation, maybe even ridicule—surely ridicule. Nora was no fool, and even with Max at her side to deflect the stares of incredulity and the patronizing smiles, she would feel it, and he couldn't say if she were strong enough to take it in her stride. But all of that was for later. For now, driving west along Highway 40 with Nora smoking at his side, he was simply glad to have her coming to his place, curious about the effect that a novel environment would have on them, and pleased by the prospect of making love to her, for once, on sheets which he knew to be clean. He wondered, too, whether he would have much trouble getting her to try the lobster. She had a spoiled child's fear of putting anything strange into her mouth—at least when it came to food.

Nora fiddled with his radio until she found a country station, and then asked him, out of the blue, if he had ever seen a play by Arthur Miller.

Max laughed from pure surprise.

"Don't make fun of me," she said.

"I'm not—who's making fun of you? I'm just, well surprised. Why Arthur Miller all of a sudden?"

Nora shrugged and fussed with her shoulder strap; she had given up arguing with him about seat belts. "Well, he was married to Marilyn, you know. And you being a teacher and all, it's just the kind of thing you'd know about. And I'm just wondering if you've seen any of his plays."

"Well, sure."

"Are they any good?"

"One of them is great—*Death of a Salesman*. I used to teach it, in fact."

"Has that ever been on TV?"

"Plenty of times."

"Maybe I've seen it and don't even know it." She looked carefully at him. "Does it ever come around, you know, to a real theater? I've never been to a real theater before."

Max's heart seemed to pump more thickly; of course she hadn't.

"We'll keep an eye on the paper," he said, "and if there's a play in town I think you'll like, we'll go there, all right?"

"That'd be nice," Nora said, but she wasn't smiling. Something was working around inside of her. "Arthur Miller was Jewish, you know."

"So?"

"So I'm just telling you." She pulled on her cigarette and looked out her window. The sun was setting in their eyes. "Arthur Miller was very good to Marilyn, you know. He kept her going all those times she was falling apart, and if it hadn't been for him, she might have died a whole lot earlier."

"And she ended up damned near killing him."

"How do you know that?"

"I've been reading up on her lately."

"How come?"

"Because there's nothing else to read in your house when I'm sitting on the toilet but *Glamour*s and *Cosmo*s."

"Well, I'm *sorry*." She pressed her shoulder to the door.

Max drove silently and listened to Merle Haggard. She was in a touchy, odd, unpredictable mood, and evidently just about anything he said was going to be taken wrong.

"I expect you've got a whole slew of books at your place," she said.

"You could call it a slew, I suppose."

"You got any I might like?"

Max looked at her. "You mean a book?"

"What else would I mean?"

"You want to borrow a book?"

"Maybe. I mean, yes—if you got something you think I might like."

Max told himself to keep a lid on his elation; he didn't want to frighten her off. "Nora, what brought this up all of a sudden?"

"It's not all of a sudden. I've been thinking about it for a while. I'm not stupid, you know. I may be ignorant—I'm not denying that—but I'm sure as hell not stupid. Lord, you should just try and talk to some of the people I work with. Or some of the men I used to go out with. You never saw such a pack of mindless hoosiers. I feel like I'm some kind of genius when I'm around them. And they know it, too. They know I'm smarter than they are. But it's all different when I'm with you, Max. Hell, when I'm with you I feel like just as big a hoosier as the rest of them. And I can't stand that feeling, Max. So I've been thinking. I've been thinking maybe I ought to start reading some things—I mean on subjects different than just Marilyn Monroe. And so I thought I'd ask you, that's all."

He wanted to cover her face and neck with kisses; he felt grateful toward her. "Nora, this is fantastic. We'll take a look at my bookshelves just as soon as we get to my apartment—how's that?"

"Just simmer down a little," Nora said. "I don't want you turning this into something I have to feel obligated about."

"Fine," Max said. "Any way you want to do it."

"Just don't pressure me."

"I won't."

But already he was compiling a reading list for her. Salinger might be good to start with—quick and funny enough to hold her. Or maybe he ought to pander to her existing tastes and give her something more romantic: *Wuthering Heights* or *Jane Eyre* or maybe even *Gone with the Wind*—there was nothing wrong with *Gone with the Wind*. Her fascination with Marilyn Monroe might put her in the market for novels about beautiful women who come to tragic ends, *Anna Karenina* or *Madame Bovary*. There was no reason why, with a little coaching from him, she couldn't tackle Shakespeare—*Romeo and Juliet* would be the perfect introduction. Shakespeare put him in mind of Tennessee Williams and Chekhov and Shaw, and Shaw put him in mind of *Pygmalion*—and here Max drew himself sharply out of his reverie. Nora wasn't asking him to make her over into someone else; all she wanted was to borrow a few books. Was he such an effete intellectual as to think that an exposure to literature could work some kind of marvelous transformation in her? And what if it could? What if she awoke beside him one morning, having devoured *Pride and Prejudice* the night before, and was miraculously transfigured into an erudite, civilized woman? Would he still even want her at all?

They turned into the entrance of the Timberlake apartment complex and passed in the flat, waning light the tennis courts, the clubhouse, the swimming pool, and the egg-shaped duckpond dotted toward the narrow end with ducks. He parked beneath a row of town houses set high above them on a steep hill laced with railroad ties. Nora, he felt, was making an effort not to appear wide-eyed. She showed him a smirk. "Nice neighborhood," she said, and stuck her Winston into her mouth and opened the door.

A long flight of concrete stairs led up to his apartment. Max followed behind her in the smoky light of dusk, marveling anew at the broad majesty of her shuddering buttocks as they labored up the stairs. He had come, in these past weeks, to cherish her outsized ass, and to view it—even more so than the obscure musculature of her vagina—as the real embodiment of her sex; the seat, so to speak, of her womanly essence, her womanly power. He loved mounting her from behind, with a pillow under her belly, his hands clamping her flat chest and her thick nipples caught between his fingers; from that vantage point the vastness of her flesh and the endlessness of her cunt made it seem as though he were coupling with something larger, more universal than Nora herself, and yet every bit as womanly: a landscape, a continent, a planet. And when he burst inside of her he knew that his ejaculation was not just a sexual, but a racial event: he was delivering his seed into the loamy fecundity of her womb, and he sensed, as he had never sensed with Janey, the real possibility of a child. As with most of his powerful instinctual reactions to Nora, it simply made no sense; Janey, at twenty-four, had been ripe for motherhood; Nora, at forty-one, had assured him she was incapable of conceiving.

He cupped her rump as she reached the final landing. She swatted his hands away. This was unlike her; usually she enjoyed sexual horseplay. And again uncharacteristically, Nora had very little to say as he showed her around his apartment. Arms crossed, eyes narrowed, she took in his fireplace, his hardwood floors, his compact gleaming kitchen with its dishwasher, Cuisinart, and trash compactor, his balcony overlooking the duck pond, his brass bed, and his entire upstairs, which was actually an open loft enclosed by redwood rails, making a kind of courtyard of the living room below. Her face was a changing palette of emotions: admiration, envy, awe—there was even a little derision in there. She had not expected him to be so rich. This was her idea of rich. Embarrassed for her, and hoping to soften the punch of all this perceived opulence, Max pointed out how badly the place needed cleaning. Nora snorted and told him he was out of his mind. She folded her arms over the redwood rail and gazed down toward the fireplace, her rear end wagging.

"What kind of rent do you pay here, if you don't mind my asking?"

Coming from one of his peers, such a question might not have bothered Max. But he didn't want to lord it over Nora by telling her the truth. "You don't want to ask that question," he told her.

"Why not?"

"Well, because it's . . ." He couldn't come up with a better word. "It's personal."

Nora hooted and slapped the rail. "Boy, that just takes the cake," she said. "Here I've had your dick up my throat more times than I can count, but how much rent you pay for this apartment is just too goddamned *personal* to talk about. I didn't know you thought money was all that sacred."

"All right," he said, and told her how much he paid.

Her butt stopped wagging. "Is that with utilities included?"

"No."

"Well, Katy-bar-the-door." Nora turned around to look at him. "Just how much are you making at that advertising company anyway?"

"Enough so this apartment doesn't break me."

"And here you are, not even thirty. You're going to be a rich man one of these days, aren't you?"

Max shrugged.

"And you're just going to eat that up, too, being rich—won't you?"

"If it happens, why shouldn't I enjoy it?"

Nora shrugged. "Don't mind me," she said. "I'm just being a bitch. I don't even know what it's *like* to have enough money, and I guess that just gets my goat."

She was being perfectly realistic; their affair had no real future; they would never share what he owned; Max's money was Max's money. Still, he was a little bit irritated with her for being so completely resigned to the facts; maybe he was turning out to be the romantic of the pair.

"How about a drink?" he asked her.

"Are you planning on joining me?"

"Sure. It's a special occasion."

Downstairs, when he emerged from the kitchen with a drink in each hand, Nora was bent forward, her hands on her hips, reading the titles on his bookshelf.

"You really read all of these?"

"Most of them."

"Well, what-all do you recommend?"

He looked around, suggested *Madame Bovary*, *Wuthering Heights, Jane Eyre,* and gave her a brief, and he hoped, nonacademic-sounding, description of each. She remained noncommittal, however, and kept on poking. Finally she selected a tattered paperback and handed it to him.

"You think I might like this?" she asked.

It was *The Adventures of Huckleberry Finn.*

When he walked into her house the next evening, miracle of miracles, the television set was off. He assumed she was in the bathtub. He checked the bathroom; no Nora. He found her instead in her water bed, sitting up against a pile of pillows, the golden sheet drawn up around her waist, reading *Huckleberry Finn*. One hand held the book; the other twisted one of her black coral earrings. He watched her for a spell with a paternal kind of gladness, and waited for an awareness of his presence to steal over her. She went on reading.

"Hey, Nora."

She looked up. "Oh. Max. Hello." She smiled and shrugged and waved the book. "I'm reading."

"How do you like it?"

"It's good. I mean, I always thought this was a children's story. But it's not. It's *mean*, you know? I think he's got a pretty good fix on people."

Max climbed onto the rocking bed and pressed his face, through the cool sheet, into her vulva. She wriggled her thighs and scooted backward. "Don't," she said.

"Don't?"

Not once that he could remember had Nora ever rejected any of his sexual advances.

"That's right," she said. "Don't mess with me that way right now."

"How about a little expert cunnilingus?"

She laughed. "No thank you."

"Why not?"

"Because I'm not in the mood."

"Well, what are you in the mood for? Would you prefer to be spanked or something? Or we could always break out the dildos—"

"What I'm in the mood for," Nora told him, "is finding out what happens next." She set her book facedown on her belly and laughed. "Poor Max. You look just like a little whipped puppy. We can't always be having sex, can we?"

"I never thought I'd regret lending you a book."

"Why don't you go and fetch me a drink?"

"And then what?"

She shrugged. "I don't know. Why don't you find yourself something to read?"

CHAPTER TWELVE

There was a jolting triple-boom of thunder that rattled the conference room windows and flickered the lights. Max, Rosemary, Mr. Spindler, and the new marketing director for Fidelity Federal, Stephanie Deluc, all looked up from their reports at once.

"We seem to be having quite a tussle," Stephanie said, and gave out a little laugh. "Meteorologically speaking, of course."

Mr. Spindler, as bald and ordinary-looking as an egg in his rumpled blue suit, grunted and forced a smile; the meeting, which was not going well, had been dragging on for two hours, and he was becoming visibly tired. Rosemary also produced a smile, drawn low over her teeth, and lifted her Balkan Sobrane from the butt-heaped ashtray that Max kept fighting the impulse to get up and empty; both women were smoking like fiends. Rosemary had dressed for the occasion in a sexless gray suit. Stephanie, on the other hand, looked primly and sweetly feminine in an off-white frilly dress the color of the ice cream substitute sold at Dairy Queens, with a big bow at the neck and a pinched waist that accentuated the heft and swell of her estimable breasts. She might have been a beautiful woman, with her baby-doll features and flawless skin, had it not been for the froggy bulge of her eyes, which had been made too big for their sockets. And then (as faint and unmistakable from where Max sat as the sound of distant music) there was the impossibility of her odor, insinuating its way past her perfume, which was a queasy mixture of the metallic and the organic, like a soup can emptied of its chicken soup. She was otherwise so perfectly put together, so calculated, so creamy cool, that this anomalous stink was the only thing that kept Max in mind of the fact that this woman was actually human.

Stephanie lit a new cigarette and said, "Why don't we move on to the media section of your report?"

This was Mr. Spindler's area of expertise, and he took over in his growly-gravelly, easily imitated voice; nearly everyone at the office did a passable Mr. Spindler impression. At the age of sixty-eight, he was semi-retired and showed up at the office whenever he felt like it, rather like a clockmaker who dropped in on his shop only to assure himself that all the clocks he had long ago set into motion were still reliably ticking. He left the day-to-day business of running the agency to his two senior partners, Ralph Arnold and Jerry Greenblatt, as well as to Rosemary. Mr. Spindler was usually on hand, however, for presentations and meetings of special importance such as this one. Stephanie thanked him when he was through with his overview of Fidelity Federal's media-buying strategies for the past ten years, and then asked him if he thought his report was complete.

Mr. Spindler shrugged. "Well, of course it's not *complete*. To give you a complete report of every marketing decision we've made since servicing this account would probably take us into next Tuesday."

Stephanie continued to smile. She had been smiling through most of the meeting, and yet the sense Max got was that she had been sitting there for two hours with a deep scowl on her face. "What I'm wondering about specifically," she said, "is why you failed to make mention of any targeting of collegiates."

"Collegiates?" Rosemary asked.

"College students," Stephanie said, and touched the bow at her neck. "Is there some reason, John, that that particular demographic is missing from your survey? Or was it simply an oversight?"

Mr. Spindler and Rosemary exchanged a glance. "We've never targeted college students," he said, "for the simple reason that college students don't have any money."

"Well, surely they have *some*, or they wouldn't be in college, would they?"

There was silence. Max, who had been largely following Rosemary's advice until now and keeping his mouth shut, opened it. "I certainly didn't have any money in college," he said. "I was lucky to keep a hundred-dollar balance in my checking account."

"But you *had* a checking account, didn't you, Max? And if you didn't have it with Fidelity Federal, you would have had it somewhere else—am I correct?"

"Well, sure."

"So you see," Stephanie said, now addressing the whole group. "By failing to make any provision for collegiates, you've simply abandoned an entire segment of the market to the competition."

"Hell," Mr. Spindler said. "They can *have* that segment of the market. We may as well start targeting bag ladies."

Rosemary sat forward and formed a steeple of her two hands; Max recognized it as his own gesture, not hers—and it made him acutely uncomfortable for her. "I think what John is suggesting, Stephanie, is that we couldn't get a justifiable return on the expenditures it would require to reach college students." Rosemary—whether deftly or heavy-handedly, Max wasn't sure—had taken up Stephanie's turgid manner of speaking.

"I see," Stephanie said. "And upon what statistical evidence have you based this conclusion?"

"It's nothing but common sense," said Mr. Spindler.

"Well, common sense is fine, John, if you don't mind gambling away your client's money on the basis of a hunch—but there is such a thing as hard, quantifiable marketing research, isn't there?" Now she closed her report. "The fact remains that you've written off an entire demographic without having conducted the simplest investigation beforehand. So what I'd like to see by next Monday is a report from your research department—"

"We don't have a research department," Mr. Spindler said.

"Of course. I think you mentioned that to me, didn't you, Rosemary? And at the same time you assured me that your agency has all the necessary depth to handle an account of our size. Now, how do those two things jibe?"

"We've been handling the account for over ten years," Mr. Spindler said.

"What I'm paid to worry about," Stephanie told him with a glassy smile, "is the next ten years."

Rosemary assured her that she would have her report by the start of next week.

"Of course, you'll have to farm the job out to an independent firm, won't you?"

"Of course," Rosemary said.

"Well, fine. But let's understand each other. This is your project entirely. I want to see only the finished report."

Rosemary held her smile. But Max could see her gray eyes start to smolder; Stephanie had just informed them that they would have to eat the cost of this pointless project themselves.

They moved on to the presentation of the creative they had done for Fidelity Federal, and which Max had spent two furious days putting together. Stephanie leafed briskly through the portfolio of print material without a single comment. During the television presentation she was inattentive to the point of rudeness, directing her gaze to the venetian blinds, the rising twists of smoke from her cigarette, or her own polished fingernails—anywhere at all, it seemed, except at the screen where the spots were fleetingly appearing. And while the radio reel was playing—which to Max's thinking contained a wealth of clever lines, some of them his—Stephanie sat as unresponsively as an old woman who had turned off her hearing aid. When it was over, she merely remarked that she had found their work "worth thinking about," then flipped open her own spiral notebook and abruptly changed the subject. She wanted to discuss the upcoming winter promotion for Cannon blankets.

"As you know, this will be our maiden project together, and I'm every bit as eager as each of you to see that it really shines. I suggest we all take notes."

So that was that. Their creative—some of it *his* creative—had been utterly and contemptuously dismissed. It hadn't even been worth talking about. Max had been trying his damnedest for the past two hours to reserve judgment, but now, watching that Kewpie-doll mouth open and close, the birdlike prissy movements of her hands, and glaring at the big snowy bow at her throat until it began to pulsate, he realized that he was so busy loathing Stephanie Deluc that he hadn't heard a word she was saying. It took him a few moments to catch up.

She had developed, she was saying, a creative strategy of her own for the Cannon blanket premium promotion; it was a concept that conveyed both the feeling of warmth and security customers got from knowing their savings were safe at Fidelity Federal, *and* that comforting feeling of warmth and coziness that Cannon blankets were famous for. "One way to go with this," she said, "would be a theme line such as *Happiness Is a Warm Blanket—and the Warmth of Saving at Fidelity Federal*. I like the way the two ideas reinforce each other—and how we're able to sell both the product and the institution on the basis of the same perception. What do you think? Of course, I'll leave the final execution, the wording, up to you—but conceptually, it seems, well, *inevitable*, doesn't it?"

She folded her hands before her like a schoolgirl who has once again recited the correct answer, and waited for their response. She didn't seem to notice that her audience sat as stony-faced as mourners at the finish of a particularly uninspired and hackneyed eulogy. Nobody wanted to be the first to speak.

"Max? We haven't heard much from you today."

Max glanced at Rosemary, who was staring resolutely at her yellow legal pad; she wasn't going to give him any help. He shrugged. "You want my honest opinion?"

"Well, of course."

"I think it's trite."

Stephanie's smile seemed to dry on her face. "Oh? And what do you mean, exactly, by trite?"

Didn't she know the meaning of the word?

"It's the kind of thing you've heard a million times before," Max said. "I mean, it was cute when Charles Shultz came up with it twenty years ago, but—"

"But of course I'm *playing* off that old line. You see that, don't you?"

Rosemary gave him a warning glance.

"Sure," he said. "I can see that."

"And furthermore, you haven't really taken the time to give this any serious consideration, have you?"

"Well, no. You just now brought it up."

"Then I suggest you do a little more thinking about it before you prejudge." She turned to Mr. Spindler. "John? What's your reaction?"

He shrugged his wide shoulders. "I agree with young Max here. It's old hat."

"I see. Rosemary?"

Rosemary carefully stubbed out her cigarette. "I think it's an idea we can certainly work with," she said. "It's a good starting point."

Of the three representatives from Spindler, Rosemary had been the most circumspect and deferential, but this was bordering on obsequiousness. It was hard to watch Rosemary grovel like this; it looked as wrong on her as the severe gray librarian's outfit she was masquerading in this morning.

"I'm glad to see that one of you, at least, has an open mind," Stephanie said. "Of course, there's always the danger of any campaign coming out sounding 'old hat,' as you put it, John—but only if the creative execution isn't up to par. I believe the strategy I'm suggesting has all the elements of a strong marketing concept. Now it's up to you, Rosemary, and to you, Max, to generate fresh, exciting and persuasive creative treatments, and once that's accomplished, I don't think we'll need to worry about sounding trite or old hat. To put it colloquially, the ball is now in your court."

"Which is where it should be," Rosemary said. "And just let me assure you, Stephanie: you're going to be very, very happy with our creative, if not positively ecstatic."

"Good. I like that kind of attitude. But let me warn you. I'm a perfectionist from the word go. I expect nothing less than exceptional effort and exceptional results from the people who work for me. That's the standard I set for myself, and that's the standard I'll expect you to live up to for as long as this relationship lasts. And as long as we all understand that, I don't think we should have any problems in getting along.''

Having delivered this sugar-coated threat, Stephanie closed her notebook and stood—producing a small wind that wafted directly into Max's nose—and gave them all another smile. Her white teeth were as perfect as the ivory keys on a piano.

He expected Stephanie Deluc to waste no time in cracking the whip. Instead—and inexplicably, if she were really the perfectionist she claimed to be—Stephanie chose to begin her tenure at Fidelity Federal by taking off the week leading up to and including Thanksgiving, and spending it with her husband in the Bahamas. She had left behind instructions, however, that she wanted to see the completed Cannon blanket campaign on the day she returned to the office. The problem facing Max was alchemical: how to create a series of tasteful, unusual ads from the raw sludge of Stephanie's sophomoric approach. For two days he was stymied. He juggled the words *comfort, warmth, security, coziness,* until he began to forget what they meant; he picked up a trunkful of Cannon blankets from the Fidelity Federal warehouse and arranged them in a dozen ways around the floor of his office, walking around them, sitting before them, and finally covering himself with one of them and waiting, like one of the dead waits for doomsday, until a sign from above summoned him to his typewriter; none came. Finally, on the third day of his ordeal, Max broke through and came up with several headlines which, if they weren't award winners, at least did the trick, and he churned out copy like a demon. Stephanie had asked him for three treatments of each ad; he was giving her four or five. With any luck, the copy could be done by Monday, and that would give the art department just enough time to complete the layouts and the storyboards before the Thanksgiving holiday. The problem Max ran into—unexpectedly and distressingly—was Rosemary.

That meeting on Monday morning seemed to have kicked something out of her. For most of Tuesday and Wednesday she was gone from the office, and the one time that she did check in on him and he complained of the rough time he was having, she had merely shrugged and asked him if he expected anything different. On Thursday she was tied up in meetings with Baumann's hams. On Friday morning Max left his sheaf of copy on her desk, and kept checking in with her every hour or so to see if she'd gotten to it; she kept putting him off. Finally, at five-thirty, Rosemary called him into her office. Everyone else he passed in the hallway was already bundled up and heading home. He found Rosemary cranked down flat in her leather chair, wearing the headphones that plugged into her tape deck. She raised an index finger as a sign that he should wait.

Max paced around the office with his hands in his pockets until Rosemary removed her headphones and cranked herself into a sitting position.

"Mozart's *Requiem Mass*," she said. "Are you familiar with it?"

"Yes."

"It's so depressing, it's not even cathartic."

Max pointedly kept his silence.

"I'm sorry, Max," Rosemary said. "I haven't gotten to your copy yet."

"Why not?"

"Why don't you have a seat?"

"Because I'm too goddamned agitated to sit down, Rosemary. What's the matter with you? Don't you realize we've got a campaign to finish by early next week? I've been busting my butt on this thing, and you haven't lifted a finger to help me. I thought our professional lives were supposed to be on the line with this project."

"They are."

"Then why are you just lying there?"

"I'm sorry, Max. You have every right to be angry."

"Never mind that. Why don't you just pick up that

manilla folder that's been sitting on your typewriter all day and read the copy inside?"

"We'll get to it," she said.

"When?"

"Tomorrow."

"Tomorrow's Saturday."

"Then we'll just have to work on a Saturday."

"Why didn't we work on it yesterday or today?"

"Because I've been negligent, self-indulgent, and un-professional. Please Max—don't be inflexible. We'll get to this campaign and we'll finish it. Just not this evening. Can you cut me that much slack?"

His anger gave way to concern, and he sat in the armchair across from her. "Rosemary," he said, "you can't let that woman get to you like this."

"What woman?"

"Stephanie Deluc."

"Ah—La Machine."

"Who did you think I meant?"

Rosemary shook her head and stared past him into the middle distance. Her eyes were milky, tired. "You deserve an explanation for my . . . listlessness. So I'll tell you. My roommate, lover, whatever, moved out on me last week. And I'm afraid I haven't been very brave about it. We were together three years, you know—a milestone for me. And I guess I've been . . . curling up on myself."

"Why did she leave?"

"Boredom, I think. She's very young—not much older than you, in fact—and I think she just got tired of living with a rather desperate, middle-aged dyke who wasn't getting any younger."

"Come on, Rosemary."

"That's what I am, Max. Anyway, I should have been better prepared for it. I saw it coming, of course. But it's like the big drop on a roller-coaster. You know you're coming to it, and you brace yourself, and then you end up screaming your head off anyway." She opened her box of Balkan Sobranes. "So that's my problem. Oh, La Machine is still my problem, and she's only going to become more of a problem as time goes on, but for right now I'm just too up to my eyebrows in grief to really give a damn about it. I'm sorry, Max. It's not fair that this should make things hard on you."

He wanted to go up and embrace her, but the bounds of their relationship restrained him. She couldn't know how fully he empathized. He, too, knew what was coming and was going to have to brace himself for that inevitable roller-coaster drop, and knew that whether he was the one to leave Nora, or she was the one to leave him, he would end up screaming his head off anyway.

When they met again at the office on Saturday, Rosemary seemed determined to portray her normal self. She was pure business, and made no mention of their conversation the evening before. As in the best times when they worked together, their imaginations meshed as neatly as a pair of complementary gears, and the copy flowed. By the end of the afternoon they had nearly made up for lost time. The only real giveaway that Rosemary was still suffering, as she had to be, did not come clear to Max until he was driving over to Nora's house: during the entire length of their six-hour working session, Rosemary hadn't eaten a single thing.

With Thanksgiving only five days away, the pressure to make plans either including or excluding Nora was reaching the critical stage. He was avoiding the problem by avoiding the phone; at Nora's house, of course, nobody could get to him to proffer an invitation for Thanksgiving dinner; at work he was having the receptionist intercept his calls, and the messages from his mother and Rachel Horowitz were piling up. Part of the difficulty was Nora's isolation. She had no contact with her relatives, and no real friends that he was aware of, and so, as far as he knew, nowhere to go for Thanksgiving unless he brought her along. That left him with two ugly visions to contemplate: Nora seated at the Thanksgiving table among his friends and trying to bear up in the withering crossfire of their scrutiny, or Nora seated all alone in some second-rate restaurant and loathing him (as she would have every right to loathe him) as she picked at her processed turkey and instant mashed potatoes. This last choice was so despicable that it nearly overcame his cowardice—but not quite. He wasn't forced into a decision until Rachel Horowitz finally caught up with him, by accident, just four days before Thanksgiving.

He and Nora had gone shopping at Schnuck's supermarket on Clayton Road, just a few blocks away from the Horowitzes' new apartment. There was a dingy National supermarket in Dogtown, but Max had insisted they drive the extra miles to Schnuck's, where it was cleaner, cheaper, and better stocked. Max was drained from his day at work, Nora was disheveled and bitchy from her shift at the White Palace, and from the moment he picked her up at work, they sniped at each other. He had never gone grocery shopping with her before, and her lack of method appalled him. She simply grabbed whatever caught her fancy, without even checking the price.

Max watched her take a box of Anacin from the shelf, waited for her to drop it into the cart, and then retrieved it, ignoring her sigh of exasperation.

"*Now* what?" she asked him, putting her hands on her hips.

"Look," he said. "These Anacin cost $2.59. Now look at these generic aspirin. Just 99 cents—and you get three times as many. Now, why do you suppose the Anacin is so much more expensive?"

"Well, I *suppose* because it's better."

"That's just what they want you to think."

"Who?"

"The people who market this stuff. Do you know what that one hundred percent of the pain reliever doctors recommend most really is? Aspirin. Pure, simple aspirin. I think it's the biggest ripoff in the whole sordid history of advertising."

"You sure have one hell of an opinion of advertising for being an advertising man yourself."

"It's made me wise," Max said, pushing the shopping cart forward. "Every American should take an advertising man shopping with them at least once."

"Only if they're masochists," Nora said, and surprised him, as she sometimes did, by coming out with a word that seemed beyond the reach of her vocabulary. "Everything in this goddamned store is a ripoff, according to you."

"Just about," Max said, and stopped in front of the pasta section.

Nora chose a box of American Beauty spaghetti and aimed it at him like a long pistol. "Any objections?" she said.

"The generic brand is just as good."

"Lord, you can be boring sometimes."

"Nora, why do you insist on throwing away your money? Is there a rich uncle somewhere you haven't told me about?"

"It's my goddamned money to do with as I please, all right?" With her red-checked headscarf, her strong cheekbones, and her expression of stony refusal, she might have been a fierce old Turkish fishwife with whom he was haggling at a bazaar. "I happen to *prefer* American Beauty spaghetti," she said.

"You only think you prefer it."

"And that's because I've been brainwashed by advertising again, right?"

"You've got it."

"Well, I don't *care*! I don't *give* a shit if I've been brainwashed." She flung the package into the cart and pointed at it. "Now, don't you lay a hand on that, you hear? We got your no-name toilet paper, and we got your no-name aspirin, and now I want my American Beauty spaghetti and I don't give a fuck if I'm getting ripped off. I'll *pay* you the goddamned eight cents difference if it makes you feel any better."

"I can't understand a woman as poor as you are just snatching things off the shelf without giving it any more thought than a chimpanzee."

"So now I'm a chimpanzee."

"I didn't say that, Nora."

"Oh? I must have imagined it."

Max swallowed his anger and rolled the cart down to

the coffee section, where he began carefully to compare prices. He could feel Nora smoldering behind him.

"Max, will you please just pick out any old can of coffee so we can get the hell out of here? I never been this long in a supermarket in my life."

"I'm not going to pick out just any old can of coffee."

"Look, I been on my feet all day long at Shit City and I'm not in the mood to keep standing around while you pick over every goddamned label in the store. I'm worn out and my feet hurt and you're driving me straight up a wall."

"I'm just trying to save you some money, Nora."

"You're just being a Jew is what you're doing."

He was surprised by how hard this hit him; he wasn't normally sensitive to such remarks. The problem was that Nora had said it. She looked perplexed and off balance in the empty supermarket aisle. One hand cupped an elbow. The other hand twisted her earring. For once this mannerism appeared about as charming as someone picking a scab; what was she doing, after all, but fiddling with a self-inflicted hole in her earlobe? Her mustard-yellow blouse, ratty green army jacket, and faded blue jeans appeared willfully shabby, the way a lesbian might dress in order to put off men. In the flat light of the overhead lights her makeup was as loud as war paint. The penciled-in eyebrows were especially pathetic. She repulsed him.

"What do you—why are you staring at me like that?"

"Don't you even know what you just said?"

"You mean about being Jewish? Hell, I was just kidding."

"No you weren't. We were at each other's throats when you said it."

"Do you really think I hate Jews? What would I be doing with you if I really hated Jews?"

"That's not the point."

"That's your favorite thing to say to me, isn't it? That's not the point, that's not the point."

"The point is how you degrade yourself when you make an anti-Semitic remark like that." But she hadn't degraded herself; she had merely revealed herself at the level where she really lived.

"I don't even know what that means—anti-Semitic. Does that mean saying something against Jews?"

"Yes."

"Well, I'm *sorry*. All right? Now, what more do you want me to do? Get down on my knees and lick your shoes?"

"Don't bother," Max said. "You've already gone about as low as you can go."

Their eyes locked.

"I don't like you right now," Nora said.

"I don't like you, either."

"But I don't *like* not liking you, Max. And I get the feeling you're *enjoying* not liking me." Nora hugged herself and moved a few yards away from him.

Rachel Horowitz, pushing a mountainously overloaded shopping cart, turned the corner into their aisle.

Fine, then; he was caught. He felt the sort of exhausted relief that an impostor must feel when his cover is finally blown. He was tired of hiding.

Rachel looked fat, rosy, and contented in her suede coat with the fox-fur collar. She'd had her hair done since the last time he saw her at the Klugmans' house. It was now a carefully sculpted bush of infinitesimal brown curls. "Max Baron!" she called out, then pushed her cart past Nora without giving her a glance. Of course: why should she have made any connection between himself and this slatternly old broad who just happened to be sharing a supermarket aisle with him? Beyond the fact that Nora existed, and that there was something problematical about her, Max had told Horowitz next to nothing.

Max got one more look at Nora—who had backed away from him still farther, and was standing with crossed arms in front of the coffee shelves, pretending, like an amateurish private detective, to be minding her own business—and then Rachel hugged him.

"Max, where have you been? Neil and I have been worried crazy about you. We've been trying to get ahold of you to invite you to Thanksgiving." She punched him rather hard, on the arm. "Come on—where have you been all week?"

He shrugged. "I've been shacked up," he said.

"With this mystery woman Neil told me about?"

"Yep."

"Well, you have to bring her—do you understand? We're both just dying of curiosity. And oh—I went ahead and invited your mother, too. You don't mind, do you? Just make sure she behaves herself, all right?"

"Come on, Rachel. You know I'm not my mother's keeper."

"Oh, yes you are. Anyway Max, you absolutely have to bring your new girlfriend to the party. Will you?"

"Would you like to meet her?" Max said.

"Well, of course—what do you think I'm talking about?"

He was about to call Nora over, but when he looked up from Rachel's riveting bright face, there was no Nora in the aisle.

He ad-libbed. He explained that he was already very late for a date with his new "girlfriend," apologized for speeding off like this, gave Rachel a hug, and thought that would take care of it. Instead, Rachel made him promise, on his honor, to bring his girlfriend to Thanksgiving, and on his honor—his heart twisting with misgiving—he gave his promise.

He waited until Rachel's cart had turned the corner, then began to search for Nora. It wasn't until he'd gotten to the frozen foods that he realized Nora wasn't in the supermarket at all. She had been chafing at the bit to get out of here, and out was where she was—maybe loitering in the parking lot, maybe hitching a ride down Clayton Road. He'd have to chase her down, and had already lost valuable time. Yet here he was, saddled with this cart full of groceries. Maybe Nora intended this as a kind of object lesson; she hated his common-sense practicality, of which she could use a good dose, and was going to force him to abandon all these carefully selected items by going after her. The hell he would, Max thought, and pushed his cart into the checkout line.

Of course everything had been diabolically choreographed to stall him. There were two old women ahead of him who moved with the maddening deliberation of tortoises. When he finally reached the counter, the checkout girl had run out of ones, and was gone an impossibly long time before she got back. And then, naturally, Nora's package of American Beauty spaghetti hadn't been properly coded for the computer, and there was another interminable wait before she was able to locate the manager, who finally got back to her with the price.

Max burst out of the supermarket with his bags clutched to his chest. It was the sixth day in a row without sun. A steady prickling drizzle was coming down. The cars in the parking lot were like a herd of cows, miserably huddling together for warmth, all pointing in the same direction. There was no guessing where Nora might be, and so he made straight for his Volvo.

She was sitting behind the steering wheel, wearing a pair of sunglasses. Sunglasses? The irrationality of it was frightening. He shifted the weight of his bags and rapped on the window. Nora waited long enough to let him know that she was doing him a favor, then opened her door.

"Why don't you open the back door?" he asked her, and shrugged to indicate his bags.

Wordlessly she craned around over the seat and unlocked the back door, but this was as far as she intended to assist him. In order to get the door open by himself he had to perform a series of off-balance maneuvers, and nearly lost his bags in the process. He dumped them onto the backseat and glared at her kerchiefed head. What had to be remembered about these passive-aggressive stunts of hers was how much forethought they entailed. Like a chess player, she'd had to think ahead three or four steps in order to work him into the ignominious position of having to open a door and get two fat bags of groceries into a car without the use of his hands. And even better, she had arranged it so that she was legalistically innocent. She *had* unlocked the door for him, she would say, and if he was having so much trouble, why hadn't he asked for her help?

Nora scooted over to the passenger side. Max got in. The car was as airless as a coffin, so naturally Nora had to light a Winston. He asked her if she would please crack her window. She waited until she had blown out a cloud of smoke which rolled, naturally, straight into Max's face, then took her window down a crack.

"Thank you," he said in a tight voice.

She said nothing. Her profile was expressionless against the rain-beaded glass. He could not get over the idiocy of those sunglasses. Wearing them on a day like this was like the self-dramatizing act of a lunatic walking down the sidewalk on a perfectly sunny day with galoshes and an umbrella. He asked her why she was wearing them.

"Felt like it," she said.

"Have you noticed that the sun isn't out?"

"Tell me something else that I don't know."

"Do you know that you're acting like a child?"

"I must be improving. Just a while back there I was a chimpanzee."

"Why did you run out on me like that?" he asked her.

She wriggled in closer to her door.

"Nora, please—talk to me."

"Why should I talk to you? Every time we talk you just end up saying something spiteful to me."

Was this true? It was true enough to make him want to be conciliatory. But he couldn't find a way in. The rain muttered on the roof of the car. They endured each other.

"Hey," Max said. "That woman I was talking to—do you know who that was?"

"I can't say that I do."

"That was Rachel Horowitz. She's the wife of my oldest friend, Neil Horowitz."

"Well, isn't that interesting."

He kept a clamp on his anger. "I was going to introduce you to her, Nora. And then when I looked up, you were gone."

"Maybe I didn't feel like being introduced."

"She's a friend of mine, Nora."

"You haven't been too hot on introducing me to any other friends of yours."

"I know. I know that. But that's going to change."

"Maybe I don't want it to change. Maybe I'm not interested in meeting your West County friends. Has that occurred to you? Besides, I didn't like that fat woman."

"You don't even know her."

"I get feelings about people."

"Come on, Nora. How could you decide that you didn't like Rachel when you didn't even meet her?"

She looked at him now. "Because I could *tell* that she wouldn't like *me*, all right? Now, why don't you just leave me the hell alone?"

So that was it. It wasn't anger that had driven her from the supermarket. It was her fear of Rachel's opinion.

His heart softened toward her, yet the action he took was impulsive and rough. He snatched away her sunglasses. There: he had guessed right. Nora reared up against the door and let out a hiss. Her eyes were pink, puffed, raw, and there were smudged circles of mascara which had bled halfway down her cheeks. Max had never seen her cry. He had wondered, in fact, if she ever did cry. But of course she wept like any other human being of normal feeling and had simply kept it hidden from him. Her vanity might have come into it, too; she must have known how crying ruined her looks.

Nora made no move to cover her face or retrieve her sunglasses. She only stared at him miserably.

Max opened the glove compartment, took out a wad of Kleenex, and moved toward her. She submitted to him, sitting motionless and keeping her swollen eyes on his as he wiped the bleared makeup from her face. He inhaled her odor—still clinging from the White Palace—of fatty meat and onion. Other men, he thought, years after the one great romance of their lives, would pick up, at a party or an airport terminal, the hint of a particular perfume, and be pierced by ageless grief for that lost love; Max would have his erotic epiphanies whenever he smelled onions frying. Nora gave a twist to her shoulders as he wiped clean her face.

"I can do this myself."

"I want to do it."

"Mr. Clean," she said. "How can you look at me like this?"

"It's not easy, believe me. You look like a drowned raccoon."

"You sure as hell know how to sweet-talk a woman."

"Hold still."

"Max?"

"Yes?"

"I'm sorry I acted so ignorant."

"I'm sorry I was being such a tight-ass," he said, borrowing one of her phrases.

"I wish we could just stop fighting."

"I don't think we can."

"Why not?"

He folded his Kleenex and started in with a clean section.

"I don't know," he said.

"Then what's going to happen? Are we just going to keep tearing each other to pieces like this?"

"It looks that way, doesn't it?"

"And that's all right with you?"

"I guess I'm willing to pay whatever price I have to pay."

"What if I'm not?"

He didn't respond to this. He continued to methodically rub away her makeup.

"What do you want from me, Max?"

"I want to keep you as long as I can."

"Why?"

"Because I love you."

"Why?"

"I'll be damned if I know."

"I'll be damned if I know, either."

When he was done, Nora asked him, sardonically, now she looked.

"Like yourself," he said.

On the way home he invited her to the Horowitzes' for Thanksgiving. She was reluctant, but he finally persuaded her to come along.

She had, after all, nowhere else to go.

CHAPTER THIRTEEN

On Sunday Nora's sister telephoned from New York City. Max would hardly have been more surprised had her dead son Charley rung her up; Nora acted as though her entire family were dead, and that was how Max saw them, banished to some murky nether realm, eternally incommunicado. Her sister Judy and her husband of two months, Bob, were driving to Kansas City, where they would be spending Thanksgiving with Bob's parents; on Wednesday they would be passing through St. Louis and Judy wanted to know, as they were on a shoestring budget, if Nora could put them up for the night. Nora gave her consent without thinking and spent the rest of the day wanting to kick herself for it. She and Judy had seen each other in the flesh only once in the past decade, at Charley's funeral, and the remainder of their contact had consisted of short conversations over the phone at Christmastime.

"I hardly know that woman, Max," Nora told him. "And what I do know, I don't like."

"What's wrong with her?"

"She just plumb out of her mind. For one thing, she's always getting married. I can't even keep track of how many husbands she's had. She keeps them for about as long as you'd keep a new car, and then she trades them in for another. And you know what she does for a living? She tells fortunes."

Nora was propped beside him against a hill of pillows, smelling fresh from her bath in the new rose-colored nightgown he had bought for her—on sale, as usual—at Neiman-Marcus. He lifted a fallen strap of her nightgown back onto her brown shoulder. "What do you mean, she tells fortunes? Is she a commodities broker?"

Nora looked at him. "I mean she tells fortunes. You know, like a goddamned gypsy. She reads palms and lays out Tarot cards and does astrology—anything some fool is willing to pay for."

"Is she for real?" Max said.

Nora snorted.

In matters of the occult, Max was basically agnostic, although his inclination was to resist any system that threw a web of causality over human life; if he believed in anything at all, it was accidents. "Has she ever read your palm or anything like that?"

"Oh, she tried. You should have seen the shenanigans she was up to at Charley's funeral. People were standing in *line* waiting to get their palms read at the wake. She was the hit of the party, let me tell you. And then when she started handing out her goddamned business cards, I damned near threw her out. I never seen such nerve in all my life."

"But is she for real?"

Nora snorted. "Even if she was for real, I wouldn't let her get near me with that stuff."

"Why not?"

Nora shrugged. "Because the last thing I want to know is how the hell I'm going to end up."

Judy's impending visit gave Max the perfect excuse. He set about cleaning her house. It was a Herculean undertaking, and Max made the mistake of telling that to Nora; she wanted to know what Herculean meant, and he told her, which led inevitably into the story of the Aegean stables, which led, of course, into the inevitable comparison to her house. "You're what's full of shit," Nora told him. He sighed and went on scrubbing. He did the floors, the rugs, the walls, the doors, the windows and everything in the kitchen right down to the oven. The task took up most of Monday and Tuesday evenings after work, and Nora gave him only grudging and token help, seizing on any pretext she could to absent herself from the scene of his labors. She took two-hour baths. She misplaced her cigarettes and had to run out for more. She decided on

Monday evening that it was time to take her car to the
shop to get the muffler fixed. When she returned he
insisted that she at least clean out the inside of the refrigerator, and then when he criticized her for the lousy job
she did, she took on the role of the henpecked husband to
play against his nagging wife, told him to get the hell off
her back for once, and stormed out of the house, slamming the door. At ten she called from the McCausland
Tap, soused and contrite, and asked him to come and join
her for a drink; Max turned her down, explaining that he
was too worn out from housework. On Tuesday she was
gone for most of the evening at the hairdresser's. When
she returned, he was surveying her living room with his
hands on his hips; mission accomplished, the Aegean
stable was spic and span. Nora came through the front
door quietly, and both of them turned and stood immobi-
lized by what was before them; she was seeing her house
as she probably hadn't seen it in years, as spotless and
ugly as a room at a Holiday Inn; Max was seeing Nora as
he had never seen her before. She had gotten herself a
permanent. Her straight black hair had been worked into
a mass of lush springy curls that floated behind her shoulders. It made her appear younger, almost girlish, and as
she stood there twisting her earring, her lips parted in
astonishment, he thought that he had never seen her
looking so simply and inarguably pretty.

Now, if she wore the right outfit and went easy on
the makeup, she might even make a passable impression
at the Horowitzes' on Thursday.

———————

Evidently the women in Nora's family shared a taste
for men younger and shorter than themselves, for coming
across the lawn from where their van stood parked was a
broad-shouldered, hugely grinning giantess in a shapeless
tent of a bright yellow dress, her wheat-colored hair in a
bun, followed by a narrow, stooped, put-upon-looking
young man wearing a ponytail and overalls who, Max

judged, was at least six inches shorter, fifty pounds lighter, and ten years younger than his wife. It came out later that Bob had quit the Merchant Marine soon after meeting Judy in Manhattan, during a consultation, and had not held a job in the six months since. He was as taciturn as Judy was voluble. She was almost *too* effervescent, in fact, with the aggressive radiance Max associated with religious converts. She looked absolutely nothing like Nora. Her eyes were chocolate-brown, and her features were rounded, flattened, slightly simian. She stood as tall and straight as a birch tree in her dress, and seemed to have no hips at all. But oddly enough (New York seemed to have made no inroads here) she sounded like Nora, with the same countrified lilting cadence to her speech and a similar graininess in the lower registers of her voice.

Throughout the introductions and the tour of the house, Judy did her best to be warm and sisterly, and didn't seem to notice, despite her professional claim to insight, Nora's distant brittleness. "What a lovely house you have," Judy gushed at one point. "Well, it's clean anyway," Nora told her. "I got me a housekeeper who comes in." "Why, how nice that must be for you," Judy said. "You've got no idea," Nora told her, and led the group into the living room for what she was suddenly referring to as "cocktails."

Bob wanted a beer. Judy said she didn't want anything, and then amended that to a glass of ice water.

"Do you know I haven't had a drink in going on fifteen years?" Judy said.

Nora looked shocked. "I had no idea."

"Well, of course not, sweetheart—how could you? We never talk. It's a shame the way we haven't kept in contact."

"It *is* a shame," Nora said, and left to fix the drinks.

Bob sat in the kitchen chair which Nora had moved into the living room as if he were afraid that he might break it, and spread his hands on the knees of his overalls. Max was trying to think of something to say to put him at his ease, when Judy took him by the wrist, led him over to the sofa, and sat him down beside her. Even sitting, he had to look up to see her face. She smelled of lilacs, and of the dusty van she'd been riding in.

"Honey, where on earth did she ever find you?" Judy beamed at Max and shook her head. "It looks to me like Nora's pattern has finally changed. Of course, I'd have to prepare a chart to be absolutely sure, but I'll just bet you that her moon passed out of Saturn on the very day that you two met."

"Do you think so?"

"It's the only good explanation."

"What's wrong with Saturn?"

"Well, there's nothing wrong with it. It's just a planet. But its influences can be very negative and prolonged. It governs a lot of unattractive traits: gloominess, stubbornness, self-pity . . ."

Nora entered with a tray that bore a glass of water, a can of Busch for Bob, and drinks for herself and Max. There was a slice of lime floating in her vodka tonic and a twist of lemon in his scotch, amenities she had never before bothered with, and Max found this small stab at gentility touching.

Judy leaned forward to accept her glass of water and took Max's hand as she sat back; her hand was as big and warm as a pancake. She said to Nora, "Honey, where on earth did you ever find him?"

"In a Sears, Roebuck catalogue," she said, drawing a sofa-shaking laugh from Judy. Bob received his beer; Max was handed his scotch with a twist; Nora sat opposite the sofa in the armchair and crossed her legs with an excess of ladylikeness. "So . . ." she said.

"Well now," Judy said, and released a big sigh. "It *is* good to see you, Nora."

"Good to see you, too, Judy."

"Can you imagine? How long has it been?"

"Not since Charley's funeral."

"Of course. My, that was a long time ago."

"Indeed it was."

There was a silence. Bob tilted his beer.

"It's a shame the way we haven't kept in touch," Judy said.

"It is a shame."

"It's a crying shame, is what it is. After all, you're the

only sister I've got in the world. Do you ever keep in touch with George or Gene or any of the boys?"

"No," Nora said. "I'm afraid I don't."

"I don't, either, I have to admit. And that's a shame, too."

Nora agreed, and the silence opened up between them again.

"To tell you the truth," Nora said, "it's been so long since I spoke to any of them, I'm afraid I wouldn't have nothing to say."

"I see what you mean. But of course, it's different between sisters. With sisters, you can't help but have a built-in understanding."

Something changed. Nora continued to smile at her sister, but in her eyes was a clinical coldness; she might have been observing her from the other side of a one-way mirror.

"Just think of all we have to talk about," Judy said.

Nora did appear to think about this. She hiked one eyebrow. "Like what?"

Judy laughed and wagged a finger. "You're just terrible, Nora—do you know that? You always did have a biting sense of humor. Even when you were a little girl, you had the wickedest tongue."

"Did I?"

"Oh, yes."

"All I remember is being scared shitless all the time."

"Oh, now. Scared of what?"

"Daddy. Or Mother. Depending on who was around at the time, and depending on which one was drunk."

"You exaggerate, Nora. We had our problems like any family. But we had our good times, too."

"I don't remember the good times," Nora said.

"Of course you do. Like, don't you remember all those times we'd all go sledding down Art Hill? The whole family together just having a fine time? You should try not to be so negative, Nora."

Nora frowned. "I do remember going sledding down Art Hill, now that you mention it."

"Why, of course. And Daddy's singing? Remember what a beautiful baritone he had?"

"No."

"Why, honey—that man could sing like a lark."

"Tell me more good things. I want to remember."

Judy batted a hand through the air. "Now, really, Nora—you don't want to talk about the past tonight, do you?"

Nora looked up from her drink. "Why, sure I do."

"Not tonight, sweetheart. We have so little time together."

Nora took another swallow and assumed a more natural position in her chair, with one of her legs hooked over an arm. "What do we have to talk about if we don't talk about the past?"

"Why, anything and everything—that's all. You know, you're looking awfully good."

"Well, thanks. So are you."

"Was your hair always that curly?"

"It was never curly at all. I just got it permed."

"Me and my memory—I swear."

"Don't you remember? My hair was so straight and black Daddy used to call me Pocahontas."

"Honey, I thought we'd agreed to leave the past alone for tonight."

Nora gave her a stare of purest curiosity. Bob cracked his knuckles. She asked him if he was ready for another beer.

"Yes, ma'am."

Nora got up to get it.

Judy turned to face Max again. "Just how long have you two been going together?" she asked him.

"Just about two months," he said.

"Well, of all things. That's just as long as Bob and I have been married."

"Well, how do you like that?" Max said, using one of Nora's pet phrases.

"Tell me this, Max. When were you born?"

"Nineteen fifty-six."

"I'll need the month and the day."

"August twenty-second."

"A Leo! Of course. And Nora's a Capricorn. No

wonder you two get along. Capricorns go to Leos just like bees go to honey—did you know that?"

"It doesn't surprise me one bit," Max said.

Judy laughed and shook her head. "I do believe Nora's moon has finally passed out of Saturn," she said.

Nora handed Bob his Busch and dumped herself into her chair with the loose-limbed insouciance of a teenager. Evidently she had given up on the gracious-hostess routine. She had a fresh vodka tonic in her hand.

"Nora," Judy said. "I want to hear all about your life these days."

"It's great," Nora said flatly.

"Well, that's wonderful. How's work going?"

"Fine."

"And what is it you do?"

"Food preparation."

"That's right. You said something to that effect when we talked last Christmas." Judy winked at Max. "And I can see how your romantic life is going."

"Can you?"

"He's a genuine prize, Nora—no doubt about that. What do you do for a living, Max?"

"I'm in advertising."

"Well—can you beat that? An advertising man! Nora, I do believe the stars are in your favor."

"I don't want to hear about the stars," Nora said.

"Honey, trying to go through life without understanding the influence of the heavens is like trying to cross a continent without the benefit of a map."

"I don't want to hear about astrology or palm-reading or any of that mumbo-jumbo right now. I don't mean to be rude, Judy—I'm just not in the mood for it at the moment."

Judy accepted this with admirable grace. "All right, then. What else has been going on in your life?"

"Well," Nora said, "I've been reading some books lately."

"Oh?"

"Max used to be an English teacher, and he's been helping me pick out what to read."

"Well, how nice."

"I just recently finished *The Adventures of Huckle-berry Finn,* by Mark Twain."

"But that's a children's book. With Tom Sawyer and the rest?"

"It's not a children's book, as a matter of fact. It's a satire, is what it is." Nora flicked her eyes at Max. "You ought to read it, you know. It's all about con men and liars and hypocrites."

Max saw that Nora didn't understand the implication of this until after she had said it, for her own eyes went flat with shock.

But Judy's ebullience—or obliviousness—did not desert her. She turned her face to her husband and said, "There he is. There's my Bob. There's the reason for my happiness, sitting right there in that chair."

Bob grinned and ducked his head and lifted an index finger away from his beer can.

"You'll never believe how we two met. You tell it, Bob."

"Hell, you tell it better. You're the one with the motor mouth."

Judy laughed. "I don't deny it. Maybe that's why we get along so well. I make up for the two of us in the talking department, don't I, Bob?"

"Well, how *did* you two meet?" Max asked.

"All right," Judy said, and placed her hands on her knees. "It happened like this. He came in one day with a friend who's one of my clients—another sailor by the name of Todd McGuiness, who I've been advising for years. So I ask Bob if he'd like a reading, too, but he says no thank you, he just doesn't believe in all that hocus-pocus, just like Nora over here. Well, we got to talking a little and what do I find out but that Bob's originally from St. Louis. And not just from St. Louis, but from right here in Dogtown. Are you listening, Nora? Do you know where he grew up? Not three blocks away from our old house, right on Yale near McCausland."

"Well, how about that?" Nora said.

"Do you know what the word *synchronicity* means? It means meaningful coincidence, and I could see that this was definitely a case of that. There are no accidents, you know—just gaps in our understanding of how things happen. So I sat Bob down for a free reading, and what do you think I saw, right there in the palm of his hand?"

"What?" Max asked.

"Me!"

Bob chuckled. "And then she looks up at me with them big calf eyes and says, why Bob, I do believe you're going to marry me. And do you know what?"

"What?" Max asked.

"I told her she was full of shit!"

Everyone laughed, no one harder than Bob.

"Well, after that," Judy said, "we had ourselves a whirlwind romance, and it wasn't four months later that Bob and I got married."

Bob was still chuckling. "I'll tell you what's funny," he said. "The funny thing is, I'll never have me no way of knowing if she actually saw that in the palm of my hand, or if she just railroaded the hell out of me."

"Oh, Bob."

"Like I tell her now"—two beers, apparently, were all it took to fully restore Bob's powers of speech—"I tell her, you're the fortune-teller; now when the hell am I going to find work? But no sir, she can't tell me a damned thing about that. She says stop moping and don't drink so much and wait and pray. Now, I have to ask you—what the hell kind of fortune-telling is that?"

"Now, Bob, things are hard all over."

"You see? She can't tell me shit about it."

"If you'd like another beer," Nora said to Bob, who was popping in the sides of his empty can as he spoke, "there's more in the refrigerator. You know where the kitchen is? Make a left down the hall and you'll see it."

When Bob was gone, Judy made light of the outburst. "Problems, problems," she said, as though experience had taught her that problems were not really problems. She pulled her shapeless dress down tighter over her knees. "I expect it's your turn now, Nora. I want to hear all about you and Max."

Nora stared into the mouth of her empty glass. "What would you like to know?"

"Why, everything. How did you two meet, for instance?"

"You don't want to know."

"Of course I do."

Nora looked up at her sister. "All right," she said. "I picked him up in a bar one Saturday night—over here at Cousin Hugo's. You know Cousin Hugo's. It's a regular dump. I was drunk and he was drunk, and I liked his looks, and so I got him back here to the house and I seduced him. And for some goddamned reason that I just can't fathom, he keeps on coming back for more. Now, is there anything else you'd care to know?"

Bob came loping in with his can of Busch. Nora passed him on the way out.

Max excused himself and followed her into the kitchen.

Her hand shook as she tilted the vodka bottle.

"You're not behaving, Nora."

"I'm sorry, Max. But I just can't help it. I got nothing to *say* to that woman. And I just can't stand it when she tries to get *personal* with me."

"For crying out loud—she's your sister."

"But she doesn't *feel* like my sister. It doesn't feel like I got any family at all. And then out of the clear blue sky this big loudmouthed crazy woman and her slimy little husband come tromping into my house because they're too goddamned cheap to get a motel room, and I'm supposed to pretend that I *love* her."

"So pretend," Max said. "It's for only one night."

"Why should I?"

"Because she's your sister. And because it'll be easier for you than fighting it like this. Besides, what are you going to do at this point—kick her out?"

She gave this some thought. "Do you mind if I get drunk?"

"Whatever gets you through the night."

"I mean it, Max—I don't want you shooting me dirty looks all evening."

"Nora, I'm on your side."

"Are you?"

"Don't you know?"

She drew him into a hard embrace. "You feel more

like family than she does—more than anybody does. Do you know that?"

Max made dinner. He stuck, at Nora's insistence, to "normal stuff": tossed salad, baked potatoes, broccoli with cheese sauce, prime T-bone steaks. Nora kept her vodka tonic beside her plate, ate like a horse, and said almost nothing, leaving Max to play the host. He tried to draw Bob out, and unfortunately was successful; there followed through the rest of the meal a bitter and obscene recitation of grievances against the Merchant Marine ("you busted your fucking balls and had to take it up the ass by a bunch of fatheads playing Navy") and when Bob finally settled down to silently chewing his steak, Max did the same. Judy, he noticed, ate with the same wolfish intensity as Nora; a carryover, maybe, from those times as a child when there wasn't enough on the table. After dinner it was discovered that Bob had drunk up all the Busch. Nora instantly volunteered to go out and get him some more. Judy suggested that Bob had had quite enough beer as it was, and Bob suggested that she shut her big trap and mind her own business. Nora protested that the trip wouldn't be any trouble, as she was running low on cigarettes and could use some more tonic, and succeeded in ushering her brother-in-law out the door, evidently so eager to escape her sister's company that she was willing to trade it in for Bob's.

It didn't take Judy long to suggest to Max that she give him a reading. He accepted without hesitation, first because he was curious to see how she operated, and second because he was—well, *curious*. She told him she would need a good strong light, and he brought in a lamp from Nora's bedroom and set it on the kitchen table.

"Have you ever had a reading done on you before?"

"Nope."

"The main thing is to relax. Now, I'm going to go into a little bit of a state here, and we'll be to be quiet for just a few minutes."

Judy held his palm so lightly in the warmth of her hand that it seemed to have no weight to it. She bent close, and the breath through her nostrils blew ever more slowly and more rhythmic. Max looked at the crown of her head in the lamplight, and the analogies that came to mind were agricultural; the curvature of her skull was like the earth, her hair was like rows of neatly plowed wheat, her scalp between those rows was like fallow ground, all of it was seen from the perspective of a hawk. She began to speak.

"There are many strong forces at work in your life. I see much pain. But I also see much joy."

Max continued to relax. This was about what he'd expected.

"You come from humble beginnings. I see a small house. But I also see a much larger one. You've come very far. This is because you're intelligent and hard-working and imaginative. There's money in your life, but I see it coming and going."

Judy's speech had changed. The lyrical Missouri cadence was gone, and her sentences were rolling out as evenly as boxcars. "There are two sides to your nature, and they are in conflict. You have a passionate side, and a side that is afraid of that passion, that needs to be in control. You put too much trust in your own mind. You need more faith." The tide of her breathing slowed still further. "Your life is heavily influenced by women. I see an old woman who is also a child—your mother—who you have taken care of in many ways, and who you resent for the burdens she's placed upon you. You need to show her more love. I see another older woman in a veil. And I see Nora. You love her, but you're afraid of something. You've made no place for her in your life. I see you first on one side of her, and then on the other. I see a marriage."

This eased somewhat the pounding of his heart, for it infused him with another shot of skepticism; evidently Judy liked to use palmistry as a matchmaking device. He was no more going to marry Nora than he was going to grow another head.

"I see another woman, a young woman, but she is on the other side. There's something wrong with her neck."

Max withdrew his hand and stood.

Judy's eyes came back into focus. "You don't want me to go on?"

"How did you know that?" he asked her.

"What, honey?"

He sat back down and tightly crossed his arms. He had never supplied Nora with that particular detail—that Janey had died of a broken neck. Neither woman could have known it. And yet one of them did. And besides— there was the rest of what Judy knew, and could not have known. How could she have known, for instance, that ever since that meeting in the graveyard, he tended to picture Sara Roth in her short black veil? Max went to the counter and poured himself another drink. He didn't want to have to think; the prospect was too exhausting.

Judy patted his hand when he joined her again at the table.

"Oh, now," she said. "Don't look so glum. Some people just get this way on their first consultation."

"I thought you were a fake," Max said. "In fact, I still want to think that, but—"

"Well, the proof's always in the pudding, isn't it?"

The somber-voiced oracle was gone, and Judy was once again Nora's gregarious, harmless, rather silly sister. "Besides, there's nothing to be afraid of, you know. I never tell people what they'd be better off not knowing. I try to stay on the positive side. And when I see something very negative, well, I usually just keep it to myself. Do you know I gave Nora a reading when Charley was just a baby, and I saw right then how he was going to die? I never told Nora, of course. I just carried the knowledge in secret all those years. Because I saw him, you know. I saw him lying right there in that section of the River Des Pères where they found him thirteen years later."

"Charley died of leukemia," Max said without force.

"Oh, my good Lord," Judy said, giving his hand a squeeze. "Is that what Nora told you?"

What killed Charley were the quantities of liquor, Quaaludes, and filthy water he took in when, at the age of fourteen, he drowned in the River Des Pères—which is

perhaps the loftiest-sounding name ever bestowed upon a
sewer. It winds in a convoluted line from North to South
St. Louis, in some spots holding no more water than a
gutter, in others, depending on the rainfall, deep enough
to swim in. Where Charley was found, near Arsenal Street,
the water had been only waist-high. While Judy had seen
him only twice in his life, she had gathered that he was an
isolated, gloomy, embittered child, abused by his father
and largely neglected by Nora, who had been an impatient and inattentive mother—something which Max had
no trouble visualizing. But this was the extent of what he
learned, for too soon Nora and Bob came banging through
the door, laughing uproariously about something.

Max made no mention of this to Nora that night, nor
was he planning to confront her with the truth. This was
her secret to give out as she chose. And anyway, he
already knew. What he wanted now from Nora was enough
confidence in his love to trust him with her secret—and
no amount of haranguing her was going to get him that.

She was not herself in bed that night. This might have
had something to do with the bed they were in. Judy and
Bob were sleeping in her bedroom; Max had pushed back
the coffee table and the television and opened out her
sofa-bed. Nora entered the living room naked, a bad idea
with guests in the house, and from the weave of her walk
he could see how drunk she was. She got into bed beside
him and turned unceremoniously upon her back. Max
wasn't sure if this contained a sexual invitation or not.
Such complete passivity on her part was unknown to
him—except for those times when he started things rolling
by applying his mouth to her. This he began to do, swiftly
losing himself in the flowery complexities of her labia,
until her thighs tightened in refusal and she sat up, taking
his face between her hands. "Just fuck me," she said.

She lay back down and waited.

"Right now?"

"Yes."

She waited stoically, like a good Victorian wife. She
felt abnormally tight as he entered her. And then there
was a further surprise; she was silent. He thought this
might be in deference to Bob and Judy down the hall, but

that didn't explain what her eyes were doing open, or why the look in them was so liquid and beseeching.

"Max," she said, just as he was starting to come apart against his climax. "Max, I have to tell you . . ."

"What?" he managed to say.

"I just wish . . ."

"What?"

"I just wish we could have a baby."

For an irrational moment he wished it, too. And then he spurted his useless seed.

CHAPTER FOURTEEN

He dreamed that he escorted both Janey and Nora to the Thanksgiving party at the Horowitzes' new apartment. It was as vast as a ballroom and flooded with guests. He couldn't remember what sort of stupidity had possessed him to invite both women to the same affair, but here they were, flanking him, each keeping hold of one of his arms, and there was nothing he could do about it now. The trouble started when he tried to introduce them to the baffling parade of unfamiliar faces passing by. He could not seem to keep the two women straight in his mind. He would introduce Janey as Nora, or Nora as Janey, and before long he lost track of which woman was supposed to be his present lover, which his former wife, who was alive or who was dead. His confusion deepened to panic, his introductions became more bungled, and as he groped for the separate threads of their identities, he saw that he wasn't with two women at all, but only one, and that woman was looking at him with such loathing that he could feel the heat of it on his face. "Can't you even remember who the hell I am?" Janey asked him, in Nora's smoky voice—then he awoke to the steady grinding of Nora's snores.

Bob and Judy turned out to be early risers. When Max got out of bed at nine, they were already gone. He went into the kitchen to make coffee, and as he waited it occurred to him that Judy might have left a note. He found it propped on the formica table against the wings of Nora's swan-shaped ashtray. She had neglected to lick the envelope shut. Max struggled only briefly against temptation, then sat down to read.

Dear Nora:

It was so good seeing you again, sweetheart, and so nice of you to let us spend the night. Take care of yourself. And take care of Max—he's a real prize. If you ever need us for anything, remember, our door is always open to you.

Love always,
Judy

There followed a phone number and a Seventh Avenue address. He was disappointed by the lack of content in her note, like a peeping Tom who has worked himself up to a lit bedroom window only to see a middle-aged woman in a bathrobe ironing one of her husband's shirts. What had he been expecting? A confession that she had told Max all about Charley? Some dreadful prediction concerning the future of their love affair, meant for Nora's eyes only? Judy had included in the envelope her business card, which read: JUDY NEIDERMEYER FOR PROFESSIONAL CONSULTATIONS. The layout was amateurish, with a border of hand-drawn stars and moons. Without thinking why, Max slipped it into his wallet.

Then Nora called out from the living room, asking him for a glass of water. He filled a Flintstones glass and brought it to her, where she sat up naked in the middle of the sofa-bed, her eyes puffed from last night's drinking, her new permanent, on the side she had slept on, crushed in like a clump of chicken wire. This was his beloved.

She closed her eyes as she drank the water.

"Judy's gone," he said.

"Praise the Lord."

"I kind of liked your sister."

"Oh, she was wild about you," Nora said, handing back the Flintstones glass. "That woman's a cradle-robber from way back. And what did you think of her new husband? My God, that woman knows how to pick 'em."

"She left you a note," Max said.

"What did it say?"

"I beg your pardon?"

Nora crinkled the corners of her eyes at him. "Oh,

don't look so innocent. I know what kind of snoop you are."

"You do?"

She laughed. "Hell, that first morning you stayed over? You must've ransacked every drawer in the house."

"I thought I was being the epitome of stealth and cunning," he said.

"You were about as stealthy as a marching band."

Max sat on the edge of the bed.

Nora sighed and put her hand on the back of his neck. "I'm feeling shaky," she said.

"You mean about the party?"

"Yes. Are you really sure you want to take me?"

He shifted his weight around on the sofa-bed, placed his hands at the fatty folds of her waist, and kissed her stale mouth. "I'm sure," he told her.

Later, as they were dressing, Nora asked him if he carried any pictures of Janey.

"No, I don't. Why do you ask?"

His tie had come out wildly uneven. He undid the knot and looked at her. She was pulling up a stocking along her big fleshy thigh.

"I'm just curious to know what she looked like. I mean, I know she was blond and had blue eyes and was supposed to be some kind of raving beauty, but I don't have me any picture in my mind, you know? Like, what did her nose look like?"

He turned back to the mirror. "Hell, I don't know. It was a nose."

"Was it a Jewish nose?"

"No. Janey didn't look Jewish at all."

"Did she have big tits?"

Again his tie had come out wrong. "Yes," he said. "She had big tits. Nora, what's this all about?"

"I'm just asking."

"But why now?"

"Because I'd like to have me some idea who everybody's going to be comparing me to today."

"Nobody's going to be comparing you to Janey."

"Liar," she said.

She wore her cream-colored blouse from Saks, a

simple brown skirt, thoughtfully low heels, and, as if she had picked up telepathically upon Max's unvoiced request, an unusually light touch of makeup.

She looked, he thought, breathtakingly presentable.

He was nervous, but during the drive to his mother's house Max did his best, for Nora's sake, to appear cheerful and unconcerned. He tried to prepare her for his mother.

"Don't let her looks fool you," Max said. "Underneath that fifty-seven-year-old exterior beats the heart of a maladjusted six-year-old. Just be patient with her."

"I'm just going to be natural with her," Nora said. "I'm just going to be my natural self with everyone today."

"Good."

"They're going to get the one hundred percent natural Nora Cromwell, and if they don't like it, they can lump it."

He hoped she would stick to this. What he feared materializing most at the Horowitzes' party was the air of affected gentility she'd put on the night they met at Cousin Hugo's.

A surprising thing happened. His mother and Nora seemed to take to each other. Once his mother had gotten over the initial shock of seeing this older woman, or maybe just *any* woman in company with her son (all he had told her was that he would be bringing along a "friend"), the two women settled down into a conversation which, for all of its easygoing chattiness, might have been taking place between two neighbors over a backyard fence. Probably what broke the ice was that Nora sounded deeply interested in his mother's complaints.

"So my doctor—that Dorfman—tells me it's only a melanoma, this skin patch on my back. But it *could* turn into cancer, he says."

"Good Lord, Mrs. Baron, that's terrible."

Max was not alarmed; his mother had been talking about her melanoma for the past two years or so, and had thus far refused to have it removed, he suspected, because of its value as a conversation piece.

"Well, what did the doctor say you should do about it?" Nora asked her.

His mother was leaning forward from the backseat. The bouquet of her perfume nearly canceled out the stink of Nora's Winston. "He says I should get it removed, but he also says there's no hurry. He says it's up to *me*. Can you imagine? Now I'm supposed to make major medical decisions. I might as well take a knife and operate on myself."

"Mom," Max said, "if he says it's up to you, he's obviously not too worried about it."

"For all I know, he doesn't want to operate because he thinks I can't pay. That's all doctors care about anyway, is their pocketbooks."

"Isn't that the truth?" Nora said. "Why, do you know there are some hospitals now that won't take you in if you don't have the money? That's right. You could be having yourself a heart attack right there on the floor of the admissions room, and they wouldn't take you in. I saw it on *60 Minutes*."

"Without money in this world," his mother said, "you get treated like a criminal."

"Amen," Nora said.

"And who has all the money? The criminals, that's who."

"Amen to that, too. I'll tell you, Mrs. Baron, when you're poor, everything is stacked against you. Why, do you realize that prices in supermarkets are higher in the poor sections of the city than they are out in the suburbs?" She had taken this information from Max. "I tell you, the whole system works against you when you're poor."

"Except for Ronald Reagan," Max said. "The poor man's buddy."

"I don't want to talk politics," Nora said.

"Me neither," said his mother.

"Hell," Max said, "you sound like a couple of Marxist ideologues."

There was a silence; neither woman had any idea what he'd meant by that last statement. But soon they started up again, chattering on now about how dangerous it was to live in the city—never mind that Nora never bothered locking doors—the two women finding agreement with each other at every turn, and the sound of their voices soothed Max like the conversation of birds; for a few minutes he nearly forgot his anxiety.

———————————

The room contained a miniature rocking horse, an empty crib, a playpen, and two different kinds of wallpaper which, like opposing armies, clashed loudly at the border where they met. There were blue and yellow choo-choo trains on one side; on the other were clusters of anthropomorphized bunny rabbits jumping rope, picking daisies, chasing butterflies, and bending toward each other to cutely, chastely, kiss. This child, Max thought (who did not yet exist in any form, for Rachel was not pregnant) was already in the process of being spoiled. He had been thinking unkind thoughts about the Horowitzes' frank and unapologetic materialism all throughout this tour of their new apartment in Clayton. They had obviously gone into hock up to their eyebrows, notwithstanding the fact that Rachel made nearly as much money as Horowitz in her job at the travel agency, for nearly everything in the apartment had been purchased since the wedding; the trappings for this nursery *in potentia*, the carpeting, the wallpaper, the furniture for the living room, bedroom and dining room from Carafial's, the VCR, the enormous microwave hulking in the kitchen, and the much-talked-about camper-van waiting in the garage which Rachel's parents had made the down payment on as a wedding present. There was something insidious in all this happy-go-lucky covetousness, and it seemed to Max a new wrinkle in Horowitz's personality that he hadn'd recognized until now. But no: it wasn't Horowitz who had changed. It was Max. This level of luxury was nothing more or less than what he and his peers had always envisioned for themselves; certainly he and Janey had owned their share of high-ticket items. And his own apartment out in Kirk-

wood wasn't exactly a hovel. What had altered his perspective were all the successive days and nights he had
spent at Nora's house. A kitchen table to him now was a
small square of flecked formica; a stereo was just a blue
plastic record player that sat on top of a rickety plywood
box; a television was a battered old thing with an unrelia-
ble black and white picture; chairs had cigarette burns in
them; couches were frayed. This lower-class vision of the
normal life was, of course, nothing new to him at all. It
had been the vision of his childhood, and it was still there
waiting for him, each Sunday, when he visited his mother's shabby house.

Horowitz was off entertaining another group of guests;
Rachel, Nora, Max, and his mother were assembled in the
nursery.

"Why, what a sweet little room," Nora said, keeping
a tight hold on his arm. Ever since they came through the
door of the apartment, Nora had been touching him,
keeping an arm around his waist, a hand in his hand, or a
hip against his hip, as if there were a current running
between them which she was afraid of breaking.

Max, on the other hand, was much less anxious than
he'd expected. After so much apprehension, the dreaded
scene, now that he was in it, was nowhere near as horrify-
ing as his fantasies. He was strangely detached. The looks
of surprise and confusion that had come over the faces of
Klugman and Sherri as they were introduced had hardly
fazed him; nor had he taken much offense at Horowitz's
excessive, artificial politeness. If they didn't approve of
the woman he was with, Max thought, taking Nora's
phrase, they could lump it. This detachment even extended to Nora herself. He was not going to monitor her
performance. She was a grown woman (when she chose
to be) and could look out for herself. This unlooked-for
equanimity in such a dangerous situation had him swaggering a little; he felt like he had two or three drinks inside
of him, which he did not—no drinks had been offered yet.
That, he guessed, would not happen until they had sufficiently ogled every bright and shining object in the
Horowitzes' trove.

"I especially like the rocking horse," Rachel was saying. "Isn't it precious? It's over ninety years old."

"Well, how about that?" Nora said.

"But the wallpaper doesn't match," his mother said with alarm—as though Rachel weren't aware of this already.

Rachel laughed. "That's Neil's idea. He's such a *goofball* sometimes. He thought as long as we were decorating the apartment, and as long as we were planning on children, we might as well go ahead and do the nursery, too. But of course, we don't know if the first child is going to be a boy or a girl, so we just went ahead and put up both kinds of wallpaper."

"So if it's a boy you keep the trains, and if it's a girl you keep the bunnies?" his mother said.

"Right. We'll just paper over the wrong one, depending," Rachel said.

"What if it's a boy and he's effeminate?" Max asked.

Rachel gave him a punch on the arm. Then she led them over to the empty crib and invited them to take a feel of the mattress. It turned out to be a tiny water bed.

"Well, how do you like that?" Nora said. She was restricting herself to comments that were as devoid of content as possible.

"It's really supposed to be much better for the baby," Rachel said. "They sleep better and they don't wake up as often. And supposedly, it cuts down on the chances of crib death."

"But Max didn't *tell* me you were pregnant!" his mother shouted.

"Well, I'm not, Mrs. Baron. Neil and I were just thinking ahead, is all. It was lots of fun, really, coming up with this room."

"Have you picked out a college for him yet?" Max asked.

Rachel narrowed her dark bright eyes at him. "You really are full of it today, aren't you?" she said.

Then she led them through the gleaming kitchen and down the backstairs to the basement garage, where the new camper-van, like a secret weapon under development, stood beneath a lone bare light bulb. It was filing-cabinet gray and outfitted (Rachel led them through it,

one by one) with three rows of plush seats that folded
down to form a sleeping platform, a color television on a
swiveling pedestal, a quadraphonic sound system, a tiny
stove and tiny refrigerator, and a wet bar that popped out
of the floor. The opulence of the amenities seemed to
form a glaze over Nora's mind as well as her eyes, for all
she kept saying as Rachel pointed out each feature were
things like, "My, my," or "Will you look at that?" But of
course, Max reflected, what were you *supposed* to say
when you were a poor southside hoosier and some privi-
leged West County Jewess was lording it over you with
her possessions? He stopped himself; something was dis-
torting his view of things. Rachel was merely trying to
entertain her guests; she had been extremely nice to Nora
thus far, and was certainly not trying to make her self-
conscious. Besides, for all she knew, Nora was an heiress.

The stairs creaked and down came Horowitz in a
voluminous gray turtleneck sweater, a glass of red wine in
his hand. "How come nobody here has a drink?" he
asked Rachel.

Rachel did not bear up well under any sort of criticism. A flush came into her bubble cheeks, and her black
eyes grew brighter. "I was just showing them around,
Neil. I can't help it if I can't think of everything at once."

"All right, all right. I was just asking you a question,"
Horowitz said, and encircled her wide waist with an arm.
"Now, who here wants a drink?"

"I could sure use one," Nora said. It was the first
definite statement of any kind she had made since their
arrival at the party.

"What's your pleasure?"

"A vodka tonic, if you've got one."

Horowitz gave a bob to his head like a waiter, and
turned to Max's mother. "Edith? What are you going to
get drunk on tonight?"

His mother laughed. Horowitz had been calling her
by her first name since childhood. "You know I can't
drink," she said. "My doctor—"

"Your doctor? What doctor?"

"You know—Dorfman."

"Dorfman? That quack? What does Dorfman know

about it? Come on, Edith." Horowitz put an arm around her shoulders. "Let's you and me get stewed tonight and talk about old times." He gave her shoulders a squeeze, squeezing out a giggle.

Max envied Horowitz's kindly, natural style with his mother. He had the knack of making her feel girlish and appreciated, as Max did not. Of course it was easier for Horowitz; he was not her son.

"One glass of white wine," Horowitz said. "How's that, Edith? Will you go for that? One glass of wine won't kill you."

"All right," his mother said. "But a *small* glass."

"That's the spirit." He turned to Max. "Scotch and water, right?"

"Right."

Horowitz indicated the camper-van with a sweep of his arm.

"What do you think of it, Max?"

"It's—something, all right."

"Isn't it? I'm in love with the goddamned thing. Ever since we got it, I keep coming down here at odd hours and just sitting in it."

"What I really like about it," Max said, "is its lack of ostentation. Come the revolution, we'll all have one just like it."

He had meant this to be funny, but heard the bad note as he hit it.

Horowitz furrowed his brow at him and tugged on his moustache.

"I'll get those drinks," he said.

———

Max and Nora circulated, and the questions that kept coming at her were amazing in their uniformity. How long had she known Max? How did they meet? What did she do for a living? Had she always lived here in St. Louis? Was she enjoying the party? Nora, braced with several vodka tonics, was soon rattling off her responses with such blithe confidence that there was no reason to suspect she was telling anything but the truth. In fact, she was lying. Max had no idea what her motivation was, for the lies that she was telling were so closely aligned to the truth, and so modest in their claims, that they couldn't possibly have served to elevate her in the eyes of her questioners. Instead of serving hamburgers at the White Palace, she now sold cosmetics at Famous-Barr; if this were a step up in the world, it certainly wasn't much of one. She and Max had met in a bar, all right, according to her new story, but she had traded in the overt seediness of Cousin Hugo's for the covert seediness of Culpepper's in the Central West End, where the more fashionable people, presumably, went to get picked up. Jack Cromwell finally got what he deserved; Nora bumped him off. She was telling everyone that she was a widow. There was something aggressive in all this lying—or was it actually defensive? Whatever it was, it seemed to give Nora a sense of power, for the shyness that gripped her earlier had disappeared. Max probably should have taken her aside and given her a severe chewing out, for her dishonesty was, after all, putting him in the deceitful position of having to back up her story. But he wasn't going to play her father today. He was even making it a point not to keep track of how many drinks she had already put away.

What he should have done, however, was to warn Nora before the Klugmans got to her that she was going to have to change her story, for Sherri, as bad luck would have it, happened to be a buyer for Famous-Barr. But the parade of guests and their barrages of questions were coming so thick and fast that Max didn't have a chance to be alone with her, and as Larry and Sherri cornered them in the kitchen, all he could do was to hold her hand and watch.

"You sell perfume where?" Sherri asked her.

"At Famous-Barr."

"Oh?" She settled back beside Klugman against the electric range that rose from the middle of the kitchen floor and twisted the fine gold chain that ringed her long goosy neck. "Which store?"

Nora took her hand away from Max's, and dug it in,

instead, around the back of his belt. "South County," she said.

"How do you like that?" Klugman said. "Sherri works at Famous, too. What is this? A conspiracy?"

"*Do* you?" Nora said, smiling hard at Sherri and tightening her grip on Max's belt. "Well, what a tiny little world."

"How long have you been with us?" Sherri asked.

"Oh, just about a week."

"Really?" Sherri was drinking a cola-colored drink which Max knew, from experience, was Diet Pepsi. Sherri never drank anything else, not even another diet drink. If you offered her a Tab, she would decline and drink water. "Who do you represent?"

"I'm sorry?"

"What line do you sell?"

"Chanel," Nora said, and lifted her chin.

"Chanel?"

"And what line do *you* represent?" Nora asked Sherri before she could get her mouth open again.

"I don't. I'm a buyer."

"Oh? And what do you buy?"

"Children's apparel."

"Children's apparel. Well, how about that?"

Sherri toyed with her necklace as she peered at Nora. The liver-colored half moons under her eyes looked especially dark in the flat light of the kitchen. "Where did you work before starting with the May Company, if you don't mind my asking?"

"Oh, here and there. I was in the food preparation business for a while."

"And you've been with us only a week and you're selling Chanel?"

"Why are you grilling her like this?" Klugman said.

"I'm just curious, Larry. It just seems odd," Sherri said, keeping her eyes on Nora, "that you'd be selling such an expensive product when you're still only a trainee."

"Would you like to know my professional secret?"

Sherri slowly blinked at her. "Yes."

"I give one hell of a good blow-job," Nora told her, and then dragged Max out of the kitchen.

Max stopped her in the hallway beside a gallery of framed wedding pictures. As the best man, Max was in several of them.

"Nora, you've got to be good today."

"I *was* being good. And then that bitch up and calls me a liar. She's lucky I didn't scratch her goddamned eyes out."

"You are a liar."

Nora shrugged and took a sip of her vodka tonic.

"Why are you doing this?"

"Doing what?"

"Lying through your teeth to everybody."

Nora protectively touched her permanent in a few spots.

"I just don't want these people thinking they've got a fix on me," she said.

––––––––––––––––

She went through phases during the party; timid and self-conscious at first, brazen and reckless later on as she distributed her phony history through the crowd, and now, as Max stood by a ring of male talkers and listened to what amounted to a dirty-joke-telling competition, there was yet another Nora, busying herself in the kitchen with Rachel, Rachel's sisters, Rachel's mother, and Rachel's Aunt Sophie, making all the chirpy noises and loose-wristed gestures of a woman who finds her true serenity in housework. Max drifted to the door of the kitchen. The women moved about like bees in a hive, miraculously failing, at every moment, to collide, step on a toe, burn a hand on a pot, or drop a dish of candied sweet potatoes to the floor. But one woman was out of sync with the rest. Nora picked and dodged through the congestion like a foreigner unsure of the local traffic laws. She was the only woman smoking, the only one with a drink in her hand. What was she even doing there, among those bossy, efficient Jewish homemakers who were, for the most part, ignoring her? She would have been much more in her element out here in the living room, exchanging blue stories with the men. Max watched her do several things that either did not need doing, or had already been done: she opened the oven door to have a look at the turkey, and Rachel's mother admonished her to shut it again; she took a sponge and made a half-assed effort at wiping down the countertop near the sink, which would only be soiled again in another thirty seconds; she lifted the aluminum foil from the top of a steaming casserole dish, looked at the contents, and then carefully pinched the foil back into place around the rim; she took a dish of pickles and olives from the refrigerator and set it on the table— again Rachel's mother said something to her, and Nora shrugged and laughed and put the relish dish back where she'd gotten it. Only Rachel was thoughtful enough to give her something useful to do. She brought out a big gelatin salad in a copper-covered mold, showed Nora which of the silver platters she wanted used, and left her on her own again. Nora frowningly fussed with a bed of romaine lettuce on the platter, then worked the Jell-O so carefully from its mold she might have been handling plastic explosives. When it emerged unbroken, she caught Max's eye; for some reason she colored.

Max returned his attention to the party.

———————

"I'll tell you why the State Department is pro-Arab," Mr. Horowitz was saying. "Because just like every other State Department before them, they're nothing but a pack of anti-Semites."

"There you go again," Horowitz said to his father.

"You don't agree?"

"I never agree with you, Dad."

"Wise guy. If you'd ever listen, you might learn."

"What makes you think they're all a pack of anti-Semites?" Max asked him. Nora had hold of his arm. Surprisingly, given the political nature of this discussion, she seemed to be paying close attention. Except for the shine of her dark blue eyes as they moved from speaker to

speaker, there was little indication that she had been
drinking steadily for the past two hours.

"All you have to do, Mr. Baron," Mr. Horowitz said,
"is take a look at the record. The president of the United
States has always been more pro-Israel than his State
Department—even Eisenhower, that back stabber. If those
guys at Foggy Bottom had their way, Israel would have
been driven into the sea a long, long time ago."

Looking at Mr. Horowitz, a small, flat-bellied man of
sixty with impressively manicured hands and a dignified
narrow face, it was hard to imagine that he could have
sired anything as gargantuan and loosely thrown together
as the body of his son. He ran a clothing store in the
Delmar Loop and was largely self-educated. Television
had been banned from the house during Horowitz's childhood, and it had not been unusual in the evenings when
Max dropped by to see the three of them, Horowitz, his
father, and his mother, all ensconced in their deep chairs
in the living room, each bent over a book. During high
school Horowitz had taken to referring to his house as
"the library."

"Well, what about the guy who's the head of the
Pentagon?" Rachel asked. "What's his name? Weinstein?
Isn't he Jewish?"

Horowitz shook his head at his wife. "His name is
Weinberger," he said. "And he's not the head of the Joint
Chiefs of Staff, honey. He's the Secretary of Defense. And
he's not Jewish, either."

"You're a very sweet and intelligent girl," Mr. Horowitz said to his daughter-in-law. "But it wouldn't kill you
to pick up the paper every once in a while."

"Well, I'm *sorry*," Rachel said.

It was just the sort of noncomeback comeback Nora
was so adept at.

Mr. Horowitz suddenly clapped his hands together.
"But that's just my point: *Weinberger!* The biggest anti-
Semite of the lot. And of course—why not? All his life he's
been carrying this Jewish-sounding name around like a
monkey on his back. All his life this Mr. Weinberger has
been trying to convince his blue-blooded cronies at the
country club that he's clean, that his credentials are in

order, that he's one of them—and all the time he knows that half of them still believe he's got one or two Jewish relatives stuck away somewhere in his family tree. The poor man can't win. Even little Rachel here is under the impression that he's Jewish, and she doesn't even know who he is."

"Will you *stop* it?" Rachel said.

"I'm just trying to make a point," Mr. Horowitz told her. "I wasn't making fun of you, dear." He went on. "Naturally the man hates Jews. All this unfair suspicion he's garnered all his life is enough to make an anti-Semite out of anyone. So what does he do in revenge? Simple. He sells planes to the Arabs. There's your Caspar Weinberger in a nutshell."

"Mr. Horowitz," Max said with a grin, "that's some of the neatest sophistry I've heard in a long time. But it's pure speculation. How can *you* know what's going on in the dark recesses of Caspar Weinberger's mind?"

"I know about anti-Semites," Mr. Horowitz said.

"But that's a circular argument."

"It's his favorite kind," Horowitz said.

Nora spoke up. "I got a question." She directed this at Mr. Horowitz.

He raised his eyebrows in the manner of a school-teacher when the slowest student in class volunteers a response. "Yes?"

"Well, if all these people you're talking about are working for President Reagan, then do you think Reagan is against Jews, too?"

"I'm sorry, my dear. You'll have to forgive me. I've forgotten your name. I'm terrible with names."

"Nora."

"Well, Nora, I'll tell you—I don't believe that our poor befuddled president hates Jews in any personal way, although I'm sure that most of his staff does. I'm sure President Reagan doesn't even realize that some of his policies are anti-Semitic, just as he doesn't understand that his own administration is a racist one."

"So he is."

"What?"

"Against Jews."

"Well, yes, I suppose I'd have to say that he is."

"Well, who doesn't hate Jews in this country, according to you?"

Mr. Horowitz thought about this. "The Jews," he said.

"Only some of the Jews," Horowitz reminded him.

Nora smiled at Mr. Horowitz and took a sip of her drink.

"Then you must think I'm anti-Semitic," she said.

The simple, nonaccusatory way in which Nora delivered this slowed, perhaps, the reaction time of the group. But soon enough the meaning came through. Mr. Horowitz looked at her with great seriousness.

"You shouldn't even say such things in jest," he told her. "Nobody here was suggesting anything remotely like that."

Nora laughed. "Why, sure you were. Didn't you just now say that anybody who wasn't Jewish had to hate the Jews? Well, here I am—and I'm sure as hell not Jewish."

Still, there was nothing unfriendly in Nora's tone. She had no concept of the gravity with which her words were being received. As far as she was concerned, she was only challenging a point of logic. Max put his hand at her waist and tugged her close; she pulled a little away from him.

"Look," Mr. Horowitz said, "we're all here to enjoy a nice Thanksgiving dinner, and nobody is more or less welcome than anyone else. Let's just drop this conversation and have a good time, all right?"

But Nora wasn't satisfied yet. "All I'm telling you is exactly what you told me," she said. "If the only people who don't hate Jews are Jews, and I'm *not* a Jew, then I have to hate Jews, now, don't I?"

This left Max breathless. Where had Nora learned to argue like Aristotle? Even Mr. Horowitz, with his predilection for loopy arguments, must have recognized a solid syllogism when he heard one. Backed up into the dead-end of his own reasoning, Mr. Horowitz sighed, briefly shut his eyes, and looked carefully at Nora again. "All right," he said. "*Do* you hate Jews?"

Nora laughed. "Well, Max sure seems to think I do,"

she said, and gave him a playful bump with her shoulder. "Hell, I didn't have no idea what the word anti-Semitic *meant* until Max accused me of it."

Now Nora's smile wavered and faded, and her hand reached up, as if for support, to one of her black coral earrings.

The group had become as still as a painting.

Nora continued to go through the motions of mingling, but her gaffe with Mr. Horowitz seemed to have taken some of the wind from her sails, and she appeared uneasy once again. In turn she was being treated with increasing coolness and reserve by most of the other guests; questions were directed to her merely for the sake of propriety, and merely for the sake of propriety Nora responded with agreeable and empty answers. She sat glassy-eyed through a detailed rehash of the Horowitzes' Mexican honeymoon and was somehow overlooked, as though she were invisible, when the packet of snapshots was passed around. Rachel finally noticed this and pressed the pictures upon her. Nora studied every photo, forcing out the proper noises of envy, but the conversation had already left her behind, and abruptly she arose from the sofa, leaving a pile of scattered snapshots in her place. Max let her go, figuring she no more wanted him to assume the role of watchdog than he wanted to play it. Later on he saw her sequestered with his mother in the dining room, at one end of the big oval table. Maybe it was only natural that these two would form their own society at the outskirts of the party; nobody was terribly interested in talking to his mother, either. Whatever the subject of their talk, there was an air about it of conspiracy, exclusivity, like two young girls sharing secrets, and Max decided to leave them to themselves.

Rachel came up to him.

"How are you doing, Max?"

"Fine, Rachel. It's a nice party."

"I like her, Max."

This surprised him. "You do?"

"Yes. Why not? She's a little different, maybe, a little unconventional—but so what? All these people around here think everybody has to be just exactly like them—as if they're so perfect themselves. She's nice, Max. She seems like a sweet person."

Rachel's perceptions were, as usual, a little too sun-drenched, but Max was warmed anyway. He was sur-prised—surprised that it would be Rachel who had come to him with this instead of Horowitz, his best friend; surprised that it would be Rachel who turned out to have the larger and more imaginative spirit. Horowitz, he now realized, had been carefully avoiding him.

Along with the turkey, which was as big as a small ostrich, there were two kinds of cranberry sauce, three varieties of stuffing, sweet potatoes with marshmallows, sweet potatoes without, a tossed salad, Nora's carefully liberated gelatin mold, a relish tray, green beans in cream sauce with onion rings on top, plenty of Rachel's home-made rye bread, and at the corner of the table opposite the turkey, an enormous glazed Baumann's ham (Max's contribution, courtesy of Spindler Advertising) studded with pineapple rings and maraschino cherries. Dessert was being held in reserve in the kitchen. Dinner was served buffet-style, with paper plates and plastic utensils, and people ate wherever they could find a place to sit. Nora and his mother had chosen to fight the crowd, and were taking their time together in line, oohing and ahhing over the fare. Max, who couldn't stand waiting in lines, excused himself, wandered off into the hallway, and looked at the wedding pictures. Klugman appeared. He hustled Max into the bathroom and locked the door behind them.

"What is this, Klugman?"

Klugman sang: "I'm dreaming of a white Thanksgiv-ing . . ."

"Are you crazy?"

Klugman sat on the toilet seat and already had out his

black film canister and coke spoon. "I'm just so drunk," he said, "that if I don't have myself a toot, I'm afraid I'm going to throw up all over my wife." He snorted through each nostril and held out a spoonful for Max.

Max sat on the edge of the bathtub and shook his head no.

Klugman shrugged and did the spoonful himself.

"I just wanted to tell you," he said, leaning back against the toilet, "that I like your girlfriend—what's her name? Nora?"

"Yes."

Klugman sniffed and blinked. His eyes looked like wet marbles. "Well, she's all right. She has a certain . . . animal attractiveness. In fact, she seems like the sort of woman I'd tend to fall in love with—not you. How in the hell did you ever end up with her, Max?"

"What do you mean she's the sort of woman you'd fall in love with?"

"I have strange tastes." Klugman looked like an abandoned rag doll, slumped against the toilet. "I just can't seem to get very sexually interested in a woman I don't despise a little bit. It's always been that way. You take a woman like Janey—shit, Max, I don't think I could even get *hard* for a woman as perfect as that. But you take a woman like Sherri—I don't know what it is. It's like being a guy who only goes for paraplegics. There has to be something missing, something wrong, before I can get the old pecker to stand up and salute." Klugman smiled. "Sick, isn't it?"

"Do you think I despise Nora?"

Klugman waved a hand around. "No, goddammit. I'm not talking about you. I'm talking about me. That's what I don't understand. I can't think of two guys more unlike than you and me. And that's"—Klugman laughed—"that's the funny part."

Max stood.

"You sure you don't want some toot?"

"I'm sure," Max said, and for some reason placed the palm of his hand on Klugman's warm bald spot. "Don't do too much of that stuff," he said as he opened the door. "You'll spoil your appetite for dinner."

_____

The line had dwindled. Max filled his plate rather meagerly, and ran into his mother and Nora as he came into the living room. They were going in the other direction for seconds. Nora gave him a surreptitious squeeze on the ass; his mother glared at him. "Where have you been?" she shouted.

"In the john."

"We're sitting in back of the sofa on those cushions—don't let anyone take our place!"

"I'll guard it with my life," Max said.

He took a seat on a cushion, propping his back against the back of the big curved sofa, and started in on his food. Behind him he heard the voice of Mr. Horowitz.

"And you should have seen his wife. Such a beauty, you wouldn't believe. And sweet as a puppy. Do you know I cried like a baby when she died? And then the way Neil carried on. You would have thought it was his own wife, God forbid, who passed away."

"It's not like he couldn't have his pick of the young girls," an old woman said.

"No. He's a very handsome young man."

"What could he see in a woman like that? I hate to say this, but she strikes me like one of the *shkutzim*."

Max set his plate down. There was probably no uglier word in the Yiddish lexicon. *Shkutz* meant dirt; *shkutzim* meant, literally, the dirty ones: those who would not or could not keep themselves clean. The poor white gentile trash. Why this should have affected him so powerfully, he didn't know; he had labeled Nora as a hoosier often enough in his own mind. But his appetite, both for the food and for the party itself, was gone. He wanted only to grab Nora and his mother and get out of there.

He dropped off his plate on an empty folding chair, went into the kitchen, and poured himself a scotch, foregoing the ice; he wanted to feel it burn. He knocked it back. Horowitz came charging into the kitchen.

He didn't spot Max until he had the refrigerator door open. "You haven't seen a plate of cranberry sauce floating around anywhere, have you?" He watched Max pour another shot. "What are you doing, drinking alone in here? Go eat."

Max swallowed his whiskey and crossed his arms.

"What do you think of Nora?" he asked Horowitz.

Horowitz frowned.

"What do you think of my date?"

"Jesus, Max—I don't know. I've hardly had time to say boo to her today."

"Come on, Horowitz. You must've picked up an impression or two."

Horowitz plucked at his moustache. "Well," he said, "she's no chicken."

"True. What else?"

"Max, I'm sorry. I really am. But you caught me at the worst possible time. I'm up to my ass with things to do right now, and we'll just have to talk later about this, all right?" Horowitz ducked behind the door of the refrigerator. "A-ha! Found you, you sly little fucker."

Horowitz emerged with his plate of cranberry sauce and made for the door. But Max was blocking him.

"Max, what are you doing?"

"I'm confronting you."

"Why?"

"Because you're avoiding me."

"Max, for God's sake, I need to get this out to the table and I don't want to have to mow you down."

But Max didn't move.

Horowitz's face darkened. "What do you want me to tell you, Max? That she's a delectable, fascinating, wonderful creature and I couldn't be happier for the two of you? Well, I can't say that. I can't lie to you."

"Then tell me the truth."

"All right, goddammit. I'll tell you the truth. The truth is, I'm worried about you. You walked through the door today with that woman on your arm and first thing I thought was that it was some kind of practical joke—I actually did. But that's how unbelievable it is, Max. What are you even doing with a woman like that? She seems like—I don't know. Like some character out of *Tobacco Road* or something. I don't understand what you see in her, and I don't understand what this whole thing is about, and I sure as shit don't understand what's going on in your mind. Why are you forcing me to tell you this?" He glared at his plate of cranberry sauce as if he wanted to fling it against the wall. "It's like you're doing this to punish yourself or humiliate yourself—I don't know. There's something pathological about it. I'm sorry, Max. I feel like a complete asshole, telling you this."

"It's all right," Max said quietly. "You were going to have to tell me sooner or later."

"I don't want this to screw up our friendship."

"Neither do I."

"Max." Horowitz's eyes were wet. "What's wrong with you?"

The diagnosis was simple.

"I'm in love," he said.

———————

Nora leaned against the mantel of the fireplace with her drink in her hand. His mother sat on a folding chair with her plate in her lap—she always ate with exquisite slowness—picking at the last of her turkey. Max came up behind Nora and kissed her on the shoulder.

"Well, hello to you," she said. "You'll never guess who we were just talking about."

His mother laughed. "I was just telling Nora how clean you were when you were a little boy. *Meshugga* for clean. That's what you were."

"What's that word mean, *meshugga*?" Nora asked.

"Crazy. Crazy for clean." His mother took an infinitesimal bite of turkey. "Not only would he make his own bed every morning without being told, but then he'd come in and make *mine*! Did you ever hear of such a thing? A ten-year-old boy, down on his hands and his knees, scrubbing the kitchen floor because he *wants* to! Who could believe? But that was Max. I don't know—maybe he got it from his father. His father was quite the dandy, you know. Me, I'm not so particular. A little mess here and there, I don't mind."

"I'm with you, Mrs. Baron," Nora said. "Max here can tell you—I'm not the cleanest person in the world."

Of course not. Far from it. She was one of the *schkutzim*. She was a character out of *Tobacco Road* whom he had brought to this party as a joke.

Max announced that he was ready to leave.

His mother's eyes widened. "But I'm not finished eating!"

"We'll go when you're finished."

"You know I can't eat that fast! My digestion—I get sick if I eat too fast. Why are you always rushing me like this?"

"We'll go when you're through eating," Max said again.

Nora peered at him. "How come you want to leave so soon?"

He told her that he was tired, that he was no longer in the mood to deal with all these people—but that wasn't the core of it. He was suffering from an intense longing to be alone with her, back at her house, upon the other-worldly island of her water bed, where the two of them belonged.

CHAPTER FIFTEEN

Nora stirred beside him, stirring the water bed.

"I'm sorry I made such a damned fool of myself," she said.

Max turned and buried his face in her hair. "You were fine, Nora. You were splendid. You were the only remarkable thing at the whole party."

"I'll bet they're still remarking about me now."

"So what if they are?"

"Don't you care what your friends think?"

"I thought I did. But no—not much."

"I embarrassed you."

"If anyone embarrassed me, it was Horowitz and the rest of those unimaginative bores. At least you gave them something to think about, for once."

"Well, maybe you should always take a hoosier with you to your parties. You know, to give people something to think about, stir things up a little . . ."

"Stop it, Nora."

"Do I ever have to see any of those people again?"

"Not if you don't want to."

"I don't."

They lay side by side in silence for a spell.

"So what are you going to do, Max? Keep me in a little box and just take me out whenever you feel like playing with me?"

He didn't answer. Outside her window the dogs of Dogtown were giving out their woozy chorus of barks and howls. Below them the furnace kicked on with a grumble.

"I'm already missing you," she said.

There was no point in pretending he didn't know exactly what she meant.

"Don't miss me yet," he told her.

"Everytime we make love, I just lay here wondering how many more times it's going to be."

"We have time, Nora."

"How much?"

"Maybe more than either one of us thinks."

She slapped the bed; the wave rolled under his back. "Don't say things like that, goddammit! I'm trying as hard as I can to keep a clear head about you and then you go and say something like that, and I lose my head all over again. We *don't* have time, Max. I don't belong in your life, and pretty soon you're going to realize that and drop me like a hot potato. Don't talk to me like I'm a fool."

"I don't think you're a fool."

"You're going to dump me, and then you're going to find yourself a nice young girl who's been to college and knows how to conduct herself and won't be an embarrassment to you. And before you know it, I'll just be this crazy thing that happened to you a long time ago that it shames you even to think about. And don't go telling me I'm wrong. I'm right."

"You're wrong," he told her. But lying there in the formless dark, on the uncertain surface of her water bed, with the furnace roaring beneath them, it was easy to imagine that they were on a raft and slipping down a river toward a sudden, steady drop-off into nothing.

"I'm afraid of having to mourn you," he said.

"I won't be dead when it happens."

"That'll only make it worse."

Nora propped herself up on an elbow. Her eyes were vividly black. "Then why don't you ask me to marry you?"

Max groaned.

"Well? Why don't you?"

"Because if I asked you," he said, "we'd probably end up getting married."

"What makes you so all-fired sure I'd say yes?"

"Wouldn't you?"

"Isn't that the point of asking? To see what I'll say?"

Max sighed and put his hand on her loose belly. "I'm not going to ask you, Nora."

She settled back down alongside him. "Tell me something else that I don't know," she said.

Lying there in the dark, his mind started working. The possibility of marriage at least bore some thinking about.

Nora Cromwell of Dogtown and Max Baron of Kirkwood were joined today in marriage in a civil ceremony at the VFW Hall in Maplewood, Missouri. The bride wore an unorthodox but nevertheless captivating work-dress of sky blue with yellow trim, set off by a matching peaked cap and newly laundered tennis shoes. A reception followed at the White Palace restaurant at the corner of Grand and Gravois in St. Louis. It was, by all accounts, a resounding success. The supper consisted of cheese fries, milk shakes, and diminutive 100 percent all-beef hamburgers charmingly presented in small cardboard boxes. Following their honeymoon trip to Antarctica, the happy couple plans to take up residence on the dark side of the moon.

Max laughed and the bed shuddered.

"What's funny?" Nora asked him.

He rolled over and kissed her dry lips.

"Nothing," he said.

Outside the window of Stephanie Deluc's tenth floor office in the Fidelity Federal Building, the first snowfall of the year was densely swirling. Inside, too, white predominated. Her broad desk was of the lightest blond wood; the chairs where Max and Rosemary sat were built of chrome and white leather; the walls, as yet undecorated, stood like empty white canvases. It was all very cool, very ethereal, and just right, Max thought, for a temperament as bloodless as Stephanie's. The only warm, organic thing in the room was Stephanie's impossible body odor.

Evidently she had not told her secretary to hold her calls during the meeting, for every few minutes the phone would ring. Stephanie would answer it, and Max and Rosemary would have to conceal their impatience as she talked at length with whomever happened to be calling.

"In that case," Stephanie was saying into the receiver, "try the West County Butcher Shop. Well, I'm terribly sorry if it causes you any inconvenience, Loretta, but you remember what happened the last time you tried to serve Mr. Deluc an inferior piece of veal. All right then. Fine. Around seven. Good. Good-bye."

Stephanie hung up and, offering no apology for the interruption, returned her attention rather wearily to the layouts spread before her on her desk. She had come back from the Bahamas with a fine tan, which had the unfortunate side effect of making her hyperthyroid eyes look even more prominent. She wore today a lavender dress with another bow at the neck; these bows appeared to be her professional trademark, as some senior executives liked to affect bow ties. She took up her pack of Merits and slowly drew one out, still frowning at the layouts.

"You shouldn't keep us in such suspense," Rosemary said.

"I'm just wondering if you've given me enough options to work from," she said, lighting her cigarette.

Max opened his mouth. "Uh, if you'll remember, Stephanie, you asked us for three treatments of each approach. We've given you four."

Stephanie shrugged.

"Don't any of them grab you?" Rosemary asked.

"Oh, these layouts are acceptable, for the most part. And the copy is serviceable, aside from a few clumsy phrases—"

"What clumsy phrases?" Max asked.

Rosemary shot him a sharp warning look.

Stephanie, luckily, laughed. "Writers," she said. "I never met one who wasn't just a little bit of a prima donna. But I guess that goes with the territory, doesn't it?"

Max managed to return Stephanie's smile.

She opened her presentation folder. "Here, for instance, in radio spot number three, just at the close of the announcer copy. *Cannon blankets, free or at special low prices—it's one offer you can really warm up to.*"

"What's wrong with that?" Max asked her.

"You've ended your sentence in a preposition."

He waited a beat to make sure Stephanie wasn't

putting him on. But she was smiling at him as if she'd scored a point. "There's nothing wrong with ending a sentence in a preposition," he said.

"Surely you went to school."

"I taught high school English for three years."

"Oh? Then surely you of all people should know that you never end a sentence in a preposition."

"That," Max said, "is the sort of English up with which I will not put."

Stephanie just looked at him.

"Winston Churchill said that when someone called *him* down for ending a sentence with a preposition. Obviously, Stephanie, you're going to end up as a kind of verbal contortionist if you stick to that old rule. It's not even a matter of archaic usage. There never *was* a time when prepositions—"

Rosemary had touched him on the arm—a clear tactile order that he shut up—and was now tapping her cigarette into the crystal ashtray on Stephanie's desk.

"Really, Stephanie, Max does have a point. Your copy simply won't sound conversational if you stick to that old rule."

"I disagree. You forget that a majority of our market is over the age of forty-five. Most of them are well acquainted with the traditional rules of grammar, and if we break those rules in our advertising, they're going to notice, and they're going to be alienated. This sentence can be turned around so that it's both conversational and grammatically correct."

"*You can really warm up to this offer,*" Max said.

"There, you see? You've proven my point."

"But listen to it, Stephanie. The punch is gone. The line just lies there now."

Stephanie ground out her cigarette. "I'm afraid we're wasting time. We can leave the fine-tuning of the executions for a later stage in the creative implementation of this campaign. For now—"

"Are you saying that you won't accept any line of copy that ends with a proposition?"

"I thought I made myself perfectly clear."

"*Security and warmth—that's what saving at Fidelity*

Federal is all about. Now, how would you turn around a line like that?"

"Max," Rosemary said.

He got a rein on himself. His right leg was jiggling and he forced it still. "Sorry," he said.

Stephanie gave a slight bob to her head. "Now, if you'll *allow* me, I'd like to take a look at these approaches as a whole." She sat back in her white chair with a sigh. "All of these executions are . . . perfectly serviceable. But none of them, to put it colloquially, really turn me on."

"What's missing?" Rosemary asked.

"Excitement. Spark. Something really *compelling*." Stephanie's smile had shifted into a candid mode; she was about to share a secret with them. "You know, I didn't spend my whole time in the Bahamas just baking my brain in the sun. I did some hard thinking about this campaign, and the more I thought, the more it seemed to me that we were actually better off with the headline that I originally suggested to you."

Rosemary, with what had to be heroic effort, maintained a look of open interest on her face. "You mean *Happiness Is a Warm Blanket?*"

"*And the Warmth of Saving at Fidelity Federal,*" Stephanie said. "Just listen to it. Don't you think it conveys the feeling we're after with much more panache than anything I've got here on my desk? *Happiness Is a Warm Blanket, and the Warmth of Saving at Fidelity Federal.* I just can't seem to get away from it. It just has that ring of *inevitability* about it—don't you think?"

Of course it did, Max thought. It was her headline.

On the way back to the office, as Rosemary maneuvered her Mercedes through the snow and snarled traffic, she lit into Max. "You amazed me," she said. "I don't think I've ever heard you being rude to *anyone*, and suddenly there you were, talking back to Stephanie Deluc like some surly teenager in the principal's office. What in the world was the matter with you back there?"

"That woman just gets my goat," Max said. It was weird how he was picking up on Nora's figures of speech. The scenario of their relationship was beginning to look like *Pygmalion*, with a twist: as the play progresses, Professor Higgins discovers that he has taken on a cockney accent, and by the end of the last act, he's on a street corner in Soho, selling flowers.

"Max, the woman gets my goat, too—but that's no excuse for a lack of professionalism."

"Doesn't professionalism include protecting your client from her own stupidities?"

"Listen to me, Max. La Machine is out for our blood. You can see how tough she's making things already, with the deadline she just gave us. She knows perfectly well we're going to be up until all hours trying to get this campaign together by tomorrow afternoon, and she's probably hoping we'll make some kind of stupid mistake in the crunch. Because that's all it's going to take: one dumb oversight or screwed-up instruction that she can point out to her superiors, and she can start the ball rolling against us. We've got to be perfect, Max. And this campaign has to be perfect—or her idea of perfect."

"Which is what?"

"Slick mediocrity."

"I don't like doing mediocre work, Rosemary."

"Do you like working at all?"

"Happiness," Max said as he came into Nora's bedroom sometime after ten, "is a warm blanket."

He tore the plastic off the thick golden comforter he had purchased wholesale that afternoon from Fidelity Federal, and whipped it out across the water bed, where she lay reading *Life on the Mississippi*. The comforter billowed down around the blanket Nora already had drawn up to her chin. Her house, as usual, was freezing; she was keeping the thermostat at a punishing fifty degrees. More than once Max had offered to help pay for her heating, seeing as how, after all, he was her roommate, but Nora stubbornly refused his "charity." He had tried another tack, suggesting that they move out to his apartment in Kirkwood for the duration of the winter; but no, it was too far to drive to work, and besides, she wouldn't feel comfortable in such a "swanky" place. So here they remained, freezing in Dogtown, swaddling themselves in two or three layers of clothing whenever they weren't keeping each other warm in bed. Nora had taken to wearing her ratty green army jacket around the house. Her closet was full of his sweaters.

"Well, now," Nora said, sitting up to inspect the new comforter. "Isn't this nice?"

"Nice," Max said wearily, "is not the word." He sat on the edge of the bed and began to take off his clothes. "What you've got there, Nora, is a warm, wonderful, comfy, cuddly, blissfully beautiful blanket from Cannon— yours free or at a special low price, when you deposit five hundred dollars or more in a savings account at Fidelity Federal." His shoes dropped to the floor.

"Poor baby," Nora said, kneading his shoulder muscles. "I do believe they've finally destroyed your mind."

"I need a drink," he said.

Nora got up to get it for him.

Max continued to undress. He was going to the closet to hang up his jacket, when he kicked Nora's purse across the floor; most of the contents spewed out. Max cursed half-heartedly and squatted and put the items one by one back into her purse. He was almost too tired to take any interest in the inventory: comb, hairbrush, tampons, loose change, compact, lipstick, Charlie cologne (odd that she would choose a cologne called Charlie and odd, too, that he hadn't perceived this before), crumpled Kleenex, several packets of White Palace ketchup, her key chain anchored by the fuzzy pink rabbit's foot, an extra pack of Winstons, and a snapshot which, when he turned it over, seemed to stop his heart.

Max had been the photographer. It had been taken on a weekend he and Janey spent at the Lodge of the Four Seasons at the Lake of the Ozarks. She was on a dock with the dark green lake behind her, wearing her two-piece cobalt-blue swimsuit, leaning back on her elbows and throwing the camera a sassy cover-girl sort of come-on look. It was a look she never gave out in real life, but which, for some reason, she had liked to affect when she was being photographed. The sun was a spiky star behind the rich mass of her golden hair—she had not been swimming yet—and her body was almost too sweetly proportioned, too buttery-solid, to be believed. He had almost forgotten about the power of real physical beauty, and felt weakened as he stared at her image.

"Find anything interesting?" Nora said. She stood in the doorway with his drink, the bottom of her heavy flannel nightgown still moving around her ankles.

"Where did you get this?"

Nora took a sip from his scotch and crossed her arms. "Your mother gave it to me," she said.

"When?"

"At the party on Thanksgiving."

"Why, Nora?"

"I *told* you I wanted to see a picture of her."

"That doesn't explain what it's doing in your goddamned purse."

Nora only stared at him.

"Nora, talk to me. Why would you be carrying this around with you?"

"I don't know."

"You've been carrying this around in your purse for almost a week and you don't know why?"

"I just *wanted* it."

"What for? So you could stick pins in it?"

She threw the drink at him, sort of. Something held her back, so that she kept hold of the glass and flung only the whiskey; it went for him in a limp arch and fell short, spattering the rug.

She retreated into the hallway and Max caught up with her, taking her by the wrist.

"Nora, I'm sorry, I'm just—well, it just knocked the wind out of me when I saw this in your purse. You can understand that, can't you?"

She nodded.

"What do you want with Janey's picture?"

"I just wanted to see what she looked like—and once I did . . . I don't know. I just wanted to make sure I didn't *forget* what she looked like."

"Why?"

She raised her eyes to him now. "Because I'm trying to keep a straight head about you."

He wasn't sure what she meant by this. But to get any further he would have to probe an area of Nora's mind that he had neither the stamina nor the courage to deal with tonight.

"Just come on back to bed," he said.

"Do I get to keep the picture?"

"As long as you put it someplace where I won't find it."

Later on, just as he was slipping past the border into sleep, Nora said, "Lord, she was beautiful."

"Who?"

"Your wife."

"Umm."

"I guess you must still be in love with her."

"Janey's dead."

"Well," Nora said. "That's one thing I've got up on her, anyway."

Max was fully awake now. "Nora, you're not in competition with Janey. You don't have to look like Janey and you don't have to be like Janey in order for me to love you. All you have to be is the one hundred percent natural Nora Cromwell."

"You must have just completely lost your mind when she died."

"I did."

"I know you did."

"How do you know?"

"Because," Nora said, "you took up with me."

The spot for the Cannon blanket premium was to be based on man-in-the-street interviews. At eight in the morning, on a dull and drizzly December day, Max was at the corner of Seventh and Olive with a video-taping crew at his back, asking passersby what their idea of happiness was. That afternoon he had Rosemary come over to the studio to help him select the takes. "Getting paid for this commercial" was one nice response from an old man

wearing a hat with leather earflaps, but Rosemary ruled it
out on the grounds that it was "too smart-alecky." "We
need to keep this saccharine and shallow and completely
inoffensive," she told him. That ruled out a majority of the
takes. No less than three people reported that their idea of
happiness would be to win the Illinois State Lottery. There
was a lot of talk about money, about love, about career
advancement, all of which Rosemary dismissed with the
epithet, "Too real." One smartly dressed young woman
thought for a moment and said—even Max had to grant
that this was unusable—"No pain." Then there were what
Rosemary categorized as the "religious" responses: Christmas all year around (it was, after all, Christmas season);
international brotherhood; being with Jesus; no more nukes.
Nobody had anything to say about warm blankets, much
less the good feeling they got from saving at Fidelity
Federal. The tape ran out.

"A completely wasted shooting day," Rosemary told
him. "You should have *coached* them, goddammit."

"I thought the idea was to get natural reactions."

"Well, we were wrong, La Machine won't go for any
of this. We need answers that come straight out of Norman Rockwell."

"People don't think like Norman Rockwell."

"They will if you pay them for it," Rosemary said.

The next morning Max was back on the same street
corner with the same taping crew asking people the same
question; this time around, however, he shamelessly read
to them the lines they were supposed to parrot, reminding
them all the while that a check amounting to union scale
for actors would be in their mailboxes within three weeks
if they could make their answers come out sounding natural and unrehearsed. A spirit of cooperation blossomed
along the sidewalk.

The completed spot ran like this: Open on a field of
blue. Super rolls up into frame: "What's *your* idea of
happiness?" Cut to a medium close-up of a woman wearing a heavy overcoat and sunglasses. Young woman: "An
armful of kittens." Cut to a middle-aged man in a fedora
hat. "That's easy—my wife's pineapple upside-down cake."
Cut to a grinning round-faced black woman. Woman:

"My idea of happiness? *Summer*time." ("You should have had her sing it," Rosemary commented.) Cut to a bright-eyed little old lady. Old lady: "Why, happiness is a warm blanket!" Dissolve to product shots of blankets, comforters, pillows, etc. Announcer voiceover: "Now, at Fidelity Federal, happiness is a warm blanket . . . with Cannon blankets, comforters, and more, all free or at special low prices. Deposit five hundred dollars or more in a savings account at Fidelity Federal, and take your pick of these beautifully blissful products from Cannon. They'll give you the same warm feeling of happiness you always get . . . when you know your savings are secure at Missouri's largest federally chartered savings and loan." Cut back to bright-eyed little old lady. Old lady: "Happiness is a warm blanket . . . and saving at Fidelity Federal!" Fade to black.

The spot so disgusted Max that he had to force himself to watch it as the supers were laid in and the copies run off at the studio. Rosemary observed that it would probably produce insulin shock in any diabetics who happened to catch it. Stephanie Deluc's critique arrived in the form of a Mailgram: "Re: Cannon spot. Congrats! A real winner. Now, let's keep up this level of execution."

By the middle of the following week, the campaign had broken.

He found Nora camped in front of the television in her raggedy green army jacket, the golden comforter from Fidelity Federal drawn up around her middle. Before her on the coffee table were assembled her Kleenex, her vodka tonic, her Winstons, a bag of potato chips, and a cup of onion dip. She was so pale that Max thought at first she must be sick; on closer inspection he saw that this was due only to a lack of makeup. She hadn't even bothered penciling in her eyebrows. Pallid and inconsolable-looking, she sat enthroned amid her luxuries, a fairy-tale princess dying of melancholia. She offered him no greeting when he closed the front door behind him, and when he lifted her chin to kiss her and inhaled her salty breath of potato chips (a vision of Janey at thirteen stabbed him), she neither accommodated nor resisted him. She merely allowed herself to be kissed.

"You look absolutely miserable," he told her.

She shrugged and kept her eyes on the television.

"Do you want to talk about it?"

"I'm not in the mood for talking."

"Well, what are you in the mood for?"

"Watching TV."

"Nora, are you all right?"

"I'm fine," she said harshly.

He hung his jacket up and came back to the sofa, sitting down beside her and drawing some of the comforter over his lap; Nora gave up her unfair portion of it only grudgingly. She was watching a rerun of *Gilligan's Island*.

"I wish you'd talk to me," Max said. "Would you like to hear about my lousy day at the office?"

"Not particularly."

"Do you mind if I lean against your shoulder?"

"I don't care."

He pressed against her, bewildered and humiliated by this need to be near her, even when she was being bitchy, or childish, or maddeningly distant, or, as now, all three. It was at moments like this that he was ready to believe, along with the likes of Sara Roth and Horowitz—those trumpeters of conventional good sense—that this love of his wasn't love at all, but a symptom of mental illness. He had to be crazy to love such a woman, crazy to think such thoughts about her and still believe that he was in love with her. But he still believed it. He wanted to curl up inside the warmth of her armpit and hibernate there all winter. Instead, he watched the show with her in silence.

Gilligan, it seemed, had discovered cannibals on the island (painted white actors with bones through their noses) and was having a hell of a time getting the other castaways to believe his story. Every time he tried to alert the Skipper or the Professor or Mary Ann to the imminent danger of getting a spear through the back, the cannibals, just a beat before their quarry turned to look, would disappear into the plastic foliage. "You see, Gilligan?" the Professor said, tapping his own temple. "A classic case of island fever."

"Nora, how can you watch this drivel?"

"I *like* it," she snapped.

His Cannon blanket spot came on.

"Here's the spot I shot last week," he said.

"This one?"

Now Nora came alive. She bent closer to the black and white picture, her lips parted in concentration. It was a continuing source of awe to her that her boyfriend's work actually appeared on television, and she displayed a solemn reverence for his commercials, however tacky, however insulting, which no amount of irreverence on Max's part could shake. Seen freshly, the Cannon blanket spot struck him as so awful, so false, so contemptuous of human intelligence, that he was ashamed in front of Nora. When it was over, he turned to her, bounced his eyebrows, flicked an imaginary cigar, and asked her in a Groucho Marx voice what *her* idea of happiness was.

She started as if he'd viciously pinched her. And then she turned a look to him of such simple, raw hurt, that he nearly believed for an instant that he'd asked the question in order to taunt her. Her eyes clouded and she abruptly stood and walked out of the living room. She wore nothing beneath her army jacket but a pair of lavender panties. She was going to freeze. Max anxiously gathered up the comforter and followed her into the kitchen.

She sat at the tiny formica table, lighting up a Winston. Already her broad thighs were pimpled with goose bumps.

He handed her the comforter and she wordlessly took it and arranged it around her middle. He took the chair across from her.

"What is it, Nora?"

"Nothing."

"Did something happen today?"

"Nothing worth mentioning. Same old shit as yesterday."

"Yesterday you weren't depressed."

She let her smoke roll out of her mouth. "Who says I'm depressed?"

"I do."

She shrugged. "Well," she said. "Maybe I am."

"What's depressing you?"

She glanced uneasily around the room. "It's the wintertime. I hate it. I hate everything about it. I hate the snow and I hate the way the house is always freezing like this and I hate the way the sky looks. I just hate it, that's all."

This sounded improvised.

"What else is bothering you?"

"Christmas. I never could stand Christmas." She drew the comforter up higher around her torso. "All Christmas ever meant to me when I was little was that I got to watch my parents go on their biggest benders of the year. I had me some real fun Christmases, let me tell you. And now all it means to me is that I'm too goddamned poor to do it up like everybody else. You know what I got for last Christmas? Nothing. Not a goddamned single thing except a ham from the White Palace." She looked at him. "I guess you must think I'm some kind of terrible person for hating Christmas."

"Jews don't celebrate Christmas."

"Well, chalk one up for the Jews."

Her mouth was trembling.

Max had an inspiration. "When did Charley die?" he asked her.

She stared at the tip of her cigarette. "I know what you're thinking. But you're wrong. Charley died in the summertime."

So she was not commemorating the death of her son tonight. But she was mourning something. He was sure of it; this was his area of expertise.

"Are you upset about—what we talked about the other night?"

"You mean about us getting married? Hell, no. I'd have to be a bigger fool than I already am to want to marry you."

"So it's not you and me that's bothering you."

She didn't answer him.

"It's just the wintertime and Christmas that's bothering you."

"That's right."

"Don't bullshit me, Nora."

She slapped the flat of her hand on the table with a crack. "I'll bullshit you if I want to bullshit you!" she screamed. "Just where the hell do you get off, thinking you've got the right to know every little goddamned thing about me? You don't own me! Nobody owns me!"

"For God's sakes, Nora—"

"*What?*"

"What's eating you up like this?"

"Nothing!" She stood, letting the comforter slide to the floor. "Nothing, nothing, nothing, nothing, nothing! All right? Will you stop *interrogating* me like this? Will you stop *mothering* me like this? I swear to God, there's something sickly about a man who mothers a woman the way you do! You won't even let me breathe. Can you just back off? Can you do that? Can you just back off and leave me the hell *alone* for once?"

He left her alone as she sat in her bath, and stalked furiously through the rooms of the house, picking up magazines and chucking them aside, flicking around the channels on her television, staring out at the frozen gray world through her windows, and then finally gave up, went into the kitchen, and poured himself a stiff vodka tonic. Midway through it he received another inspiration. He went down the hallway and opened the door to the bathroom.

Nora was lying slack in the steaming water, her knees raised up higher than her head.

"One question," Max said, "and then I'll leave you alone."

"What?"

"When's your birthday?"

Nora sunk down deeper into the water.

"Tomorrow," she said.

CHAPTER SIXTEEN

He remembered Janey's twenty-fifth birthday, her last, and how she had stood naked before the mirror in the bedroom and bemoaned the passing of her looks. Her skin, she said, was going dry; wrinkles were cropping up around her eyes and mouth; her bottom was dropping; her breasts were beginning to sag. It was all pure fantasy, of course, but the more Max insisted on the ripe perfection of her beauty, the more stridently Janey had rejected the evidence in front of her eyes. She was like a fabulously wealthy miser who can only brood on the idea of poverty. By the light of this memory she appeared just as silly and shallow as Sara Roth liked to paint her; she had even gone so far as to declare, absurdly, that her life was already behind her—never mind the fact that she happened to be right. And so, Max told himself, if the terrors of aging had frightened Janey out of her senses at the age of twenty-five, certainly Nora had a little temporary insanity coming to her on the eve of her forty-second birthday. Maybe that was why she had refused to have sex with him last night, or why, this morning, she had spoken to him only in glum monosyllables. But he was afraid that wasn't all of it. He was afraid that she had taken the same hard, dry, dispassionate look at their future as she had surely taken of her own aging face in the mirror this morning. And what was there to see? Nothing—their future was as blank as a movie screen once the illusion was over and the lights had come on. If he had any courage at all, what he would give her for her birthday would be the favor of a clean break. Instead, he intended to bribe as much time as he could from her with his love.

Luck was with him. That morning in his office, as he looked through the entertainment section of the *Post-Dispatch,* he saw that *Some Like It Hot* was showing tonight at the Tivoli.

He called Nora at the White Palace and sang her a round of "Happy Birthday." Max couldn't carry a tune to save his life, and his awful attempt drew a grudging laugh out of her.

"You're crazy, I swear."

"How are you feeling today, Nora?"

"Old and washed-up."

"If you're so old and washed-up," he asked, "how are you managing to hold on to a twenty-seven-year-old lover?"

Like a fool, he'd asked the very question that must have been preying on her mind. She didn't answer.

"When do you get home tonight?"

"Five or so."

"I'll be there at six. Wear your Halston blouse and that nice brown skirt you wore to the Horowitzes'. We're going out on the town."

"I'm not sure . . . I'm in the mood for going out."

"Get in the mood."

"Well, where-all are we going?"

"Ah," Max told her, "but that would be telling."

He left the office at five, drawing a dark look from Rosemary—only receptionists and secretaries, she liked to tell him, abandoned the office promptly at closing time—and fought the homecoming traffic in two directions in order to pick up a box of chocolate-covered cherries and a bottle of Stolichnaya vodka. The gifts were intentionally frivolous; he did not want to put any pressure on her by bringing her something expensive. The light touch seemed to work. After putting away several chocolate-covered cherries and a stiff drink of Stoly on the rocks ("It almost tastes like milk," she marveled), she appeared to be his Nora once again and, as if to prove it, pulled him down to the living room floor, where they made up, achingly, for time lost in bed last night. She was as easy to manipulate as his mother, so long as you remembered they were both essentially children in the guise of grown women; but even as Max thought this, he doubted it was true. Every time he felt certain he had a handle on Nora, he found himself gripping the air.

She peppered him with questions during the drive north to the Delmar Loop, but Max steadfastly refused to reveal his plans. And then, when she saw what was on the marquee at the Tivoli theater, she flashed him an inquiring grin, gave out a hoot, and flung her arms around his neck, blocking his view of the traffic.

"Jesus Christ, Nora—are you trying to kill us?"

"You sweet man," she said. "I think I owe you a blow-job."

The Tivoli was St. Louis's only repertory cinema, and the only theater, too, where lemonade, granola, and herbal teas were available at the concession stand. The crowd in the lobby was made up mostly of scruffy academic types and some angry-headed punkers—nobody Max was likely to know. Yet he found himself, against his will, furtively scanning their faces for anyone at all who might recognize him. He tightened his hold around Nora's waist, but her unsuspecting warmth only made his guilt burn hotter. He'd thought, or hoped, that the Horowitzes' party would have exorcised once and for all his fear of being seen with Nora; evidently his shameful cowardice was more deeply embedded than that. When, when was he finally going to get past this despicable glitch in his heart? What, for instance, was he planning to do when the Spindler office Christmas party rolled around next week and pushed the question right into his face? Lie to her again and pretend he was simply working late next Thursday? Sit her down and explain to her in a fatherly way that he was not inviting her for her own good—that if she'd felt self-conscious and uncomfortable at the Horowitzes' party, then such a gathering of glib advertising slickos would positively demoralize her? Or would he own up to his love, swallow the bitter pill of his reputation, and present her to the disbelieving crowd, Rosemary, clients, and all?

He asked her in a congested voice if she wanted any popcorn.

"No," she said. "I think it's starting." Then she led

him, with the pure excitement of a child, into the darkened theater.

Max had seen *Some Like It Hot* before, but only now did he see that it was better than just a very good movie, and that Marilyn Monroe was something more than a very good actress. What made him want to keep drinking in the sight of her—never mind the script, never mind, even, her performance—was some hypnotic quality in Marilyn herself, some perfectly pitched, perfectly balanced *uneasiness* between her vulnerability and her power as a woman. And then there was her amazing fleshiness. It looked as if he could reach out and encircle the pliancy of her waist through that black and white flatness. She was—like Nora, after all—as dense with her own particular being as a crystal of lead. Max touched Nora on the wrist, but she was elsewhere. She'd been sitting bolt upright all through the movie with her arms tightly crossed, and when he looked at her, as often as not, her lips were moving along devoutly with the dialogue. She did not laugh at the laugh lines; she was in a sphere too rarefied for humor to reach. When he took her hand, her fingers closed tightly over his, but this, he sensed, was a mere muscular reaction taking place outside the pale of her concentration. She was enthralled.

Now Marilyn, like a dippy, lascivious, superbly fleshed angel, appeared in Tony Curtis's doorway and said, "It's me, Sugar."

Nora drew in a sharp breath.

Max reached inside her coat and cupped her between the legs.

"Have I ever mentioned," he asked her, "how insanely in love with you I am?"

She firmly took his hand and moved it to the arm of his seat.

"Just watch the movie," she told him.

But there was a thin smile of happiness on her lips.

"She was a regular holy terror when they were making that movie," Nora said. "She was always two or three hours late, and when she finally did get there, she kept flubbing her lines. I mean the simplest lines. You remember that part where she comes in and says, 'It's me, Sugar'? Well, that took something like fifty takes before she got it right. She kept saying things like, 'It's Sugar, me.' Finally the director, Billy Wilder, had to write out the line on a card and hold it up for her. Can you imagine?" Nora paused to put a Winston into her mouth, and before she could bring her match to it, a waiter smoothly interceded with his lighter. Nora showed him an amused smile. "One of these times," she told him, "I swear I'm going to beat you to the punch." The waiter politely laughed and moved off. Nora picked up the Beaujolais which she had earlier pronounced to be "pretty good," took a hefty swallow of it, and went on. "But that's the amazing thing. The whole time she was making that movie, she was so depressed and so fucked-up on sleeping pills, why, the poor woman could hardly even walk. But every book I read on her says that was her best performance of all time. And it *was*. You saw how good she was, didn't you, Max?"

"Yes," he said. "She was—angelic."

Nora beamed at him. Another waiter stopped by the table and performed a series of moves as deftly as a magician: he refilled Nora's wineglass, giving the neck of the bottle a neat twist as he lifted it; he whisked away her small white porcelain ashtray, dipped his hand into the pocket of his tuxedo jacket, produced another ashtray, and slipped it next to Nora's elbow; he brushed away with two strokes of a small metal bar the crumbs beside her bread plate; with one pass of his palm he lined up her silverware so that it once again lay at right angles to her dinner plate. Nora watched him go, looked back at Max, and giggled, covering her mouth with the back of her hand. "It's like a room full of Max Baron clones," she said. "Everyone here is just as persnickety as you."

"It must be nice to get paid for it," Max said.

They were at Tony's, and all around them in the quiet intensity of the dining room the tuxedoed waiters were circulating as smoothly and soundlessly as shadows. The last time Max had been to Tony's, he'd never made it as far as the dining room. That was the night of Janey's graduation from college, when the two of them had given up waiting for a table in the cocktail lounge, and had driven instead to the White Palace at Grand and Gravois. Nora had been working there at the time, and it was not at all impossible that she had been the one to sell them their cheese fries, shakes, and bellybombers. An irony as huge as Everest loomed over that connection, but for the moment Max couldn't see a shred of significance in it. Across from their table, behind Nora's head, hung a fat chandelier in the stairwell (the maître d' had led them into the dining room by walking backward up those stairs with a face as composed and humorless as a bailiff's) and against that glittering globe of lights Nora's profile shimmered. There was no finer restaurant in St. Louis than Tony's, and certainly none more expensive, and Nora was taking it all in, Max thought, with just the right proportions of bedazzlement and sarcasm. The salad cart arrived. It took three waiters, with the reverence of acolytes preparing the Mass, to toss, dish up, and serve their salads. Nora watched them with an imperfectly restrained smirk until they had all three glided away with their cart, then picked up her salad fork—which one of the waiters had thoughtfully tipped to the side of her plate, just in case, God forbid, she didn't know which fork to use—and dug in.

Max started in on his own salad, which had an undertone of sweet olive oil that was absolutely delicious, and noticed, as he raised his head, that on the other side of the room, past the low-hanging chandelier, a woman whose boyish figure and close-cropped red hair were remarkably like Rosemary's was getting up from a table. His stomach seemed to lift and bump his heart. Rosemary had turned and was rooting for something in her purse. Coming up beside her were Stephanie Deluc and a short fat man with a heavy beard. They had been there, on the other side of the chandelier, the whole time he'd been sitting here with Nora. Apparently they were leaving. He considered in his panic simply ducking his head and letting them go—but no, Rosemary might still spot him and come over to the table. He stood. "Excuse me for a minute," he said to Nora.

"Where are you going?"

"I'll be right back."

He moved through the dining room with his heart knocking at his rib cage like a clenched fist, and caught up with Rosemary's party.

"Well, will you speak of the devil?" Rosemary said. She looked lovely in her velvety green dress. "We were just talking about you, Max."

"Nothing nice, I hope."

"I was singing your praises to the heavens, as usual. You know Stephanie, of course. This is her husband, Ralph Deluc. Meet Max Baron—my star writer."

Max shook hands with Ralph Deluc, a surprisingly squat and ugly counterpart to a woman of Stephanie's buxom charms—another anomalous chink, he thought, in the queer armor of this woman's personality—and then shook hands with Stephanie.

Ralph Deluc nodded his gnomish head at Max and said, "Stephanie informs me that you're quite the wordsmith."

Max gave a dumb, sheepish shrug. "Did you all have a nice dinner?" he asked them.

Stephanie laughed and put a hand to the throat of her black sequined dress. "It was positively sinful," she said. "You feel like you ought to go out and do charity work after a meal like that."

Rosemary touched Max on the arm. "Max, what are you doing here? Nobody in their right minds even *thinks* about coming to this place unless they're on an expense account." This drew a laugh from Stephanie and her husband. "Where's your date?" she asked him.

Now the fist of his heart came unclenched. He willed himself not to glance in Nora's direction.

"She's in the ladies' room," he said.

"What rotten luck. I would've liked to have met her."

Ralph Deluc was tapping his wristwatch. "We've got to be running," he said.

"We told the baby-sitter we'd be home an hour ago," Stephanie said.

Again his vision of Stephanie blurred and wobbled; he hadn't thought of her as having children.

Her husband gave an impatient roll of his fat shoulders and said, "Very nice meeting you, Max. Keep up the good work."

"Oh, he will," Rosemary said, and winked at him. "Don't you worry about that."

"Good to see you, Max," Stephanie said.

Then the three of them were off and moving down the stairs and gone behind the big chandelier.

When he returned to the table, Nora's brow was furrowed at him. Her salad plate was gone, her wineglass refilled. She was fiddling with her earring.

"Max?" Nora dropped her hand to the tablecloth. "Who were those people?"

Max pulled out his chair and bumped it as he moved to sit down; a waiter materialized to help him in. "Thank you," he said to the waiter's retreating back.

"Max?"

"Yes?"

"Who were those people?"

Just some people I know. It could have been as easy as that. *Mr. and Mrs. Harry Schmendrick and their lovely daughter, Lucille.* How could she have known the difference? Instead, as if he were angling for Nora's outrage, he told her the truth.

"That was my boss," he said. "Rosemary Powers."

"Which one?"

"The one with the red hair."

"Well, who were those other people?"

He took a swallow of his wine, which tasted bitter. "The woman was Stephanie Deluc. I've told you about her. She's the client at Fidelity Federal, La Machine, as Rosemary likes to call her. And the man with them was her husband."

Nora began to twist her black coral earring again.

A waiter appeared and held his salad plate at a tilt; Max told him he could take it away.

"Why didn't you introduce me to them?" Nora asked. The whole restaurant seemed to sink a few inches.

"I, well, they were in a hurry to go."

"Oh."

"Evidently Stephanie had told their baby-sitter they'd be home an hour ago."

"I see."

"And her husband looked like he was about to drop a calf or something. Nora?"

"What?"

"I haven't really told you much about Stephanie Deluc, have I? It's the damnedest thing. In most ways the woman is a complete automaton. But there are these certain strange glitches in her personality—"

Nora dropped her hand and faced away from him. He caught a rare, momentary view of the curve of her eyeball; she blinked and the surface of it flooded. She looked back at him with shining eyes.

"Why didn't you introduce me?" she asked him again. "Don't lie to me, Max. Tell me."

"I . . . don't know why."

Nora studied him for a moment. Then she reached for the bottle of Beaujolais as a waiter hurried over to assist her. "I can pour my own goddamned wine," she told him.

"Very good," the waiter replied with a tight smile, and slipped away.

Nora filled her wineglass to the brim. She drained it in one long pull, as if she were drinking water. Then she looked at Max with what struck him as a terrible sad clarity. "I'm forty-two years old tonight," she said. "Do you think I'm a fool?"

"No. I don't think you're a fool."

"Good," Nora said. "I just wanted to make sure we got that straight." She set her purse on the table. Then she arose from her chair, dropped her balled up napkin onto the tablecloth, and swaggered off through the dining room, forcing a waiter to roll his dessert cart out of her path. She passed him without breaking stride, started down the stairs, and disappeared behind the bright bloated ball of the chandelier.

Max waited. He waited as the entrees were elaborately served—his stuffed quail, her New York strip—and waited as their dinners grew cold. He had them pack up the food and bring him his bill, and when he saw the total, he handed it back and ordered a double scotch on the rocks and continued to wait.

But Nora never reappeared at the table.

———————

She had managed somehow to talk the hatcheck girl and the parking lot attendant into handing over her coat and his car without being presented with the tickets—both of which were still in the pocket of his sport coat—and Max had been forced to take a cab back to her house. His Volvo was parked out front with the keys in the ignition. But her house, for once, was locked, and her rusty Impala was gone.

He called her when he got home, and he went on calling ten or twelve times a day until, on the third day of his misery, a recorded voice informed him that her phone had been disconnected. Each time he drove into Dogtown, he found her house just as he had left it before: as closed-up, silent, and indifferent to his yearning as a tomb. He paid a visit to the White Palace. He was told that Nora no longer worked there. She had simply come in on Monday morning and quit. Had she given any reason? No. Did she say what her plans were? No, she hadn't said. Well, was she taking a leave of absence or had she quit the place for good? Nobody takes a leave of absence, he was told; once you quit this place, you're gone.

Max became physically sick, which he almost didn't mind; it only seemed just that his body should mirror the fevered, aching, nauseated state of his soul. But in two days, almost against his will, he was better, and after work he made what he told himself would be his final stop at Nora's house.

The letter was taped to the side of the black mailbox which he had installed on her lawn not one month before. He didn't even bother trying her front door. She was gone, and the certainty of it quieted him. He stood for a spell with the envelope in his gloved hand, watching the snow fall on her roof and lawn. Then he went into his car, started up the engine, and slowly worked open the envelope.

Her handwriting was unfamiliar to him. The only other written document of hers in his possession was the torn corner of notebook paper bearing her name and phone number, which he had brought home with him after their first night together. He was surprised by the letter's length; there were two densely filled pages. Her handwriting was labored and childish, tight at the start and then progressively looser and loopier; she had probably been drinking when she wrote it. She had put the date at the top, and had set up the salutation and valediction where they belonged. He would not have noted such things an educated writer. But coming from Nora, it was heartbreaking. Somehow she had dredged up this long-buried schoolgirl knowledge and correctly applied it, as if she feared she were going to be graded. At the last, she had not wanted him to think her ignorant.

December 20, 1983

Dear Max:

By the time you read this I will be gone. I cant tell you where I'm going because you'll try and follow me, knowing you. All I can tell you is I'm allright and I'll be taken care of just fine. So don't you worry, please. I'm not worried about you. You'll do fine. Things will get better for you now that I'm out of your life. You'll find yourself a nice girl whose decent and you won't be ashamed of and raise a family and forget all about me (if you're smart).

This is very hard for me to write and I know I'm botching it. Also, I'm a little drunk right now, which is the only way I can write this letter.

I'm sorry for the way I walked out on you at

Tony's. You've been so sweet and good to me in so many ways you didn't deserve it. But I knew when you didn't introduce me to your boss & those people that you'd never be able to take me into your life all the way (I guess I knew it before, but not in the same way—does that make sense?) and so I just had to go. I don't blame you for it. I never did belong in your life and there wasn't no way you were going to fit me into it, and so now it's all for the best. (Even if you don't believe me.)

I already miss you, Max. I miss you so much. I feel like hell and I guess your feeling like hell too and I'm sorry. You won't believe me, but I'm doing this for both of us and if I told you where I am it would only make it harder on us both, so I won't.

I have to tell you something. I lied about Charley. He wasn't good & sweet like I said. He was a fuck-up from the word go just like me & Jack. He was wild and mean and we never did get along. I didnt even like him as a baby much. He had the devil in him. Starting at age 11 he got into drugs and when he was thirteen he drownd in the River De Pere. They found qualoods and alcohol in his bloodstream. It's the worst thing that ever happened to me & I'll never get over it as long as I live. I think sometimes he did it to get back at Jack & me, and I wouldn't blame him if he did. We were horrible parents and we raised him shitty. I was just as bad as Jack in my own way. I never have been good for anybody (you included) but I'm going to try my damndest to change that now & be different. Anyway, Charley is the only thing I kept lying about to you (the rest is true).

I could lie to you now and make up some place where I went, or make up some reason for leaving that's not true. But I dont wnat any lies between us now. So instead I wonn't say anything at all. Someday you'll be glad I did this. I didn't belong in your life & was only going to screw it up.

Don't ever ever think that I don't love you. I

love you now and I always loved you and I'll love
you for as long as I live. Try not to hate me.

Love,
Nora

PART THREE

CHAPTER SEVENTEEN

Max reordered his life. He took up, once again, with his nightly regimen of Great Literature, plowing through the remainder of Shakespeare and then plunging into the darker waters of Dostoevsky, whose mood of grim fatalism nicely matched his own. He picked up again with his Friday night get-togethers over at the Horowitzes' (Klugman was in the process of an unsurprising divorce, Rachel was blissfully pregnant, and Horowitz seemed to be slipping ever more rapidly into a smug middle age), and every Sunday he dutifully parked his body at his mother's house and endured her hysteria and infantilism largely by ignoring her. He firmly resisted the overtures of women, which seemed to be coming especially thick and fast since Nora's departure—as if the scent of aroused sex were still bristling on his skin—but he managed to stick to his monkish self-discipline and did not date; his heart was simply too bruised for handling. In the daytime he concentrated furiously on his work; at night he did battle with his various griefs. Some of the time he didn't even know what he was mourning—Janey dead, Nora gone, or some piece of his personality that had been lost, the part that savored life, that took joy in its own appetites, and which, like a spurned lover, had packed up in exasperation and deserted him. But most of the time he knew precisely what kept him pacing the floor of his apartment and flipping over in his bed like a churning watermill: Nora refused to go. He still wanted her.

It wasn't until the spring that Rosemary finally cornered Max in a booth at O'Connell's and got him to tell the story of his mysterious love affair. It was odd talking about it. Already that period of his life, so remarkable, so peculiar, so intense, so unconnected to anything he had known before or since, seemed oceans away from the life he was living. It was as if he'd returned from a long sojourn in some wildly exotic locale, the outback of Australia, the frozen tundra of Mongolia, the rain forests of Borneo, and now, four months later, set up again amid bland and familiar surroundings, it boggled belief to think that he had ever made the trip at all. Indeed, the only concrete evidence he had of Nora's existence was in the negative: a gap in his bookshelves where *Huckleberry Finn* and *The Portable Mark Twain* had stood, a house in Dogtown where nobody lived, a White Palace restaurant where she no longer worked, a valedictory love letter with no return address.

"You didn't have any idea where she might have gone?" Rosemary asked him.

"No. The problem was, I didn't know anybody she knew—except for her sister in New York."

"Did you call?"

"Yes. But Judy hadn't heard from her either."

"She could have been lying, you know."

"That wouldn't have changed anything."

"What about her house? It seems awfully odd that a woman who hardly owns anything would leave everything she owned behind."

"There was a For Sale sign on the lawn the last time I checked, back in February. I talked to the real estate company, but they wouldn't tell me a thing."

"Naturally. Did you try a detective agency?"

Max looked up from his knotted swizzle stick.

Rosemary took a sip of her Old Bushmill's, sat back against the booth, and shrugged. "That's what detectives are for, you know."

Max shook his head. "The point is, she didn't want to have anything to do with me. She knew how to get in touch with me. And she chose not to."

"So far."

"She's gone, Rosemary."

This evening Rosemary was wearing her Left Bank outfit: maroon turtleneck sweater, brown leather jacket, black beret. She slouched forward onto her crossed arms and contemplated the whiskey in her glass. "I would've liked her," she said.

"You would have?"

"Yes, goddammit. Why not? I'm *sure* I would've liked her. Why didn't I ever get to meet her?"

Max hesitated. "You almost did meet her," he said, and went on to tell her what he had omitted from his story, about the night at Tony's when he'd pretended Nora was in the ladies' room, when in fact she had been watching Rosemary's party from the other side of the restaurant. The confession failed to lighten his heart. The shame of it still burned with its original heat.

Rosemary studied him with a deep frown. "Poor baby," she said. "You really botched it, didn't you?"

Max finished off his drink.

"So you denied her."

"That's a way of putting it."

"And she knew it, too, didn't she?"

"Yes."

"And you've decided not to forgive yourself, haven't you?"

Max's throat thickened. "It seems to me there are certain things you don't have the right to forgive yourself for."

"You could always look at it from the Catholic standpoint. Peter denied his own best lover three times, and he certainly didn't go to hell for it."

"I'm not St. Peter," Max said. "And if Nora turns out to be Jesus Christ, we're all in deep trouble."

Rosemary laughed and signaled the waitress for another round.

Neither one of them said anything until their drinks arrived.

"So what if you hadn't been ashamed of her?" Rosemary asked him. "What would have happened then?"

"Maybe I would have asked her to marry me."

"I wonder why she didn't stick around long enough for you to propose."

"I wasn't going to propose to her, Rosemary."

"Because you were ashamed of her."

"Yes. My God—do we have to keep coming back to that?"

"It seems to be the crux of it, doesn't it?" Rosemary reached across the table and gave his hand a squeeze. "I'm sorry, Max. You don't need me to make you feel any guiltier than you already feel. Should we talk about something else?"

"No. It's a relief talking to you about her, Rosemary. Everyone else only seems to see her as some kind of projection of my neurosis. But you seem interested in *her*."

"Well, like I said, I would've liked her."

"Why?"

Rosemary shrugged. "Because she was poor and had a lousy job and had no prospects of anything better, and yet she still refused to let you take care of her. Because she had the chutzpah to seduce you in the first place. And because . . . well, because she had the bravery and clearsightedness to leave you when she did."

"You like her because she left me?"

Rosemary smiled at him. "Don't you?"

The question was a dizzying one. But yes—he did. Certainly she'd shown more bravery and clearsightedness in her decision to leave him then he'd been capable of at the time, or was probably capable of now. And she'd looked good, admirable, and fiery, swaggering through that dining room and nearly upsetting that dessert cart in her path as she willed her way out of his life.

For all he knew, it had been Nora's finest hour.

———————

In April Stephanie Deluc had a new inspiration, which she shared with Max, Rosemary, and Mr. Spindler at a hastily called meeting in her tenth floor snow-white office. The bow at her neck was sky-blue, and the underlying odor she emitted was like a distant whiff of burning rubber.

"I wish I'd brought the article to the office," she said. "Although it does surprise me that not one of you has read this week's *Advertising Age*."

"That's usually the last on my list of things to do," Mr. Spindler said with a pleasant smile.

"Well, it shouldn't be, John. The trade magazines, and *Ad Age* in particular, are your best method for keeping up with the latest-breaking trends in the industry—and that's especially important in a market as isolated as St. Louis. But, be that as it may, the name this article gives to this new trend in creative, and I think it's a pretty good name, is Reality Advertising. What it sets out to . . . Max? It looks as though you're enjoying a private joke."

Rosemary had sternly warned him about his propensity for talking too much at these meetings with Stephanie, but Max was unable now to keep his mouth shut. The longer he dealt with this woman, the more deeply she seemed to get under his skin. "Well, listen to it," he said. "Reality Advertising—it sounds something like 'jumbo shrimp,' doesn't it?"

"Meaning what?" Stephanie asked him.

"It's a contradiction in terms. I never thought advertising had much connection with reality."

Rosemary closed her lighter with an emphatic clack. "Why don't you let Stephanie finish her thought?" she asked Max.

"Thank you," Stephanie said. "Now . . ." She folded her hands primly in front of her, schoolgirl fashion. "The spot this article cites is the one currently running on television for Anacin. I'm sure you've all seen it, but let me just reiterate the gist of it for you. We see a coal miner in close-up. No attempt is made to pretty him up. His hair is mussed and wild and his face is streaked with dirt. His delivery is gruff, halting—this obviously isn't any smooth, artificial announcer hired for this commercial, but a real human being speaking his mind. He says something to the effect of, 'When I get a headache, I can't afford to mess around with any halfway measures. Not in my line of work. The pain gets me right here (and he points to a place in his forehead) and I need real relief and I need it fast. That's why I take Anacin. Because in my line of work, a headache is nothing to treat with kid gloves.' That's the spot, basically. It absolutely *rivets* our attention, because for once we have a real human being speaking to us on real human terms about a problem we all share. Instead of the usual blue-skies-and-candy backdrop to our sales message, we employ a straightforward, hard-bitten view of reality, and because our presentation is so credible, the viewer is *convinced*. This seems to me a wholly new and fresh creative approach, and I want you to know that I'm very, very excited about it. And I want to see what we can do with it in our upcoming campaign for the 'safety and security' story at Fidelity Federal.''

Stephanie showed them all her glassy smile and waited.

Rosemary ground out her cigarette. ''Let me just play the devil's advocate here for a moment, Stephanie. I agree that such an approach worked well for that particular product. After all, there's nothing pretty about a headache. But how would such a treatment work for Fidelity Federal?''

''That was my very next point. I think it fits like a glove. Who are our customers? By and large senior citizens who are terrified of losing their life savings. They don't want to gamble with their money; they don't want to speculate. They remember the Depression and they know how unpredictable life really is. Their worries are real—and we have a real solution. Here, their money is safe. Savings here are backed up by one hundred thousand dollars in FSLIC insurance, and your rate of return is guaranteed as well. Now, I think we can sell that institutional perception through a creative execution that doesn't pull punches, and that's grounded in hard reality. So what I want to see from you, Rosemary, and from you, Max, is a spot so real, so uncompromising, so hard-hitting, that you can taste the grit of it in your mouth. And if we can accomplish this, we'll have a television presence that sets us completely apart from every other financial institution in the market.''

Rosemary smoothed her skirt and hiked up her smile. ''If I could, Stephanie, let me play the devil's advocate just a little bit longer. It's true that the bulk of our money comes from elderly people who are worried about the safety of their savings. But it would seem to me that our job is to assure them, to *comfort* them with the notion that the big bad wolf isn't going to get them after all, so long as they save with us. What do we want to frighten them for?''

"I'm surprised at you, Rosemary. I thought you prided yourself on your reputation as something of a creative maverick. Those campaigns you did for Vandeman's Beer, for example, so many years ago. Those spots broke a lot of rules—mentioning Anheuser-Busch by name, for instance—and were considered genuine groundbreakers. Are you telling me now that you've lost the fire in your belly? Am I to assume that you're no longer interested in taking creative risks?"

"Of course not."

"Then do you think yourself capable of coming up with a television spot along the lines I've delineated for you?"

"If that's the assignment, of course."

"That's the assignment," Stephanie said.

Interior: greasy-spoon diner. On counter in foreground sit the remains of a meal; in the background is a grill, racks of Campbell soups, coffee machine, etc. Open on middle-aged woman in soiled uniform clearing away dishes. She is neither attractive nor unattractive; neither is she plain. She has severe, striking features; her mouth is wide; her hair is jet-black and arranged in a bun, from which a few loose strands are hanging down. Her makeup is heavy-handed. She looks tired and her movements are rather slovenly. Her speech is touched by the soft, lilting cadences of out-state Missouri; nevertheless it is a St. Louis accent, from Dogtown or the South Side. Obviously she has been through the mill, but beneath her surface frowsiness is a kind of dignity, a certain bravery and clearsightedness. She addresses the camera casually—placing the viewer in the position of a patron at the diner—as she goes about her work. WOMAN: If I'm anything at all, it's a survivor. But Lord, it hasn't been easy. (*She finishes wiping down counter and slaps a hamburger onto the grill.*) WOMAN: Still, with what I've managed to lay aside on the wages I earn, and what with an occasional alimony check, I've got me a little nest egg saved

up. It's not much. But it's all I got in this world. And I
know how uncertain this world can be. (*She crosses back
to lunch counter, picks up cigarette she's left burning in
ashtray, and smokes.*) WOMAN: That's how come I keep my
savings at Fidelity Federal. They pay a top return, and
maybe more important, that money's insured to one hundred thousand dollars by the FSLIC, an agency of the
federal government. (*Camera tightens in.*) WOMAN: Look—
saving at Fidelity Federal hasn't solved all my problems.
Not by a long shot. But it *has* given me one less thing to
worry about. And for a woman like me, that makes a lot
of difference. (*Freeze frame on woman as she stares off
pensively past camera: super: Fidelity Federal.*) ANNOUNCER
VOICEOVER: Fidelity Federal . . . in an uncertain world, it's
one thing you can be certain about. (*Fade to black.*)

Once the inspiration seized him, Max was carried
along on a wave of exultation and guilt, and the words
seemed to appear of their own volition on the yellow
second sheet in his typewriter. He shot up from his chair
and paced his office, then sat back down and read the
copy. It was exactly what La Machine was looking for.
The damned thing would work, as long as he could find
the right actress; under his informed and impassioned
direction, the spot would fairly shimmer with reality. Had
he thought that Nora was still in the St. Louis area, and
might catch the spot, he would have squelched the idea
the moment it came to him. But she was far away—he
was sure of it—and would have no way of ever guessing,
as she streaked down the Pennsylvania Turnpike with her
Winston hanging from her mouth, or batted her eyelashes
at the paper-products salesman in a cocktail lounge in
Phoenix, or scratched her elbow as she waited for her
change at a 7-Eleven store in Monterrey, that Max had
so ruthlessly used her, swapped her beloved image for
a buck, and was now feeling the shaky triumph of a blas-
phemer. The stains were adding up on his soul; it wasn't
enough that he had betrayed Nora when they were together. Now that she was gone, he was going to sell
her down the river as well. And why not? His heartache
had to be good for something. He was merely putting

it to constructive use. And wasn't this, after all, the traditional wellspring of art?

"Art, my fucking ass," Max said aloud as he pulled the copy from his typewriter. He nearly broke into a run as he made for Rosemary's office; he needed to get it into her hands before he had a chance to second-guess himself.

Rosemary studied it for a long time, then removed her reading glasses, held up the yellow sheet of copy, and pointed to it.

"Anybody I know?" she asked him.

From the desk of Stephanie Deluc to:
John Spindler, Rosemary Powers, Max Baron.

RE: "Reality Advertising" Institutional TV Spot

Bravo! Better, even, than I had anticipated. You are all to be congratulated on the high level of quality and the complete credibility of this execution. The principal seems all at once the prototype of the social class she represents, as well as a distinct individual. She is not someone we would care to know personally, of course, but she *is* someone we can believe in as she speaks—a genuine, hardbitten, unsentimentalized working-class drudge who's "been through the wringer" and "tells it like it is." Truly an inspired creation! I'm very excited about this, and have already commended you on it to the board of directors.

Questions and reservations:

1) Is she too sleazy? Does her hair have to be coming undone, for instance? When the copy direction reads that her uniform is "soiled," does this mean big sloppy ketchup stains, or what? We don't want to make her too slovenly—the danger with this character is that she will appear merely disgusting. On the other hand, we don't want to clean her up to the point that she loses credibility. Strike a happy medium.

2) Nix on the smoking. Showing our principal smoking a cigarette as she delivers the sales message is out of the question. The negative impact could be tremendous. Come up with some other business to keep the eye occupied toward the end of the spot. (Maybe having her unwrap and chew a stick of gum might do the trick—but I'll leave the fine detailing up to you.)

3) I want final authority over choosing the actress. She must not be anyone recognizable in the market. If you need to send to Chicago for talent, I think our budget can absorb that. Meanwhile, I suggest you hold auditions at the earliest possible time, narrow the field down to two or three candidates, and show me the head sheets.

The flight will begin on May 1. I need a finished cassette of the spot by this Friday to show to a meeting of the board of directors. Please let me know when you'll be shooting and where, so that I can make arrangements to be on the set. Again, congrats on a job well done!

                                        Stephanie Deluc

———————————

Elizabeth Ritter, five feet seven inches, 135 pounds, brown hair, green eyes, age range thirty to forty-nine, took one more moment to look at the script, then rolled it into a baton, crossed her arms, and approached the far end of the conference table from where Max and Rosemary sat. She narrowed her eyes, threw back her head, and declaimed in a belligerently upbeat tone of voice, "If I'm anything at all, it's a survivor. But Lord, it hasn't been easy!"

"Uh—Elizabeth?"

She stopped herself in mid-sentence. "What's wrong?"

"I think maybe it's just a little too . . . ballsy," Max said.

"I thought you wanted it ballsy."

"Well, yes. But more of a *restrained* ballsy, if you know what I mean. I don't want her coming off like Ethel Merman."

Elizabeth frowned and nodded, absorbing, as was her professional duty, another inadvertent insult from another director who was failing to communicate what he wanted. "Restrained ballsy," she repeated.

"The woman is exhausted," Max said. "Her whole life has exhausted her. But she's still tough, still strong, because she has to be—do you see what I'm saying? If anything, she's a little bit languid, but in a hard-edged way."

"Languid in a hard-edged way," Elizabeth said.

Max was rubbing with both index fingers the bridge of his nose. "Let's just try it again and see if we come any closer."

Beside him Rosemary sighed and lit up another Balkan Sobrane.

Elizabeth struggled through the reading uninterrupted. Then she slapped her thigh with the rolled-up script and gave her head a furious shake. "I was too strident, wasn't I? I could *feel* I was too strident."

"You were fine," Rosemary said with a smile.

"I was almost there," Elizabeth said. "Can I give it another shot?"

"I'm afraid we don't have the time. But thank you, Elizabeth. We'll be making a decision later on this afternoon, and you'll be notified."

Elizabeth pressed upon them her new head sheet and resume, which the talent agency did not yet have on file, and departed with a bright "Have a nice evening." These brave exits were becoming almost as depressing as the performances. Max began to massage the bridge of his nose again.

"That was number fourteen," Rosemary told him. "Anything positive to say?"

"She seems like a very nice person," Max said into his cupped hands.

"Max, it's nearly five o'clock and we're not any further along than we were at noon."

"Nobody's been right."

"What about—" Rosemary checked the list on her yellow legal pad. "Here. Claudia Resnick. I thought she was just fine."

"She's too pert. She looks like an aging cheerleader."

"All right. What was wrong with Lynette what's-her-name?"

"Steiner. She's from the East Coast, Rosemary."

"So?"

"So she wouldn't know a Missouri accent if it bit her on the ass. You heard what she gave us. She sounded like Scarlett O'Hara."

Rosemary stubbed out her cigarette. "Listen to me, Max. We're looking for an actress to play a role in a television commercial. We're not looking for the reincarnation of your lost lover."

Rosemary was wrong. They were indeed looking for Nora, or for a close approximation of her. Watching himself watch this absurd parade of hopefuls who were pretending, whether they knew it or not, to be the woman he loved, had to have been one of the most bizarre and disconcerting experiences of his life. He felt like Prince Charming at the end of his rope, having already tested every female foot in the kingdom, and now despairing of ever finding the one that would fit the fragile glass slipper—or in this case, the dirty tennis shoe—that belonged to his mysteriously vanished beloved. The audition had been dragging on for more than four hours, and Max didn't think he could endure the sight of one more anxious actress giving out her grotesque imitation of Nora. He was sorry he had ever written the goddamned spot.

"Who's next?" he asked Rosemary.

"Katy McCormick. She's one hell of a good actress, Max."

"I know Katy."

"And she's had very little television exposure—which makes her just what La Machine is looking for."

"She's too young."

"Max—"

"She's not even thirty, Rosemary, and the woman in this spot—"

"Dammit, Max!" Rosemary slapped the table. "We're running out of time and we're running out of actresses, and I've just about run out of patience! You promised me up and down when I recommended this spot that you wouldn't let your private feelings interfere. Do you remember?"

"I remember."

"Good. Now, I'm bringing Katy in here and I want you to watch what she does with an open mind."

Katy's performance was far and away the best of the lot. She had the accent down (it turned out that she had grown up in South St. Louis), and her characterization, even if it was only faintly reminiscent of Nora, was convincing on its own terms.

Later that afternoon Rosemary presented Katy's head-sheet and resume, along with those of two others, to Stephanie Deluc, who for once displayed good judgment, and selected her.

"It dies at the end," Max said.

Dan Green, the director he had requested from Technivision Studios, nodded, twisted the ends of his handlebar moustache, and crossed his arms over the light meter hanging from his neck. He frowned in contemplation of Katy McCormick. "She needs to be doing something," he said. "Some kind of business."

"How about if she's smoking a cigarette?" Katy McCormick said, who, perched atop the lunch counter in front of the mocked-up grill in front of a flat painted to look like a wall of greasy linoleum tiles, was at that moment smoking a cigarette. "I'm good at smoking cigarettes," she said.

"Forget it," Max said. "I had her smoking in the original script and the client scotched it. She wants it absolutely real—but only to a point."

"So I guess that rules out scratching my crotch," Katy
said.

"By all means, go ahead and do it," Dan told her.
"We just won't tape it." He stepped up to Katy and
inspected her from all sides, as if she were a perplexing
piece of sculpture. She wore a dirty blue uniform (the
effect was achieved by throwing it on the floor of the
studio and having Tom, the grip, walk all over it). Her
dark brown hair was up in a bun, with a few loose tendrils
licking down. Her eyes were made up with purple shadow
and plenty of mascara, and on Katy's inspiration they had
left off the obligatory PanCake makeup so that her skin
would appear pallorous under the lights. Katy had aged
her face with shadows and lines, and she possessed,
something like Nora, a strong jawline and high cheekbones. But of course all Max could see was the distance
between the reality and the attempt. Katy's performance
so far had been restrained and intelligent, and her
accent was so close to perfect that it made Max uneasy
to hear it. But Dan was right; there was still a missing
element.

"Something, something," Dan said, and kept twisting
one end of his handlebar moustache.

Then it hit Max.

It had been so obvious that he'd missed it, like a
pencil behind his ear. He approached Katy with a knocking heart, and with an actress's instinct for obliging self-
display, she offered him her profile. There, in the middle
of her left earlobe, was an indentation no bigger than a
freckle.

"Your ears are pierced, right?"

"Right."

"Do you have your earrings with you?"

"I left them in the dressing room."

"Let's see them," Max said.

They were tiny pink roses. Max coached her on the
movement he wanted, and they ran through the spot. As
she neared the end of her speech, Katy reached up and
began to absentmindedly twist her earring, and he saw,
with a dizzying uprush of triumph and longing, that in this

single gesture was crystallized the essence of Nora's specificity.

Now he felt suddenly sick to his stomach, and sat down in the canvas director's chair. He took in a deep breath; he had the urge to bolt from the studio.

"It works," Dan said.

"I know it works."

Dan turned to B.J., the cameraman, and said, "Let's record."

They had it in one take. Dan put his stopwatch to it and showed it to Max.

"Twenty-nine and a half," he said. "That, ladies and gentlemen, is what we refer to in the business as the miracle take."

There was a clacking of high heels on the concrete floor. Coming briskly toward the set from the far end of the studio—which was as vast and gray as an aircraft hanger—were Rosemary and Stephanie Deluc. Although Stephanie was here, technically, as Rosemary's guest, she was the one who led the way, clipboard in hand. Max arose from his chair and introduced her all around; Rosemary already knew everyone here. Stephanie had brought in with her a faint tang of chicken soup. Although he'd known she would be coming to the shoot, he hadn't expected her so soon, and felt—wrongly, of course—that what was going on here was none of Stephanie's business. This was nothing new; whenever a client showed up on the set, he or she was viewed by the actors and crew with the same suspicion that a group of dissident artists might show to the state censor during an unannounced official inspection.

Rosemary was checking out the greasy-spoon set with her hands clasped behind her back. "Didn't we just have lunch here?" she asked Stephanie.

"Well, it's hardly Cafe Balaban," Stephanie said with a laugh, touching the bow at her neck, and it struck Max, uneasily, that she had actually said this in order to impress everyone. She turned to him now. "Please don't let us interfere with the creative process," she told him. "You just keep on working and Rosemary and I will just stand back and observe."

Max gave a shrug and forced a smile. "I think we're done," he said.

"Already?"

"Well, I think that luck was with us."

"But I thought we'd booked the studio until five. Aren't you going to use the time you've got to see that it's absolutely perfect?"

"Sometimes you can ruin something by overworking it," Max said.

"And sometimes you can just railroad something through and fail to come up with the optimum result," Stephanie said with a brittle smile. "And besides, I'd hoped to be able to give a little input here."

Rosemary interceded. "Max might be right, Stephanie. Sometimes things just come together on a shoot, and you can get it on the second or the third or even the first take. I've seen it happen. Why don't we just take a look at what we've got, and then decided if we need to keep on shooting?"

Stephanie turned to Dan Green.

"May we see what you have?"

"Absolutely," Dan said. He spoke into his headset. "We want to see the last take, Stan. And make sure we've got enough audio out here, please."

They all gathered in a half-moon around the monitor, Max standing to one side of Stephanie, Rosemary to the other.

"How long did you say you've been at it?" Stephanie asked him.

"Just about two hours."

"Two hours? Well. Maybe you are the boy genius Rosemary claims you are—if it's perfect, that is."

"You'll have to decide that for yourself," Max said. The anger in his voice was barely concealed and he doubted it had escaped Stephanie's notice. He kept his eyes on the monitor. He heard Stephanie light her cigarette with a sharp intake of air. The spot came on. A plume of smoke discharged from where Stephanie stood and dispersed in front of the screen. She watched most of the spot in silence, but when there were perhaps seven or eight seconds left of it, she abruptly began speaking over Katy's lines.

"What—wait a minute! What's that? What's she doing?"

"Stop tape," Dan said into his headset.

The spot was already over.

Stephanie pivoted and pointed a finger at Dan Green. "I want to see the end of that again."

Dan spoke into his headset again. "We want to see the last half of the spot again, Stan. Try 0750."

"What didn't you like?" Rosemary asked her.

"Just wait a minute and I'll show you." Stephanie sounded grimly pleased.

Max tightened his crossed arms and his heart kicked against his right fist.

The tape scrambled. It stopped on a freeze frame of Katy with her mouth partway open and her eyes closed, then started forward as she moved from the grill to the counter, and said, ". . . an agency of the federal government." Now Katy paused and frowned pensively and reached up with her left hand to the earring in her right ear. "Look," she said, "saving at Fidelity Federal . . ."

"There!" Stephanie shouted, waving her clipboard at the monitor.

"Stop tape," Dan said.

Katy McCormick, eyes closed again, mouth open, stood frozen with her fingers bunched at her ear.

"All right," Stephanie said to Max without looking at him. "What on earth is she supposed to be doing there?"

"She's fiddling with her earring," Max said in a low monotone.

"Why is she fiddling with it?"

His heart kept thumping against his fist. Stephanie, with her mouth crumpled, her eyes bulging, her armpits letting loose with their secret emanations, appeared to him fragile, stupid, utterly ridiculous. He had no fear of her. She was trying to get at something he would simply not let her near; he was like a parent shielding his child

from an assailant. Nothing she could do was going to
move him.

"I asked you a question. Why is she doing that with
her earring?"

"Because," Max said.

"Because? What do you mean because? Because
why?"

"Because that's one of her mannerisms."

Stephanie was blinking at him now. "It's not in the
script," she said. "I saw no reference to anything like it in
the script that I approved, and I know that I never would
have approved of any such thing. It's . . . well, it's disgusting. You may as well have her picking her nose."

"You expressly said," Max told her, "in the memo
that I received, that I was free to come up with some
business at the end of the spot to replace the bit with the
cigarette you cut out. Don't you remember that?"

"All right. You came up with something, and I don't
like it. I want it out."

"Rosemary?" Max said—she was staring at the frozen
image on the monitor and refused to look at him—"how
do you think it comes off?"

Stephanie did an odd thing. She tugged at his sleeve,
like a little girl who was being ignored. "You're not
talking to Rosemary, young man. You're talking to
me. I'm not discussing this with you anymore. I'm telling you. I want it out. Now, how do I make myself any
clearer?"

"You don't know what you're talking about," Max
heard himself say, losing his stomach. "The spot is
perfect the way it stands. You take that bit out, and you'll
ruin it."

"Excuse me," Stephanie said. "But I seem to have
lost track of who the client is here."

"Oh, for chrissakes," Max said, deciding, in a crazy
instant, that he would rather be a human being than an
advertising man. "I'm so sick and tired of your stupidities,
Stephanie. You don't know what you're talking about and
you never have known what you were talking about. The
only reason you haven't fallen flat on your ass up there at

Fidelity Federal is that you've had an agency working for you that's good enough to save you from your own incompetence. If you want the fucking spot changed, change it yourself, because it's obvious to me and everybody else here that you don't have the faintest idea of what the hell you're doing. And one more thing—" He felt the mad transcendental glow of a martyr about to die for the greater glory of something. "You stink. You *smell* bad. Hasn't anybody ever told you that, Stephanie? You smell like a rusty old can of Campbell's chicken soup. You're an expert in the field of product marketing—so just how is it that you've never heard of deodorant?"

Max remembered only two things about what happened next: how Rosemary refused to look at him, and how many long years it seemed to take him to walk the length of the studio until he reached the exit sign.

———————

"How could I not forgive you?" Rosemary said. "All you did was precisely what I've been wishing I had the nerve to do for the past fifteen years in this business. What you did was very brave, very noble, and incredibly stupid."

"I wonder just how stupid it was," Max said.

"You'll find out soon enough."

Rosemary balled up her sandwich wrapper and lobbed it into the trash bin a few feet away from the bench they were sharing. They were in Oak Knoll Park, just a block from the office, facing the artificial pond, with its spiraled chrome sculpture sunk halfway into the glassy water. The spring was in full flush. Birds called to each other, the trees looked girlish with their modest displays of green, and the grass of the park was dotted with other people out on their lunch hours and bright yellow dabs of dandelions. Max supposed that in the next few weeks or months he would be doing plenty of solitary bench-sitting, and hoped the good weather would continue, for as of this morning he was out of a job.

"I just wish this wouldn't have to make things tough on you," Max said.

"You didn't think of that when you told the bitch off, did you?"

Rosemary gave a shake to her head and took his hand. "Forget I said that. I'll muddle through. What I'm worried about is you, Max. You really fucked up, you know. I don't even think you realize how badly you fucked up."

"I'll tell you when I fucked up," he said. "When I wrote a spot featuring somebody who was supposed to be my old lover mouthing banalities about Fidelity Federal. That's when I fucked up."

"And now you've redeemed yourself by getting yourself fired—is that it?"

Max withdrew his hand from hers and leaned forward onto his knees. "I don't know, Rosemary. I don't know anything right now—except that I don't regret it."

"You will."

He looked up at her.

"When do you think you're going to find work again, Max? Do you think it's going to be easy? Maybe you think that because you're a good writer, and good writers are always scarce, that someone is going snap you up just like that. Well, it's not going to happen, Max. I'm telling you this because I'm very, very fond of you and I'm worried about you, and I don't want you to be deceived about what you've done."

"Tell me."

"You told off a client. Not only did you tell off a client, but you told her off in such a way, and in front of such people, that the story's got to be all over town by now. Do you think Katy McCormick or anybody else over there at Technivision is going to be able to keep such a delicious secret to themselves? By the end of this week there won't be a creative director in St. Louis who hasn't heard of your little exploit, or who doesn't think you're one hell of an admirable guy for doing it, or who would hire you if you were the last copywriter on earth. You've established your reputation, Max. You're a writer who tells off clients." Rosemary put an arm around his shoulders. "I'm sorry. I just didn't want to see you go through six months of job-hunting before it dawned on you."

Max sat up straight. "You're assuming that I still want to be in advertising," he said.

"Well, what else are you going to do?"

Max shrugged.

"Maybe there's an opening at a White Palace," he said.

CHAPTER EIGHTEEN

His mother died in August, just a few days before Max's twenty-eighth birthday. He later calculated that at the very moment the Bi-State bus must have crushed her against the parked Chevette on Olive Street, he was sitting with Harvey Fishman and his son Randy in the office of MidAmerica Home Building Supplies, wearily defending a piece of shlocky freelance television copy he had hacked out for them that morning.

"Where's your brain?" Mr. Fishman shouted at him. "Where's your intelligence? Don't you listen when somebody tells you something?" Fishman the elder, a sour and agitated old streetfighter who had never acquired the rudiments of civilized behavior, sat in his high-backed chair with his yellow face sunk between his shoulders. He jabbed at the copy on his desk with a thick forefinger. "I tell you I want Randy saying that we guarantee—you hear?—that we *guarantee* we'll undersell the competition by ten percent, and where do I see it in here? Why spend my money on advertising when we don't even tell them about the ten-percent guarantee? Are we just pulling our peckers here or what?"

"The whole fucking point of the whole fucking spot and he fucking leaves it out," Fishman the younger said. Randy was leaning against a tall file cabinet and staring suspiciously at Max. He wore a meticulously sculpted hairdo, an expensive snug-fitting suit, and a thin gold chain around his hairy neck. He looked like a Jewish pimp.

Max had yet to have a meeting with these two which hadn't deteriorated into a shouting match, although Max himself had never raised his voice. It was Rosemary who

282

had lined him up with this account; she'd gotten the lead from a radio rep and passed it on to Max, explaining that the account was too small for Spindler to bother with. He knew better, however. Rosemary had done it as a favor.

From the outset it had been understood that Randy Fishman would act as the on-camera spokesman; Max had already produced two spots for them (the type of cheap, amateurish thirty-second screaming sessions that came sandwiched between public service announcements on late night television) and Randy had turned out to be even more of a disaster than he'd feared. He took direction no better than a houseplant, he had all the charisma of a bodyguard, and nothing could be done with his hoarse, mushmouthed, assaultive delivery—but no matter. These commercials were such congenital shlock that nothing, really, could ruin them. Shlock, for the most part, was all that Max had been doing since leaving Spindler. He had given some consideration to returning to teaching, but his pride wouldn't allow it. And so the work he had been getting (much of it funneled to him by Rosemary) consisted of quickies for auto parts stores, furniture warehouses, second-rate car dealerships, failing restaurants, and everything he had produced in the past two months or so blended in his memory into one manic bellow. As hard as Max scratched for these nickel-and-dime accounts, and as spartan as his life-style had become (he had vacated Kirkwood and now lived in a much cheaper apartment in Richmond Heights, not far from Dogtown), his money problems were only worsening. He had three thousand dollars in the bank as an untouchable emergency fund. Meanwhile, he was lucky to be pulling in five hundred a month, his mother still required his assistance, and he was in no position to do anything but sit there and take the hysterical abuse—mixed in with an occasional aerosal burst of saliva—which Mr. Fishman was spewing at him from the other side of his chipped oak desk.

Max waited for him to finish. And then he quietly pointed out that the ten-percent guarantee was included in a super at the end of the spot, with an off-camera announcer underscoring it with his voice.

"Wait one goddamned minute," Mr. Fishman said. "I got Randy here as the spokesman and now I'm forking out another two hundred dollars for another announcer to deliver one lousy line? How *else* can I throw my money out the window?"

"It's nothing but rape, what these announcers get paid anyway," Randy said, evidently forgetting that he himself hadn't exactly balked at getting paid.

Max reminded him that it wasn't a matter of choice; union scale was union scale.

"Unions! A bunch of fucking modern-day pirates. That's what your unions are," Randy said.

"We're getting off the subject," Mr. Fishman said. "I want to know why the hell we need a second announcer when we got Randy in there already."

Max, of course, had thought this through. The ten-percent guarantee was the major selling point, and he hadn't wanted it mangled by Randy's murderous delivery. But what did it matter? Garbage was garbage, and they were arguing over the shape and color of the can. "Mr. Fishman," he said—and in his weariness he felt as old as the old man he was addressing—"if you want Randy to deliver that line, I don't have any objection."

"Objection? What's to object? That's what I want."

"Fine," Max said.

Behind him Randy snorted, as if to say, "You'd better believe it's fine," and then, as Max's eyes were drawn to the serene oceanic blue of the sky outside the window, the feeling came over him.

Everything sank—Mr. Fishman and his desk, Randy and the filing cabinet, himself and the chair he was sitting in—as if the foundation of the building had turned to water. An intense presence, female and familiar, was enfolding him like a silent whirlwind, and he was overwhelmed by a sensation of purest longing and regret. He himself was the object of that longing and the subject of that regret. This thing had come to say good-bye.

Once before in his life he'd had such a feeling. It was on a night almost three years before as he'd stood at the kitchen window, washing the dishes from supper, and watched a thunderstorm tearing up the western sky. The same impression of longing and regret—longing and regret that were not yet his own—had hit him, paralyzed him, leaving his hands like drowned things in the soapy water, and he knew, before the phone ever rang, that something had happened to Janey.

Now all he knew was that he had to get home.

Max stood. Mr. Fishman's eyebrows shot up.

"I'm sorry, Mr. Fishman—but I have to go."

"You what? What are you talking about? Sit down."

"I'm not feeling well."

"Are you crazy? We're in the middle of a meeting!"

"I have to go," Max said, and simply left the room.

Until the moment that he got back to his cramped apartment and answered the ringing telephone, he had been convinced in his marrow that something, somewhere, had happened to Nora.

As usual, his mother had been the last thing on his mind.

————————

Her death was as clownish and pathetic as her life. His mother had gone downtown to buy him a birthday card. Why she would have trekked all the way downtown for the strangely juvenile Hallmark card with the grouping of boyish possessions on the front (baseball bat, glove, magnifying glass, slingshot) which was the only thing found in the paper bag at the site of the accident, would have to remain a mystery—as would her reason for suddenly darting out, in the clear, sane sunlight of that August afternoon, into the path of a Bi-State bus that was heavily swinging in toward its stop at Sixth and Olive. Attempting to reconstruct his mother's thoughts was surely an exercise in pointlessness, but Max could not stop trying; maybe she'd suddenly realized, having bought the card, left the store, and crossed the street to her bus stop, that her son was not going to be eleven years old on Thursday, but twenty-eight, a grown man. She'd bought the wrong card! What she should have bought was that other card— the one with the wooden duck decoy and the pipe on the front. But was it still on the rack? Had someone come in and bought it, the last copy? Would the store close in two minutes? She had no time to lose—and so across the street she flew. Or maybe, Max thought, she had merely been dreaming, of the meat she was going to order from Simon Kohn's butcher shop for the birthday dinner she would be cooking for him, or what she was going to say to those goniffs at the graveyard if they didn't get Janey's grave into shape—and simply stepped off the curb and out of this life, not watching or caring where she was going. The driver of the bus had been a middle-aged black woman named Sissy Stubbs. The pun, of course, was irresistible; his mother's life had been stubbed out as carelessly as a cigarette. Mrs. Stubbs had maintained, with good justification, that she had never even seen Max's mother lunge out in front of her—which might have explained why, once his mother was pinned against that parked car, the bus had kept on rolling. She suffered multiple fractures of the spine and an epic catalogue of internal injuries. Her coma lasted only fourteen hours, and she died toward dawn, as Max was having a cup of coffee alone in the hospital cafeteria.

Just as he had three years before, when Janey died, Horowitz carried Max almost single-handedly through the ordeal; he made arrangements for the funeral, offered his apartment as the place to hold the *shiva*, and put Max in touch with his father's lawyer, a clean, soft-spoken old gentleman named Sidney Sachs. Sid explained sadly to Max that there was no case to make against the Bi-State corporation. There were plenty of witnesses, and all agreed that his mother had acted like someone in a trance; nobody driving that bus could have reacted in time to save her. Max pursued it no further. If he'd wanted anything from the Bi-State people, it was simple justice, and justice was not on his side in this case; as always in his mother's life, this final ridiculous pratfall had been nobody's fault but her own.

———————

Because his mother's house was a warehouse of junk,

and his apartment in Richmond Heights too small, the *shiva* was held at the Horowitzes' apartment in Clayton. For everyone's convenience they trimmed the traditional eight days of mourning to two; by the second day the stream of visitors had narrowed to a trickle, and there were long stretches when the only people present were Rachel, with her piece of black lace pinned to her hair, Horowitz, in his dark blue suit, and Max, in his stocking feet. During these lulls they would drink coffee, listlessly pick at the sea of delicatessen food which various guests had deposited on the big oval table in the dining room, and carefully reminisce—carefully because there was so much about his mother that was better left unsaid—until the sound of the doorbell would summon them again.

The moment a guest came through the door, Max seemed to know the depth of sympathy, the quality of sorrow, the texture of discomfort that was in that person's heart. He was as sensitive as a radar dish. When Klugman shook his hand, Max felt his own stomach become shrunken and shriveled like a walnut, and knew just how ravaged Klugman was by his divorce; he was embarrassed for his mother's embarrassed boss, Lou Stein, a colorless man in a bow tie who brought in a tray of desserts from Pratzel's bakery and stayed less than five minutes; when Rosemary appeared with a bottle of Wild Turkey (a sweetly inappropriate gift, as nobody ever drank at these Jewish versions of a wake, but ate instead), what flowed out from him was the same firm, clear love that was flowing out from Rosemary.

But nobody's entrance undid him like Sara Roth's. The gut connection between them—maybe like the connection he still felt to Nora—was something he could neither fathom nor deny, and the moment she saw her lined, exhausted, once-beautiful face at the door, he started to cry again. She had come alone (Bill, she explained, was out of town on business) and carried with her a bunch of daisies. Max held on to her tightly as he wept, and what he felt coming from Sara was a complexity of cross-currents: sadness at this death, regret that she had never liked his mother better, love and worry for Max, and the old revivified pain of Janey's death. He remembered her at that other *shiva*, so similar and so different, when Sara herself had sat in her stocking feet in that row of low wooden mourner's stools, next to Max and Bill and Max's mother, trying to hold up and be brave and play the cordial hostess in her condition of thunderstruck grief. That was the idea of the *shiva*—to keep the mourner occupied, to fasten the mind on the here-and-now—but Sara wouldn't have it. She spent most of the time, to everyone's dismay, locked up in her bedroom. People knocked lightly on the door. Some of them she would admit; others she would ask to go away. "I just can't suffer fools right now," she'd told Max, one of the few visitors she'd allowed in her bedroom. "I can't censor myself right now, and I'm afraid I'll say something to somebody that I'll regret later on."

Now Sara was on the other side of the situation, a guest who had come to pay her respects, and for a half an hour or so she politely greeted whoever had to be greeted, and remembered whoever had to be remembered from that other *shiva* of three years before, then took Max aside in the kitchen.

"I'll bet you could use some fresh air," she said. "You want to go for a walk?"

Max put on his shoes.

It was a Sunday, and the weather was all wrong for mourning. It was unusually mild for a St. Louis August afternoon. The sun shone benevolently; the wind was playful. Sara hooked her arm through his, and as they walked down Wydown Avenue past the stately trees, the dignified brick houses, the occasional jogger or old woman with her poodle, Max had the feeling that he was an invalid, perhaps a dying man, being escorted around the block by a visiting relative for the short time until he would have to be delivered again into the hands of his nurses. Neither one of them felt the need to speak for a while. Then Sara broke the silence.

"How did everything turn out with that woman? What was her name?"

"Nora." It still undid him to push those soft, open-ended syllables out. The heart, Max thought, had plenty of chambers, enough to accommodate everyone you had ever loved or would love, and now one chamber began to freshly ache beside the one that was already aching, to create a kind of harmony of loss. "She broke it off last winter," he said.

"She broke it off? I wouldn't have expected that."

"It turned out she had more guts than I did."

Sara stepped up their pace.

"So is it all over and done with?" she asked him.

He would have lied to Sara just to be done with the subject, but he was incapable of lying; there was no space between himself and his feelings.

"I think I'm still in love with her," he said.

"You mean she still has a place in your heart?"

"I mean I still want her."

"You'll get over it," she said. "You'll meet another woman and fall in love again, and you'll get over it. It's only a matter of time."

Max saw no advantage in disputing her. Besides, his obsession for Nora was becoming harder to defend with the passage of time, even to himself. But there it was—a fire that refused, against all laws of physics, to burn itself out. He did not speak to anyone about Nora now. Horowitz, for instance, was under the delusion that Max had long since purged himself of his fixation for that woman out of *Tobacco Road,* and attributed his lack of interest in women to the morbid tenacity of his grief for Janey.

Sara looked at him appraisingly. "You've put on weight," she said.

Max instinctively touched the bulge of his belly. "You noticed."

"How much have you gained since I saw you last?"

"Fifteen, sixteen pounds." One unexpected effect of near-poverty—or maybe it was just unhappiness—was to make him much hungrier than he had ever been when he was making plenty of money. His face had grown rounder, and when he lay on his back, he could see the curved horizon of his belly.

"It doesn't look good on you," Sara said. "You should lose it."

"Maybe now's my chance. I remember after Janey's death I practically became anorexic."

"Me too. I got sick from not eating, in fact."

Sara tightly clamped his arm and gave out a rough sigh. "I'm so sorry, Max. I'm so sorry for you, and for your mother, and for her whole rotten life. You were the only good thing in it, you know."

A resurgence of tears clamored in his throat; he swallowed them back. He was sick of crying. "I loved her, Sara."

"I know you did."

"But the thing is, I never could stand her."

"I never could stand her, either, Max. Who could?"

"Horowitz. Janey." He thought about adding in Nora, but then thought better of it.

"Well, good for Janey and Horowitz. The fact is, she wasn't easy to like."

"I was her son. I could have learned how to like her."

"You can't force yourself to like somebody, and you shouldn't condemn yourself if you don't."

But he wasn't really paying much attention to Sara's retorts at they walked down that sun-struck street; he wanted only to talk.

"There was this one Passover when we were having the seder at the Horowitzes'. I must have been ten or eleven. Anyway, it got to the part in the seder where we were passing around the maror, and Mrs. Horowitz had committed the terrible infraction of putting nuts in it. My mother was convinced she couldn't eat nuts—they got stuck to the walls of her intestines, or some such crazy thing—and she made a terrible scene about it. You didn't know her when she was younger and at the peak of her energy, Sara, but she was much worse, much more hysterical, and capable of real viciousness. I tried calming her down, and that only made her put her back up higher, and finally Mr. Horowitz told her to leave the table if she couldn't comport herself like a human being. Well, that did it. She used the same line on him as she used on you that time out at the graveyard—about his shit smelling just as bad as hers—and then she went for his eyes with her fingernails. Horowitz and I had to pull her away. After that she ran out screaming from the house and threw herself into the middle of Raymond Street and lay there kicking and raving like a little girl having a tantrum. All the neighbors came out to watch and she put on one hell of a show for them. She kept yelling at the oncoming cars to run her over and put her out of her misery—and I remember standing there on the Horowitzes' front porch and wishing that one of those drivers would just take her advice and put us *both* out of our misery. I couldn't stomach the fact that she was actually my mother, Sara. I wanted to see her dead."

"And you say you were how old when this happened?"

"Ten, I think."

"Do you want to take responsibility now for something you thought when you were ten?"

"That's not it."

"Well, what *is* it?"

"It's that . . . that's the way she died, finally. By throwing herself into the street."

"And what does that mean?"

"I don't know what it means. But I can't stop thinking about it."

"I'll tell you what it means. It means your mother was the kind of hysterical woman who made a habit of throwing herself into the street. That's what it means and that's *all* it means. Were you wishing for your mother's death?"

"You know I wasn't."

"Then what's the problem here?"

"I despised her," Max said. "She was nothing but a shame and an embarrassment to me when I was growing up and—" Nora suddenly appeared to him, shrouded in the sickly violet light of another, more recent shame, but he pushed her out of the picture; it was his mother he meant to talk about now. ". . . and when I got older, nothing really changed. I just learned to mask it better. Not once, Sara—not once did I ever go to see her because I wanted to. Everything I ever did for her I did purely from a sense of obligation."

Sara stopped walking and withdrew her arm from his.

"Is that why you're torturing yourself like this? Because you fulfilled your obligations to your mother?"

"It's because of the way I felt."

"Who cares how you felt? How you felt has nothing to do with it."

They were standing at the green edge of Jackson Park. Sara faced him with crossed arms, a slight wind moving the translucent outline of her salt and pepper hair. "I've got a question for you," she said.

"All right."

"Do you think that if there is a God, He approves of us?"

Max smiled. "I don't see why He would."

"Let me tell you something that might surprise you. I do believe in God. And it's not some cheerful, avuncular Santa Claus sort of God I believe in, but one who knows what's what. And of course He doesn't approve of us. Why should He? But He sustains us, Max. You and me standing here are proof of that. And He doesn't sustain us because we're such wonderful company to have around. He sustains us because He loves us, and He loves us simply because we belong to Him. That's it. There are no conditions. Everyone's completely overblown this idea of approving of people, of *liking* people. You get thrown in with certain people in this life, most of whom you had absolutely no say in choosing—your parents, your children, whoever you've had the strange luck to fall in love with, maybe a friend or two—and those are the people it's your duty to love because those are the people who belong to you. It's not *necessary* to like them or admire them or approve of them. If love were contingent on that, what value would it have?"

The wind continued to play with her salt and pepper hair. Max felt like sitting down on the grass to take in the weight of what she was saying, but he kept standing, barely maintaining his balance, as her words clicked into place like coins dropped down a slot.

"Do you think that after all these years I still delight in Bill's company? He's smug and he's childish and he's horribly repetitious and most of the time he simply bores me to tears. But I stay with him because I love him and because we belong to each other. Who cares how it happened? And you know how I felt about Janey. I probably liked her less than anyone who knew her. She was vain and silly and terribly materialistic and simply skipped through life assuming that everyone she met thought she was God's gift to mankind. She irritated the hell out of me, Max, and from the time she was two years old we were at each other's throats. But I want you to know that nobody, nobody, loved that girl more than I did . . . do." Now Sara's voice caught and she lifted her chin. "I don't berate myself for not having liked Janey better. It wasn't in my power to like her better. But I loved her and I fulfilled my obligations toward her—which just might be the very same thing, when you come right down to it. You loved your mother and you fulfilled your obligations toward her, and that's all that can be reasonably expected of any human being. You look around you, and you determine who really belongs to you, and then you act accordingly. The rest of it is out of your hands." Sara watched him steadily. "Do you believe what I'm telling you, Max?"

You take a look around you, you determine who really belongs to you, and then you act accordingly.

Of course he was grasping at straws—but what else was there to grasp at? Max managed to contain himself until the *shiva* was over and he was back in his own apartment with all his motivations and priorities lined up as carefully behind him as the titles on his bookshelf, then dialed Judy's number in New York.

Although Nora had given every indication of genuinely despising her sister, there was still the outside chance that the two of them might have been in touch since the last time Max talked to Judy, back in December. And if not, he thought, then maybe he could prevail upon Judy to do a little psychic detective work on his behalf. After all, if she had managed, by simply looking into the palm of his hand, to spot Janey's broken neck across the void, how difficult would it be for Judy to zero in on her own living sister as she went about her business (Max assumed) somewhere in America? So his love had finally dragged him down to this: he was seeking supernatural assistance from a sorceress. Maybe it was only fitting that his obsession for an ignorant lower-class woman should end up rendering him as credulous as a loyal reader of the *National Enquirer;* he may as well have been sending in a coupon from its back pages for a phial of holy water from Lourdes. Well, so be it. Max had been hit between the eyes by the Irrational too often in the past few years for him to go on denying its existence. The very fact that he had lost his heart to a woman such as Nora proved there were more things in heaven and earth than had been dreamt of in his philosophy. Besides, what could it hurt to give Judy a call? He was not unlike a terminal cancer patient resorting to the services of a faith healer. The worst that could happen was that he'd wind up in the same boat he was in.

It was Nora who answered the phone.

Max was so unprepared to hear her voice that he couldn't find his own.

"Hello," she said again. "Who is this?"

Now he couldn't decide if he wanted to talk to her at this point, or, if he did want to talk to her, what tone, approach, or logic he should employ.

She waited.

"Mister," she finally said, "if this is the way you get your kicks, you are one sorry motherfucker."

Max opened his mouth and closed it.

Then he softly replaced the receiver in its cradle.

He decided that it would do no good to warn her that he was coming. She might forbid it, and he wasn't sure he could steel himself to act directly against her wishes. On the other hand, if her wishes weren't known, he was free to act on the assumption that she might take him back. The best thing would be simply to show up at her door.

He converted the entire three thousand dollars in his savings account to traveler's checks, then booked a flight to New York for the next morning. It was, of course, impetuous, unwise, and dangerous, and he was leaving himself absolutely nothing to fall back on. But what did that matter? Nora was there.

And there was nothing holding him here.

CHAPTER NINETEEN

I t was Max's first sight of New York, and as he watched it tilt and swerve in the silvery light outside his window, he thought, how strange that his strange love should have brought him as far as this strange city; how strange that the whole immensity of New York should exist, as far as he was concerned, for no other purpose than to house Nora somewhere within its labyrinthine innards. He could hardly think of Nora outside the context of Dogtown, and it seemed that she would expire, like a fish, in the element of any other place. But she was alive down there, all right, smoking a Winston, eating a bologna-and-white-bread sandwich, sedating herself in front of a television, and could have no way of knowing that at this very moment he was in a holding pattern in the blue sky beyond the skyscrapers, preparing to swoop down, like an angel, to reclaim her.

While he still felt an undertone of grief for his mother, the thought of an imminent reunion with Nora provided a counterpoint of nervous exultation. He was brimming over with love. It sprang out like a golden net to include everyone he had left behind; his mother and Janey, both rendered more simple and innocent in death; Horowitz and pregnant Rachel, stalwart in their normalcy; bereft and agitated Klugman; Rosemary still slugging it out in the trenches of a business she despised; Sara Roth, with her sleeplessness and sad clarity. They were oddballs, all of them, hopeless cases, and he loved each of them best at the points where they were weakest. He even allowed himself the illusion that he loved everyone in this cabin, the rather dumpy stewardess, with her rather ducky walk, the snoring businessman across the aisle wearing the pink earplugs, even the drawling pilot, whose face he hadn't seen: he felt like grabbing a microphone and notifying them all that he was on a mission of love, and asking for their blessing.

Instead, he asked the stewardess for a grapefruit juice. He would have preferred a real drink, but clearheaded-ness was required today. Max sipped his juice and en-dured his excitement as the city reeled and glittered underneath him. Finally the pilot announced that they were headed into LaGuardia. The drone of the engines dropped from baritone to bass, the plane began to sink and, Max thought, it fits. Down he went again. The way to Nora had always been a descent.

—————————

He overtipped the cab driver, then stood with his overnight bag on a corner of Sixth Avenue and Fourth Street, gazing with an open mouth at the carnival that was the West Village in the summer. The crowds surged in all directions with the sort of urgency he associated with the last hours of Pompeii; pigeons exploded from the side-walks; all around him was a riot of horns—people seemed to be leaning on their horns for the sheer hell of it, or maybe in the hope that a loud noise would cause the gridlock to dissolve, for the traffic was utterly stopped. This, emphatically, was not St. Louis.

As he made his way up the narrow channel of Fourth Street he saw a pimply young man selling poetry for a dime, a white-faced mime kissing the hand of a man in a three-piece suit, two drag queens walking arm in arm, each with an ice cream cone, an oriental ventriloquist with an oriental dummy on his lap, a string quartet in blue jeans, lifting up above the raucous noise of the city the oddly pastoral strains of Vivaldi. Every restaurant he passed was filled to capacity, every window packed solid with eaters, drinkers, newspaper readers, avid gesticulators. In the window of the Pink Pussycat Boutique were frankly displayed collection of whips, edible underwear, erotic leather goods, and a grouping of impossibly long, heroi-

cally thick dildos jutting upward like a cluster of stalag-
mites—if Nora hadn't gone shopping here already, they
should certainly pay a visit; she would be like a kid in a
candy store. Most of the males Max passed appeared to
be gay: lean, meticulously groomed, and leading airily
from the pelvis as they walked. Everyone moved at the
same burning pace; nobody paid the least attention to the
directives of the streetlights; not one person would look
Max in the eye. He had never seen such a concentration
of jazzed-up humanity. Of course he was as jazzed-up as
everyone else, mostly because of his own urgent business,
but partly due to osmosis, and soon Max was charging
ahead with the rest of the anxious herd, crossing the
streets against the commands of the lights, until he saw
it—the sand-colored wedge-shaped building at the corner
of Seventh Avenue which bore the address on Judy's
business card, housed at the street level Jimmy Day's Bar
and Restaurant, and harbored, somewhere amid all those
inscrutable windows, Nora.

The recklessness of his adventure suddenly came clear
to him. What did he know, except that Judy lived in that
building and that yesterday Nora had answered the phone?
He knew nothing at all, except for the monumental fact
that she was here, or that somebody in that building
would know of her whereabouts, and standing there trans-
fixed on that corner of Sheridan Square, as the multitudes
stampeded around him, he panicked. He seemed to have
forgotten how to move his limbs.

He realized it would be a mistake to simply show up
at her door. She might not be home, for one thing. And if
she were, there was no guarantee that she wouldn't be
sleeping off a hangover, or be in some other way indisposed. He should call her first, and give her the time to
collect herself before she faced him again for the first time
in eight months; he owed her that much. Max went
into Jimmy Day's. The place was high-ceilinged, dripping
with plants, and ringed round, like so many other restaurants along Fourth Street, with picture windows that revealed the diners to the street, the street to the diners;
New York, evidently, was a city that liked to look at itself.
A waitress directed him to the pay phone at the back.

Judy answered.

"Well, of all things!" she bubbled when Max identified himself. "Max! What a surprise! How in the world are you doing, honey?"

"I'm fine, Judy. You?"

"Well, now, I couldn't be better—especially now that I'm a single woman again."

"What? You are? What happened to Bob?"

"Let's just say Bob proved to be something of a disappointment. But that's me, you know. Here I get paid for advising other people on how to avoid mistakes in their lives, and then I just turn right around and make one dumb mistake after another. But that's all water under the bridge now—and besides, you didn't call up just to hear about me, did you?"

"Nora answered your phone yesterday," Max said.

Judy fell silent. Then she gave out a rough sigh. "Max, I'm sorry I had to lie to you that time. But I gave Nora my word of honor that I wouldn't give her away if you ever happened to call—and you know how it is between sisters."

"How long has she been there, Judy?"

"Ever since she left St. Louis."

"Is she there now?"

"Max—"

"Please, Judy. I need to talk to her."

"I can't guarantee she'll come to the phone."

"Would you please give it a try?"

"All right," Judy said. "Just hold on."

The phone was silent at the other end for what seemed like days. Max leaned his forehead against the cool metal of the telephone and tried, as if his will could perform such a thing, to quiet the hammering of his heart. Then he heard footsteps and a clattering noise and Nora's husky voice.

"Max?"

"Hello, Nora."

"Max, are you all right?"

"I'm fine."

"Say something else."

"I'm in New York."

She said nothing.

"How are you doing, Nora?"

"I'm about to shit a brick! What in the hell are you doing in New York?"

"I came to see you."

"No you didn't. That's just plumb crazy. You didn't come all the way up here just to see me."

"All right. I came up here to see the Empire State Building. I've always wanted to see the Empire State Building, and I thought as long as I was in the neighborhood—"

"It's at Thirty-fourth Street," she said.

They listened to each other breathing over the line.

"How did you know I was here?" Nora finally asked him.

"You answered the phone yesterday."

"What? When?"

"I was the obscene phone caller with nothing to say."

"That was you? Why didn't you say something?"

"I didn't expect you to answer. And I guess . . . the cat got my tongue."

"Max, have you gone straight off the deep end or what? Don't you have yourself a girlfriend back in St. Louis by now?"

"You're my girlfriend," he told her in a clogged voice.

"Don't say that! That's just crazy. Too many goddamned things have happened. For all you know, I just might be a whole different person."

"Are you?"

"No. But I'm not the same, either."

"Neither am I."

Max listened to his own breath rasping into the receiver. He hadn't counted on meeting this type of opposition, and that had been stupid of him. Throughout the whole euphoric rush that had transported him from St. Louis to this pay phone at the back of Jimmy Day's, he had blithely ignored the facts: it was Nora who had left him in the first place, and it was Nora who had known all along how to get in touch with him, and hadn't bothered.

"You don't sound exactly overjoyed to hear from me," he said.

She didn't respond to this.

"Have you missed me at all, Nora?"

Still she didn't say anything.

"Have you missed me? I'd appreciate some kind of answer."

"Yes. All right? I missed you."

"Do you still love me?"

"Don't ask me that."

"All right. I'll ask you something else. Do you want to see me?"

"Lord, I don't know! Where are you, anyway?"

"Downstairs at Jimmy Day's."

"Oh, shit."

"What's that supposed to mean?"

"That means you sure as hell know how to put a person's back against the wall, is what it means."

"Do you want to see me or not, Nora?"

"I don't know, goddammit! How the hell do you expect me to know anything when you just up and *spring* yourself on me like this? It's not *fair*, just showing up like this, Max!"

"It wasn't fair just walking out on me like that."

"Look—I'm sorry for the way that happened. I *am* sorry. It hurt me like hell to have to leave you like that. Just don't you go thinking you're the only one who got hurt by this thing."

"Fine. Now that we've established that we've both been hurt, *do you want to see me or not?*"

"Not if you're going to take that sarcastic tone of voice with me," she said.

Here they were again, Max thought. It was just like old times.

"All right, Nora. Here's what I'm going to do. I'm going to get myself a table by the window, order a cup of coffee, and just keep getting refills until closing time. And if you're not here by then, I'm going to take a cab back to LaGuardia and you'll never hear from me again. That's what I'm going to do. Now you can do any goddamned thing you want to do."

In the silence that ensued he was certain she was twisting one of her earrings.

"Give me fifteen minutes," she told him, and hung up.

————————

To hell with clearheadedness, he thought. He ordered an Irish whiskey neat and poured half of it into his lukewarm coffee. He checked his watch: four minutes to go before Nora's fifteen minutes were up. The scene in Sheridan Square was as exuberant and outlandish as a medieval carnival; a brass band stood on one corner, blaring so loud that he could hear it through the window; a black man peddled phosphorescent green hoops, thickly piled down his neck, arms, around his waist; a bearded man glided past on a skateboard.

He turned back to his whiskey and saw her.

She was standing by the horseshoe-shaped bar with crossed arms, looking for him in the wrong direction. She wore blue jeans, a vivid yellow blouse, a leather vest, and a pair of fancy cowboy boots he didn't recognize. Her blue-black hair was straight again, and clasped back in a ponytail. A waitress balancing a tray full of drinks on one hand approached her, gracefully pivoted as she pushed the tray above her head, and said something to her. Nora turned. She spotted him and touched the base of her throat for an instant. He did not wave. Then she took a step in his direction and the old insanity of love took hold of him again: she would never reach his table. It was far more likely that the floor would yawn open and swallow her, that she would be plucked up by the ponytail straight through the ceiling, or that she would disappear in the next moment like a mirage, than that the world would prove so generous as to allow him to hold her again.

And then she was standing before him, palpable, nervous, herself. Even now, after so much time away from her, he couldn't say if she were attractive or not. Her face was Nora's face: that was all the value he could attach to it.

He stood.

"You really are a crazy man, aren't you?" she said.

"Maybe not."

"Well, welcome to the Big Apple. You're looking good, Max."

"I've gotten fat."

"Hell, you've just put on a little weight, is all."

"You look wonderful, Nora."

"Do I?" She touched her hair above one ear, and finally granted him a smile. He'd forgotten how dim and small her teeth were. "I'm sorry we bitched at each other over the phone like that," she said.

"I've missed our bitching sessions, if you want to know the truth."

"You always were a glutton for punishment."

"Was I?"

"Why else would you go out with me?"

He didn't tell her why else. He sensed that restraint, for the time being, was going to be his best strategy. They went on eyeing each other, and the silence between them seemed to gain depth. Nora in her edginess reached for one of her earrings, and Max, unable to check himself, took an awkward half-step in her direction. She raised her chin.

"No," she said. "Please don't try and touch me."

This stung. "Why not?"

"Because I know what used to happen when you touched me."

"Was it that awful?"

"You know it wasn't."

"Then why not give it another shot?"

"Please, Max."

"Not even a friendly hug after all this time?"

She shook her head.

"Well," Max said, sitting down, "it wouldn't have been friendly, anyway."

Nora sat across from him. "Tell me something else that I don't know." Then she hurt him still further by asking: "So where-all are you going to be staying while you're here in New York?"

He glanced at his overnight bag on the floor and

decided on a politician's response. "That all depends," he said. "I haven't really made any arrangements yet."

She did not offer him an invitation.

Max kept a tight grip on himself. Nothing was settled yet. He hadn't come here counting on a struggle, but if he had to fight to win her back, then he would give the best of himself to that fight. The main thing was not to surrender to any premature despair. That would only weaken his position. He forced a smile for her.

"So what are you drinking these days?"

She took the news about his mother very hard. For a long while she smoked her Winston in silence and stared off, the muscles gone slack in her face, at the crowd in Sheridan Square. The setting sun slapped everything with an unreal golden patina, like Technicolor. He thought, but couldn't be sure, that for an instant her eyes brimmed with tears. Then she looked at him and picked up her vodka tonic. "God, I'm sorry, Max. I liked your mother, you know. She was . . . real down-to-earth. You poor baby. Everybody always seems to up and die on you."

"Not everybody."

She sighed. "It's all so fucked-up."

"You were just telling me how everything was coming up roses."

"Everything's always fucked-up, one way or another."

She sipped her drink and shrugged and summoned up a smile. "Anyway, I got no reason to complain. Things are one hell of a lot better than they used to be, let me tell you. Believe it or not, Max, I'm really doing fine. I'm doing better than I've ever done in my whole life, in fact."

And then she was off and running and waxing poetic about the glories of New York.

"It's called the Bleecker Street Cinema, and it's right over there on Bleecker Street. You know where that is?"

Already she seemed to have acquired the famous geocentrism of New Yorkers. How was he supposed to know where Bleecker Street was?

"It's this wonderful place where all they show is old movies—something like the Tivoli back in St. Louis, but even better. Do you know the first week I was up here they had a Marilyn Monroe festival? Three days of nothing but Marilyn Monroe movies. I took a whole Sunday off and saw *How to Marry a Millionaire* and *Gentlemen Prefer Blondes* and *The Seven Year Itch,* and I swear, I thought I'd died and gone to heaven. But New York is just chock-full of nice things like that. And you don't got to have money, either. They got free concerts in Central Park and street fairs happening all over the place, and hell, all you really have to do for entertainment is leave your apartment and stand out on the sidewalk. St. Louis was just this place where you were stuck and had to live. But New York is this one big circus. Of course it's much more dangerous here. You really do have to watch yourself. And everything from going shopping to going to the post office is a much bigger pain in the ass, and this neighborhood is so full of fairies, it's enough to make you puke. But all in all, it's worth it. I feel alive here, Max. I feel like I'm really alive for the first time in my life."

This cut. Hadn't she felt alive when they were lovers?

Max was asking the questions, but it was Nora who was guiding the conversation, for they were staying resolutely in the here-and-now. Later, he thought, they could get to the unfinished business of the past, and after that, the unfinished business of the future. But for now he wasn't losing anything by letting her handle the reins. And besides, she was talking about his favorite subject: herself.

"Judy's been real good to me," she was saying. "Oh, I know how I bad-mouthed her back in St. Louis—and she's still just a bullshit artist when it comes to her astrology and the rest of it, if you want my opinion—but she's treated me like a real sister ever since I came up here, Max. In fact, she's the one who got me my job. One of her clients, George Stefanos, is the man who owns the restaurant where I work and it was Judy who lined me up with him. It's really not half-bad. It's right down here on Fourth Street, so I can walk there in no time. It's kind of a cute little place—Greek food, you know: gyros and that type of thing. Waiting tables is still a pain in the ass, but it's a damned sight better than dishing out shitburgers, let me tell you. And another nice thing is, I only got to work three or four shifts a week, what with the money I made from selling the house."

"So you sold it, then."

"It was mine to sell, wasn't it? Turns out Jack Cromwell was good for one thing, anyway. I ended up with nine thousand dollars after taxes." She sat back and grinned at him. "Now, how do you like that?"

So Nora had money, and he did not.

Things were getting curiouser and curiouser.

Next she informed him that she had been using her spare time to study for her high school equivalency examinations.

"So believe it or not," she said, bouncing her eyebrows at him, "pretty soon I'm going to be a bona fide forty-two-year-old high school graduate."

It was everything he could do to keep from going over and hugging the life out of her. "Nora, that's just fantastic. That's just . . . Jesus, I'm proud of you."

"I'll bet you never thought that would happen in a million years, did you?"

"I've never known what to expect from you."

"Well, it's been a real bitch so far, let me tell you. But Judy's been helping me out, especially with the math parts, and I mean to stick with it. And guess what else? I'm thinking about taking a course or two at City College after I get my diploma. I already got their brochures and the whole works you need to apply with. And you know what I'm thinking about taking first? American literature. That's right. Hell, I've already read a whole lot of Mark Twain, so I figure I got at least part of it licked. And then who knows? Maybe one of these days you and me can sit down like a couple of regular eggheads and just—" Nora caught herself, laughed into the back of her hand, and shook her head. "Lord, just listen to me go on," she said.

Max was smiling for her, but behind his smile things were getting murky. So she had changed, and changed for the better. The filthy air of New York City had proven salubrious. She looked good, a little fuller, a little more rounded in the face, as if this were an outward sign of the new roundedness of her spirit. Of course he didn't be-grudge her her happiness—how could he? He was sup-posed to be in love with her, for chrissakes. Yet the truth of it was, this news of her recent string of successes was paining him. He was jealous. He didn't know what he was jealous of, precisely, but the bitter fact remained: whatever was making Nora glow like this, it had nothing to do with him.

He asked her in a husky voice if she was glad he came.

Her mouth crumpled and she looked away into the shadowy crowd along Sheridan Square.

"That all depends," she said.

"On what?"

"On what you want."

"You know what I want."

She slapped the table. "Damn you, Max! I *don't* know what you want. I thought for sure you would've picked up with somebody else by now and forgotten all about me. And now here you are, and it doesn't make a goddamned lick of sense! I've got a life now. Can you understand that? For the first time in my life I've got me a life, and I'll be damned if I'll let anybody take that away from me. What do you want from me? I know you got no interest in marrying me, and I know you can't go leaving your job back in St. Louis, so just what is this trip all about? Did you just want to come up here and fuck me a few times for old time's sake or what?"

He was on his feet now, his hands planted flat on the table between them.

"I want it back," he said.

"What?"

"Us."

"There isn't any us anymore."

"How can you be so sure?"

"Because," she said, pulling on her cigarette and averting her eyes. "I'm . . . living with someone at the moment."

Max slowly lowered himself back into his chair.

Now Nora looked at him, and her eyes were wet with sympathy.

"I'm sorry, Max. I'm sorry you had to come all the way up here to find out."

He was overcome with exhaustion. It was as if this period without Nora were a steep mountain he'd been scaling, this meeting with her the dizzying summit, and now that he'd arrived, he found there was no air to breathe, nothing to lean on, and no place to sit down—nothing but this bone-deep weariness and defeat—and all he wanted was to close his eyes, give up the struggle, and fall backward the way he came. As if to counter this impulse, Max widened his eyes and blinked.

"I thought you were living with Judy," he said.

"I was, when I first got up here. But then George came along."

"George."

"George Stefanos. I believe I mentioned him to you—the man who owns the restaurant? He's been Judy's neighbor down the hall for years, and one of her clients, too. Hell, practically the whole apartment building comes to her for readings. Anyway, George is crazy about all that horseshit—astrology, Tarot, previous incarnations, pyramids—you name it, he's a sucker for it. I never seen such a superstitious person in all my life. He crosses himself every goddamned time he gets into a cab—which maybe isn't such a bad idea, now that I think about it." Nora, as if remembering what Max had to be suffering, worked the smile off her face. "Anyway, he was sitting right there, having coffee with Judy, the day that I walked in. And it wasn't one month later that I moved in down the hall with him."

"What you'd call a whirlwind romance," Max said, and then remembered that it had taken less than a week before he moved in with Nora. "George Stefanos. He's Greek?" he asked her, as if this could make any kind of difference.

"That's right."

It had been dull, blind, solipsistic of him not to have considered the possibility that Nora had taken a lover. She had been here since Christmas, was a woman with a powerful sexual appetite, and was not without, he knew too well, her own special brand of magnetism. He'd been

obsessed for so long with Nora's unfitness for him that
he'd failed to see that she might be perfectly suited to
somebody else. He found himself hating this faceless Greek
restaurateur, then reprimanded himself for it. What, after
all, had George Stefanos done except to fall victim to the
same inexplicable passion as Max? No two men in the
world had more in common. They were soulmates sharing
the same prison cell.

"He's a good man," Nora went on. "Of course, he's
nothing like you. I mean, he's not what you'd call sophis-
ticated. He hasn't even been in this country very long. He
came over here from Greece just about five years ago,
after his wife died, and he's been working like a nigger all
this time to get to where he is. Lord, you should see that
man work—twelve-, fourteen-hour days, six days a week.
He's solid and he's dependable and I think he really loves
me. And another thing: I think I'm good for him. I was
never any good for you, Max, and I hated that feeling
something awful. Hell, I've never been any good for nobody, until George came along."

The extent of his pain must have been showing on his
face, for Nora abruptly lowered her eyes to her drink.

"You forgot to mention one thing," Max said.

"What's that?"

"Whether or not you love him."

"Sure I do."

"In the same way you love me?"

She kept her gaze on the ghostly crowd in Sheridan
Square.

"That's a trick question," she said.

Hope flared in his chest like a weak pilot light. He
swallowed what was left of the watery drink in his glass.

"Would you do me a favor?" he asked her.

"Depends on what it is."

"Introduce me to him."

"Oh, shit, Max! What in the world would you want
to meet him for?"

"I guess because I'm curious."

"What if I just *tell* you about him?"

"Please, Nora. I want to meet him. I want to see him.
I want to see you two together. I'm really not sure why—

maybe it's because I want to come away with some first-hand knowledge of what your life is like if I can't come away with anything else."

His campaign had already started. Already he was being duplicitous, withholding information, playing his cards close. What he really wanted from a meeting with George Stefanos was to take his measure of the man in the flesh and determine just exactly what it was that he was going to be up against. For he understood now that he wasn't giving up. The only other option he had left himself was to return to St. Louis, crawl into a hole, and give himself over to something tantamount to death. He was desperately in love, his love had put him into desperate circumstances, and the notion of taking some kind of desperate action, far from frightening him, infused him instead with a strange and concentrated calm. This was the sort of calm, he thought, that must have possessed Tennyson's light brigade in the moment before they made their crazy charge at Balaklava—never mind how that charge actually turned out, or that the officers who ordered it were some of history's biggest fools. He leaned forward.

"I've come an awfully long way just to run straight into a brick wall," he told her. "Don't you think you could do me this one small favor?"

"I didn't ask you up here, you know." And then, perhaps to soften this, she added: "Besides, wouldn't it make you terribly uncomfortable, seeing me and him together like that?"

"I couldn't feel much worse than I already do. Come on, Nora. He doesn't have to know who I am. Just tell him I'm an old friend from St. Louis—one of your managers at White Palace, any goddamned thing. I happen to know you're a terrific liar. Why should he suspect anything? I look more like your son than I do your lover, anyway."

"Thanks a lot."

"Is he jealous?"

"No. Which is funny—I mean, with him being Greek. Most of these Greeks would just as soon kill you as to catch you looking at another man. But George isn't that way at all."

"Is he at the restaurant now?"

"He's always at that goddamned restaurant."

"Then what do you say we go over there and have an ouzo?"

Nora studied him for a moment.

"You really are a crazy man, aren't you?"

CHAPTER TWENTY

The air was delicious, bursting with oregano, cinnamon, lamb drippings sizzling on charcoal. Rapid-fire bouzouki music sputtered overhead. There were only seven or eight tables in the place, all occupied, and so closely jumbled together that from Max's angle the diners appeared to be knocking elbows. Two black-jacketed waiters maneuvered through the narrows like dignified rats in a maze. At one end of the room stood a long and none-too-clean-looking steam table, behind which a black cook, his hair in corn rows, scurried.

This restaurant, Max thought—if you ignored the obvious cultural distance from Dogtown—looked custom-made for Nora: chaotic, earthy, and not quite up to American standards of hygiene. She stood beside him, her purse held close to her chest, surveying the restaurant with a stony apprehensiveness. One of the waiters gave her a friendly wave. She acknowledged it only with a curt bob of the head. Here was a Nora he'd never expected to see: the queenly girlfriend of the owner of the establishment, maintaining a cool reserve with the help. But of course, he was forgetting how much distress this must have been causing her. Under normal circumstances she was probably just one of the boys—as foul-mouthed and convivial as any seventeen-year-old dishwasher with a half-smoked joint in his jeans.

She led him to a table near the window, where a man with shoulders like a buffalo's sat alone, assiduously hunched over a tabloid newspaper. Beside him was a cup and saucer that looked, next to his bulk, like something filched from a little girl's toy tea service. The sleeves of his white shirt were rolled up high above his elbows. On the crown of his head his bald spot made a pink bull's-eye. Max saw that he was tracing the lines of copy before him with a thick forefinger, and that his lips were moving to sound out the words as he read them.

"George," Nora said.

He went on reading, moving his lips. The paper was *The Midnight Globe*.

"George. Hey. *Malakis*."

Max had no idea what the word meant. But that Nora was speaking so much as a syllable of Greek, that she had already traveled so far into another man's world—and a world which Max knew nothing about—pierced him as if he were watching them passionately kiss. He tightened his grip on the handle of his overnight bag.

George looked up and an easy white grin broke out across his face, bracketed by a bristling walrus moustache. He looked, to Max's discomfort, something like Horowitz: there was the enormity of his torso, the walrus moustache, the broad face and heavy jowls, and a similar mix of sadness and kindness in the eyes, which were as black and wet as ripe olives. But just as disconcerting was how old the man looked: somewhere in his fifties. Of course, by any conventional measure, this was how old the lover of a woman in her forties should have been—yet for some reason Max had been expecting a much younger man.

"Who are you calling *malakis*?" George asked her.

"You. Taking a break in the middle of a rush like this."

"Who owns the place? Huh? Can you tell me that?" He directed his black eyes to Max. "Hello."

"Hello," Max said, surprised that his own smile came so naturally.

"George, I want you to meet Max. He's an old friend of mine from St. Louis, and he's up here for a visit." Nora's voice was tight.

George hoisted himself partway out of his chair and extended his hand to Max. He had the sort of a handshake you'd want to hang on to in a hurricane. "Very nice to meet you," he said. "Very nice."

Max told George that it was very nice to meet him, too.

"Sit. Please. Have a seat," George said. Nora chose the chair which put her at the farthest distance from George and from the only place remaining for Max. She opened her purse and got out her Winstons. Max sat, set down his bag, and tried to affect a relaxed slouch. George was nodding and smiling. Nora shot two furious streams of smoke out her nose.

"So . . ." George said. "So . . ."

"Max just got in from St. Louis a little while ago," Nora said in her constricted voice.

"St. Louis, *Missouri*—right?"

"That's right," Max said.

"Cowboys and Indians, yes?"

"Well, no. What you're thinking of is quite a bit farther west."

"What are you talking about? Of course cowboys and Indians!" He gave the table a definitive smack.

Hadn't Nora already set George straight on his geography? Or maybe she'd hardly breathed a word to him about her hometown, her past life. That would have been just like her.

"Jesse James. You know Jesse James?"

"Well, sure," Max said.

"Now you tell me: where was his hideout if it wasn't Missouri? Am I right? And what about the Pony Express? Missouri!" George sat back, chuckling. "You see, I know a little something about the American West. Louis L'Amour. You ever read him? He's my number one American writer."

"Hell," Nora said. "All you ever read are them goddamned tabloids."

"They help me with my English," George explained not to Nora, but to Max. "*The New York Times*—who can understand it? But these—" He tapped the cover of his *Midnight Globe*. "These are simpler."

"So what were you just reading about?" Max asked him.

"The Shroud of Turin. You know it?"

"I've heard of it."

"Amazing. They say science is . . . . stumped. Is that the word?"

"Stumped," Max said. "That's right."

"Just incredible."

"It's a lot of crap, is what it is," Nora said. She shifted her weight unhappily in her chair. "Can we get us a drink, George?"

"Sure, sure."

He signaled a waiter. Nora ordered a vodka tonic; Max asked for an ouzo; George was sticking to coffee. If he took any notice of Nora's glumness, he gave no indication. He seemed in perfect boyish high spirits. The whole time they were talking, he'd been straightening up the table for his guests with a fussiness that reminded Max uncomfortably of himself. He folded away his paper with meticulous care, ironing out the creases with the edge of his hand. He rearranged a cluster of objects in the center of the table—mustard and ketchup bottles, napkin dispenser, sugar bowl, salt and pepper shakers—with the exactitude of a video director setting things up for a product shot. Even now he was brushing away invisible crumbs and smoothing out imaginary wrinkles from the waxy blue-checked tablecloth. Don't bother, Max silently advised him—none of these charms and hexes are going to keep the wolf away from your door. He's already here, in fact, sitting at your table. This is what Max was thinking. But he was having a hard time really seeing himself as the dangerous interloper. The problem was, he'd already taken a liking to this man. Nora was right; he seemed generous, good-hearted, simple. So even if he failed in his purpose, Max allowed himself to think, at least Nora would remain here in good hands. Their drinks arrived. Max took a swallow of his ouzo—ice-cold and licorice-sweet—and sat up straighter, banishing all such defeatist thoughts from his brain. He was indeed the wolf at the door, the dangerous interloper, whether he approved of George or not.

"Nora has fun with what I read," George said.

"Makes fun," Nora corrected him.

"You see?" George rolled his eyes indulgently in Nora's direction. "The professor. She graduates high school, and next year she goes to college, and all the time she's reading Mark Twain. So I'm too stupid for her, she thinks. Well, all right, I say to her—now *you* run a restaurant! You see? Now *you* run a restaurant, I tell her, and we'll see how stupid I am." George winked at Nora. She smiled wanly back.

That things could have become so contorted that Nora was now berating her mate for his lowbrow reading habits was too much for Max to quickly digest. He tasted his ouzo again and said to George: "I like your restaurant. It seems . . . very homey."

"You like it? Have you eaten here?"

"Well, no."

"Then for all you know, it's shit—am I right?"

Both Max and George laughed. George looked at Nora; she had her gaze fixed in a neutral space between the two men. "No, but seriously," George said, "I try to make this a nice place. Nothing but real food, you know—everything from scratch. And of course, I've got the best goddamned waitress in New York City working for me right here."

"Horseshit," Nora said.

"You see? Real New York chutzpah. That's what the customers like."

Hearing George come out with a Yiddish word gave Max a jolt of cultural vertigo—the sort, he supposed, that you could get only in America. He sipped at his ouzo again.

"You like that, eh?"

"Yes. I do."

"Order us another round, George."

"You okay tonight, Nora?"

"I'm fine."

"You sure?"

"I'm *fine*."

George shrugged and waved at the waiter. A sticky silence ensued. Max polished off his ouzo. George began brushing more imaginary crumbs from the tablecloth. Nora lit a new Winston.

"So anyway," she said, swallowing her smoke, "Max and me go way back."

"Is that right?"

"He was my manager at that hamburger place I told you about."

"Well, how do you like that? And are you still in the restaurant business?"

"No," Max said. "I'm in advertising now."

"Advertising! Well, well. That's big potatoes—am I right?"

Max smiled at George over his empty ouzo glass. The ouzo, the frenetic restaurant, the bouzouki music, the fact that he was actually in New York and that this unreal scene was taking place at this table—all of it was going strangely, maybe dangerously, to his head. His misery was in remission. He felt instead well-oiled, muscular, untrustworthy.

"I guess you're up here for business," George said.

"Well, no. Not exactly. Unless you want to call it business of the heart."

Nora moved some phlegm in her throat.

George looked a little confused.

"You see, I chased a woman up here from St. Louis."

George's bushy eyebrows went up. "Ah-hah," he said. "All the way to New York? But tell me this: Why would a young man as handsome as you have to chase a woman so far?" George turned his grin to Nora and gave her another wink. She took a frowning swallow of her vodka tonic.

"Do you really want to hear about it?" Max asked him.

"Well, sure. Why not?"

"All right," Max said, determined not to look at Nora. "I think we were very much in love with each other—or at least I know that I was very much in love with her. But I didn't handle it right, George. I was cowardly, and shortsighted, and I never really gave her credit for her intelligence. And she was smart enough to catch on to all of that. So she ran up here to New York, I've come running after her—and now I'm determined to get her back."

"It sounds serious," George said.

"I've never been more serious about anything in my

life," Max told him. "The problem is, I don't think she understands that. I think she's convinced herself that this is some kind of adolescent infatuation, or some kind of temporary insanity on my part, and that it's just going to fade away with time. But she's dead wrong, George. And there's another thing she's wrong about. I've changed. I'm not the same guy I was back in St. Louis. I don't undervalue her anymore. And I'm not going to betray her again like I did. But she'll never be convinced of those things until she puts them to the test." A feathery cloud of smoke drifted across the table.

George was studying him now with the same concentration he had given to his tabloid. "Is she in love with another man?" he asked him.

"I really couldn't say at this point," Max told him, and then sensed that he had gone too far.

An uneasy light worked to the surface of George's eyes. He turned to Nora. She met his gaze with a look of utter flatness. Now he turned back to Max, giving a roll to his massive shoulders, and knit his big fingers in front of him on the table.

"Do you mind," he said, "if you tell me who this woman is?"

Max glanced at Nora's drawn face and decided he had tortured her enough. "Not at all," he said. "She works at Macy's, in the cosmetics department. Her name is Mildred Rogers."

Nora burst out laughing and slapped the table. "I tell you, George—it's all he's talked about since the minute he got up here. Mildred, Mildred, Mildred—yak, yak, yak, yak, yak. The poor thing. You'd think there wasn't nobody else in the whole goddamned world but Mildred Rogers."

"That's just about the case," Max said, meeting her eyes.

Brazening it out like this with Nora, so that they formed, if only for a few moments, a conspiracy of two, produced an intimacy and excitement that bordered on the erotic. And evidently, it was enough to put George's suspicions—however deep they might have gone—to rest. His jowly face relaxed, he plucked at one end of his moustache, and the light in his eyes softened. "So . . ." he said, smoothing out an area of tablecloth in front of him. "So . . ."

"So I said to him, Max—why don't you just give up? From everything you've told me about this woman, she's just not worth it. Cut your losses and go home and find a woman who's right for you, who's more up to your level. That's what I told him. But I may as well have been talking to a brick wall."

"What Nora doesn't understand," Max said, "is that telling me to give up on this woman is the same as telling me to just crawl off someplace and die. That's how much she means to me." He knew how melodramatic this sounded, but he also knew that Nora, with her taste for sappy country music and biographies of doomed movie stars, was probably the right audience for such tumescent rhetoric. And besides, as he spoke it, it didn't feel in the least like an exaggeration.

Nora's brow puckered. She began to slowly rotate her glass between the palms of her hands. Max willed her to look him in the eye, but she kept her gaze resolutely on her drink.

George leaned candidly forward on his hairy crossed forearms.

"You love this girl very much, eh?"

"Very much."

"Then let me give you some advice. You talk to her. You *tell* her how you feel. Screw your pride—you understand? The main point is, communicate! Isn't that right, Nora? Don't be proud, my friend."

"Thanks, George. I won't be."

"Aren't you going to be late for your date?" Nora asked him.

Max looked at his watch. "Oh, brother. I guess I lost track of the time."

"You talk to her," George said again.

"I will."

"Good luck to you, my friend."

"Thanks again, George."

Nora was on her feet and slinging her purse strap over her shoulder.

"I see you later," George said to her.

"You have yourself a good night," she told him, and ushered Max out the door.

The crowd in Sheridan Square seemed to have doubled since the onset of darkness. Nora led the way—to wherever they were headed—at a swift New Yorker's clip, keeping hold of Max's arm as they threaded upstream through the onrush of bodies.

"Are you mad at me?" he asked her.

"Lord, I don't know. But I never seen you act so nervy—that's for damned sure."

"He seems like a good man, Nora. I like him."

"Why shouldn't you like him?"

"Because he's got what I want."

She picked up their pace.

"What does *malakis* mean, by the way?"

"Jerkoff, basically. You ever want a Greek to tear you limb from limb, just use that word on him."

"Thanks for the tip."

She snorted. "God, I hated lying to him like that. He's just like a little boy sometimes. He'll believe any goddamned thing you tell him. It's no *fun* lying to a man like that—it's like picking on somebody helpless."

"I got a charge out of lying to him, if you want to know the truth."

She glanced at him. "What's happened to you, Max?"

"What do you mean?"

"You used to be such a straight arrow."

"Nobody's a straight arrow," he said.

"George is a straight arrow. I can tell you that right now."

They dodged more bodies.

"Where are we going?"

"Back to my apartment. I got some good liquor up there."

"Don't you think we've drunk enough?"

"No."

"Aren't you afraid of what might happen up there?"

"I won't let it happen."

They had arrived at the entrance to the apartment building on Seventh Avenue. Nora took a key chain thickly shingled with keys from her purse and opened the way into an outer vestibule. Another lock, another key, and they were in a dull green hallway, facing the elevator. Max set down his overnight bag and worked the blood back into his fingers. Nora kept punching the button, saying, "Come on, goddamn you. Come on."

Two young men came through the door of the vestibule, bumping shoulders, their laughter ricocheting off the walls. One was wiry as a monkey and carried a bulging bag of groceries. The other looked like he might have just come from a Mr. Clean look-alike contest; his head was hairless, he wore a gold hoop in one ear, his chest burgeoned impressively.

The elevator came open. Nora stepped to the back and slumped against the wall, crossing her arms.

"Hold the door, please!" called out the one with the groceries. "Will you please hold the door?"

Max, polite as always, held the door. Nora aimed a look of exasperated disgust at the ceiling. The two men came aboard.

"Thank you *so* much," the one with the groceries said to Max. "You *absolutely* saved our lives." The door closed, trapping an atmosphere of liquor and cologne. The one with the groceries wore a sleeveless undershirt, and while his upper arms and shoulders were finely muscled, he did not appear healthy; his face was sallow and brutally pockmarked; there was a yellowish cast to his eyes. He seemed to take notice of Nora for the first time. "Why, if it isn't the Daisy Mae Yokum of Seventh Avenue! How are we tonight, Nora sweetheart?"

"I told you before, Danny—knock it off with that Daisy Mae shit."

"But you know I only mean it fondly, Nora. You are *such* an American original."

"Look who's talking."

This cracked Danny up. He leaned backward against the stalwart chest of Mr. Clean, feigning helplessness, and then recovered himself sufficiently to flash his eyes at Max. "And what do we have here?" he asked Nora. "A new acquisition? You *must* introduce us."

"He's not your type."

"Let me guess. He's your son."

"He's my father."

"No! And yet he looks like a perfect Adonis. What's the secret of his youth?"

"He doesn't take it up the ass."

This sent Danny into such paroxysms of laughter that his grocery bag started slipping down his thigh. The elevator opened. Nora stalked out. Max picked up his overnight bag and followed.

"Good-bye, Nora darling! Good-bye!"

The hallway was painted a grim bone-white. Nora was moving once again at her impatient New Yorker's pace, the heels of her boots rat-tatting on the cement floor. "Lord, I can't stand fairies! I know they're human beings and all—so don't you go snapping at me, Max. I just don't like them, that's all. And from what I can tell, this neighborhood is the queer capital of the world. Why, do you know that me and George and Judy are the only normal people in this whole damned apartment building? It's enough to make you sick. Oh, some of them are tolerable, I suppose. But not the ones who make it their business to keep *reminding* you they're fairies—like Danny back there." They were at her door now, and Nora was stooping to work the key into the lock. "And the crazy thing is, they all seem to like *me* for some reason."

"It's because you make such a good sparring partner," Max said.

She looked up at him.

And then he was leaning helplessly against her and brushing his dry lips across her cheek.

"No."

"Just kiss me for godsakes, Nora."

"*No.*"

But then her mouth was on his, her hands had seized the flesh below his shoulder blades, and her tongue was spearing his heart. She kissed him with such ferocity that it almost seemed an expression of anger. Her odor, as much as her touch, overcame him, and for an instant he lost himself.

An instant later she twisted free of their kiss and shoved him roughly away at the collarbone. Her back clunked the door.

"Damn you, Max! *Goddamn* you!" She stepped away from the door and whipped her ponytail across her shoulders. "Didn't I ask you not to touch me?"

"You were right with me just then, Nora. You were right with me just then and you know it! Why did you push me away?"

"For the same goddamned reason I came to New York! To get away from you."

"Why did you want to get away from me?"

"Because we got no business being together. Don't you—" She shook her head as if to clear it of something. "Don't you understand I'm nothing but a dead-end for you? Don't you want a family someday, Max? Don't you want to live a regular life and raise some kids and be a normal human being?"

"Not particularly."

"Well, I know *better,* goddammit! I swear to God, you're as much a little boy as George is! You *will* want those things, Max. And I can't *give* them to you. If I'd stayed with you in St. Louis, you were going to wake up someday and look at me and realize that, and the next thing you know, we'd be tearing each other's throats out. I know what I'm saying, Max. Don't you know what would've happened?"

"That's your scenario, not mine."

"Lord, how can a man as intelligent as you be as stupid as you are?"

"Come back with me to St. Louis, Nora."

Her ponytail went whipping across her shoulders again.

"You're not even listening to me! You're not even arguing right!" Her chest heaved and she blinked at him. "And let's say I *did* go back with you to St. Louis. What've you got to offer me that's better than what I got now?"

"How about a marriage?"

"Oh, shit! Max, whatever gave you the stupid idea I

wanted to marry you in the first place? I never *liked* being married. I was never any damned good at it."

"Does George know that?"

"He's getting used to the idea."

"Then come back to St. Louis and *live* with me, Nora."

"I like it here. All right? I like it up here and I'm staying up here. I'm never going back to that cow town. No way, Jose."

"I can always make other arrangements, for chrissakes."

"Don't bother. I'm staying here with George."

"Do you love him, Nora?"

"Stop asking me that question."

"Do you love him or not?"

"I'm *staying* with him. He loves me and he's good to me and he's not going to burn me—all right? Why in the hell should I throw everything I've got straight out the window for a man who's ashamed to be seen with me in public?"

There it was. She'd finally hit the root, the exposed nerve.

It was Max's turn to cross his arms.

"I've changed," he said. "That sort of thing won't ever happen again."

"And *I'm* Marilyn Monroe! Say any goddamned thing you want to say, Max—why should I believe you?"

He had no answer for this.

"And let's say I did go back with you. How long do you think it would last? Do you think you're still going to want me ten years from now, when I'm fifty-two and you're not even forty?"

"Yes."

"It's all *words*, Max! It's all nothing but pretty words. I have to keep reminding myself that that's the thing you're best at—because let me tell you, you really had me going back at the restaurant. You really had me going there, all right."

"Nora, how in the fuck am I ever going to convince you of anything if you don't believe a single word I say? What do I have to do? Slit my wrists? What do I *do*, Nora?"

"Go home," she said.

A door opened and a tall black man wearing a bathrobe and a towel wrapped around his head like a turban stood smiling at them, a can of Budweiser in his hand.

"I just wanted to say," he told them, "that I think you two are doing a fabulous job. A first-rate bang-up performance. But do you think you could lower the volume just a bit? I've got *Grand Hotel* on the VCR, and I'm afraid it's really paling by comparison."

"Go fuck yourself," Nora told him.

"I knew you'd understand."

He withdrew into his apartment, softly closing the door.

Nora turned back to Max. "I think you'd better go now," she said in the same constricted voice she had used at George's restaurant.

"You still love me."

"That's your opinion."

"Please don't bullshit me, Nora."

She raised her chin. "I'll admit that . . . something still happens when we touch."

"We both know that. I'm talking about something else."

She did a girlish thing; she stamped her foot.

"All right—so what if I do? What does that *change*, Max? You think love is some kind of magic wand you can just wave over everything to make everything all better? We come from two different sides of the track, and nothing is *ever* going to change that." She scratched her neck. "I'm staying here with George. All right? I'm not saying it again."

He was gratified, in a miserable way, to see her eyes fill up with tears.

"I'm sorry, Max. I *am* sorry. But I just can't go risking everything I've got for a few pretty words from you."

Then she turned, turned the key, and went alone into her apartment.

When Max came back to himself—he had no idea how long he'd been gone, much less where he might have gone to—he was facing the blank white, utterly indifferent wall of the hallway. He took all the air he could into his lungs, then pushed it all slowly out his nose. He was not going to panic. It wasn't over yet. He had no idea what he was going to do, but he knew in his bones that he was going to do it. He picked up his overnight bag and saw that the black man with the turban was standing once again in his doorway.

"Do you know something?" he said.

Max just looked at him.

"Greta Garbo's got nothing on you."

CHAPTER TWENTY-ONE

Katy McCormick, doing her impersonation of Nora Cromwell, reached for a rose-shaped earring and said: "Look, saving at Fidelity Federal hasn't solved all my problems. But it *has* given me one less thing to worry about. And for a woman like me, that makes a lot of difference."

"Fidelity Federal," intoned the off-camera announcer. "In an uncertain world, it's one thing you can be certain about."

Brandon Black, creative group head at Sussman, Sherman and Rice, the twenty-third largest advertising agency in the world, punched the rewind button on the VCR, ran a hand through his thick blond hair, pushed backward on the steel rollers of his chair, and joined Max once again at the conference table in his office. It was actually the sawed-off trunk of a redwood tree, polished, laminated, and shaped approximately like the continent of Australia. Black himself looked like an advertising man's notion of what an advertising man should look like: as handsome as an aging male model, his expensive blue suit rather rumpled, his shrewd blue eyes showing equal parts of boyish energy and jaded calculation. He lit another Camel Light. "I can see why Rosemary Powers is so high on you," he said. "It's good stuff. Unusual. I especially like that last spot, the one with the sleazeball doing the on-camera. Crazy idea. What kind of reaction did it get?"

"It never ran. The client pulled it at the last minute."

"Crazy idea. I liked it."

"Well, thank you," Max said, tugging at the crease in his pant leg. "Of course, it can't measure up to a national spot—"

"What are you talking about? We spend a hundred thousand dollars every three days on spots that don't have half as much savvy. What'd that thing cost you, by the way?"

"Seven thousand."

"Jesus. And I guess you can still buy a Coke for a nickel in St. Louis, right?"

Max smiled. Black returned his attention to the resume folder. Black's praise was something Max knew he had to steel himself against; he'd been getting plenty of praise these past weeks, and not a single offer. Black's name was the last on a list of names that Rosemary had gathered for him; if nothing came of this interview today, tomorrow Max would have to start calling agencies cold, starting with the A's. He watched Black close the folder and lean back with his hands locked behind his handsome head. He squinted at Max, pursing his mouth.

"Can I get into some areas that are none of my business?"

"Go ahead."

"You had a fine career going back in St. Louis, from what Rosemary tells me. You were a rising star. You were going to get noticed. What the hell are you doing in New York?"

Max shrugged. "What are *you* doing in New York? This is supposed to be the pinnacle, isn't it?"

"You want to hear the truth? If I had it to do all over again, I would've stayed in Baltimore. There's nothing wrong with being the big fish in the little pond. It's more *fun*, if you want to know the truth. But that's not my point. The point is, when I came up here seventeen years ago, you could still get in. Things were moving, shifting around. It was the late sixties, you know—Doyle Dane, Della Femina, Freberg, all that stuff was happening. Now it's a fucking gridlock." He went on squinting at Max. "Has anybody really told you yet how things operate in this town? I mean for creative people? Has anybody done you that service?"

"I wish you would," Max said.

"You make your money here by showing absolutely no loyalty whatsoever to anybody. Any writer or art director who thinks he owes something to his boss in this town is a shmuck, pure and simple. There are simply too many agencies, too many opportunities. You come on at one place, you work on one or two accounts for one or two years, you add some snazzy shit to your portfolio, and boom, you're off to some other agency. That's how it works. You sit around at one outfit and wait for a raise and what do you get? Five percent? On the other hand, you go someplace else, and you can expect anywhere from a ten to a twenty percent hike in your salary. You're no better. You're no different. You're just making twenty percent more than you did yesterday, that's all. It's like a flea circus—everybody hopping around, across, back, and forth.'' Black unhooked his hands from behind his head long enough to take a deep drag on his cigarette. ''So let me ask you this, Max: who do you think your competition is right now? It's not some guy who really needs a job, and it's not some talented freshman up from the sticks. It's a seasoned New York professional who's already been at five or six agencies, is already making forty grand, and sees a way to turn that into fifty. That's who you're up against.''

Max steeled himself against this warning just as he steeled himself against Black's praise. If he allowed himself to think about the odds, he'd go to pieces.

''Let me ask you some more things that are none of my business. How long have you been up here?''

''Seven weeks.''

''How many interviews have you gotten?''

''Ten or eleven.''

''Any offers?''

''No.''

''Any second interviews?''

''One.''

''But nothing doing?''

''Nothing doing.''

''And people like your work?''

''Generally.''

Black squinted at the ceiling for a spell, then redirected his squint at Max. ''Are you staying up here with friends?''

"I'm on my own," Max said.

"Where?"

"A furnished room. The Washington-Jefferson Hotel."

"Which is where?"

"Forty-ninth Street."

"*West* Forty-ninth Street?"

"Right."

"Holy fucking shit. Is it depressing or what?"

"Well," Max said, "I haven't committed suicide yet."

"But you've been thinking about it."

"Luckily, I haven't had that much leisure time."

"One last question and then I'll cut this out. How much money have you got in the bank?"

"Around a thousand."

Black let out a whistle. Then he unknit his hands from behind his head and leaned forward. "Max, I like you. You're a very talented guy, and obviously you've got a lot of balls. I only wish we had an opening for you. But we don't. I'm sorry."

Max took this in.

"Well," he said. "I do appreciate the time you've given me. You seem like you'd be a terrific person to work for. I'm sorry, too."

Black nodded at him.

"Will you take a piece of unsolicited advice?" he asked Max.

"It depends on what it is."

"Go home," Black said.

———————

Max walked the twenty-three blocks from the offices of Sussman, Sherman and Rice at his recently acquired, urgent New York pace. It was drizzling lightly, already dark, and felt more like the middle of December than early October, but Max had been choosing to walk whenever he could in this city. The other means of getting around were either repugnant or impractical: the subways might have been designed by Dante as conveyances for damned souls into hell; the overcrowded buses were nearly as bad; he had no business squandering his diminishing assets on cabs. Besides, walking like this—powering past the omnipresent hordes on the sidewalks, engulfed by the hostile roar and squeal of the traffic, reduced to the status of an insect by these towering walls of glass and steel— served to sharpen his sense of struggle, focus him on his purpose, and to strangely brace and energize him, not unlike a steambath followed by a plunge in an icy river.

He was constantly and consciously playing such tricks on himself. His real enemy was not the city, and it was not the sewn-up provincial world of New York advertis- ing, and it was not George Stefanos—it was realistic think- ing. Certain facts were poison to dwell upon: that Nora (whom he had not spoken to since the night, seven weeks before, when she'd shut her door in his face) had meant just exactly what she said; that his chances of landing a job were about as good as his winning the New York State Lottery; that he'd left himself nothing to fall back on, not even a contingency plan; that his money, and hence his time, was running out.

He plotted each move in his day with the grim calcu- lation of an assassin. Over coffee he would revise his list of creative directors that Rosemary had supplied to him: who among them were still possibilities, who to call back, who to wait for a call from. He would inspect his check- book and determine, to the dollar, how much he could allow himself to spend that day. Then he would clean his room, clean himself up, straighten his tie, and go down to the street to use a pay telephone: there was only one public phone in the rooming house, and Max had been warned off by more than one resident for monopolizing it. Once he used up his leads, he would go back to his room and revise his list, and, if there were no interviews to be had that day, devise a plan for getting through the remain- ing hours ahead of him. He tried to forget himself at the museums, the Central Park Zoo, the libraries, the second- hand bookstores. Already, he had been to the top of the Empire State Building, to the South Street Seaport, the World Trade Center, the United Nations Building, and, just for the ironic hell of it, the cosmetics department at

Macy's. Once or twice a week he would shell out the money for a movie—usually a double feature at one of the revival houses—and had learned from bitter experience to avoid any movie with Marilyn Monroe in it. He would kill some afternoons reading *The New York Times* over a cup of cappuccino at an outdoor café usually on the Upper West Side—but never in the Village, where there was always the outside chance of running into Nora. Otherwise he simply walked the streets with his driven, unflagging stride.

The main thing was to return to his room in a state of utter exhaustion. He would have two drinks—no more, no less—of cheap gin or vodka on ice, fix himself something on his tiny stove or eat something he'd picked up at a deli, crack whatever second-hand paperback he was reading, and only about half the time, after all of this, have trouble falling asleep.

His dreams were vivid, cogent, obsessive.

He had one recurring dream where he arrived at a shoot for a TV spot, with the actors, crew, and client all in attendance, and realized, in a hot panic, that he had forgotten the script, and couldn't even remember what the spot was supposed to be about.

One night he dreamed that he was living on the street, among the bag ladies and the other hollow-eyed homeless souls, and was rooting through a trash can—not for food, but for a stack of resumes that he had foolishly dumped there for some inexplicable reason. Other hands joined his, scrabbling through the garbage, so that their fingers bumped, and when Max looked up and saw two crazed-looking women in filthy overcoats, he recognized them: one was his mother, the other was Janey.

Max had thought that Janey's death had taught him all he needed to know about loneliness, but he was wrong. This was loneliness of a different order, with no boundaries and no islands of relief, and for days at a time it congealed in his chest in a knot of physical pain. He made no friends. Outside of Nora, Judy, and George Stefanos, who weren't even aware that he was here, the only people in this city who knew his name were the

creative directors he'd spoken to, some of the boarders
and staff at the rooming house, and the gentlemanly owner
of the second-hand bookstore on Ninth Avenue where
Max went once or twice a week to replenish his small
library. Days went by in which he used his voice so
seldom that, when he finally did speak—to ask for a
newspaper, a corned beef sandwich, a pint of Cossack
vodka—the resonant low rumble seemed to belong to
somebody else.

And yet his letter-writing had been minimal. He wrote
only one letter to Horowitz, and only one to Sara Roth—
both of them falsely upbeat and intentionally vague. Even
his letters to Rosemary were becoming fewer and farther
between. He had no taste for either concealing his predic-
ament or for hearing himself complain, and until something good finally broke, he imagined, his correspondence
would probably dwindle down to nothing.

Max was eating meagerly, and this, along with his
daily marathon walks, had burned off most of the weight
he'd put on in the past year. He was becoming, he sometimes thought, as hardened and half-crazy as any native
New Yorker

Max walked until he spotted the vertical neon sign of
the Washington-Jefferson Hotel. His hair was dripping wet
from the drizzle. The blister on the heel of his right foot
was howling. Tomorrow, he told himself, now that Rosemary had run out of names, he would have to go to the
Forty-second Street Library, get out a copy of the Red
Book—which gave detailed information on every advertising agency in the country—and begin to work his way
through it. There were hundreds of agencies standing
between himself and failure. With enough diligence—but
here he shut his mind off. It was better not to think. He
braced himself for the sour smell of old men and rotting
carpet, then entered the lobby of the rooming house.

He passed the grotesque potted palm, the cluster of
crusty-looking armchairs, the empty magazine rack, the

row of white radiators, and there, as always, was Carl, hunkered down behind his desk. Carl served as the front line of the hotel. No visitors were allowed upstairs without Carl's permission, and he was the sole operator of the hotel switchboard. In Max's room, above the rusty sink, was an intercom, and every long once in a while the buzzer would sound and Carl's scratchy voice would come through to announce that someone at some agency had actually returned one of Max's calls. Otherwise he was as cut off in his room from the outside world as a caterpillar in his cocoon.

When, or if, Carl ever slept, Max had no idea, for he was always there at his desk, day or night, his eyes fixed on the small black and white television mounted above the mail slots, a Chesterfield stuck up high between his fingers, his perennial coughing fit either subsiding, coming on, or breaking out. Carl's cough had an ugly, tangible sound—like taffy being pulled apart in his lungs. Max couldn't recall an instance when he'd asked Carl how he was doing that Carl hadn't responded with his laconic "The same." Over these long weeks that cryptic phrase, "the same," had taken on, to Max's ears, a certain gloomy profundity.

Now Max approached his desk and there was Carl, as unchanged as a painting in a museum, his gaze glued to the barking television, his Chesterfield streaming between his fingers. He rearranged some sludge in the pit of his throat.

"Hello, Carl," Max said.

Carl gave an almost imperceptible nod to his head.

"Any mail for me today?"

Carl shook his head no.

"How are you doing tonight, Carl?"

"The same."

Max looked at him: the old gray face, the sparse hair, the nose as shapeless as a pastry that hadn't come out right. He thought of asking Carl if there was ever a time when he *didn't* feel the same, but then thought better of it. The bitter old man would only think that Max was trying to be a wise guy.

"I'm the same too," Max told him, and then ascended the musty stairs, the rattle of Carl's coughing fit diminishing below him.

He couldn't help thinking, each time he entered his room, of Raskolnikov from *Crime and Punishment*, skulking miserably into his shabby compartment, an ax handle sticking out of his coat pocket, a pair of bloody socks stashed under the bed. Dostoevsky would probably have found a room like this inspirational. There was a half-refrigerator, a tiny stove with two burners—only one of which worked—a rust-mottled sink, a wobbly bureau, a bed with a mattress that sighed into a shape like a spoon when Max lay on it, a dirty window looking out onto a dirty Forty-ninth Street, and a solid oak writing desk which was the only decent thing in the room. Down the hall was the communal bathroom, equipped with one shower stall, one toilet, two sinks, and two urinals—at the bottom of which sat fat white tablets of some kind of disinfectant that made the entire floor smell like Luden's Wild Cherry cough drops.

Max poured himself a gin on ice and sat on the sagging edge of his bed. Tonight was going to be particularly rough. Brandon Black, for all his kind attention, was the first of his interviewers to tell him point-blank to give up. It seemed to carry the weight of a stern judge's sentence.

He asked himself: What if I fail?

He answered himself: Shut up.

He sipped his gin.

Next door Mr. Fischer began to shuffle around his room. At any moment Rodgers and Hammerstein would start bleeding through the wall. It was all Mr. Fischer ever put on his record player. Four or five nights a week, starting around eight o'clock, the concert would begin: *Oklahoma!*, *South Pacific*, *The King and I*, *The Sound of Music*. At some point, Max had deduced, Mr. Fischer would drift off to sleep under their cornball influence, for the last band on the last record would usually go on playing through the night.

Tonight it was *Carousel*.

Max listened for a while, got up to make a fresh

drink, sat back down on the sagging edge of his bed, and went on listening. He began to fall under its cornball influence himself. During "You'll Never Walk Alone" Max thought that he was going to cry, and then thought that a good long purgative weeping session might be just the thing he needed.

But he didn't allow it.

CHAPTER TWENTY-TWO

The restaurant was half-empty, and looked smaller and dirtier than the last time he'd been here, nearly two months ago. This was probably due to the late October ight striking through the windows, which filled the air with tumbling galaxies of dust motes, lit up the grease smudges on the glass partition above the steam table, and revealed the areas of the floor—beneath the tables, along the walls—where it hadn't been properly scrubbed. There was no sign of George Stefanos, no sign of Nora. On the speakers overhead, in place of the traditional bouzouki music, a shmaltzy string arrangement of "Yesterday" yearningly swelled.

A waiter with a pencil moustache asked him how many there were in his party.

"One," Max said. "Is Nora Cromwell working here today?"

"You bet."

"Could you seat me in her section?"

The waiter led him to the small table in its niche by the window, where Max had first seen George Stefanos studying his copy of *The Midnight Globe*.

"Who should I say—"

"I want to surprise her," Max told him with a smile, and sat down.

The waiter handed him a dog-eared menu. Max set it aside and nervously scanned the restaurant.

The gray double doors to the kitchen flew open and Nora burst through, holding a folded tray-stand in one hand, and balancing a big oval platter loaded with food on the high-held palm of the other. She spotted him as she made her turn. She hesitated, her eyes going flat, and her platter gave a dangerous wobble. She recovered her composure sufficiently to move to a table where three men in business suits sat. She snapped open her tray-stand with a flick of a wrist, bowed from the waist, and set down her platter; she glanced back at Max over her shoulder; she took a pad from her apron and studied it for a moment; then she began to serve, moving counter-clockwise around the table. Something spilled, or she knocked something over—Max couldn't tell which from his angle. She whisked a rag from her apron and began to mop up in front of one of the men, who grinned broadly at his companions, took Nora by the elbow, and when she inclined her head, spoke into her ear. She said something back. The table exploded with laughter. Then, leaving her customers and her empty platter behind her, she cautiously approached Max's table, as if she were wading in water, and wasn't sure of what depths lay in front of her.

She wore a white blouse, a black bow tie, a red apron, a black skirt. Her hair was piled up in a blue-black bun that was threatening to spill loose. There was too much blue eye shadow on her eyes, which were still as flat as in the moment when she first spotted him. Her mouth was set in a straight line. Her jaw was squared. He wasn't at all sure how to interpret her expression. She touched the bow tie at her neck, crossed her arms in front of her chest, and went on staring at him.

He swallowed, as if to push his heart back down where it belonged, and said, "Hello, Nora."

"Hello." Her voice was scarcely audible.

"Aren't you going to take my order?"

"What do you want?" she asked him carefully.

"A bottle of your best champagne."

"We don't got no champagne."

"It doesn't matter. Congratulate me. I got a job today."

One of the men at her table craned around in his chair to signal for her.

"One of your customers wants you," Max said.

Nora kept staring at him.

"Where've you been, Max?"

"Here in New York."

"Since when?"

"Since the last time I saw you, basically."

Now the man who wanted her attention snapped his fingers high over his head.

Her eyes blinked at each snap. But they didn't veer from Max's face.

"What do you mean by basically?" she asked him.

"I had to go back to St. Louis for a few days," he said. "You know, to pay off my landlady, put my furniture in storage, that sort of thing. But otherwise I've been in New York."

"Nora!" the man finally called out.

She abruptly turned and stalked back to her customers. There was some talk, some laughter from the men. Nora wrote something down on her pad. Then she stuffed it into a pocket of her apron and returned to Max's table.

"Did you really get a job?" she asked him.

"Of course I really got a job."

"What kind of a job?"

"Advertising."

"Like doing what you were doing in St. Louis?"

"Like doing what I was doing in St. Louis," he said. "It's a small agency by New York standards. But it turns out that's all for the better. I'll be getting paid more, and have much more responsibility than I would've started off with at a larger agency. The old guy I'll be working for seems awfully nice. And the funny thing is, he's from St. Louis originally—which might have been one of the reasons he hired me. I was damned lucky, Nora. For a while there it looked like I was going to have to pack up and go home."

Nora glanced away from him and then looked at him again—as if she didn't expect to find him still sitting there when she took a second look.

"You been up here all this time?"

"Yes."

"And now you got a job in advertising and you're staying up here?"

"I'll start looking for an apartment tomorrow."

"Well, where the hell are you living now?"

"In a furnished room. On Forty-ninth Street."

"*West* Forty-ninth Street?"

Max smiled. "That's right."

Her left hand went up to one of her earrings—she was wearing the pair of black coral earrings he had given her back in St. Louis.

"How come you did all that, Max?"

"Because I'd run out of pretty words," he said.

She went on twisting her earring.

"So look," he told her. "I'm celebrating tonight, and I want you to join me. I'll cook you dinner. Nothing fancy—there's not a hell of a lot you can do with the so-called kitchen I've got right now. But it'll be nice, Nora. I promise you that."

He finally deciphered the look on her face. She was frightened.

"Don't say yes and don't say no," he told her. He was writing down on a napkin the address and phone number of the Washington-Jefferson Hotel. "Just think about it. What time do you get off work?"

"Six," she said, again so softly that he could barely hear her.

"I can have everything ready by eight."

"Max—"

"No. Don't say yes and don't say no. Just think about it."

He pushed the napkin toward her.

She finally brought her hand down from her ear.

"You look great," he told her, standing now. "I especially like the bow tie."

Then he walked out of the restaurant.

Realistic thinking was still his enemy. Back in his room, Max tried to bring a Zenlike concentration to his preparations for dinner, screening out everything but the task at hand. But thoughts would sometimes leak through: What made him think this desperate ploy would induce her to leave George Stefanos, now that she'd already stayed with him so long? What made him think that if she did show up, her intentions would be anything other than just friendly? What would happen if she turned him down once again, and this time shut his own door in his face? What then? What would he do tomorrow?

Eat the leftovers, he told himself, and went on fixing dinner.

He'd thought about trying to cook on that pathetic stove, with no counter space at all to work on, and had decided instead to buy some expensive cold cuts from Zabar's. The Nora he'd known had practically lived on cold cuts anyway. He laid out in a delicate fanning pattern the strips of roast beef, corned beef, ham, pastrami, and brisket on a plate, and on another plate the cheeses—including American, in case Nora wouldn't touch the others. There was rye bread, pumpernickel, and again, in deference to Nora's tastes, a loaf of Wonder bread. He'd even bought a jar of mayonnaise for her. The Stolichnaya and the champagne were chilling in the refrigerator. The table was set. All that was left was for the candles to be lit.

The buzzer sounded.

"Mr. Baron?"

"Yes, Carl."

"A lady here to see you—" Here Carl fell into a fit of stringy coughing. When he got back his breath, he added: "A Miss Mildred Rogers."

"Thanks, Carl. Tell her I'll be right down."

Max knew he didn't have to hurry now. He went on lighting the candles.

COMING SOON FROM THE AUTHOR OF

SOMEWHERE OFF THE COAST OF MAINE

WAITING TO VANISH

AND

THREE-LEGGED HORSE

SOMETHING BLUE

by

ANN HOOD

THE BEST IN INNOVATIVE
CONTEMPORARY FICTION

SOMEWHERE OFF THE COAST OF MAINE
by Ann Hood
"The author is brilliant..."
--The New York Times Book Review

GOOD ROCKIN' TONIGHT   by William Hauptman
"Excellent...as promising a book as I've seen come out of Texas in
a good long while."
--Larry McMurtry

LOSS OF FLIGHT   by Sara Vogan
"Tough, touching, upbeat..."
--Newsday

HENRY IN LOVE   by Marian Thurm
"Buoyant and original fiction..."
--The Philadelphia Inquirer

OUR HAPPINESS   by Tom Jenks
"Tom Jenks has written an utterly convincing and, at times,
almost unbearably suspenseful novel of domestic disintegration;
of the way in which happiness shades into unhappiness, our most
mysterious of losses."
--Joyce Carol Oates

A SOLDIER'S DAUGHTER NEVER CRIES
by Kaylie Jones
"Amiably fresh and funny..."
-- Kirkus